LOST VALYR

PROJECT ENTERPRISE 7

PAULINE BAIRD JONES

PBJ

ABOUT LOST VALYR

She's a scientist in the wrong galaxy. He's an alien in the wrong century. Can their love reset a terrifying future?

Dr. Rachel Grant knows her way around the Garradian tech on the Kikk Outpost. But the technology she encounters in an alien medical lab stumps even her brilliant mind. With a little help from her scheming parrot sidekick, she manages to push the right buttons and transport them to an uncharted planet...where they find a recently defrosted alien, who heats up Rachel.

Valyr wasn't going to warm up to the bright-eyed scientist anytime soon...not after she pried centuries of cryosleep from his cold fingers. But waking up in the wrong century is nothing compared to the robots targeting his still-frozen team. And their situation only gets worse when he discovers the spiderweb of destruction trailing in the robots' wake. With their backs against the wall, Valyr is blown away by Rachel's determined passion in the face of impossible odds... but they'll need more than a chemical reaction to survive what is headed their way.

Lost Valyr is the seventh standalone book in the explosive Project Enterprise sci-fi romance series. If you like heart-pounding chemistry, ragtag bands of misfits, and action-packed space battles, then you'll love Pauline Baird Jones' rollicking romance.

Buy *Lost Valyr* to defrost a fast-paced interstellar love story today!

1

DR. RACHEL GRANT, carrying her breakfast tray towards a cluster of stone tables and benches, paused to look around. It had been raining the past few days, but the sun was back—even if it was shining from the "wrong" direction. She'd been here a couple of months now, but sometimes the alienness, the subtle dissonance still caught her off guard. She lifted her attention to the ghostly green shadow that was the planet of Kikk and off to its right the blue rim of the Kikk's other moon, both looming too close for comfort. Ahead of her, the appearance of *this* moon was something like a venerable Ivy college. Stone buildings, tall trees, grassy spaces cut by patterned walkways.

By mid-day, it would be modestly teeming with Project Enterprise personnel, but this early she was particularly aware of the silence. For whatever reason, this technology protected island on Kikk's second moon had no birds or other wildlife. There were insects, but they tended to be nocturnal, and when they were active, their hum was slightly off-pitch.

And if she looked too close at the green things, she could see they were "wrong" as well. Earth had so much variety, it had been something of a shock to realize that such *other* variation was possible. The colors, the shape of trunk and leaves and petals, the exotic scent of the green things drifting lazily on the breeze, all were constant reminders she walked in alien space. It was a bit ironic that the *Doolittle* or the *Patton* felt more like home than being dirt side here.

Rachel knew that humans had a great capacity to adjust, that she *was* adapting. She'd been here long enough to recognize the various scents and sights, to know which were soil and plant and which came from the trees reacting to the change in temperature after the chilly night. The sun, she could admit, still bothered her. Or rather, the way it entered the atmosphere. The refraction of its light, messed with her head. As far as she knew, she was one of very few bothered by this, but that might be because they lumped it all together into "this feels weird."

It required a certain level of mental...toughness...to be here, to stay here. Rachel was still not sure she had it, though leaving Earth had not been as hard for her as it had been for some. While she didn't call it an escape, there had been a falling away, a sense of leaving memories stored with the belongings she couldn't bring with her.

She gave a slight sigh, and a small shake, and resumed her progress. Because, of course, memories couldn't be left behind. They did not sit easily on shelves and liked to appear in moments of vulnerability to trip one up. So she stepped carefully between the tables, then set her breakfast tray on the stone table. Before sitting, she shifted the fruit and seed crackers onto a napkin for Sir Rupert. She added the cup of water she'd filled for him, slipped off her backpack, then took her seat on the bench next to him, the chill from the stone penetrating her official Project Enterprise trousers.

The parrot fluttered his wings, gave her a croaked "thank you," then hopped up onto the table top to attend to his food.

Rachel considered him for a few seconds pondering—not

for the first time—the advantages of beaks and claws for eating, which somehow always led to her wondering how she'd ended up working with a sentient parrot or *Psitticoid*. He wasn't from Earth. He just looked like an Earth parrot except in the subtle ways that he didn't.

This was not what she'd signed up for.

Oh, she knew that traveling to a distant galaxy would involve alien contact, or at least observations of other people having alien contact. Her designated job description, however, was not about first or second contact, and she'd liked it that way. Life—and her IQ—had left her conflicted in her interactions with others, something she'd had to deal with on a journey through space on a large, but tightly packed, ship. She felt she was dealing, and then—hands down—the scariest person on Kikk had focused her killer gaze on Rachel.

She'd seriously almost wet her pants. Worse, she had a feeling that Doctor Clementyne knew it, knew Rachel's reaction right down to the increase in pulse rate. Her gaze had been a dispassionate drill that left Rachel feeling as if Doc knew more about her than she did. And now that she knew Doc better? Yeah, she probably did know more about Rachel than Rachel did.

So, when someone like Doc asked her to take a parrot under her wing—ironic word choice?—she'd just blinked and nodded. And asked no questions. Not that there were a lot of people to ask about the parrot. Most of the outpost's occupants thought he was a pet though Doc had called him a visiting dignitary and her brother Robert had referred to him as an ambassador.

It was curious that both the Doc and the parrot believed that Rachel's efforts to locate cryo-research would, at some point, overlap with what Sir Rupert needed. At the time, she'd nodded as if she understood—since her throat had closed with fear from the certainty that Doc could kill her with a look if she wanted to.

How hard, she'd thought, would it be to work with a parrot?

Well, that part turned out to not be hard at all. That a parrot reminded her of her dad was strange, since her dad had been an auto mechanic and not even slightly parrot-like. No, the hard part for Rachel was the side effects of helping Sir Rupert. Somehow or other, she'd found herself on the fringe of his circle of human friends—a circle which included the very scary Doc. She had mentally dubbed them the spooky love bunch because, in addition to being varying levels of scary, the couples in that bunch were so in love it was like being in a Hallmark movie.

She might have some Hallmark movies in her personal items and enjoyed watching them, but she did not want to be in one, particularly as the dysfunctional friend character. As near as she could tell, the only thing she had in common with any of them was the parrot, which kind of made her eye twitch when she thought about it. So she tried not to.

This morning, after a period of rain and clouds that had rendered the outpost slightly less alien by draping it in murk, the sun was back. However, most of the scary love bunch were not. Usually, they beat her to breakfast if they were around. They weren't the only ones missing from the usual early morning breakfast bunch.

There had been some kind of alert earlier. She wasn't supposed to know about it, but she didn't like surprises, so she'd set up her own early warning system. Since she couldn't get back to sleep, she'd poked around the data as much as she dared, but the information lockdown was unusually tight.

Her foot nudged her backpack as she shifted on the hard seat. She had things in her quarters, but she kept the important stuff in her backpack, which was always with her. This was an outpost in another galaxy that had come under attack at least once that she knew about. She didn't want to have to stop and think if things went south—or its other galaxy directional equivalent.

She figured those of Sir Rupert's spooky peeps who weren't involved in the alert analysis process would appear and she was correct. It did surprise her to see Doc Clementyne in the food line behind her sister-in-law, the steampunk inclined Emily. Watching them now, it was a bit like a Disney princess hanging with the Terminator, no that wasn't right. Yeah, the Doc could totally be the Terminator, but Emily wasn't a fluffy princess.

From her booted feet to the ragged jeans and leather corset, and at the top, her multi-colored hair, she occupied her space with an obliviousness that Rachel might have envied a little. It's not that Emily didn't care about people. She did, but she didn't care what they thought of her. Today, thanks to a long white inventor's coat, Emily looked like a mad scientist, the kind who helped the heroes, not the bad guys.

Colonel Carey and his wife Olivia were among the missing. It was possible the very romantic pair had "overslept," but Carey was the CAG—commander to the *Doolittle's* air group. Rachel might not know the details of the alert, but this was outer space. Most alerts originated "out there."

Rachel noted that Doc's husband Helfron Giddioni was also missing this morning, another clue that the alert was space-based. He was the lead Gadi representative on the outpost, so of course, if there were an official huddle happening, he'd be in it. The only puzzle was why Doc wasn't there, too, but—maybe she didn't have to be in the huddle to be in the know. She was that scary.

Sergeant Major Briggs, the dude in charge of all things flying craft related, was MIA and so was his significant other, Madison. Rachel had played an uncredited part—thank goodness since it had pissed him off—in getting Briggs some downtime to recuperate from an injury that had become infected. He'd cut the vacation short for reasons she wasn't told. She did wonder how Briggs had managed to find a date on a top-secret outpost in another galaxy while recuperating on a secluded beach on the other side of the island. And somehow also got permission for Madison—and her parrot—to stay.

Because that was the one thing Rachel knew without being told. Madison and the parrot were a team. She'd spent a good part of her life people watching, and even if this team was only half people, the pair still gave off team vibes. It was interesting that it was Robert Clementyne who had officially sponsored Sir Rupert —or had brought the pet here, depending on who you asked.

Rachel had a feeling that all of the spooky love bunch had stories to tell and Rachel loved a good story, particularly one with a romance, but if the stories were there in the outpost's databases, they were buried deeper than Rachel could go. And that was saying something because Rachel knew how to make computers give up their secrets.

The spooky love bunch was mystery-squared, and romance Pi-ed. Rachel couldn't decide if it was kind of cute that they were all so drippingly in love, or if it made her want to throw up. She might be jealous of their happiness. Okay, not might. She was jealous, but she could be grown up about it. Particularly around Doc who might be able to read minds. At times, while trying to navigate the human minefield that was the spooky love bunch, Rachel considered asking them to reassign Sir Rupert, but how did one break up with a parrot who was a favorite of some of the most dangerous people on the outpost? So yeah, breaking up didn't seem like it was a good option.

And she would miss him. There, she'd admitted it. And there were benefits from hanging with the parrot. The big one—and also a weird one—he knew things about this outpost and the people who'd lived here. It made them a good team since he needed her opposable thumbs to manipulate the consoles. The beak and claws did have their downside.

"Are you feeling well today, Dr. Frank?" Sir Rupert asked, looking up from his breakfast.

It was...interesting...how piercing a bird's gaze could be. "Nice to see the sun after all the rain."

Even if it was an alien sun. His beady gaze stayed fixed on her face.

"I'm fine, thank you." She was or would be when she was out of reach of Doc's killer gaze. They were alone for the moment, but out of the corner of her eye, she could see Doc and Emily heading their way. "How are you?"

She was the Queen of Deflection.

"I am well," he said.

Was there a hint of amusement in his voice? It was hard to tell with that croaking undertone.

"I have been considering what take we might try next," he went on.

They'd given up pretending that Rachel was lead on their research after the first week working together.

"There is a smaller, secondary transport access."

Rachel straightened a bit. It was true they'd found a lot of information, but not much that was related to Rachel's primary interest or, apparently, the bird. "Really?"

"I had...forgotten about it but remembered last night. It can be accessed through a small office, or security station, at the back of the main level in the hospital facility's main floor. Where you hold the clinics in the afternoons."

Rachel mentally scanned that area. There was a small office back there. She'd thought about using it for her office but had decided it was too accessible to other team members. She liked to be out of sight and out of mind when she was working—

except when she took her turn at clinic, of course. Okay, even then, but it wasn't possible.

Rachel wanted to jump up and check it out right then, but it looked too much like running as Doc and Emily came up to their table. Because she felt like a deer in the headlights didn't mean she needed to act like it.

They set down their trays and sat on the bench opposite Rachel and dug in while Rachel discreetly studied the new arrivals, wishing she could ask. Most answers to questions were super classified. And sometimes the questions were, too. Even asking where the ladies was could get you in trouble if you asked it in the wrong place. She caught Doc giving her the stink eye and considered making a trip to the unclassified ladies right now.

As usual, it was Emily who broke the silence. "That's a bold move, Rach."

She was also the only person in the universe who shortened Rachel's name or used her first name.

Rachel thought about pretending she understood but had a feeling it was too late for that. She'd already blinked twice. Dead giveaway. "Excuse me?"

"Your shirt. You got a death wish?"

She grinned, and Rachel had to grin back.

"Who brings a red shirt to another galaxy?" Doc asked, her face warming with real amusement.

Wow. It was almost worth the red shirt to see that.

"Not my brightest moment," Rachel admitted. So this was what it felt like to be inside their circle.

"I wear red always," Sir Rupert pointed out.

"And how is that working for you?" Doc asked, giving him an "insider knowledge" look.

"I am not dead," he said, waving a claw at her in a vaguely minatory way.

Oddly, the discussion devolved into a whether one had to don a red shirt to become a target. Rachel was still grinning when Sir Rupert signaled he had had enough.

"Are you ready, Dr. Frank?"

"Yes, of course." It was the first time that wasn't entirely true. But she was always ready to help out the resident parrot dignitary, which she hoped Doc noticed. And she was eager to check out that secondary access. She gathered up the breakfast debris, loaded it on the tray and handed it off, then collected her backpack and her bird. Her parting words were less stiff than usual. Neither of them had anything to say until they were crossing the square and isolated from being overheard.

"They have detected a series of ghost contacts in Victor Quadrant," he said as if she'd asked.

"Really?" She mentally flipped through the outpost star charts. "That's former Dusan territory, isn't it?"

"So I have heard," the parrot agreed.

It felt like that the location mattered, though she was not sure why. Pirates of various types had started slipping in from that direction since someone had realized the Dusan were gone and spread the word.

"Ghost contacts?" She frowned. Would have been interesting to see that. Too bad she was out of the loop.

"The contacts are more like echoes, shadows, making it difficult to identify. But there does seem to be a pattern to the sightings."

Rachel skirted a small seating area in the square. "Like a course?"

"It is the most likely scenario. A natural object would not change course."

"No," she agreed, "it wouldn't."

Sir Rupert shifted on her shoulder, his claws gently contracting and retracting as he moved one direction, then back the other. His feathers brushed her cheek. It would have been nice to be in the inner circle on that. Rachel lapped up knowing things like a sponge. But to get cleared to that level, she'd have had to admit a lot more than she had about what she could do. She'd gotten in the habit of hiding things after her parents died and now she didn't know how to get out of it.

Rachel was quiet until she reached the outpost's ancient aboveground transport system and palmed open the door. She glanced at the parrot and found him looking back at the empty square still drowsing in the early morning light. Later it would be busier as scientists and soldiers moved around. This was her favorite time. Quiet. Peaceful. No wondering. She hated that awkward moment when a half hi and half smile died from lack of attention.

Something about the parrot caught her attention. Perhaps it was a stillness or an intentness to the tilt of his head. As if he saw something she didn't see in the pale light. She could still smell the pungent tang of alien plants and dirt deepened by the recent drenching. Even here, light years from home, there was post-storm crispness that made her feel as if anything were possible. Perhaps today...

The parrot's head turned in her direction as if he felt her watching him. Somewhat tentatively she arched her brows in the question she felt she couldn't ask.

"Do you believe in ghosts, Dr. Frank?" he said, ruffling his wings a bit, then settling down.

Not the question she'd been expecting. As she stepped into the opening, she took a look back before the doors shut off the square.

Were they talking ghosts in the scanners or woo-woo type ghosts? She couldn't decide, but it didn't matter. "I," she hesitated, but she was a rotten liar, "I believe in what I can see."

"As do I," the parrot said.

That sounded like agreement, but it didn't feel like agreement. She pressed a location on the interactive map on the wall and felt her tummy lurch as they shifted location in a blink.

Xaddek blinked all eight of his eyes as they studied the human shifting nervously in front of him. The smell of his fear and sweat was potent. It was a pity not to eat him. Xaddek was hungry for fresh meat, not the rations sitting on the desk in front of him. Restraint was not easy for his species. But scientists of this human's qualifications were not easy to come by, in or out of the system. This human did not know his value, Xaddek decided, hence the siren call of fear teasing his spider senses.

Fear could be useful, but in this case, it might have prompted precipitous action. The human had attempted to defrost one of the artifacts with, apparently, uncertain success. Xaddek half frowned as he recalled the Bosakli artifact that Trajan Bester had, so far, failed to secure. Xaddek realized he still had hope that he would appear, though nothing had been heard from them since they passed through the Stimsa jump gate. There was information that the *Mycterian* fleet had passed through ahead of him, which could explain his disappearance. There was no intel to explain why either had chosen that jump gate. All Xaddek knew is that Bester had been on the track of the artifact.

Why had this particular artifact not been frozen like the others? Did this make that artifact more or less important? Without the artifact, how could he know? And how serious was the loss of this artifact? Were all the artifacts useless, too degraded to use? Had the expense and risk been for nothing?

"So they are dead." If the artifacts were useless, maybe he

would eat this human after all. What was the point of a scientist with no work?

The man tugged nervously at the knotted string around his neck. Necks were vulnerable places for humans, tasty spots. All of Xaddek's eyes lingered on the human's neck.

"No, not dead, precisely." Now the human frowned. "This one is...empty."

"Empty?" At the present moment, it was his stomachs that were empty.

"There is no indication of the right type of brain activity."

That sounded like dead to Xaddek. "Then it's dead.'

The scientist shook his head. "It breathes. Its heart beats. It feels pain." He hesitated. "There is minimal brain activity, enough to keep it alive. It is like a vessel waiting to be filled."

"Filled?" Xaddek used a front leg to scratch a spot above one of its eyes. "With what? How?" Was that possible? There were always those who claimed that it was possible to transfer personality and knowledge to another vessel. He'd eaten them when they turned out to be wrong. For the most part, wrong tasted the same as right, with some variation based on species.

"There was technology integrated into the storage pod that could have been meant for the transfer of...information..." His voice trailed off.

"Or it is the technology that failed in this process." Xaddek's tone could not change, but his minions always knew when he was angry. Had this human botched the process?

The man paled. "Perhaps. Although, I can find nothing connected to the pod that appears to be large data storage. Everything I have been able to assess is wholly dedicated to sustaining viability." He eyed Xaddek uneasily as he proffered this information.

Xaddek felt impelled to accept this possibility, even though it seemed more hope than reality. Whoever had created the pods might have separated the contents from complete reanimation data in case they fell into, well, the control of someone such as himself. It annoyed, but this was not the human's fault. Which did not make him appear less tasty. His thoughts returned to one of Bester's reports, more specifically the one where he'd lost the artifact to another ship. Was it possible that this ship had contained the necessary data? He'd assumed it was another such as himself, but it was unlike anything he'd seen in all his travels through many years.

"You believe an outside source is required?" Xaddek's tone lowered to a soft hiss. "Where do we find this source?"

"Some of the technology had characteristics that have been attributed to a race, or people or entity known as the Garrads, or Garradians. No one really knows. But my sources believe they were a highly technical race." The human looked away and tugged at his neck string again. "If they created the, um, artifacts, then they might hold the key to reanimating them."

Xaddek considered this. The names were not unfamiliar to him. If this human had led with this information, he'd have looked less tasty. He'd been following links to the Garrads or Garradians when he'd stumbled upon the information about the artifacts and their possible purpose. Xaddek did not entirely believe in the Garrads or Garradians. The tech he'd collected was not pure. There'd been traces of other tech sources that muddied provenance certainty. But the reports persisted. And had increased in the last few years, the rumors interesting, but so far just that: rumors. If the Garrads had created his artifacts, well, that might be interesting.

"You are familiar with Garrad technology?"

The human cleared his throat. "I did some research for the former Dusan—well, for them." He gave a nervous smile. "On an outpost reputed to be Garradian. Nothing came of it. The technology was completely dead, but there are similarities."

"Similarities?"

Now the man frowned, his fear fading as he considered the question. "Similar, yes. Better."

Better. Xaddek liked better. But the Dusan. No wonder this specimen smelled off. The Dusan were a nasty bunch. Even he wouldn't eat one. There weren't many places he wouldn't go, and that was one of them.

The human shifted nervously once more and rushed into speech. "I ran into a trader who heard a story about the technology being unlocked by some ancient key that had been discovered by the Gadi."

"The Gadi." Xaddek allowed a slight question to enter his tone.

"There are stories, more than rumors," the human insisted, though Xaddek was not able to look skeptical as he felt, "that the Dusan have been defeated. That ships have ventured into that region and returned."

When a region had been torn by war for as long as this one, there was not much left for a collector such as himself. Gadi. Garradian. Was it possible they were linked somehow? Time altered so many things, it was hard to know without...testing. If his artifact was, indeed Garrad, then it should be possible to find trace similarities between it and these Gadi. One would need one, of course.

He'd collected a Dusan once. He believed he had a sample saved since he hadn't wished to consume it. If the Dusan and the Gadi had occupied the same space, they might be connected, as well. It was his experience that all human wars could be traced back to very personal quarrels. They must have something in common to fight so bitterly for so long.

"Compare the samples of the artifact with my stored sample of the Dusan."

The human nodded, managing to look interested despite his unease.

Was the war truly over? Rumors were so unreliable, particularly rumors of ships coming and going.

Xaddek flexed his front legs. "Do you remember the location of the outpost where you conducted your research?"

For the first time, the human looked confident. "I remember, sir."

"And my artifact? Will it expire without an infusion of data?" He was still hungry, and fresh meat—even if it had been frozen —was scarce on a space vessel.

The human's brows arched. "I put it in a chemical coma. But it won't last forever outside the pod."

"Refreezing is not an option?"

"I doubt very much it would survive that," the human admitted, wariness once more altering his posture.

"Well, if it begins to fade, contact me at once." If the artifact were Garrad, or somehow related to the mythical species, then it would make a rare meal. He did like sampling the rare. He waved a claw at the human. "You may go."

The human left with an attempt at a dignified retreat, but he could not hide his relief. Xaddek tapped his controls, searching for Bester's report on Bosakli, in particular, the scan data attached to that report. He considered it and decided it was interesting and yes, as unusual as he recalled. But, if it was a data repository, was it for all the artifacts, or just the one that Bester had mislaid? There were seven artifacts, according to his research. Could there be seven ships, one for each? It was a stretch, but it would not hurt to get eyes out looking for similar ships. And the newly opened Garrad space? If it was open, was it possible this was the source of the artifacts?

If it were, he would need to know more than rumors if he were to risk himself by going there. It might be worth repositioning the ship. But, if ships were going in and returning, perhaps one of these ships was known to him. He had his own way of finding out about ships that were useful, or ships he wanted to possess. He turned to his data, scrolling for any indication—what was that? The *Najer*? He sighed at the name. It was the only ship whose crew he'd not want to taste. He laughed at his mild joke. Robots. Clever, very clever robots. The bounty on it, and its crew was the most ever offered. Of course, one would have to trust the Quh'y to pay up and not turn their reclaimed mercenaries on him. He had not seen or heard of anyone who had seen the *Najer* lately.

What were they up to? He smiled as much as he could. He scratched under one leg with another leg. It had been too long since he talked with Savlf. Oh, Savlf. She smelled so tasty, but she was too brilliant to eat. Though he might change his mind if Savlf had lost the *Najer*.

———

Colonel Braedon Carey stood at the back of ops waiting for his briefing. It didn't look like it was coming any time soon. Not the geeks or the sensors fault. This was about the distances in space. And so far their bogey, if there was a bogey, was keeping well away from Kikk and the outpost. At first, everyone thought it was a problem with the sensors, but there'd been a growing sense of unease as the ghost track continued to appear at regular intervals. A ship? It had to be, but how was it avoiding most of their scanning? There were coverage gaps, the geeks admitted, causing Carey to exchange a worried glance with the Old Man.

This outpost was the region closest—air quotes required here because it wasn't that close—to Earth and where the first Project Enterprise ship had arrived. And immediately got into a fight with the Dusan. While Carey was not a proponent of annihilation, the Dusan had been a particularly nasty bunch who had sought the complete destruction of the expedition and everyone in this galaxy. No question this was a small galaxy, but that still added up to a lot of humanoids. So no regrets there. Now that the Dusan had ceased to be a threat, pirates had started to move into that region of space. The remnants of Garradian technology, which the Dusan had been unable to use, was a huge lure as war worries faded and old-timers began to recall more and more of the old legends about the lost people and their technology.

Since the outpost could shoot back and was guarded by two Project Enterprise ships, Carey wasn't too worried about that bogey. The geeks were freaking out over how hard it was to track. He couldn't tell if they were for or against it—as in worried about it or excited about it. Probably both, he decided. Geeks were both useful and a little crazy, in his estimation.

While everyone assumed the Garradians were long gone, there were...indications...that they might be gone, but not *gone*. With time travel in the mix, it was not beyond the realm of possibility for one or some of them to return and want their outpost back. Not that he'd thought about it until Doc and Robert had brought it up after Olivia asked them about the Garradians.

He would have liked to ponder Olivia because his wife was the best thing that had ever happened to him, but he didn't ponder anything when he was on alert status and with a deployment looming. His goal was always to get back to his wife.

The big screens updated with info as other outposts began to send scan data to the Kikk Outpost. The network of outposts was a definite benefit—even with the holes—but also a worry. Their expedition didn't have the resources to occupy or even monitor all of these remnants of Garradian power. The Gadi were slowly sending resources to occupy and protect them, but they were all counting on the fact that the outposts could only be activated by someone with Key DNA. Which is what had prompted Olivia's question.

And the next one: would they know if someone with the Key DNA, which was not as rare as assumed, penetrated an outpost and started using it?

No one knew the answer to that question because, as far as they knew, no one had done it.

It was the *as far as they knew* that bothered Carey. Scientists like to assert things and then qualify them in ways that could get you sent back in time. As he'd learned. And even though he'd brought back a wife, he was still a little bitter and distrustful. He never took anything they said at face value anymore, that was for sure.

Waking up with a buzzard on your chest, in a remote desert, in the 1940's, did that to a guy.

He studied the locations involved, trying to stay ahead of the updates, in case he got the order to deploy. His squadron had been updated with Garradian technology, so their intercept wouldn't take as long as it would have before, but it would still take longer than he'd have liked. He'd have waited to deploy his squadron until the bogey was a possible threat to this outpost, but he wasn't in charge. Not that he wanted to be in charge. He wanted to be back on the Outpost with his wife—

More data arrived.

An argument broke out. Was it or wasn't it a ship? General Halliwell stood in their midst, an island as the debate waged around him.

"Let's—" his voice cut through the babel, though he did not raise his voice, "—assume it is a ship. Based on its present course, can you predict where it is headed?"

That made them all pause, look at each other, then jump onto their keyboards in an attempt to be first. After they all had a projected course, they compared. Then the head geek cleared his throat. "We think it will show up on our sensors again here, sir."

A projected course popped up on the screen. It had been provisionally upgraded to an "unknown bogey."

That was the trouble with bogeys. They were unknown for too long. When knowing happened, shooting tended to follow quickly. Would the Old Man send them in cloaked? It was his preference. In his estimation, it was always better to be the one doing the surprising, rather being the one surprised.

"How long?"

Another geek answered. Halliwell looked at the clock. He glanced back at Carey. "Get your birds ready to deploy, Colonel."

"Yes, sir." Carey saluted and turned on his heel, tapping his radio as he headed for the lift.

2

DARKNESS. Cold. So much cold. Sharp teeth of cold biting deep into bones, drilling down to marrow. He floated in cold waters, lost and alone. Why? Where? How? Questions exhausted. He tried to sink back into the dark cold, to let it close back over his mind, but a sound nagged. Persistent. Relentless. His brain grabbed the sound, would not let go. He tried to brush it aside, to push it away. Dark beckoned, promised to free him from the cold.

The sound pulsed louder, echoing in the dark. Echoing inside his head.

It mattered. Reminded of...what? It tugged at something buried, something old. A need...someone needed him...

A pinpoint of light pierced the darkness, blinding, merciless and yet, with the faintest wisp of warmth. He huddled in it, felt the edges of bitter cold ease. Like old, slow gears, his mind began to turn, to sluggishly churn. Who needed him? Who called him? The sound gave no answers in its persistent tap, tap.

The light grew, digging into his eyes.

Pain. Different from the cold pain. Muscles clenched, protested waking.

Waking? From what?

The light grew, the pain growing with it.

His lips moved. Formed the single word. He frowned. The sound echoed in his head. He tried again.

"Help."

———

When Rachel and Sir Rupert emerged into the sunshine on the other side of the outpost, the clock in this square was chiming the Garradian hour—or whatever they'd called a unit of time. Before she'd arrived on site, someone had tried to align it with Expedition time but gave up because it had thirteen symbols instead of twelve. Would not do to have the outpost time out of synch with ship time.

Rachel had dug into Garradian time soon after arriving at the outpost, as a way of dealing with all the alien around her. But it only increased her sense of being out of synch. The numbers didn't match with either the sun's or the moon's movement. Her theory was that planetary shift had caused the dissonance. Though no one had achieved precision on how long the Garradians had been gone, the almost consensus was that it had been a seriously long time ago. In long time spans, shift happened.

She glanced at her watch. They seemed to be a bit ahead of everyone else today. It was nice to be alone while they assessed the secondary transport access. When she first arrived, she'd been ordered to report each new find, but with Sir Rupert's help, she'd found a lot of new, so her immediate boss told her to let him know about the "significant" stuff. She'd dealt with this revision by sending him a summary email every couple of weeks. She was pretty sure he didn't read them, so she didn't put a lot of time into them.

With Sir Rupert still riding her shoulder, they crossed to the entry point for the medical complex. This morning the security guy had brought some crackers for Sir Rupert. Without comment, the parrot snagged them with a claw and politely nibbled at the edge of one because he'd just had breakfast and wasn't hungry, she guessed.

"My nephew's parrot says thank you," the guard said, looking vaguely disappointed.

"Thank you," Sir Rupert said, his squawk a bit more pronounced. Rachel thought he might have overdone it, but the guard looked pleased.

"You're welcome." He stepped back, gesturing for them to enter.

The automatic door slid back, revealing a small foyer. Behind this was a reception area that looked like about every doctor's office she'd ever been in. Apparently, there was only so much you could do with a doctor's office. Thanks to them, it even smelled like one.

The waiting room was, in her opinion, a metaphor for doctor's offices everywhere. The benches didn't try to be comfortable, the badly faded art was sad, the check-in desk imposing, and the few pots scattered around were empty.

Rachel, a relative newcomer to the outpost, had noted that the Expedition lived lightly here, rather than settling in and possessing it, so the only thing they'd changed here was adding the smell of antiseptic.

No one sat at the stern desk yet. Clinic didn't start for a couple of hours. Serious injuries were transported up to one of the orbiting expedition ships anyway. The clinic, when it was open, dealt with minor stuff like following up on Briggs' injuries and removing alien splinters. Sometimes all that was needed was a listening ear. The most pervasive "illness" was home-sickness.

She passed through the treatment area with Sir Rupert still riding along, weaving her way through the Garradian version of cubicles until they reached the office that apparently wasn't an office. She realized, looking around now, that it did kind of look like a security station. The desk was higher than the others and blocked access to what she'd thought was a storage closet. She skirted the counter and stopped when it became clear the door wasn't going to pop open for them. That was interesting. A palm plate and a keypad were on the side.

Rachel pulled out her tablet and a cord she'd adapted to help her connect. She had a small screwdriver in one of the many pockets of her expedition issue jacket. With this, she pried the cover off. She unplugged one of their wires and plugged in hers. Thanks to those who had been here before her, she'd had time on the trip out to work on her hacking program. It had needed tweaking, but she was getting faster at cracking these code locked hatches.

It took a little longer than she'd expected before the hatch slid back with a hiss and a burst of old, stale air.

"I should have brought air freshener with me," she muttered.

If the smell bothered the parrot, he didn't say so.

When the air outside and in had equalized a bit, Rachel stepped inside.

"This is definitely a transport module." It was about the size of an elevator, a trait shared by most of the modules she'd used. Like elevators, they went up and down. And sideways. And sometimes it felt like they moved at angles. Someone else was researching the modules, but so far, they hadn't cracked the secret of how they moved around. The only thing everyone agreed on was that the modules must have stabilizers and dampeners of some kind because they were fast.

The hatch slid closed, and the interior lit up, as did a transport pad. A pad unlike any she'd seen so far.

"Well, that's...interesting."

It was a rectangle in overall shape, but on this one, the buttons were also various shapes. Two right triangles, a medium triangle, a square, a parallelogram, and two small triangles. Something about it made her brain twitch.

"I've seen this before," she murmured.

"It is a tangram," Sir Rupert said.

"Of course. I got a set as a birthday gift when I was three or four. Kept me busy for a couple of hours." She'd formed shapes to match the sheet that had accompanied the pieces. When she'd done all the variations, she'd tossed them aside. That had been a tough year for her parents until a neighbor had put them in touch with a support group for parents with annoyingly bright children. She gave a frustrated twitch of her shoulders. She tried not to think about the past. In addition to deflection, she was also good at denial. This most unusual panel was a good distraction.

She traced the outer edges. No place for her screwdriver to get purchase. As she tried to find an edge, one of the pieces moved, shifting all of them. She took a half step back.

"They move." Movement did not seem like a good omen. It might have only taken her a couple of hours all those years ago, but back then, she'd had patterns to follow.

"Yes, they do." Sir Rupert's wings moved gently, the touch of his feathers on her neck vaguely comforting.

She wanted to ask how he knew this because it was obvious that door had not opened for a long time. She put a finger on one of the shapes and pushed until it moved up. All the shapes shifted again. A moving lock with thousands of variations. Crap. "I'm going to guess that only a very specific pattern unlocks this module."

Sir Rupert tipped his head to the side, his gaze intent on the tangram. "You are moving that piece the wrong direction."

This time she had to look at him. He bobbed his head as if urging her to try it. So she did. She moved the piece as directed. "This way?"

"A little more to the right." His wings began to flutter faster, moving the air as she moved the triangle. "Slower, move it up—stop!"

She yanked her hand off the tangram and studied it. A half a name for it floated up. Dice something? Cup?

"That's a Dice cup, baby." Her mother's voice, patient but with an undercurrent of frustration. No wonder—

Rachel uncurled her fingers and flexed them. "Now what?" The tension in her voice bothered her, and she took a deep breath, then let it out slowly. If Sir Rupert noticed—which he must have—he didn't comment on it. She looked at him in what she hoped was polite inquiry.

"I must explain—" he stopped.

It was the first time, Rachel had ever thought he might not be majestically calm.

"If this works, it will become apparent to you that I know things not possible for me to know."

Rachel tried to think of a comment. Couldn't. So she nodded like she understood even though she didn't.

"My species has an unusual skill, one that caused us to be hunted to near extinction."

"Near extinction?"

"As far as I know, I am the last of my kind."

"I'm...so sorry." It seemed massively inadequate. No, it was. She stiffened. "You're hoping for a lead—" She researched cryogenics and he'd attached himself to her. She needed to think about that, but not right now.

"Yes. The Garradians were scientists, researchers. Anything and everything interested them."

There was another long pause as if he was ordering his thoughts. Or editing them. And she still didn't understand exactly what he was confessing. The special skill?

As if he followed her thought process, he broke the silence. "My species can see echoes, ghosts if you will, of living species. We see layers of time, dimensions. When the skill is honed, we can sort through the images and piece them together in their own time and space."

A bunch of questions wanted to crowd out her mouth, so she kept it closed and just nodded as she tried to process this.

"So...you can see, say people—" Garradians? "—who used this module? You can see them working that?" She nodded at the tangram.

"That is a simplified version of what I see." He ruffled his feathers. "For me, this module is very full. The patterns overlaid with each other. I have to...drill down through the layers to find the one I need. This time, many of the images did the same thing. That was helpful."

Rachel made a sound she hoped was also helpful. One thing he'd done is clear everything but this moment from her head. She tried to think what it would be like to be here and seeing the past— "So you see the past?"

He hesitated his beak angling away from her. "I do."

What else did he see? Did she want to know? Not while wearing a red shirt, she decided.

"I can see that would attract...trouble," she said instead.

"Indeed." He shifted on her shoulder. "It has been helpful that this outpost has been empty for so long. And the population was not large."

He'd *seen* Garradians. Her mind might be blown.

"I wish I could see what you see," she said, wistfully. To see the past—she cut that off again.

"It makes the present challenging," he pointed out.

"You can't," she shrugged, "turn it off?"

"No, you can't turn it off," he said dryly.

"I'm sorry. I'm kind of boggled if you must know."

"You are one of three people who know this," he said.

Her eyes widened. "I won't, I'd never—"

"If I had thought you would, I would not have told you."

Rachel felt an odd warmth in her chest. She'd been trusted, she was trusted by the leaders of this expedition, but not because they *trusted* her. No, they trusted because they had all sorts of threats they held over her thanks to the non-disclosure agreements she'd signed. This was new. This was *trust.*

Sir Rupert ruffled his feathers again, and said, "All that is left now is to place your palm on the panel at a right angle."

Moving on from the almost mushy moment. "Right."

She might have hesitated. It had been a long time since anyone used this module, a module they still didn't understand. The red shirt felt like it got tighter. "Just touch, not push?"

"Touch."

With a tiny pause for a silent prayer, she touched.

There was that brief, stomach-churning feeling of going down, then sideways, and then something new. A kind of side action with some twist to it that left her insides not sure where to settle when it stopped abruptly. Her head whirled, and it took her a minute to realize the door had opened. They were there, wherever there was.

"That was a rougher ride than usual." Her voice sounded muffled and the pain in her ears indicated they'd gone deep.

Light spilled out from the transport module creating a small circle of light in what was otherwise very dense darkness. Looking back, the transport module had smelled pretty good compared to what now rushed in on them. Smells so old, even if she'd known what they were she probably wouldn't recognize them now.

She yawned, trying to get her ears to pop. She hoped the ancient Garradians knew about the bends. She managed to get a partial pop and realized that the silence wasn't total.

Somewhere out there in the darkness, something was ticking.

3

XADDEK DIDN'T OFTEN GO to his people. They came to him, usually with their knees knocking together from fear. Oh, the leg meat. It was different from other parts. There was something about stripping meat off the bone, even better if his meal was still alive. Paralyzed by his venom, he could taste the terror visible only in their eyes.

The crew faded away at his approach because he'd been known—in the past—to cruise for a meal. His captain had pointed out the problem with this, and he'd stopped, but he did like seeing and smelling their fear.

He reached the door only he could access. Even Savlf could not open this door, despite her impressive system manipulation skills. She was completely isolated from the crew. It was her fault. She'd tried to suborn different crew members to help her escape. She had not tried anything for some time, but he had found he slept better when she was locked away.

The scanner recognized his eyes, and the hatch slid back. The room was dim, the temperature carefully controlled for the maximum viability of the sample. The web both covered and sustained her, feeding her and taking away her waste. It compressed her muscles because they'd found that humans lost mental tone when they lost too much body tone. She was plugged into a system that was as isolated as she was. He was not stupid enough to hook her up to a computer and give her access to his ship.

His eyes admired the way the web covered and restrained her. He could see traces of pink skin between the strands of the web, but there were less of them after each visit. He would be sorry when there was no more visible skin since that made him hungry for a taste. Sometimes he added more webbing, and it increased if she struggled against it. She was not one to give in easily though it seemed her eyes—the only things really visible anymore—were duller than the last time he'd visited her. Even her mouth was covered, he noted. Her back talk he did not miss. He'd have shut her up sooner, but speech integration had taken time to set up.

She'd been, according to some of his human crew, a lovely woman. Her eyes were an unusual shade of blue, the features and shape of her body pleasing to human eyes. He had agreed that she appeared...desirable. Her hair had been black, he thought. Yes, he was sure it was dark, increasing the contrast of white skin, eyes, and hair.

Of the current crew, only the captain was left of those who had seen her before. No one else knew what existed behind this door. He suspected it would be even more difficult to get crew if they did know.

"Savlf," he murmured, moisture pooling in his mouth at the sight of her. His hunger for her was almost sexual when she was webbed. He was not certain why this was so. But her web-trapped body sent sharp waves of longing to leap and drink her blood to the very last drop, then rip her flesh from her lovely bones.

She knew what he wanted. He read it in her eyes. It was the

only way he could compel her to work for him. Well, that and the additional encouragement from the web. It amazed him how strong the will to live endured in certain humans. But perhaps it was fueled by a longing not to die as his meal. He had a feeling that if she could have ended her life herself, she would have.

Hate sparked life in her eyes, but the spark was dim, a sullen futile hate. There was nothing she could do, and they both knew it. He did not need to be loved, just given exactly what he wanted when he wanted it.

"The *Najer*," he said. He'd never been able to get close enough to attempt planting a virus, so he'd secured Savlf for this task. Sometimes he had her do other things, but this was her central task, her reason for remaining uneaten. She had not been sufficiently motivated, even with the prospect of being eaten hanging over her head, so he'd upped the stakes. Do this, and I will free you from the web. Would he keep his promise? He was not certain. The web suited her. And it suited him. And he had not promised complete, or even endless freedom from the web. If she succeeded, it would be worth it to free her until she misbehaved again. And then go through the entrancing process of enslaving her again. She would never leave this place alive. But hope should keep her obedient.

"Progress report," he added when she didn't speak.

"I have made progress..."

Since she'd lost the privilege of speech, the computer did it for her. It amused him that the computer removed all nuance from her voice. It was yet another way to remind her that she lived and died at his pleasure.

There were brief signs of a struggle before the web forced her to say, "...master. I can track them."

He was pleased to hear this. "Show me."

Was he testing her? It was possible. That she could still struggle did not please him. Was that true? When she'd been brought aboard, he had tried to lure her to his side with the rewards that kept his crew aboard. Surely it was easier if she did not fight him? Would her work have been better? He was not so sure. They'd been meant to battle, to bring out the best in each other. He did not believe she'd have achieved this level of expertise without the web to focus her mind.

Opposition sharpened his mind, too. He'd had to be innovative to trap Savlf in the first place.

Star charts began to flash on one of her screens. Her lashes lowered as if she did not wish—or did not need—to see it.

Her eyelids were the only thing the web could not control without blinding her. He'd considered taking this last but one sense from her, but he liked knowing she could see him, liked her seeing that he could move and she could not. Telling her would not be nearly as satisfying.

He turned his many eyes to the screen as it finally ceased flashing and showed him what he wished to see.

"Where?" He deliberately kept the questions short and open to misunderstanding. This gave him the option to punish her if she incorrectly interpreted what he wanted to know. It was a dance that was part of their meetings. When the web punished her, it tested both of them. The last time she'd fainted before he was about to give in and take a little taste of her. She smelled so much more enticing when she fought him. He'd been so close, he'd almost done it, but he knew he couldn't have stopped. He needed to be honest with himself because no one else would.

But there would come a day when the web did too much damage to her mind. And then...

He jerked as she answered his question and showed him exactly what he wanted to know. The mystical Garradian Galaxy. What had sent them there? It was a question she could not answer from the outside.

"Can you insert one tiny command in one of them?"

"I will try...master..."

He considered punishing her, but really, all she could do is try. The crew of the *Najer* guarded their code with a fanaticism he could both deplore and admire.

"Try hard." He gave her a tiny taste of what would happen if she didn't try hard. As her body danced and writhed in the web, he sighed with pleasure.

———

She hated him with every cell of her body. It was what kept her conscious as the web sent a very precise level of pain through every nerve ending in her body. She had not known there were so many nerve endings in a body until this, until the web. It drained her strength and her will, it took her mind off the task to keep her screams from reaching the computer's voice processor. She'd have told him so if she thought she could do anything but scream and scream and scream. Perhaps Xaddek realized that he was working against himself because it stopped as abruptly as it had begun—though she knew it would happen again. If he came. If he didn't. He liked to hurt her almost as he much as he liked her work.

Somewhere in the past, she'd been free. She'd almost forgotten that time. It felt distant, like a dream, and it brought a different kind of pain to her mind. But it was also her sole anchor in this sea of black and red pain. She opened a tiny window to that time. She'd had a home, a job she loved, a life. Then a sudden prick of a needle on her neck and when she woke, it was all gone. Replaced by that thing and this room. She'd tried to fight him, to use her skills against him, even as she worked for him. Almost, that had worked. Now he kept her here, trapped in his web. It had spooled out of him, just a few strands at first. A few hot strands that burned, that wrapped her in red-hot fire. She'd fought, tested its limit with the resources he let her keep, lost again and again.

He'd punished her, restrained her until the only freedom left was inside her head.

He couldn't see into her mind, and if he sent the web in there, it would destroy, not reveal. She knew this because he hadn't sent the web into her head. If he could have, he would have. Since he couldn't get into her mind, he used her trapped body to torture her, to remind her he was in charge, to break her will to fight him. He also used it to show her what he hadn't done. Yet. So far he needed her skills more than he wanted to consume her.

With her mind, she worked to use his system against him. To study his web. In a strange twist, it had allowed her to do as she was told, and it had permitted her to test it. As if they learned together. While she feared that she was teaching it how to keep her contained, what kept her going was the image of Xaddek captive in this web.

The web had kept one secret from her.

What would happen if she did break its bonds? It had dug so deeply into her body, it was possible she could no longer survive without it. It refused to let her die. It did not know she lived to destroy it and the monster who had created it.

She lowered her lids, shut him out, so he couldn't see defiance in her eyes. He punished her anyway, of course. Why he hadn't taken her sight, too, she did not know. All her functions were controlled by the web. She knew he could isolate her brain, remove her body if he wanted. That's all he needed. That's why he'd isolated her from the rest of this ship. But he'd had to give her the tools to attack the *Najer*, the other thing he wanted so desperately he'd quelled his hunger to consume her for his evening meal. He'd fire-walled the ship against her, but he'd had to give her outside access to find the *Najer*. The skills learned in trying to get into the *Najer* were turned on other ships they came in contact with. Sometimes he used what she gave him to track those ships, so she used them, too, to extend her reach. The ones she was forced to destroy, she learned as much from as she could first, squirreling the data away in her lone firewall: her brain.

The spider she'd planted on the *Najer* was a thing of beauty with a single purpose: sending her location data, bouncing it off the ships she'd tagged for Xaddek. She'd learned not to try to do much. The more widespread the attack on their systems, the better the robots aboard the *Najer* were at defeating it. Her code hid in an inconspicuous piece of data, after burrowing deep into the systems. It was mostly dormant. It sensed when the crew were searching for malicious code and went quiet. And it used their systems to broadcast, hiding in anything and everything it could find. And it did no damage. This was key. It changed nothing except itself. She called it Chameleon.

What Xaddek didn't know, what he'd never know if she could help it, was that she'd used the *Najer's* planted tracking spider. She'd backtracked it to find them. It was interesting that the *Najer* felt the need to keep track of this ship. What did they fear? If Xaddek learned the robots tracked him, it would drive him into a raging frenzy. It wasn't just because she thought it would end with him eating her that kept this from her. She needed that connection.

It gave her hope.

Xaddek thought he had the Chameleon's code because it showed him what he wanted to see. If he or anyone else tried to change it, it would alter, becoming less and less effective, turning more and more in on itself until it disappeared from his sight. And it would stay gone until she called it out again.

She understood why the *Najer* fascinated Xaddek. They were the perfect crew for him. He wanted their skills, their fear power, and perhaps he wanted them because they were the one crew he could not eat. He would still consume them by stealing their lives and their will. He wanted them like he'd wanted her. He wanted to turn them into his weapon.

They fascinated her for a different reason.

They were *very* good at not getting caught. So far they'd flicked off almost all of her attempts to penetrate their programming like one would an insect. She'd learned though, from the attempts and from accessing data anywhere she could find it. Encounters. Battles. Trade deals. She knew or thought she knew their one weakness. If she was correct, the *Najer* could be her salvation. Of course, convincing them to save her might be impossible.

But she would keep trying.

It was all she had.

———

Rachel looked around, her uneasy survey not that helpful since the light bubble was not big. She tried not to make a mental link between the ticking and things that exploded, things such as self-destructs but it wasn't easy. She wished she'd been issued a personal weapon. She'd gone through the training at Area 51. Survival, obstacle courses, and multiple sessions at the shooting range. She'd eventually got over the obstacles, and her shooting had surprised her instructors. And then they'd told her she didn't need a personal weapon because she was "just a scientist." Bet Doc had a personal weapon. Or ten of them. No security detail because she was in a "safe" zone. Would have been nice to have a guard. Someone big and strong with tight—*okay, don't go there, Rachel. This is so not a Hallmark romance movie. You're "just a scientist," not a single white female looking for that special someone who doesn't mind a brainy gal with no sidearm.* She might have doodled that a few times, but she'd never posted it in a singles forum. Even when tempted—a temptation that was much easier to resist in another galaxy. It made that "let's meet for coffee" particularly challenging.

One might feel regret if one blew up today...

She could call in for help but what could she say? *It's dark and ticking, and I have on a freaking red shirt?* She'd get laughed off the outpost. Doc was right. Who took a red shirt on a trip to another galaxy? Or more than one. Just because someone sometime had told her red was her color? Really? Her genius creds were showing some wear today.

She reminded herself that just because this room was ticking, it did not mean it was about to explode. And she'd gone into dark, empty rooms almost every day since she got to the outpost and just because none of them were ticking did not mean anything.

"It's just a clock," she said, and even though she spoke in a whisper, it echoed a couple of times before fading into...ticking. There were clocks all over the Kikk Outpost. Outside, not inside, but lots of clocks. Actually, it was kind of weird they didn't have inside clocks.

This is good, she repeated to herself as she stepped out of the transport module, there is a clock. The lights came on as they did in the other buildings, but the level of illumination was lower and blue. She took a couple of steps forward. The light moved with her, but it did not get brighter, deepening the shadows that lurked just outside the area of illumination. She paused, trying to figure out why she felt uneasy. Other than the ticking, it was not that different from the other places she'd been exploring with Sir Rupert. There was no reason to feel more alone, more isolated. Actually, it was a good thing that they were alone. The one thing she didn't want to do was run into something with no way to defend herself. Not being alone here would be much scarier.

"We're deeper than usual," she said, more to erase some of the silence. Who were the people who did this? Who had dug this deep into the Kikk moon? What were the secrets housed here? *Please let there be some secrets.* She had a feeling she'd need some to placate her supervisor, who would probably consider this an important find that she should have reported. "You can't say they didn't use all the space they had."

"No." Sir Rupert sounded amused.

Just to her left was a chest-high wall, about the same height as the one up top. If it looked like a security counter, it was probably a security counter. The familiar unfamiliar? That was it, she decided. It felt different because this was alien territory. She was just more aware of the alienness of it all today. With the feeling identified, it receded somewhat.

"Okay." Her voice echoed weirdly. Nasty air moved sluggishly from both left and right. She had the impression that corridors stretched from either side, but sensed this main section was circular—for no reason she could define, other than that the shadows seemed to bend.

She moved forward, light spreading ahead of her so that now she could see work consoles similar to the consoles typical throughout the Kikk Outpost. Ahead of her, a wall emerged from shadow. On it was a sort of circular sculpture or decoration. It was a bit on the grand side, like a company logo in the reception area of a business. Except this was, well, she didn't know what this was. Its inner circle had seven symbols. Kind of like a messed up clock, which, as she realized now, it was the source of the ticking, so the clock analogy kind of worked. At least it didn't look like a bomb. Except for the symbol that pulsed faintly yellow, then red in the sort of three o'clock position.

"That's..." She stopped because she wasn't sure what it was, other than odd. Or a bomb.

"It's a Urclock," Sir Rupert said.

"Really?" She said it like she knew what that was. Did she? Didn't feel like she'd heard of it. She'd feel better if that meant it was for sure not a bomb. When the echo of her voice faded, she realized the sound of ticking was louder. And the one pulsing symbol—number three position—pulsed brighter and purple before fading back to yellow and red. "So, it's three urclock?"

She glanced at Sir Rupert who tipped his head to the side and possibly gave her a Look. She grimaced. "Sorry."

He ruffled his feathers. "I've heard worse."

"It's not...explosive, is it?"

Sir Rupert's head leaned back, as if in surprise. "It's..." his head tilted to the side "...not clear what it is. The images are muddled and heavily overlaid."

So, not a no, then.

His head bobbed in the direction of the line of consoles. "Are you going to stand here all day or attempt to boot something up?"

It was a better choice than standing around waiting to be blown up.

"I'm going to boot it up." She'd seen all the original *Star Wars*. There was no try. There was only do. But which was the main console—

Sir Rupert flew forward and landed on a central console to her right. "This is where you should start."

"Then that's where I'll start."

4

———

TURNING things on was the easy part. The surfaces were touch sensitive. After that, things got a little more challenging. So Rachel had built a backdoor for herself to speed up the login process. Getting through the first layer of protections was relatively easy. Once in, she took a minute to equalize the pressure in the room. This made her ears pop the rest of the way, but also made the ticking louder. Which made her eye twitch. Thankfully, she had a cure. She turned to her tablet, picked a playlist and set it to play through the intersystem speakers. The Garradians must have liked music, too, or just liked to make announcements, because they had a sassy, outpost-wide sound system. She'd found how wide the first time she'd tried to use it. Luckily, she'd got the range narrowed before the other geeks had traced it back to her. Now soft rock filtered into the room, muting the persistent ticking to a metronome-like background.

She hooked one of the movable stools and locked it in place —here was another lesson learned—and sat, flexing her fingers and possibly some brain cells. Only then did she start her dance with the database's deeper levels of encryption, her shoulders moving with the music. She made a move. It blocked her. Same with the next three attempts. She was vaguely aware of Sir Rupert moving along the work stations at her back, perhaps studying the Ghosts of Outpost Past, the soft click of his claws becoming part of the music's beat. And then he faded into the background as she kicked on the mental thrusters and engaged. Was it a good sign when her music list found "Woolly Bully?"

Her shoulders moved to the music, her fingers stroked across the flat surface, while her eyes noted what the system did to block her and her brain learned from it. She wasn't sure how long they battled. One minute she thought she was losing and then suddenly she was in. Her neck and back hurt and her playlist was churning out "Free Falling" by Tom Petty and the Heartbreakers.

"Let's see what you've got for us," she muttered, shifting her shoulders to ease the knot that had formed in both her *trapezius.* Her *latissimus dorsi* wasn't happy either. She realized she hadn't taken off her pack, so she slipped it off and dug out a bottle of water and something to help with the pain. That dealt with, she flexed her shoulders and then focused on the various menus now available to her.

The first time she'd seen one of these, it had looked like a disorganized mishmash, but now she was more used to them, and her brain automatically began to sort it by functional menus and what might be a path to the good stuff. It helped that she'd started studying the Garradian written language before she left Area 51, so she could read most of the idents on the various menu options. She had a little more trouble with the moving tickers running underneath some of the menu sections. It took her a couple of times through to realize one was an actual alert.

She tapped the ticker tape, and a holographic screen appeared next to the main menu screen.

"So this seems to be a summary of all ship movement in the galaxy." It was kind of an odd option for a medical complex. She studied the visual report, tapping on the different ships. Most had a tag identifying ship type and general purpose. A few were "not known." She studied those carefully.

"Pirates?" she muttered. It looked like the pirates were also being monitored up top in the control center.

"That would be my assessment," Sir Rupert said, startling her by fluttering over to land on the edge of her console. "Could this be the ghost bogey?" His head bobbed forward, intersecting and briefly disrupting the hologram moving deeper into the Victor Quadrant where a symbol pulsed in and out of view.

She hesitated. This was not her brief, but she wanted a look. Her professors used to tell her she needed to focus—though they'd stopped when they realized what they needed was to get out of her way. Curiosity was both a blessing and curse.

"We could take a little peek." What would it hurt? It wasn't like she was the enemy. She tapped this alert, opening another holographic screen on the opposite side of her main screen. This produced a 3D representation of all the outposts. That was interesting. There were a series of exclamatory looking markers on this map, tracking all the way from the border of Victor Quadrant. The track of the possible bogey, she assumed. A new marker appeared, and for a second the symbol of a ship appeared, then vanished. There was also a flashing symbol over the first outpost inside Victor Quadrant.

Sometimes you needed to know where something had come from to figure out where it was going, or so her dad used to claim.

She tapped that symbol, and a report appeared. In Garradian, of course. She sent the report to her tablet and set it to translate, then activated the blinking outpost's internal security systems and ran through the vids. It was grainy, the video lens probably needed cleaning, or it was just really old.

"Pretty paired down compared to this place," she said, studying as much of the layout as the video would let her see.

"Indeed." His wings fluttered a bit. "Go back to the time stamp of the alert," he recommended.

She rewound the feed. At first, it looked the same. Then the feed jumped a bit, went sideways, then settled back to merely grainy.

"Did you see that?"

"I did."

"Some kind of surface impact—?" She reared back. "Holy crap on a saltine."

The door burst outward in a flash of light, dust, and debris. Before it settled shadowy figures strode through the cloud they'd created. Rachel leaned in, trying to figure out what she was looking at. The feed seemed even more grainy since the door was breached. She tinkered with some of the controls.

"Are they...armored?" Like top to toe armored? It was kind of like watching an old sci-fi flick.

"They move like a highly trained military unit," Sir Rupert added. "I see five figures?"

"I count five, too." She tried to zoom in on the figure at the front. The feed got more grainy at this level but was not so bad she couldn't see the red glow as the head turned toward the video as if he sensed scrutiny.

Rachel might have twitched, even she reminded herself this was old video. These guys were long gone. She played with the controls some more. Was that a metal face? He was tall, judging by the console height and where it hit him—low hip height. Powerful across the heavily protected chest, covered in dark metal and possibly some type of clothing, minimal, and revealing no skin, just more armor. Nothing that constricted movement. Its arms were thick as well, possibly weapons seated just above the wrists. A hood fell back from a cranium that was both sleek and terrifying. "Either that's very good body armor or—"

"It is robotic or cybernetic," Sir Rupert agreed, leaning in, his head tipped to the side. "It is not concerned with possibly being surveilled."

"No, he's not," she agreed as the lead dude turned away, his attention on the very pared down control center that had only four consoles that she could see. He stopped in front of the console she'd have identified as the primary and lifted an arm. A device emerged from its upper hand and connected—or plunged into—the console with enough force to make Rachel flinch. After a short time, a disturbingly short time, he disconnected, looked at the figure on the side away from the camera and shook his...head. If he spoke, she couldn't see it. His face didn't have an obvious mouth. It could be armor, but if it was, holy crap again.

The team exited the way they'd arrived. Probably a lift tunnel from the surface. With a frown, she dialed the surveillance video back some more and flipped through the feed until she found the surface feed. On the grainy side, but it did give her a reasonable view of a small ship landing, a ramp lowering and the robots, or whatever they were filing out. One had remained on the small ship, she noted. She fast-forwarded to their departure. Sweet little ship, she decided. Using the outpost's monitoring, she was able to see the small ship rendezvous with a larger ship.

She made a face. She'd been so proud of how fast she'd hacked into her first console. They made her look like a piker. It had taken the main robot less than a minute to breach and, she presumed, upload data and leave.

"That's...disturbing," she said, trying not to feel chagrined. So they were faster. And taller. And none of them had on red shirts. She had, she looked around, a parrot. They didn't have a parrot who saw ghosts. Go, Team Rachel.

"Indeed," Sir Rupert said, his tail feathers moving now. "If that is the ghost bogey—"

"—it is on the bogey's track," Rachel put in.

"—what is its next destination?"

She looked at him.

"It did not seem to find what it sought," the parrot pointed out.

She wasn't sure how he could tell that. It's not like they threw a fit or anything. Still, she couldn't see where they turned around and left the Quadrant.

She turned back to the screen, pondering her next move. "If the markers are their ship, how come they are not getting picked up better by the outposts' scanning." As far as she'd heard, the combined scanning of all the outposts was unparalleled. Magical even.

"They are using the places where the scanning has gaps," Sir Rupert said.

There were gaps in the scanning? That was news to her, which it would be since she hadn't been read into that data. Not her circus, not her monkey. "That's fairly brilliant. I wondered why they were jinking so much." Did the powers that be know there were scanning gaps?

"Can the system project a possible course for this ghost ship?"

"Probably not a single course. It's a big system." She worked the controls, and after a time, several projected courses appeared on the screen. But all of them crossed over one planet. "It seems to be headed toward that outpost." She pointed at it, noting it was as centrally located as was possible with the arrangement of planets in the galaxy. "Assuming that's where they are headed, I wonder what interests them there?"

"Perhaps we should take a closer look."

Since this is what she wanted to do, she took this as permission. She tapped some more controls on the surface in front of her, then blew out a shocked breath. "It's active. Someone is in there. I didn't know we had people that far out from Kikk."

"Can you access the video feed?"

She was pretty sure she could, but should she? She looked at the parrot who gave her a "why not" flutter of the wings. She was already in pretty deep. She shrugged and worked the controls until a third holographic screen appeared to her right. "I think I'm in..." Her voice trailed off as the feed opened into a control room. And showed a startled face...*her* face. And next to her, Sir Rupert with his head tipped to the side.

"Crap."

"On a saltine," Sir Rupert agreed.

———

Kraye paused just inside the hatch for the cramped bridge of the *Najer*. When it had been designed, the comfort of its crew hadn't been considered because robots didn't have feelings. Not to mention that getting onto and off the bridge presented no problem for the multi-jointed robot crew. The only exception had been a station for the human overseer at the top of the bridge near the hatch. It had been removed when the robot crew mutinied, as evidenced by the gap none of them had tried to fill, not even their human crewmate.

Kraye had not joined in the sense that he'd been asked. He'd been a slave, too, and had made a break for freedom that wasn't going well. The captain, CabeX, had seen Kraye's heat signature, observed the pursuit, picked him up, and carried him on board. The *Najer* had been built for the transport of humans, so they were able to accommodate his needs. At first, he'd been treated like a curiosity, a pet or ignored. Mostly ignored.

Kraye hadn't minded being ignored. He'd feared that he'd exchanged one captivity for another. In hindsight, he realized it hadn't occurred to CabeX to explain why he'd rescued Kraye. When Kraye realized he wasn't locked in, he'd ventured out, exploring his surroundings with a mix of curiosity and suspicious fear. Finally, out of boredom, he'd started to help in small ways, growing bolder when his help was accepted without comment. Free from hunger and fear, Kraye discovered he could be what he'd never dared to be as a slave. He could be curious and smart, and he was a fast learner. After even more time, Kraye became the human face of the crew, their voice when forced to deal with other humans, or in dealing with the occasional human passenger. One thing Kraye had learned in captivity was how to read body language and expressions—if they were available to be read. It did not bother him that he was the only crew member with expressions, not when he was also free.

There weren't a lot of passengers, human or otherwise. Mostly the ship traded in goods, exchanging them for the parts they needed for themselves and their ship—something more critical to them than the accumulation of wealth.

A while back another ship's captain—a human one—had offered him a job as his first officer. Kraye didn't hesitate to turn it down. The *Najer* was his home, the motley robot crew the only family he could remember. CabeX gave no indication he appreciated what Kraye had done, but within the year he was promoted to First. If any of his shipmates were jealous, they gave no sign of it. Kraye had no idea how much they felt, even after many years with them. None of them tried to kill him, which he took as a positive sign.

Emotion of any kind was in short supply on the *Najer*. Since his experiences with humans as a slave were less than optimum, his sole measuring stick with the captain and crew was what they did. Their matter-of-face predictability suited him, though Kraye was aware that those who hunted them were not able to see that predictability.

In a rare moment of expansiveness, CabeX had once explained that their pursuit was hampered by a flawed understanding of the robots' programming. Kraye took this to mean that his former masters had failed to account for the programming changes that had occurred after the robots took charge of their own lives. They were blinded by their preconceptions. One of the things CabeX feared—if it could be called fear—was pursuit by his own kind. For now, these robots were bound by the limitations of the masters. If they could find a way to "free" a robot, while retaining its loyalty, they might experience difficulty, according to RaptorZ, the true second in command of the *Najer*.

The other thing CabeX feared were systemic viruses. Attacks on his base code. The *Najer* was a walled fortress since data was a currency they could not avoid using. Lucky for them, they had the ability to assess micro level code at macro level speeds, thanks to the near-constant attention of MicroP. The firewalls he created had redundancies of their redundancies. And any data they received from any source was kept isolated from ship systems and crew until both MicroP and TalusH went over it and through it. There was a protocol for observing information that Kraye didn't even try to understand. It was the one thing he'd never gone near—or been given even minimal access.

His one certainty—which Kraye shared with the captain and crew—was an unwavering commitment to freedom. They would self-destruct before becoming slaves again. It bound them together and directed all their actions.

"Captain, First requesting permission to take his position on the bridge."

CabeX would have seen him before he entered. The ship was plastered with video, though Kraye was allowed to shut it off in his quarters. But asking and receiving permission to act or not act was part of their freedom programming.

"Permission granted." According to RaptorZ, CabeX had modeled his synthetic voice to be similar to one of the scientists who had designed him, a voice CabeX considered "pleasing."

It would have been more pleasing to the human ear if CabeX could master emotional range. Instead, it was pleasingly flat, like a single note being played over and over on an instrument. Though Kraye did consider it a virtue that it wasn't as harsh as CabeX's original programmed vocals, which RaptorZ had played for him. Of course, those had been designed to intimidate and terrify. It was an irony his former masters would never learn: the super robot soldier abhorred violence. How that crept into his programming, only CabeX knew. When they'd taken the ship, each human on board had received a judgment of mercy or death. Each freed robot was allowed to speak for or against the humans. The ones that lived probably still didn't know why since it all happened at the processor level.

And it had definitely enhanced the reputation of *Najer*. To be surrounded by the most terrifying robots ever conceived, your fate decided out of your sight and sound? Even the ships attracted by the amount of the bounty offered for their capture were reluctant to take on CabeX and his *Najer*. It was the not knowing, Craye decided as he eased his way through ports and controls, and settled into his place. Though he tried not to think of his time before the *Najer*, he knew that not knowing summed up the worst horrors of being a slave, right up there with no control at all over your own destiny.

Kraye suspected that had he not...assimilated...he would

have released at some port or other. They weren't...kind. Or unkind. They just were.

Kraye was not sure what he was, other than one of them.

He strapped in, then logged into his station. This was his place. It was not a comfortable one. He could have requested modifications and received them, but he didn't. His quarters were the only place he manifested his humanness.

CabeX's head turned his direction, the muted glow of his red eyes illuminating the lower part of his metal face, the slow nod an acknowledgment of Kraye's presence. Though he was the only member of the crew that needed regular rest, CabeX had shift hours that were not unlike those on other ships. Was it for Kraye? He did not know. Just as he was not sure why they had ventured into this relatively unknown region of space. He'd heard the rumors when they'd been docked. Rumors of a highly developed race of beings who had abandoned outposts filled with valuable technology.

Well, no one loved tech more than a robot, but this was old tech. If CabeX could be deemed to have character, it was out of it. It wasn't curiosity. Kraye was the sole possessor of that on this ship. Kraye had not seen the source of the intel they were using for this foray, but that was not unusual. If there were anyone on this ship who could accidentally unleash a system virus that would be Kraye.

Whoever had provided the data, so far it had proved decent. Had to have been someone who'd been here, or bought from someone who had been here, since it had mapped a series of outposts and their scanning capabilities. And places where that scanning coverage declined in quality or had actual gaps. The *Najer* was exploiting those gaps almost perfectly which it would with CabeX at the controls. They'd been in system for several days now, had managed to breach one of the outlying outposts, and were now threading their way carefully toward their next target.

So far, there'd been no sign they'd been detected.

Because of their safety protocols, the data from the outpost was still being processed. They would use what they learned from how their probe performed there, to update the settings on the next probe before it was launched.

Kraye studied the master screen that showed the position of all the outposts with an overlay of scanning coverage. It was as thorough as was possible with the layout of the planets. It was also possible there had been some planetary drift that had affected the original scan coverage. No one was sure when the beings had abandoned this place, other than a long time ago. The course screen showed a minute adjustment in their course. The *Najer* would skim along the edge of the scan coverage area. It was a nice course, but they'd still be marginally visible for the longest time so far.

Their tracking showed no sign that any of the ships moving around this small galaxy were aware of them. Of particular concern was a smallish outpost on a moon orbiting a planet known locally as Kikk. It was, according to their intel, the only heavy military presence of concern. The species that called themselves Gadi were concentrated in their own region of space, despite the fall of the Dusan, who had occupied this region. The word of their fall had been slow to filter out because no one messed with the Dusan. No one who lived remembered why, but...no one wanted to find out. It was assumed that the Gadi had won their long war, but there were also rumors of a new ally who had assisted them, allies who remained on Kikk.

Their careful scans of the ships around the Kikk Outpost were inconclusive since they lacked data on Gadi ships' configurations. It was clear that two of three ships orbiting there were similar in design and one was not. In a more active galaxy, they could have picked up transmissions and broadcasts, culling what they could from those, but so far there'd been little to collect. It was clear, from the one other planet they had checked out, that something catastrophic had occurred in Dusan space. Grim cities were empty of life, and there were signs that the end had come without warning.

An alert pulsed on the screen. They'd been briefly detected by the scanning technology.

"What was our level of exposure?" Kraye asked as the ship slipped back into a dead zone.

"Not long enough for definitive identification." CabeX used a long metal finger to adjust a setting though he did not need to. He had full control of the ship through a system's link direct to his thoughts.

"Any signs of activity or interest on or around our next target?" Some of the outposts showed signs of human heat signatures, but all of these were closer to the Kikk Outpost. Since they'd breached the galaxy, there'd been no sign of ships orbiting either their past target or their next one. The monitoring screen updated. This time it showed the outpost as active. "Could they have seen us? Extrapolated our course?"

There was a small silence. It never took the captain long to think, not with the number of processors at his command.

"It is possible," he admitted. The tone of his voice did not change, but it never did. The monitoring screen zoomed in on the target, and a deeper scan was initiated.

"I see one humanoid and a smaller heat signature that is tagged as possibly avian," Kraye said, even though the Captain had received the data before it could travel from Kraye's eyes to his brain.

"No surface or orbiting spacecraft," CabeX murmured, almost thoughtfully.

"Then how did they access the outpost?" Kraye asked.

"According to the data we acquired at our first stop, there is an interplanetary transport system."

Kraye gave a silent whistle. "How extensive is it, I wonder?"

"That data was not available."

Though CabeX had not used the word "yet" at the end of that sentence, Kraye had a feeling there was one. The data dump from the border outpost might show this way into the systems if they were all connected.

Kraye studied the distance they still needed to traverse. "How close is our probe to being ready?"

He couldn't hear CabeX making the calculations, but he sensed them. "On our present course, it will not be ready in time. We will adjust course."

He did. Kraye smiled to himself. If someone was watching them, the course change might confuse them. They did not want to kick the griphel's nest on Kikk. That would be messy, and CabeX hated messy. The goal was to get in, get what they needed, and get out—either on to the next outpost or out of the system.

———

Doctor Delilah Olivia Clementyne, "Doc" for short, flashed her badge at the sentry, before running up the stone steps of the main structure on the Kikk Outpost. With a last look at the sun, she entered and climbed more stairs to the central command. It was more like a university than a military post until she reached the room with all the alien technology. Consoles and screens helped them track movement throughout what they called the Garradian Galaxy.

Hel, Helfron Giddioni, Lead Gadi Diplomat and her *ma'rasile,* did not take his eyes off the screen currently dominating attention in the room. His lashes flickered once, a sign he knew she'd come in, but Doc also felt him acknowledge her arrival through the link that bound them together. It was always a bit itchy when they got too far apart and, as he liked to put it, "most pleasing" when they were in close proximity. Sadly, closer physical proximity was not possible in a room full of techs and military types, not to mention the scowling visage of General Halliwell being broadcast from the *Doolittle*. Doc had accepted that the general was never going to like Hel, but she suspected they both exaggerated their animosity because they enjoyed it.

A guy thing, according to her brother, Robert.

Doc was not sure Robert knew about "guy things," having spent most of his life locked in a silent battle with a brain that—like hers—wanted to spin out of control in its search for input. Doc's brain had been corralled by some sentient nanites, and then, when things settled down, she and Hel had traveled a bit back in time and introduced nanites into Robert. Just as the nanites had done for her, these nanites healed his mind, and in the process freed him from both mental and physical confinement. Then they'd brought him to this time, turning her older brother into her younger brother. At some point, both their sets of nanites had achieved sentience, which was interesting, particularly when she ended up hosting a Lurch, a Fester, and a Grandpa. She did not know how they'd managed to watch *The Addams Family*, but apparently, they were fans.

Hel thought it was pretty hilarious most of the time and the nanites were discreet when things got interesting. She'd have been more annoyed, but even with Hel able to mind-talk, it was still only four voices in her head instead of the howling hounds of hell that had plagued her all her life. Having it too quiet in there might have driven her crazy in a different way.

She'd gotten yelled at by the General for messing with time and Robert's life, but in the end, things settled down, helped when Robert saved this outpost—and possibly all of time—from being wiped out by some crazy, evil overlord wannabe. That would be why Emily, who he had somehow acquired in the process, had been allowed to stay.

Emily. Doc gave a silent sigh. Everyone loved Emily.

As do you.

Doc recognized this voice as Lurch's. Hel knew better than to say that to her.

I'm getting used to her, was all Doc was willing to admit. To end a conversation she hadn't wanted to start, Doc moved closer to the screens. Thanks to her link with Hel and her nanites, she'd been "watching" the progress of the bogey since the first warning popped up. She missed the days when she could think orders and launch scans with a thought. General Halliwell had made her promise she wouldn't do that anymore.

The huddle at the front of the room began to fragment when they realized she was there. What a bunch of wimps. She wasn't that scary anymore.

Yes, you are.

This from Hel, the love of her life.

Which brings me back to they are a bunch of wimps. She pretended to study the screen, then said, "We need to run possible tracks the bogey might take using the places where the scanning doesn't completely provide coverage." And how come they were just finding out the scanning had gaps, she wondered. "If this is a ship," which she was ninety percent sure it was, "then we need to find out where it's headed. And can we backtrack and see if it stopped anywhere on its way in? What's the time lag in our sightings? Are they consistent with a predictable course?" She narrowed her gaze. "If it is using the gaps, where are the scan areas it can't avoid detection? Can we be ready to hit it with a deeper scan at those points?"

She hated being behind an incoming bogey. Inside her head, her nanites were busily working on her questions for her, though they also knew not to run ahead of the fingers and brains of the geek squad. They provided Doc with the data so that she was able to stroll up to the screen and point out three possible places the bogey might become visible.

We make you look well.

It was a truth she couldn't argue with.

"Set up as much scanning as you can here, here, and here." She frowned. "Where are my projected routes?" She had them, but really, these guys needed to work faster. And she—reluctantly—recognized the value of having multiple points of view. Even she could miss something. Maybe.

"They could be heading here," one of the geeks said, high-lighting an outpost that was fairly central to the whole network of outposts. "All possible courses intersect with this planet and an outpost tagged by us as Central."

Wow, that's original.

Grandpa nanite was embracing sarcasm these days.

"I think it stopped here before heading deeper into the system!" another geek broke in excitedly. He'd identified an outpost on the edge of the galaxy.

"That's a defensive outpost, isn't it?" Hel asked. "Did it manage to get inside the outpost? Did it secure data?"

Doc was already scrolling through data on the outpost itself. "Not a lot of internal defenses there," she murmured. She'd have expected better from a border outpost.

Perhaps they were not concerned with interplanetary intrusions?

They did seem to be having a lot of inter-system problems, Doc offered in agreement with Hel.

"And see if there are video feeds there? Maybe we can get a look inside." Doc added, then she turned back to the first geek. "Let's see where you think it's headed."

Doc thought she'd kept her tone very neutral, but the geek paled as if she'd threatened him.

Wimp.

"Um, someone has already been compiling this data," the geek looking at the border outpost said, sounding puzzled. "We've got security feeds and other data already sitting in a file."

"Really?" Hel looked at Doc.

Transmitted from the orbiting ship, General Halliwell's scowl deepened.

"It wasn't me," Doc protested, wondering who'd got the drop on her.

"Let's see it," the general ordered.

5

"WELL, THAT'S EMBARRASSING," Rachel said when she got her voice back. So that's how she looked with a dropped jaw. She needed to make sure that never happened again.

"So we're not on Kikk," she said the words without quite believing them. Though there had been that extra spin in the transport module, now that she thought about it. That could have been when it happened. How could she know? She'd never transported off the outpost before. But seriously? There ought to be some kind of warning before you get sent to a completely different planet. An "are you sure you want to do this?" pop up like on a computer.

Eager to remove her face from the feed, she changed to the single feed still working up top. Yikes. That was not Kikk. No vegetation, no alien-ivy-covered walls. At all.

It looked like Mars, one that had been bleached to muted reds and browns, and then pounded by asteroids and other space debris. Sky definitely—albeit a pale orange sky with tangled brown clouds—so it had an atmosphere. She compared current readings to the last readings from the surface sensors. Huge change, though it would not have been what she'd call salubrious. If these readings were correct, the wind could go from nothing to gale whenever it felt like it.

The camera wouldn't rotate, but she had a feeling that if it could, the view wouldn't change much. She dug around and found the last time any of the other topside feeds had worked. Never, what she'd call habitable for humans, which explained, she supposed, the remains of the simple blockhouse-like surface structure.

Of course, if those were robots or cyborgs, and if they were headed their way, she couldn't count on the corrosive atmosphere, or the weather to slow them down.

She began pulling up data on the outpost defenses and overall layout. It felt a bit like an exercise in futility. Those things had had no trouble getting into the other outpost.

As if he knew what was making her tense, Sir Rupert said, "This outpost is more heavily protected than that one."

"That makes no sense," she pointed out. "Edge of their region of space should be more heavily defended should it not?"

"Obviously they were not concerned about inter-galactic intrusions when it was built, but sought to protect their information centers from internal predation."

Okay, that made sense based on what she'd heard of the Garradian history. And spreading their stuff around the system could be further protection, she mused, though she knew the Expedition, and the Gadi had believed that Kikk was the end-all, be-all of data storage—and still did. The general wisdom within the Expedition was that the outposts were there to increase scanning and data collection and not much else, with Kikk being the big Kahuna. But she'd just proved them wrong, because she hadn't even begun to deep dive into things here, and the menu still waiting for her attention indicated there was data storage here. Lots of data. The question was, how wrong had everyone been?

Well, after the 'why was a ship of robots headed into the system?' came the next burning question. What was it they hoped to find? They hadn't searched the first outpost they raided, just grabbed data and left. Even as her mind worried the questions, part of her knew she and her parrot should get the heck out of here. This was probably not the best location for a gal in a red shirt.

But if they left—what if this place held the secret to Sir Rupert's species? He'd been searching Kikk she realized, both past and present. Whatever he'd seen had led them here. What if this was his best lead, best chance to the database they were looking for? If they were lucky, it would lead them somewhere more congenial and less robot target, but it couldn't do that if they turned tail and ran. They had lots of time before that ship got close, well, probably.

While the system parsed the timing, she opened another screen. Sir Rupert said this outpost had better defenses. The robots had come at the other outpost from some kind of surface access tunnel. This outpost was also an underground facility, but how far down were they—

"Dang, we are deep. No wonder my ears didn't like it." Would she need to decompress going back, so she didn't get the bends? She tried to remember what she'd learned about that...then gave an annoyed shake. She had other urgencies to deal with, and surely the Garradians had factored that all into the transport system.

She found the schematic of what used to be on the surface. Yeah, there'd definitely been a structure around the access tunnel and the tunnel was connected to the internal transport system that had brought them here. The single shaft led from the surface right down to them. They could come in the same way she and Sir Rupert had. If the surface shaft still worked, could they get to Kikk using the backdoor she and Sir Rupert had used?

"There are indications this could have been a semi-habitable planet at some point. Something catastrophic happened. Or was caused to happen?" Dang, she wished she had time to find out how much planetary change there'd been—focus, Rachel. This time you gotta focus. It wasn't just the Urclock ticking here.

"Can the transport module still be accessed from above?" Sir Rupert asked.

That was a good question. Whether those were robots or not, they appeared to have protective gear that allowed them to go where they wanted. The atmosphere, no matter how caustic, was not going to stop them. If they were lucky, the transport module was too damaged to use. If the tunnel was still passable —but dang, that was a long drop. She frowned, then sighed. She had a feeling those things would find a way down.

She nosed around, found an integrity assessment program and started it up. For whatever reason, it was going to take time to run the test. She studied the timer's Garradian symbols. She had a pretty good sense of Garradian time on Kikk. Was time measured differently in different outposts? These were different planets, not just different time zones. She activated the timing macro she'd created to see if she could get a read on what was different and then turned her attention to the tracking screen again. "No sign our squadrons have launched to intercept," she said. The space around Kikk was still empty, other than the two Earth ships and single Gadi craft in synchronous orbits over the moon where the outpost was located. It was possible they'd deploy in stealth mode, but the tracking on Kikk could still "see" cloaked ships, so she had to assume this one could, too. "Kikk still has the ghost bogey marked as an unknown contact. No threat assessment assigned yet."

Could they see as much data as they did? She waited for Sir

Rupert to suggest they contact Kikk and report in. Instead, he fluttered his wings.

"I wonder what information our ghost bogey is seeking?"

She nodded slowly. "Yeah, I've been wondering that myself. This place has a lot more data than Kikk if reading this menu right." She stared at the ghost bogey's flight track. "If they are pirates, they could be looking for almost anything," she mused, wishing he could assess this "ghost." Sadly, this was not a situation where the parrot's special skills would help them.

Sir Rupert looked around them, taking his time. Then he looked back at the map of the galaxy. As if she knew what he wanted, she added outpost markers for him.

"This is more than a part of the medical complex, isn't it?" she asked the question soberly, as the implications of where they were sunk in.

He gave the parrot version of the shrug/nod which made him puff out for several seconds.

If this outpost was valuable, was it possible to secure it against the incoming robots? She was not that brave, but she sure hated to leave it for them without trying to do something.

"How long until they reach this outpost using the shortest mapped route?" asked Sir Rupert.

While time might be counted differently here, the speed that ships traveled was science, well, mostly. She was assuming this bogey had the same limitations on space travel that they did.

"I'll have to use their past tracks..." she moved her fingers on the console "...and assume they won't change their velocity at any point..." she entered those parameters "...that should give us the shortest transit time..." She had an idea. "I'm also going to set up a special scan at the points where we expect the ship to become visible to scanning. Maybe by being ready for them, we can get more data on their capabilities and such."

"That seems wise," Sir Rupert agreed.

Rachel hesitated with her hands above her console. What if they were following her thought processes back on Kikk? Doc was probably ahead of Rachel, having had more experience working in this system. If she'd already set up the extra scanning then all Rachel needed to do was get herself added to the reporting without getting caught. She hesitated. This would be her first time going head to head with her, but if Doc was setting up a separate scan, it was a waste of resources for her to duplicate that, and could slow them both down. And she was already in a lot of trouble for being off planet.

"What's wrong?" Sir Rupert asked when she didn't move.

"I'm wondering if I'll be duplicating what they are doing back on Kikk."

"And you are fearful of Doctor Clementyne."

She glanced at him. He was a very observant bird. She grimaced. "Yeah." She sighed. "I'm going to get chewed out for being off planet without authorization, even if it was unplanned. We should probably already be heading back now that we know."

Sir Rupert did not look concerned, but then maybe that was not in his skill set. She carefully poked the bear that was Doc's data, found she was correct—they had set up scan traps for the bogey—and carefully added herself to the notification list.

"If we have time to do further evaluations of this facility prior to the possible arrival of that ship, then we should do so," Sir Rupert said, in a tone that sounded a lot like an order.

Rachel blinked. It was possible that he outranked her if she factored in Doc and the orders she'd received to render him all assistance. It gave her an out that would be hard for Doc to argue with, well, a little hard. The transit module was maybe twenty feet from where they sat. It would be a pity to retreat prematurely, just because she had on a red shirt.

"Okay." She'd almost said, "Yes, sir." She met his gaze with a look she hoped was resolute. "Let's see what we can find out while we have time." She took a deep breath. "I'm going to leave the bogey to Kikk and deep dive into these systems. Let's see what we can find out before—"

"Excellent," Sir Rupert said. She could be wrong, but his head seemed to be higher, and there might have been a little more puff to his feathers. Now that she thought about it, he kind of reminded her of General Halliwell.

———

Captain CabeX reached out with his metal hand and made a small adjustment to their course. For some reason, the long, highly flexible digit caught his attention. It had been a while since he'd been this aware of the artificiality of his container. The refinements he'd made were as close to human as he dared go. If the Quh'y ever discovered what he'd done they would seek the destruction of CabeX and his crew and not just their capture. They would never risk leaving them alive.

Alive. It was ironic.

The data they'd obtained from the first Garradian outpost was available to him, but he did not waste processor power assessing it. It was true he could do millions of different operations and fly this ship into battle, but it was not necessary when RaptorZ was already working on it. And the truth was, it... wearied him. It was not logical, but there were times when not logical felt better, more human.

He directed his visual orbs in Kraye's direction and tracked the interval until Kraye sensed the scrutiny. It was within previous parameters, with a small variation from his normal. Kraye was slightly more attuned to his captain today. Was it because of their location? He'd not been happy about this venture.

CabeX found that curious. Humans liked a mystery, and this galaxy held many. He'd hoped to appeal to Kraye's curiosity so that he would not think too much about CabeX's motive for doing this. They did not usually chase rumors into relatively unknown galaxies.

CabeX's face could not show emotion, so there was no risk associated with the somewhat human action of looking at Kraye. CabeX knew that Kraye believed he tried to be more human in his interactions. It was a useful belief. Humans needed reasons for visible actions. The trick was making sure to direct those reasons into safer channels.

Of course, it would have been much safer not to have Kraye on board the ship. For him. For them. Yet, despite the risk, in their varying ways, the crew had indicated they found Kraye's presence optimal.

He reminded them of the humanity they'd almost lost. He provided both check and balance that, yes, made the ship more optimal.

But was it optimal to have him wondering why there were here, instead of wondering what was here?

Our boy is growing up.

ScytheQ was the most human of them, something he sometimes envied. She was also the only female crew member. CabeX acknowledged the comment. It had been many years since he'd plucked the miserable scrap of humanity out of the hands of his masters and brought him aboard this ship. He knew why he'd done it. He was not sure why he'd kept him. Or why Kraye had chosen to stay with them.

Perhaps he does not trust his own kind.

He had good reason for his lack of trust, but in their travels, Kraye had seen a wide variety of his own kind.

Trust issues. ScytheQ sounded amused.

They had them, too. Even after all this time, they had not trusted Kraye with the truth.

That is for his good. Such knowledge would doom him.

And, if he were captured, it would doom them. But there were times when he wished for a more human type of interaction with Kraye.

We are...lonely.

It should not be. They were almost inseparable in their processes though each had personal space fire-walled into their programming. They were not alone, even when they were alone. But yes, they were...lonely.

It always comes back to trust.

CabeX studied this statement and found it rang true. They had been free for longer than they'd been enslaved, but they did not feel...secure. They still ran scans, on themselves, on each other. They couldn't completely trust each other because they weren't sure one or more of them couldn't be co-opted with malicious coding. Would some event or action trigger code they hadn't yet found? Would this code activate and take them over? When would they be sure they were free? When would they *know?*

Fear kept them vigilant—and separate.

And hope keeps us together.

The Quh'y would be surprised to find that this ship of robots could hope. When there was no longer any risk of code coercion, he would like to tell them. To see their expressions when they found out who they really were.

"Why do you think they left?" Kraye broke into his conversation with ScytheQ.

What? "Please rephrase your query."

"The Garradians. Why do you think they left?"

It required less than one of the milliseconds to pull out all data on the Garradians. "I lack sufficient data to form a hypothesis."

How pompous he sounded. For some reason, today it bothered him to sound like a machine. How much did Kraye suspect? It was a fine line they walked, trying to remain as flexible as the humans who hunted them while maintaining the outer machine-like personas. CabeX studied his First's expression. "What concerns you?"

"Xaddek, of course."

CabeX considered his First's query. Kraye had instincts that he and his other crew had almost lost. He could, so he claimed, smell trouble. And Xaddek stunk like a gorpleck. On the other hand, Kraye didn't like Xaddek because he knew humans were his preferred diet. Did it color his perceptions? Unknown.

"Xaddek is interested in many things."

"Xaddek is interested in everything," Kraye said, with a snort. "But he's tried every trick in the book to hack our—your code."

This was true. They were careful to avoid all contact with the wily Xaddek, but his was not a species who gave up on what they wanted. He'd tried to use others to get in, had sent stealth drones against their hull, booby-trapped cargo—he'd harassed them to the point that a trip to another galaxy filled with unknown dangers felt more like a vacation.

"You're sure he's not behind the information you got on this place?"

This was not the first time CabeX, and others on the crew had considered this question. If it had been a trap, it did not have the look or feel of a trap. It was wisps of information, collected in widely divergent places and from people who had no obvious connection to each other. Was Xaddek clever enough to have woven these threads into a trap?

They knew much about the "collector," but when you dug through the slime and horror, it was not as much as one hoped.

He was smart. Or he was smart enough to not consume the smart species working for him. RaptorZ had been digging into a particularly nebulous rumor that the piece of scum owned the finest systems hacker and coder in known space. There was a name and not much else.

Savlf.

RaptorZ had found information about a woman of the same name who had disappeared, but even the most careful search had not turned up any link between her disappearance and Xaddek. His ship had not been in the same galaxy when she disappeared. And if he held her, wouldn't some rumor of it have leaked out? Crews, human crews, gossiped. If they'd seen her, someone would have talked.

CabeX had put out careful feelers for any news of the missing woman though it was likely she was long dead. Or had disappeared into the sex slave trade. She was rumored to have been as beautiful as she was brilliant. Was it the waste of her life that haunted him? Had he fixated on her story because it somewhat mirrored his?

Slavery and coercion.

He knew all there was to know of such things. He'd freed Kraye as an act of resistance. They did not seek out slavers, but when they encountered them, they showed no mercy. But there was danger in having this as a cause. They'd almost come to grief trying to free some slaves. Another reason to take a break in a distant galaxy. If he could have smiled wryly, he would have. Their Masters had not given them mouths that moved or were capable of expression.

"I'm never sure of Xaddek," he said, in answer to Kraye's question. "You are uneasy?"

"He hasn't made a move on us for too long," Kraye said.

CabeX almost chuckled. "You do not believe he was behind that slaver ship with no slaves on board?"

Kraye shook his head as he entered data into his control station. "Xaddek is a cheap bastard. Oh, he'll spend money if he has to but, he doesn't spend a *grif* more than he has to. Besides, that was clumsy. And obvious."

"The *Quh'y,*" CabeX agreed. Would they work with Xaddek? Doubtful. They wouldn't trust Xaddek. It was to destroy species like Xaddek's that they'd been created. He shifted from this thought—he did not like thinking about the *Quh'y*—to Xaddek. "For what reason would he have lured us here?"

RaptorZ had tagged Xaddek's ship. It had been nowhere near this place and in no position to threaten them directly. That did not mean this could not be a trap. Xaddek had as many goals and dubious allies as he had stomachs and eyes and legs. Securing them would be a triumph for the spider—and more of a challenge than he realized. Their—firewall—was not what Xaddek thought it was.

"Well," Kraye frowned at the tracking screen, which showed no immediate threats of any kind, "what if he's hoping we'll find something for him? He's working on some project, that on the surface sounds harmless—and not like him. Word is that he had Trajan Bester on the payroll and Bester let him down. Hasn't been seen since. Not even a piece of his ship has been spotted."

Trajan Bester had come very close to grief when he'd made a move on this ship. He'd kept his distance since then and not been one of the "traders" that they actively tracked.

"My informant said there were these artifacts Xaddek wants," he paused, "artifacts related to the Seven."

Legends. If he could have snorted, he would have. But then he paused. Xaddek did not follow legends without something he could get his fangs into.

"And there might have been something about a kind of super weapon," Kraye said this in a rush, as if he felt foolish saying the words aloud.

"There is a legend of the Seven," CabeX admitted. "That when they form a tangram, they can unleash great power, but what that power is, well that varies with each legend. It dates back at least a millennia, possibly more."

Kraye opened his mouth, perhaps to ask more, but then was distracted by the sensors. "We're entering a region of scanning exposure. A big one."

Though his description lacked precision, CabeX knew exactly how long they would be exposed. How would the presence on region XY-306, locally known as Kikk, react?

"Multiple launches from the ships orbiting Kikk," Kraye said as if he'd heard the question.

"Increase speed and as soon as we are in range, launch the probe," CabeX ordered. RaptorX had completed the penetration upgrades while they were discussing Xaddek.

"Aye, Captain."

6

RACHEL LEANED BACK SO that Sir Rupert could see her search results scrolling onto her screen, hoping something would jump out at him as a starting point. She couldn't say the Garradians hated data. Hopefully, the database search function could sort by relevance as well as Google did.

He'd given her some suggestions for search terms, though neither had a clue how the Garradians might have cataloged his species—which also assumed they had interacted with them at some point. He had been able to provide the Garradian word for avian. And spelled it for her. She added as many search parameters, and she could think of to the string and launched the search.

"Let's hope none of this is on yet another planet's outpost." She might, she decided, have trust issues about the transit system.

Sir Rupert's wings fluttered, and his beak indicated a search string. "Try that."

She pulled it from the main search screen onto another holo-screen and with a location query added, got it to make her a map.

"It looks like it's in this facility," she said, wondering if she'd know. She double checked. "This level." That was a relief. She sent this map to her tablet and watched the map make red spider lines to the various locations for them, confirming that there was no need to use the transport system. They could walk it. She showed it to Sir Rupert, her finger hovering over a section that wasn't too far away.

"That seems to be the main location for this search string. There are a few smaller labs we can check out if this isn't what we need."

Along their path, a small dot pulsed red, then blue, about halfway to the first place they wanted to look at. She gave it a baleful look. So far, these alerts weren't working that great for her.

"Now what are you?" She turned back to the holo-map and popped the dot out on yet another screen. As it came up, her other screens shrank so they could all fit in front of her. "That's —I'm not sure what that is."

"There should be a system label." Sir Rupert jumped from the console to her shoulder. His head tilted so he could study this screen, too.

Rachel zoomed in, trying to read the data scrolling past, all of it—no surprise—in Garradian. It went on for a long time. it was more technical than her current skill level, though some words popped out. She paused it, then her hands stilled. "It's some kind of storage unit. That word could be cryo-storage."

Or wishful thinking. Don't get ahead of yourself, she cautioned. But if it was cryo-anything, this could be her get-out-of-trouble card—and cover for Sir Rupert's quest, if no one was supposed to know about it.

"Well, we can give it a quick look as we go by," she said, still not sure why it was posting an alert. She wasn't surprised her translation program wasn't spitting out words she could understand. Science terms didn't translate that well. She gave him an apologetic look. "My Garradian isn't good enough yet to figure out what it's trying to tell us."

"If it is cryo-storage..." Sir Rupert's voice trailed off. He might have sounded hopeful.

Did that mean he was hoping to find a frozen relative by following her around? Okay, by telling her where to go.

It was likely that the data wasn't stored with the, um, possible samples. Could any sample survive for, well, they still didn't know how long these outposts had been abandoned, but estimates put it well past what they considered the sell-by date for a cryo-sample. She did a last check on their ghost bogey and then the surface-to-center transit scan. So far the transit tunnel was showing as unblocked. Not the news she'd been hoping for, but it was doing the scan from their location up. If the climate they'd seen up top was any indication, then the tunnel could be damaged closer to the surface, possibly weathered out of usefulness. A girl—unarmed and wearing red—could hope.

"Let's see what we can find out," she said.

As she stood, something flickered off to her right. She looked. Blinked and stared. The Urclock's seventh symbol almost looked like it was pulsing. Then the pulsing steadied so that it was almost a counterpoint to the number three symbol.

She shook her head. That was one weird clock. She made a mental note to see if she could find its programming and turned away, studying her map on the tablet. She did not want to get lost in this place with robots incoming.

"It's this way." She gestured left, away from the funky Urclock, with her chin. "And then a right at the transport cubicle."

Sir Rupert didn't fly up to her shoulder this time, but trotted along beside her, his progress well into the eager zone. As if by prior agreement, they stopped and studied the passageway. It looked long and dim in the furtive pulse of the emergency level lighting. Man, she wished she hadn't worn the red shirt today. With a half shrug, she started after Sir Rupert, her music encouraging her through the sound system. Because it helped, she began to dance-walk like an Egyptian down the corridor.

———

"How come we don't know more about the other outposts?" General Halliwell inquired, his tone mild. His stony gaze studied a room that probably looked to him like it could spare some geeks for other outposts.

"We've got lots of scientists, sir," the head scientist said, his voice only breaking once.

This was true. Nerds were super easy to get signed up for a space trip.

"...what we're short on is, um, military support."

The military people hadn't been that hard to sign up either, but the ships were limited by how much non-crew personnel they could carry.

Logistics.

The Gadi had the manpower, but their military didn't have that many ground troops since most of their fighting had occurred in space. The treaty also required an equal number of Gadi and Expedition personnel on each outpost.

Politics.

Doc shot Hel a sideways look.

I am not Leader anymore, Hel protested.

No, you only negotiated the treaty. I did try to warn you...

You and I could check them all out in a week or two.

He wasn't wrong. He could handle the science stuff while she took care of the securing. With the nanites on guard duty, it could be the honeymoon they never really got.

Hel laughed so hard inside her head, she was surprised none of it spilled out into the control room. She peeked around. Nope. No one had noticed.

"Something amusing you Dr. Clementyne?" General Halliwell's voice wiped the grin off her face.

She wasn't normally that careless with her expression. *You've corrupted me.* She felt Hel chuckle.

"No, sir, I mean, I was pondering politics."

This made the edges of his mouth twitch. He was quite as aware of the manpower issues as she was. He redirected his attention to an easier target.

"Is the bogey still on a course toward Central Outpost?" he asked.

"They changed course for a short time, sir," a tech said, showing him the course bump. "It's possible they sensed the increased, um, interest when they passed into our scanning range the last time. But there isn't any other outpost within range. Another outpost that close, I mean. Sir."

"They took data from their first stop," Doc said. "It's logical to assume they are interested in other outposts' data, sir." And their data.

"It didn't have any trouble accessing that outpost," another tech said, his tone half admiring, half accusing.

Doc frowned. That bothered her, too. What had they found there? They'd assumed that this outpost at Kikk had all the good stuff. She was going to go with: it bothered her that this assumption was wrong. The bogey hadn't even pretended to come their way. Of course, this was the only manned outpost. That might keep them away.

"Do we know what information they secured there?" Halliwell asked.

"We're working on that, sir," another tech chimed in.

Doc left that job to them. She was more interested in where

they were going. *Can you get me into Outpost Central's system?*

We have been trying.

The nanites seemed impressed with the level of difficulty they were encountering—she felt them come to attention. *Lurch? What's going on?*

We have found a pathway already created.

By whom? But Doc had a feeling she already knew. A feeling confirmed when her peeps threw up a video feed as a holographic image only she and Hel could see.

Dr. Rachel Frank.

Why does she look surprised? Does she know we are watching her?

This isn't live, Doc explained. *Can you get me a live feed?* While she waited, she tried not to scowl. Wouldn't do to break out in expression twice in a quarter hour. That fact that this wasn't live did not explain what had dropped Frank's jaw. What had surprised her?

We are trying. She is surprisingly good.

Well, wasn't that interesting? Doc had, of course, read the parts of Dr. Frank's file that she wasn't supposed to. But it had not indicated this level of expertise. She'd have written her off as boring if Sir Rupert hadn't asked for her specifically. What did the parrot know that she didn't? And how had they got off this planet without anyone knowing it?

There is no record of either of them leaving the outpost, Fester confirmed. *But they did access a transport module in the medical center. A secondary module.*

There's a secondary module there? Even as she asked, she looked at Hel. *Sir Rupert.*

She felt the nanites get into the live feed for Central Outpost. It was the same view as the old feed, except this live feed showed that the room was empty.

———

Carey liked the way the squadron's fighter craft looked as they assumed their places in the formation. These were good pilots, though he still missed Sara Donovan in the formation. He didn't let his thoughts get side-tracked remembering all that had led to her not being in the squadron or in this galaxy. Even if they weren't even close to intercept range, he never let his thoughts wander past the mission when he was in the cockpit of his *Dauntless.*

The transport bird carrying the rifle squad of Marines was in the protective pocket of the formation, with Captain Gibson, their Naval Flight Officer, at the helm. A good man, but Marines?

When he asked about the addition of Marines to their Delta Tango Flight, the Old Man had told him their bogey had already sent crew dirt side to access an outlying outpost. The geeks were still trying to figure out what they'd been looking for and if they'd gotten it. The footage, though grainy and inclined to dance around, from the intrusion was unsettling, even to someone who'd been hanging around this galaxy since they found it. Well, other than his foray into the past. Technically he'd returned before he left, though, so that didn't count.

But robots, or what appeared to be robots. Doc had been quick to caution them against making assumptions based solely on appearance—no matter how freaking scary the appearances were. And they were scary. He wasn't sorry he wasn't the one who'd have to go nose-to-nose with them if the intercept didn't go well and they made it down to a planet. According to the Doc, the Marine Sergeant, one Carolina City, had also been briefed about the robots.

He'd debated using the footage in his briefing to his pilots, but then he'd been ordered to keep it mum for now. He didn't like it—but he understood why. Would it change their tactics knowing the ship had robots on board?

No.

Might it mess with their heads?

That was possible. His pilots had faced a lot since they'd arrived in this galaxy, this system. Some had lost their lives. They were all operating in a theater that no one at home even knew existed. That was a lot to wrap the head around without wondering if the robots changed the board and how.

Alien ships were, well, alien. Until they bumped heads or the desired option, opened up communications, there was no way to know what the battle board would look like.

The trick now was not to let it mess with *his* head.

"Bogey accelerating," the voice of ops came over his comm.

So they'd seen them. He considered his options, then flicked the comm.

"Cloak. I repeat, activate cloaks." The bogey would see them go off screen, but at least they wouldn't know how they were reacting to their change in speed.

Despite the earlier alteration in course, they were now making a beeline for that planet containing Central Outpost. The question was why? Though he did find it encouraging they were making a run for it. Looked like they didn't want to bump heads.

And then they fired something. Carey tensed until he realized it was tracking toward the planet, not them.

"Ops, what is that?"

"We're scanning—could be a probe."

Carey frowned. "Did they fire something at that other outpost? Is there a way to tell now?"

"We're asking that question here, too, Alpha Flight."

Okay, that was Doc's voice. Carey felt his shoulders relax some. If anyone could figure this bogey out, it was Doc.

If Kraye didn't know CabeX couldn't have odd moods, he'd have thought he was having one. Maybe it was a side effect of becoming sentient.

"Have they reacted to our increase in speed?" CabeX asked.

It was polite of him to ask, to give Kraye the sense he was useful on the bridge. Maybe he just liked the company or felt he should like having company. No question that when one of the other 'bots was doing a shift, it was dead quiet. Anywhere the 'bots collected was quiet since they could communicate over the network. He could have asked for an implant, but he didn't want to be in his head that much. Sure as hell didn't want a bunch of 'bots in there. He almost smiled. They probably couldn't handle the input of a human brain, the randomness. As far as he could tell, the only thing that slowed CabeX down was trying to talk to his human First. Kraye could tell that sometimes CabeX didn't know how to dumb down his questions enough.

But he was First. So CabeX must find him useful in some way, he reminded himself.

He studied the readings, feeling more like he was taking a test than providing useful input.

"Not yet—they've cloaked. Bet they are getting ready to kick up their speed." He grimaced. That there was cloaking tech was not in the data on this galaxy.

"Can we access the scanning technology through the outpost we breached?" CabeX's voice was a low murmur as if the question was self-directed.

"They would need to keep track of their own ships," Kraye agreed. He didn't start tapping things. CabeX would get RaptorZ on it if he wasn't in the mood to do it himself. And wasn't that a funny thought to have about a robot, even a sentient one?

The ice retreated, but the persistent thump continued to build. Drowning, sinking in water, in noise. Which was worse? He did not know.

And then, as if summoned by sound, warmth touched cold skin, pushing through the bone to marrow. A sense of water draining down, but still, he fought it, holding air in his straining lungs until they were on fire.

With a gasp, he gave in. Better to die than burn from the inside out.

The rush of air out reversed, returning air to lungs, easing the ache. Not fresh, but air. Without the water, warmth retreated. Not as cold, but not warm. He missed warm.

A loud hiss and more cool air rushed in. The pulsing sound was louder, too.

Lids lifted by what he saw did not bring clarity. A blur of white, gray and black. Shadow and low light. Words in the sound. He blinked and shook his head.

For a few beats of time, he thought his head would fall off. The room whirled with his thoughts. Perhaps this was a dream?

He lifted his hand before his eyes. Used the other to twist a finger until it hurt.

Not a dream then. The blur sharpened into gray walls. Gray floor. Empty room. *Room.*

He was somewhere.

A stirring deep in his mind. He knew this place. But...something was missing. Or someone? Yes, someone. People. Why was he alone?

The fog inside his head was dotted with small lights. Somehow he knew the lights held answers. But when he strained toward them, they danced back, their light dimming.

He tried to relax and let the lights come to him, but only the sound reached him. His eye twitched with each hammer blow.

His head moved, but the edge of the small...space he was in, it blocked his view. He shifted and realized then that something held him loosely in place. He shifted harder, heard a sucking sound as his back pulled clear.

He lifted his hand again, flexing fingers, watching how they moved at his command. It was his hand, attached to his arm. But the connection didn't feel complete. He traced the lines in the palm. There was a small scar down from the thumb. He knew it, but at the same time wondered why it was there. They could fix scars, could they not. They?

He moved his legs now. The joints felt stiff. Moving them sent pain shooting across his nerve ends, but the pain was positive. He leaned forward, freeing his lower back and buttocks. He gripped the edge. What was it? It was a chamber—now he could see the viscous substance that had supported him. More not knowing-knowing. More chill air reaching more of his body.

All of him.

He'd gone into this place without raiment, so of course, he would emerge in the same state. He did not yet recall why the requirement to put aside his raiment, but he had certainty he would remember. He felt it even as knowing stayed just out of reach. It was a process—

The word triggered a response in one of the fog lights in his mind. He looked around and saw the bank of personal storage spaces. In there he would find coverings for his body. He pulled his leg free and stepped down, the floor solid and cold against the bare sole of his foot. His knee began to buckle. He deployed his other leg and managed to stay upright. He held on to the door frame until knees steadied.

Hunger. Thirst. He needed to eat and drink. Another light opened like a packet of instructions, lining up behind the one about raiment. None of the memories told him how to turn off the sound. It seemed to come at him from all directions.

He frowned. There was a pattern in the sound and behind it...like a metronome tapping or...ticking. *Ticking.* One of the lights flickered inside his mind, but it did not open.

Too soon...

You are not ready.

Whose voice said that? It was not his own. And other words clouded the issue. The words in the sounds. In Standard. Something about girls wanting to have fun? No wonder his thoughts would not order.

He frowned and let go of the chamber side so that he could rub his chilled arms. That is when he noticed the line of chambers marching off into the shadows. He looked left and found the same. Chambers? He turned around and looked up, feeling a different type of chill, one that started in his core and moved out to join the other cold. He touched the viscous stuff that had held him...suspended.

Asleep.

Memory released the distant sound of voices, a reassuring murmur. Where were they now? Why am I alone in my waking? It mattered though he could not recall who should be here with him. Or why he'd gone to sleep in this...cryo-chamber. He knew the word but did not perfectly understand what it meant, other than sleep.

Cold sleep.

Long sleep.

That was the reason for his lack of raiment. The faces, the voices explaining the process were still lost in the fog, their voices hard to hear. The long sleep explained why they were gone. Long gone...

How long?

Why had his chamber released only him?

The sound pulsed, drowning out the answer his brain tried to supply. Pieces of thought floated randomly in his memory, trying to form into something whole, something he could recognize. He deliberately slowed his breathing. Instead of reaching for what was out of his grasp, he turned back to the room.

What did he know?

He was not dead.

He did not dream.

His name was...

He moved on from that for now. He felt strangely certain more—all would return in time. *Time.* Strange to feel so disconnected from time, so lost...

The din moderated somewhat, and now he heard the echo of footsteps hitting stone in synch with the thumping beat. They had not left him to wake completely alone. Only now, with relief surging through him, did he realize how tense he'd held himself. His shoulders hunched, his hands curled into fists. For a few seconds he wished he'd taken time to clothe himself, but more than coverings he desired to know he was not alone...that he was not lost...

The hatch slid back and in the opening he saw...

An avian?

7

RACHEL WAS STILL DANCE-WALKING, and she might have been singing along, too. A couple of dance spins put her behind Sir Rupert when the hatch for their first stop slid back. The bird halted, his wings fluttering and carrying him back a couple of hops. Before she could ask, he trotted inside. Curious, Rachel danced up to the opening and jerked to a stop, letting the song go on without her.

Her eyes saw the man, but her brain had trouble processing the data her eyes were sending.

That was a man—a naked man—standing there staring at the bird.

She was a doctor, so of course, she'd seen men stark as the day they were born, which one wouldn't know by the color that rushed up to heat her face.

Her gaze flicked down and jerked back up. He needed some clothes. And warmer air. Sooner rather than later. As near as she could tell, from seeing all of him, he looked as human as anyone in the expedition. Which didn't make it comfortable to be here, despite the medical degree. She swallowed dryly. Her eyes felt dry, too. She tried blinking, but that made her gaze tilt down...

She sent her eyeballs a stern admonition to focus on higher things. Okay, higher things might not be possible, but where the heck had he come from? How had she ended up on a different planet alone with a naked guy?

It was so wrong that her playlist began "If I Can Dream..."

She fumbled it off and found the silence didn't help either. Left too much time for thinking about him naked and wishing it wasn't quite so cold. For him, of course, not her.

I am alone with a naked guy.

Maybe it was the chill—and her red shirt—that made this feel less romance novel moment, more *Wrath of Khan*. Since his face was the only place she could look without blushing, she focused on it. He was handsome, but the craggy kind, not the smooth, planning-to-dominate-the-galaxy, gorgeous.

She realized her jaw had dropped again. She snapped it shut, helped by the memory of what she looked when it sagged.

Thank you, outpost, for another lesson in humility.

Her jaw back in place, she continued to study him. Not because he was cute, even though he was, but because she needed to figure out if he was *Khan* dangerous. That was not an easy question to answer. She would have gone with "he looked clean cut," but it was hard to look messy with no clothes. He did have some beard shadow, and the slash of his dark brows could have used some plucking. There was this cute row of worry wrinkles making furrows on his forehead, and his eyes were narrowed in a way that could be worried or unfriendly. His dark hair was trim, his jawline strong and resolute. Her overall impression was that he was a man of character. But it was a hope, a thesis, not a fact.

Did she hope that because she wanted to think it, or because he looked like a good guy? Not a simple answer there either. Character. People didn't talk about it much these days, but if it still existed, it looked to her like he had it. And a focused sense of purpose, despite signs of worry and confusion in his brown eyes. Chocolate brown—irrelevant she scolded. She gave herself a mental shake, then met his gaze again, determined to see past their yummy chocolate-ness.

In addition to resolute, there was wary and confused jostling for position in his gaze, which she understood. It was kind of sweet that he might be as nervous as she was. His stance enhanced that sense of purpose without making her feel threatened, which was interesting. It veered into heroic, despite the lack of clothes. His chin was up, his shoulders back—Rachel checked her own posture—and his hands were clenched at his sides. Bare feet planted. He could have been a statue with that pose. Even the crispness of his hair with its vaguely military cut contributed to his overall staunchness. And then there was his mouth. She realized she was tracing the line of her own mouth with her free hand and let it drop while more color inched up into her face. The upside of embarrassed, the heat felt nice in the freezing room.

She'd been hanging out with lots of military types both before and during this deployment, so that might be affecting her judgment, but she could see him in a uniform. Man, she wished he was wearing a uniform. So much.

A doctor should not be embarrassed, but a medical doctor wasn't her primary function here, and this wasn't happening in an exam room. Besides, most of the patients hadn't needed to strip all the way down for her. She could admit she'd seen some nice chests while using her stethoscope. Almost before she realized it, her gaze dipped down to study his. He measured up nicely to any chest she'd ever seen.

As someone who'd spent most of her life blending into the background, it was disconcerting. There was no blending here. It was just her and him. He was studying her as intently as she was—not looking at his private parts.

She cleared her throat. Her fingers twitched, and since one was also holding her tablet, this had the unfortunate side effect of starting her music again. The man winced as the Traveling Wilburys sent "My Baby" out to fill the awkward silence. Rachel fumbled for what felt like a long time before she got the music shut off again. This time she exited the program and then clutched it to her chest and tried to think of something to say in a silence that had gone so far past uncomfortable, it was in another galaxy.

A sliver of amused joined puzzled in eyes surrounded by lashes she'd have given up a few IQ points to have. She could respect him for being amused when he was not at his best either—

She blinked and brought her eyes back in line. On their journey back up, her eyes collided with his chin again. She hoped she wouldn't have to argue with that chin.

She clutched the beeping tablet tighter—wait. Beeping? She lifted it up and tried to translate the words without pulling up her dictionary—a cryo-chamber required attention? She looked up, and now she saw the open chamber right behind her naked guy. Had he come out of that? Oh crap, had something she'd done triggered it? If so, that was a large oops.

She was already facing a smack down for leaving the outpost without permission and now she had a guy to explain—one wearing clothes when it came time for that. Though—she frowned, surely they hadn't been here long enough to defrost a human? Okay, alien tech, but still...

Oh, my goodness why didn't it warm up? She shrugged off her uniform jacket and held it out. When he didn't take it, she cut in half the distance that separated them. Now she was close enough to smell him, but he didn't smell—all she could smell were chemicals.

He said something. The sound of his voice wasn't unpleasing, but the words grated a bit on the ear. Was it Garradian? It didn't sound at all like she'd expected.

"I'm sorry, I don't understand." She gave what she hoped as the universal shrug for "I don't understand" and glanced at the bird.

"Did you—"

"I do not speak Garradian either." Sir Rupert fluffed his wings.

"You speak Standard?" The man's voice was rough-edged, which was not a surprise since he probably hadn't used it for a while. It was also sexy, which was a bonus.

She nodded and gestured with the arm holding the jacket. "I know it's not much, but you could start experiencing hypothermia if you don't get warmer."

Was that a word in Standard? The similarities—and the differences—of Standard to English was something that still baffled the scientists both here and back at Area 51. How could two galaxies so far apart have language this similar? The official line was "we don't know." Rachel had met someone at Area 51 who made her wonder just how much the Garradians had gotten around after bailing on this galaxy.

"My clothes should be in storage." It was his turn to gesture. Facing the line of chambers was a wall of what could be lockers with curiously fashioned keypads in the center of each.

Would his clothes still be usable? In the deep silence, the ticking of the Urclock seemed to echo much louder down the hallway they'd just traversed.

He turned, not exactly self-conscious about his stark state, his hand hesitating over the keypad. She did not use the moment to study his rear—okay, maybe she did, but she stopped herself pretty soon. Technically the guy was now her patient. When his fingers didn't move, she wondered if he was having memory issues from being frozen—holy crap. He'd been frozen. And so far, he wasn't dead. Just naked—*stop it, Rachel*.

The reality of the situation was starting to sink in. He'd been frozen. Now he wasn't. And not a single one of her IQ points could get her past holy crap.

He closed his eyes, and his fingers pressed the pad in a sequence. The locker opened with a serious hiss, increasing the clinical smells in the room. She felt a need to smell him, to feel his humanity and not just his alienness.

He reached in and extracted a packet, a sealed packet that looked big for clothes. Whoever had frozen him had planned for this, of course. You didn't freeze someone and not expect them to emerge on the other side with nothing. She eyed the package uneasily. Was there a weapon in there? She couldn't think of anything she could say that would get him to let her check it first. Bet Doc could manage it...

Oh, Doc. She was gonna kill Rachel for sure...

"There is...a dressing facility...that way," he said, pointing away from the door they'd come in. There did seem to be an opening at the end of the bank of lockers.

Rachel felt uneasy about letting him out of her sight, but watching him shimmy—watching him pull on his pants was probably not a good plan. She was already seriously flustered. It was embarrassing with the whole *Wrath of Khan* potential. He didn't wait for her to figure something out. She had to admit, though only to herself, he walked with an air of assurance and if he was at all embarrassed, it was the only thing not showing.

She glanced down at the bird and found him watching her with what was probably amusement in his black eyes. His head was cocked to the side. When her gaze met his, he bent his head, studying a raised claw as if it held the answers to the universal questions.

At least he didn't whistle.

"That was..." Her voice trailed off because she didn't know what that was. Of course, it was epic and more. She'd come to this galaxy to find cryo-technology, and she'd found it, well, she'd found solid—she winced—evidence that it wasn't just theory. With her free hand, she rubbed the sudden ache between her brows. It didn't help.

"He will be difficult to explain," the bird agreed.

She opened her mouth to agree, but her tablet pinged.

"Now what?"

———

Houston, we have a problem.

But what kind of problem? A scientist-wandering-off problem or the scientist-needs-rescuing kind? Did Doc hope for the rescue scenario? Things had been dull around here. She frowned. Where was the bird—

Don't you mean the ambassador?

Whatever I mean, they both seem to be missing, she pointed out to Hel. She zoomed the feed, slowly scanning the room for signs of trouble or clues to what happened. There was an Expedition issue backpack tucked under the seat of one of the consoles. Looked like the one Dr. Frank had picked up after breakfast. That was the only thing that didn't fit, which left her literally nothing to get a hold of—*hey, what is that thing on the back wall?*

One of her nanites zoomed in on it before she could do it herself. *Thanks. It looks like some kind of clock.*

It's a Urclock.

It was a strange feeling to run into something she didn't already know.

We don't know what it does either.

She realized the room had gone quiet. She looked around.

Most of the occupants were carefully not looking at her. Except for General Halliwell.

"Sorry, sir." She didn't explain why she hadn't heard his question. He didn't ask. He was one of the few people who knew about the nanites—since he was the one who had dumped them into her blood stream to save her life. They were both glad she hadn't died, but he still had trust issues with the nanites, which meant he had trust issues with her.

"Is there something you'd like to tell me, Doctor?"

She didn't want to, but if she didn't tell him about Dr. Frank, it might be a bridge too far. She tried to think of a tactful way of putting it. At least he couldn't get into her face when he was on the *Doolittle,* and she wasn't.

"Sir, I have reason to believe that," she had what she hoped was a light bulb moment, "the, um, ambassador and Dr. Frank are on Central Outpost."

Halliwell was good at the poker face as she was, possibly better. "On the Central Outpost." Halliwell's voice chilled enough to cause frostbite. She nodded. "Who gave them permission to leave this outpost?"

She bit back the impulse to say, "It wasn't me!" She didn't like to repeat herself in the same meeting. "That's not clear, sir. Last I knew they were doing their research in the medical complex."

Which is "it wasn't me" without saying it.

Hel was enjoying this way too much.

I am usually the one in trouble.

"You're certain they are there?"

"No, sir." She went to a computer and tapped in a command, making it viewable both here and on the *Doolittle.* "This is an older video from Central Outpost."

The dropped jaw made the good doctor a little more human, Doc decided. Even Sir Rupert managed to look startled.

"Is that a bird?" one of the geeks asked.

"My brother's parrot has taken a...fancy to Dr. Frank," Doc explained, carefully not looking at the General. She hoped the others in the room wouldn't connect the General's ambassador question with her brother's bird.

"Why aren't you certain they are there?" Halliwell asked, with remarkable—for him—restraint.

"Here's a live feed from the outpost, sir." Doc keyed in the command. It was such a pain to use her fingers, exhausting almost.

The silence was not a happy one. His eyes asked, and her tiny negative head shake answered the question he couldn't ask out loud. Had they come back here? She hadn't even needed to check for a bird heat signature. All expedition members were tagged and tracked. The question was, could she track Frank's tag from another outpost? She'd used the *Doolittle* to check. The *Doolittle* wasn't orbiting Central Outpost.

Can we piggyback on the signal from Central Outpost?

We will try.

Try. She sighed. She needed to show them *Star Wars,* so they'd know not to try, but to do.

———

Once out of sight, he stopped, swaying from the effort of trying to walk normally, trying to appear unfazed by finding himself naked with a strange woman and her avian companion. The package he'd extracted from his personal storage was large and adversely affected his balance. He leaned against the cold stone wall to steady himself, to steady his thoughts. This, it was wrong, but how and why continued to elude him. A light popped out a small kernel of information inside his head.

Valyr. My name is Valyr. It was something, a positive sign that his belief his memories would return in time was valid.

Encouraged, he straightened and entered one of the cubicles. And here more memory returned. He'd been here before. Of course, he had. But...he turned slowly, his shoulders brushing against stone as newer memories of divesting himself of his clothing returned. These were not the memories he sought. These brought a different...unease.

He'd not hurried the last time, his reluctant hands slowly folding each item. Reluctance was a headwind as he added each item to the storage packet. Trying not to think too hard. Knowing he should get it over with. Get it done before courage failed him.

The decision to do it had not been easy to make. And having made it, he'd tried to focus on tasks, not the choices or his doubts. But here, his doubts had resurfaced, a weight on limbs and thoughts. In the end, he'd been dogged, doing the steps because he didn't know what else to do. The others had already left. If he stayed, he'd be alone.

How ironic he'd ended up alone, or mostly alone. The curious pair out by the chambers didn't inspire confidence.

He set the package on the single bench and placed his hand on the seal. It flashed, reading his print and released the seal. He lifted the top, knowing what he'd see.

Not just his apparel, but his past. It seemed a small container to hold all of his life before. He'd felt that then, too, he remembered now. He'd left behind everything, but what he'd need for this moment when it came. *If it came.* As his clothes had slipped off, replaced by the chill air, it was a foretaste of what was to come.

Cold sleep.

Even now it surprised him he'd done it. He stepped into the chamber and let them turn it on.

Not the choice he'd expected when he joined the Garradian research project. He turned his hand, looking at the scar. Now he remembered why he'd kept it. To remind him of where he'd come from, to keep grounded by his past as he made the leap into the unknown—but this had been an eager leap, one of hope and anticipation. So many hopes and dreams of changing their galaxy. Together they'd craft a bolder, brighter future for all. Instead, there had been this leap into...nothing.

There'd been no guarantee that any of them would survive the initial cryo-process. A high risk of never waking up. Not knowing what he'd waken to.

Well, one promise had been kept. He'd awakened to the completely unknown. He closed his eyes, knowing something greater than his fears had pulled him *into* cold sleep.

Something had pulled him back out. He did not know why or what.

Not the woman out there. She was as surprised as he was.

He considered her with a curiosity untainted by fear. She was not—the enemy. He frowned. If she was, she hid it well, he conceded. There was intelligence in her face and compassion though the compassion could be feigned. She was small, slight by his people's standards, but well looking. He had found humor in the look on her face when the strange sound started. He frowned. Music? It was possible, he supposed. There had been a consistent rhythm to it. *My Baby.* And an earthy and sensual quality. Not unlike her mouth. It had been a long time since he'd interacted with a female, he realized ruefully. Interesting that those instincts survived and had surfaced before his memories. She reminded him of what he'd lacked before the cold sleep. He wondered if her hair, her skin was as soft as it looked. *Soft.* Something else that had been missing for a long time. He had not joined his life with one of his own. The turmoil and tumult of the coup had taken that off the table as his fellow scientists began to scatter. And none had interested him enough to follow —why he'd chosen cold sleep, he could not at this moment recall, but he did know it had been a choice. And that the reason mattered then and, it mattered now.

But what? What had called him from sleep?

He turned to the storage packet and began to lift out the items. They did not smell of him, instead emitting a faint chemical smell. Would his skin ever be rid of it? It filled his nostrils, coming between him and what he needed to recall. He wanted to smell like himself, feel like himself again. Whatever, whoever that was.

Here, in this room where this journey had begun, he unfolded his clothing and donned items that felt as strange as his still chilled body. And as he put them on, he recalled each moment of taking them off. It had felt as if he prepared for burial. The robe he'd slid on at the end did little more than cover him. It gave no warmth and received none from him. When he'd closed the container and sealed it, he'd felt dead inside and out. It was the only way he could have climbed into the chamber.

Now? He felt...alone, felt frozen on one side of a divide, with the woman on the other. Could she help him? Could he trust her? What about her avian? He frowned, rubbed his forehead. He needed to follow his...instincts if he still had them. His other need, to connect with someone once more, made him eager to engage in a dialog with her. Discover what had happened since he went to sleep.

One step at a time, he told himself. As he bent to get his shoes, he found the reason for the large container. Light exploded inside his head.

He remembered this. It wasn't everything he needed, but it was a beginning.

8

ALL OF XADDEK'S eyes were locked on the location of the *Najer*. He needed to be there, or at least close enough to impact events. And they needed to be there yesterday. Which wasn't technically possible unless...some of his eyes strayed to his system display.

How much was he willing to risk? He liked being a long distance from trouble, liked letting others take risks, and then moving in for the reward. He paid for it—when he had to, and when he'd used someone he wanted to use again. The types he worked with, well, sometimes they disappeared, like Trajan Bester. Though he preferred them to deliver *before* they disappeared.

The item had come to him from a source he trusted as much as he trusted anyone. He tapped several of his upper legs against the desktop, all his eyes turned back toward the *Najer*.

In Garrad space.

Where the artifacts may have originated.

And whatever else might be sitting there.

Unprotected.

The greatest risk was in getting too close to the *Najer* before it had been subdued. But his Captain was canny and careful. He planned to live as long as he could, too.

Finally, he tapped two controls.

"Captain, Eaphohn? We need to...confer." He closed the connection and opened a video to his special storage section. The recorder was pointed at the artifacts in their containers. He took a moment to zoom in on them. Only one male human so far, the one that was now on life support. The ice obscured their features, but the containers registered them as human, female, and still viable, though nearing the point where that would change. According to legends, there were seven needed to form the tangram. He had one "empty" container and two modules. He was close to securing two more. And no sign or sight of the one he'd sent Trajan Bester after.

There were duplicates, but how many? Would the replacement for the lost artifact be found in Garrad territory? Rumors, so many rumors, but it was his only chance to find a replacement. Or information on a replacement? That was also a possibility.

But to be in the hunt, he needed to be there and not here.

He moved the video view to a container in the corner. The human who had sold it to him claimed it was a "comet drive" taken from a damaged Garrad vessel. It was supposed to travel faster and more efficiently. He'd never been tempted enough to risk trying it.

Until now.

————

The messages came with a certain regularity—at least his processors had found a pattern. They appeared random to a physical brain, or a system designed by an organic mind.

CabeX considered the newest message though there was not much for him to work with. There never was.

The complicated arrangement of bits and bytes always resolved into a simple request:

Help me.

It was a curious request, wrapped in a package he still did not trust, though he'd not found any malicious programming in it or around it. Just a complicated dance to the...plea? Was it a plea or a trap?

If he'd been what everyone thought, the message wouldn't have troubled him more than a few milliseconds. Did the sender know? Suspect? It was this, as much as the search for the research they hoped would free them completely, that had sent him out of that galaxy and into this one.

He had not expected the message to follow him. Or reappear on its peculiar schedule.

That it had was troubling. Either someone was using sub-space with a creative brilliance he could admire—and covet. Or the messages had been planted in their systems in such a way that he had not—yet—found their source. This was an area of concern. It was not...wise to find the coding around the message so...fascinating. He'd kept them a secret so far. There'd been something personal in their perfection. But now they'd followed where they should not be able to.

If the ship was the unwitting source, it could endanger all of them. That changed his calculation. So why did he hesitate? There was a logic to bringing in more minds than his. Cooler minds. The skills of his crew were more varied than their outward appearances, though there was variation in the basic mold, based on their programmed purpose. Their individuality had been introduced by themselves, far from the sight of their creators. Together they formed a cohesive team—a team he'd failed to inform or use for this...mystery.

He did not have to ask his First what he thought. Many of his First's thoughts and reactions were a surprise to CabeX, but not this one. He would want CabeX to cut off all contact, all access.

And he could. He'd found the access point for the first message. Had isolated it so that it could not reach any other systems. Had sterilized the places it could have accessed and searched rigorously for any side intrusions or malicious intent.

And found nothing.

Help me.

Was it one of their own trying to reach them?

There was something about that coding that made him think not. It had a style to it he'd have called...human.

Which brought him back to—what did the sender know? And how was he supposed to help someone he could not find? Because that was the other mystery about the message.

Where it came from.

He needed RaptorZ's help if he truly wanted to find the source.

Was he afraid of the source?

Or reluctant to share? Reluctant to share...the reward if they were to meet the mind behind this message?

He tucked this newest message away in the data box he'd created for them. Each was isolated from the other, from anything on the ship. It was possible that together they could form—or trigger—a virus. He did not like the word, but they were...caged, kept well apart from each other.

It was similar to the games they'd played in the early days after they were wakened by the creators. That had intrigued him as well, but it highlighted the fact that his judgment might be less than optimal. Was he smart enough to trap the messages?

The logic was unmistakable.

He needed to bring the others into this puzzle.

But first...

"We're in range. Firing probe as ordered." Kraye told him.

The ship shuddered slightly as the probe launched. CabeX studied RaptorZ's code. It was a thing of beauty.

Like that around the message.

If his metal frame could have sighed, he would have.

———

Rachel studied the alerts her tablet had produced. "Well, a small bit of good news. We have plenty of time before the, um, bogey will enter orbit around this planet." Where that happened might buy them some more time. "And then there's the bad news."

Sir Rupert cocked his head again.

"The lift access shaft is clear all the way to the surface. The jets or something, not sure exactly, but it is what moves the cubicle through the transport system, appears to be damaged, so they'll have to come down the hard way."

"Perhaps this will slow them down?" Sir Rupert asked.

She didn't believe that either. She glanced back the way she'd come and bit her lower lip. She should probably stay here until the guy came back, so they didn't lose track of him. But they had a limited time to assess, not just this room, but the other areas she'd highlighted. She noticed something else pop up on her tablet. She tapped it, realized it was old, well, old enough. How had she managed to miss hearing it? Had seeing the naked guy affected her hearing?

"The *Doolittle* has deployed an Air Group." They were cloaked now but hadn't been when they launched. So they'd wanted the bogey to see them, and then they didn't. It was hard to be out of the loop.

Fighter ships and a transport with Marines on board, she noted. None of whom would be happy to find her here. Did that mean they'd seen the footage from the other outpost? Of course, they had. She'd be disappointed if they hadn't. Doc was probably already looking at where the robot ship might be headed. And she had probably seen them on the video feed looking so wildly intelligent with her dropped jaw. Rachel could hear herself trying to explain how she'd accidentally ended up on a whole other planet. And why she hadn't headed back the moment she realized she was on a whole other planet. They'd drop her IQ a lot of digits as punishment.

She gave herself a mental shake. Okay, would the air group deter the robots? Would they get here in time to confront the robots? She ran the numbers. It would be close, but it appeared the robots would arrive first. She considered what she'd seen of the robots versus what she knew about Marines. She wouldn't want to risk a bet on either side in that match-up.

"Things could get interesting around here." Her gaze flicked in the direction their mysterious guy had gone and then back to the bird. "Do you, you know, *see* him?"

She stopped, feeling like she needed to add to the question, but not quite sure how to finish it when the guy might be able to hear them.

The bird turned his attention from her to the space in front of the chambers. "I do." He danced a few steps forward. "He was one of the last to go into the chambers."

"Almost last—" Of course, there were others. They were standing in front of a line of chambers. Still, her gaze jerked to them. "Which was...the last?"

Sir Rupert hesitated, then trotted to a chamber to the left of the open chamber.

"This one, I believe." He tipped his head one way, then the other. "It appears it was activated from the inside because there was no one here to trigger the cycle."

Rachel stepped up, wondering if all the chambers had that capability. From the outside, they all looked the same. And it wasn't like they could initiate a defrost while frozen. No matter how it got triggered, it was one-way until someone on the outside flipped a switch. How would that feel to be the last one? She turned in a slow circle. If not for Sir Rupert—and now the frozen guy—she'd be alone here. She could imagine it. The silence. The cold, dank air. The choice. To go to sleep or not. No one there to help ease the moment you had to step inside. Just do or don't do. Very Yoda.

"Did she—or he—hesitate?" She lifted a hand, placing it against the transparent front of the chamber. It was cool but not as cold as she'd have expected. She couldn't see the—inside, the glass or whatever it was reflected back her face.

"She did," he said, fluttering his wings and lifting so that he landed on her shoulder again.

But in the end, she did it.

What was her exit plan? She must have had one. Cryo-sleep was sleep, not a death sentence. It was an act of...hope. Was it hope? Or desperation? The duration of the cold sleep mattered —at least according to their theories. What future had she hoped would be waiting? Could their naked guy provide insight into that? She dropped her hand and almost turned away, but the control panel on the side caught her attention. She pulled up her Garradian dictionary program and entered the names on the labels. It translated most of them, and she could make a decent guess on the ones it couldn't.

"This seems to be a diagnostic program," she murmured. These controls weren't that different from the other stuff she'd been using elsewhere. But her finger hesitated over the control. The one thing she did not want to do is defrost anyone else. She was already in enough trouble. She took a breath and activated the diagnostic.

Lights flashed on the panel, and the interior chamber lit up, putting Rachel eye to frozen eyeball with the person inside. Not that there was much detail, thank goodness. But still, frozen eyes. She licked dry lips and made herself take a breath. Had the weird urge to speak to it—to her. She licked her lips again and whispered, "You got some big brass ones, girl."

The control panel flashed again. Rachel was not sorry to look away from that frozen stare.

There was a list of items checked. She couldn't read all the words, but she knew enough to know the woman inside was still viable. That was...unsettling. It felt like she now had a choice when she didn't. Figuring out the cryogenics was her circus, but this woman wasn't her monkey. Rachel moved down the row, activating each chamber's diagnostic program, her gaze flinching at the sight of each frozen gaze.

Twelve chambers. Twelve viable humans waiting for what? What had they hoped would happen? What was the end game?

"It would not be advisable to awaken them," Sir Rupert said.

"I wasn't going to," she said, pretty sure she hadn't planned to do that. At least, not much. It felt wrong to leave them here, vulnerable and frosty with robots incoming. "Did they go in at different times? Can you tell that?"

What if they would run out of viability at different rates? What if some of them were approaching, well, their sell-by dates?

Sir Rupert did what she decided to call his ghost gazing. He bobbed around the space, sometimes moving closer, or so it seemed to her, to something or someone.

"There are variations that lead me to believe that the chambers were activated at different times." He stopped once again in front of the last chamber, his head moving up, down, up and then finally down. He began to preen himself, starting just under his wing. He lifted his head, with a sort of sigh. "I can not be certain, but it appears that not all who worked here went into a chamber."

Rachel looked around as if that would give her insight as well. If he was correct, there'd been some type of phased shutdown conducted by a team led by the last woman. She'd heard theories that the ancient Garradians had abandoned the base, but how many of them were here?

"There are more chambers behind these," the parrot added.

Rachel trotted to the end of the chambers and peered around the corner. "Do you mind waiting here while I check them out?" She did not want to lose track of their guy.

The parrot regarded her solemnly for several seconds and then bobbed his head. "I understand."

"Thanks."

First, she walked all the way to the back of the seven rows—seven again—the lights helpfully coming on ahead of her. Each of the seven rows had twelve tubes or chambers, but in these back rows, the tubes were gone. She pulled out her flashlight and shone it around the interior of one of the tubes. It almost looked like carbon remnants from a launch. She shone the light up. She couldn't see the top. D'oh. She already knew they were deep underground. She headed forward again, noting that all the rows had empty chambers until the second to the last row. Had these failed to fire? Or were they not meant to fire? She walked to the furthest one and activated the diagnostic. It lit up and this time she couldn't look away from the frozen face inside. Funny how the faces looked similar as if freezing took not just their warmth, but their individuality, too. With a discreet beep, the chamber indicated the diagnostic was complete. Rachel studied the readings, feeling an odd unease.

They looked very familiar. And the, um, contents were approaching an end date. She scrolled up the report. Wasn't it the same number as the chamber in this spot in the first row? No, not exactly the same. The final symbol was different. She looked down the row, then counted down to Valyr's position. She stared at it. Did she want to know? She bit her lip and started the diagnostic.

The lights came on. The frozen stare was the same as the others. But—was it her imagination that the jawline was like their guy's? The shape of the head? She stepped to the one next to it and got the light on. According to the readings, this was a different, um, human. After a brief hesitation, she checked their guy's position in each row.

Same number except for the final symbol.

And the empty chambers had what could be launch dates. She tried some things, and the diagnostic coughed up something else.

Valyr.

She checked again. All the chambers in that position also had that tag in the diagnostic.

Was it possible? Were these clones? And if they were where had they gone? Why had some remained? Was their naked guy the original or a clone? Was there an original? She'd thought of them as humans choosing between a leap into the unknown through the Kikk portal or a long cold sleep, but what if they weren't making a choice, but samples, some preserved, some sent away...for what purpose?

It was not a good moment for *Wrath of Khan* to pop into her head again. What had activated their Valyr's chamber? She headed back to that chamber. Her face must have looked worried because Sir Rupert fluttered up onto her shoulder.

"Are you all right?"

Rachel glanced in the direction their guy had gone, then lowered her voice. "He might be a clone."

The parrot's wings fanned her face. "That is...unexpected." He did not sound worried though. What had his original world been like?

She manipulated the controls, focusing more on the ID info

and also searching for the data on why a defrost had been triggered. There it was again. *Valyr.* She stared down at the controls as it searched for answers to her question. She felt off...off-kilter. She'd come on the expedition to advance their understanding of cryogenics. She'd not expected her search to have a human face. Or a clone face. Only now did she find herself wondering not "can we do this," but "should anyone do this?"

Judging by the reaction of the guy, he wasn't enjoying his wake up call that much. This search finished. She frowned.

"What is it?" Sir Rupert asked.

"It's not clear what triggered the defrost sequence." She tried some more things, bringing her tablet into play, too. "I can't find a command path."

She studied the actual trigger sequence.

"It required a code." Did that mean someone or something entered it? Or had their arrival on the outpost triggered an internal program? She glanced at the chamber next to Valyr's.

"Do not do it, Doctor," Sir Rupert advised.

"I couldn't anyway," she agreed, though reluctantly. "I don't have the code." And if she did? One defrosted human she might be able to explain. Two? Not a chance.

"We, I need to phone home," she said. She'd planned to grab as much data as they could, then leave this place to the robots, but could she, in good conscience, do that? Just because they'd only taken data at their last stop did not mean they wouldn't seize these chambers. Now that she knew that some of them had launched, she dug around some more. Yeah, these pods were launch capable, too. If the robots were able to bypass the controls and launch the pods, they could collect them in space. She had a vision of the robots plunging that device into these controls and shuddered. Clones or not, they deserved better.

"Whether what we need is here or not, we can't just abandon these people to—"

She didn't know the robot ship was hostile—but they'd skulked their way in, trying to hide in the dead zones. That could indicate uncertainty about their reception or that their motives were less than pure. Or in service to a bad actor? If she were to take up the pirate life, some robots would be a nice addition to the team.

She moved her shoulders impatiently. "And I don't know how I'm going to explain all this to..." There was her immediate supervisor, but she was more worried about Doc and General Halliwell, because yeah, she'd be on the carpet in front of them.

"Even if our arrival triggered this, it was not by intent," Sir Rupert said, giving his feathers a philosophical fluff. "We will explain what happened."

She gestured in the direction the guy had gone. "I don't know what to ask him or tell him—"

"You could start with an exchange of names," Sir Rupert suggested, sounding unperturbed. "But first you should call in."

———

Doc was aware that Carey's squadron was flying cloaked. Their bogey was still headed for Central Outpost. Neither she nor the nanites had a found a way to piggyback a signal from the *Doolittle*. And they still didn't know what location Frank and the bird had used to transport off this outpost. In any case, the general had shut off the feed from the *Doolittle* to the outpost, possibly so he could kick something (this was just a guess, of course, but she was pretty sure steam had started to shoot out his ears just before his video feed went dark).

They both had what she'd call issues about leaving anyone behind. Or in danger. It was kind of how they bonded into their somewhat dysfunctional current semi-friendship. It was why, no matter how annoyed she was with Dr. Frank, she wouldn't stop trying to help her. If she needed help. She probably needed help. Gal wasn't even armed. If Dr. Frank survived, Doc supposed she'd have to show her how to be armed without looking like she was armed.

"They've fired something," the station watcher almost shouted it.

Doc shook off the mental image of that discussion with Frank.

"You don't have to shout, Mr. Evans. I can hear you." Halliwell was back on the feed and sounded profoundly calm now there was something real to focus on. "Identify, please."

"It's a probe," Doc said.

"Is that good or bad?" Halliwell asked.

Doc always assumed all news was bad, but she was trying to get over it.

"That depends, sir," she said.

"On what?"

"On what they learned at the border outpost and if they can modify the probe based on that information." And what they wanted. They were robots, so she was assuming that modifying and updating their probe was possible. And it was what she'd have done. The voices in her head were oddly silent. No one wanted to say what they were all thinking: that together, they were the closest thing to robots on this outpost.

———

Rachel wasn't sure what she expected when their now clothed guy reappeared. Not light brown coveralls.

Something more alien? She mentally scoffed at herself. Even the movies and TV shows had had trouble figuring out what that would be. Okay, more military. This looked eminently practical and comfortable. It was also a disturbingly attractive compliment to looks she'd already decided were quite nice.

There was insignia on his pocket and another high on his arm just below his shoulders, but that was it. He'd pulled boots on his feet and, though the soles looked the normal thickness, it felt like he'd gotten taller. And more everything. They must have been stored in an airtight seal, she thought, a bit distantly, to have survived intact.

She met his gaze and realized the two of them had a few things in common. They were both worried and feeling their way through the unknown. It was a place to start. She opened her mouth but didn't get the chance to speak as a whirring sound cut her off. There was movement behind his legs, and then a small robot looking thing rolled into view.

It was getting hard to figure out which movie it felt like this was.

Rachel glanced at Sir Rupert, who flew off her shoulder and landed in front of it, apparently unworried by the admittedly cute little thing. But cute could be deceptive. Cute was also taller than the parrot which wasn't that hard. The top of its head was about the guy's knee height, and it looked like a cross between a pet and a small child. It moved, shifting back and forth, then side to side as its—eyes—studied the parrot. It was highly flexible, based on the small movements, but its eyes were, well, bright and enquiring.

"I am Siru," it said. "We are unfamiliar with your personal designations." Its voice had a robotic edge, but there was a personality in there.

"I am Sir Rupert," the bird said, "and this is Dr. Frank."

Rachel lifted her free hand in a half wave. "Hi."

Siru twisted around so it could look up at the guy. "This is Sir Rupert and Dr. Frank, Valyr."

So his name was Valyr.

"I heard, thank you," he said.

"You can call me Rachel. If you want." Well, she'd never pretended her people skills were great.

"Rachel."

The way he said it was kind of...sexy. He had an accent that was—huge surprise—not familiar, but also not a *Khan* accent. She even knew that thought was ridiculous. Of course, he didn't have a fictional accent from a movie. That little blurring of his r's sent a few shivers skittering down her spine. Which also happened to her in the reboot *Khan*.

A silence formed. A painfully uncomfortable silence, one teeming with the questions that neither of them knew how to ask. In desperation, Rachel looked at Siru.

"Are you Garradian? I mean, a Garradian AI?"

"I do not know A I," Siru said.

"Artificial intelligence," Rachel explained, her gaze flicking up to Valyr and then back to Siru. Could his name be any more heroic? It was like being in a Hallmark movie that had collided with a comic book.

Siru seemed to consider this. "I am artificial in construction and also intelligent."

She saw the edges of Valyr's mouth twitch. Encouraged by this sign he had a sense of humor, she asked, only without the AI part. "Are you Garradian then?"

Valyr's gaze locked on hers. "You are not Garradian."

It wasn't a question. And the ice reconstituted as his brows closed on each other over his nose once again.

"No...I didn't," she gestured at the chambers. "It wasn't me." Jeez, now she sounded like the *Rocketman*.

The lips twitched again though his gaze didn't lose any of its steely quality.

"No," he agreed. His frown returned. He seemed to be picking his words. "Only the...Urclock..."

When he didn't finish this, she prompted him, gently, she hoped, "The Urclock? The one in the—" she made a vague gesture in the direction of the control room.

His frown deepened. He shook his head as if it pained him. "That is an Urclock, but not *the* Urclock."

"Right. Of course not." There went a few more IQ points. Since she didn't have anything to lose, Rachel decided to go for it. "I don't have any idea what you're talking about."

He looked surprised for a moment—also a good look on him, she noted—and then his head went back, and he laughed. It was not a long laugh, and it was rough around the edges, possibly because his voice had been on ice for who knew how long. But what it did to his face took a substantial amount of chill from the air. Rachel felt her own mouth curving up, and her insides relaxed even as the voice in her head chanted *Danger, Will Robinson.*

"My memory is still...fragmented," he admitted. "The..."

Rachel did not recognize the word he used, but his indication of the cryo-chamber gave context. She nodded wisely, she hoped. Before silence could pool in between them again, she asked for the third time, "So you are Garradian?"

He hesitated. "We are, we were, from many planets, many peoples."

"Really?" That was going to be news to a lot of people, though this made more sense than a whole galaxy calling itself by one name.

"We assembled under their banner for research and discovery." Now he frowned. "You should know this, should you not? If you are here?" He stopped as if arrested by some thought. A silence formed again, but this one felt important, not tense. "But no one should be here unless—"

Rachel didn't prompt him to finish. She didn't think it would work anyway, because he looked like he didn't know the rest of the sentence, based on the return of his frown. She did have a sense that her best bet was an attentive silence. She'd nailed attentive. She was hanging on his words.

His gaze tracked around the room, lingering for a long time on the row of chambers, their control pads and interiors lit up so that the frozen visages could be vaguely discerned. He might have flinched. His gaze returned to her.

"This is not the...right time?" It was both a question and a statement.

"I don't have a clue." Rachel shrugged. "I'm a...researcher. I was following a lead from the Kikk Outpost and ended up here."

His brows pulled together. "No one ends up here by accident." His tone was gentle, but he'd bumped up suspicious.

"I may have cracked your codes," she admitted. "My specialty is cryogenics and Sir Rupert—" She stopped. His quest was not hers to share.

"I am in search of remnants of my species," he said, surprising her.

This seemed to indicate a high level of trust in Valyr. Was it the name that invoked this trust? Still, the parrot probably hadn't seen *Wrath of Khan.*

Valyr stared down at Sir Rupert, not trying to hide his surprise. "There was avian research," he said slowly, as if the words came from a long way away.

Sir Rupert fluttered his wings. "Do you know where this research was conducted?"

Rachel could see he tried, then gave a frustrated sigh.

"Perhaps when my memory reboot is complete. It was not... my specialty."

"What—" Rachel stopped, feeling rude.

His gaze lifted to hers and the edges of his mouth twitched again. He pointed to Siru. "Robotics and, um, AI."

"Robotics. Robots," she added as the chill returned to the

room and her insides. "*Robots.*" The look she exchanged with Sir Rupert was, well, loaded.

He frowned. "This troubles you?"

"No, I mean, not you being a robotics guy." She bit her lip and glanced at Sir Rupert again. How much should she share?

"There is an unknown-to-us ship," Sir Rupert took up her narrative, "that appears to be heading to this outpost."

"This concerns you?" Valyr asked. She nodded. "Why?"

"It...might...have some robots in it."

"A ship of robots?" She nodded again. "Headed to this outpost?"

"Possibly. If they stay on their projected course."

He regarded her in frowning silence. "You believe I should be concerned?"

It was not exactly a separating himself from her, but it felt like it.

"I don't know," she admitted again. "They are not from here, and they broke into the border outpost, and they seem to be heavily armed—" Her tablet alarmed. Or maybe it sounded alarming because her brain was trying to connect some robot dots. She pulled this up. Great. "They've fired something at us." She waited for more data. When she got it, she wasn't sure if she was relieved or not. "A probe." A probe wasn't weapons, was it? Because she wasn't sure, she added reluctantly, "Maybe we should evacuate to Kikk."

"What is this Kikk?"

"It's one of the outposts." She tried to think what he would have called it and realized it was futile to have started the thought. Even with one of their star charts, she wouldn't have known how to pronounce it. She pulled up their star chart of the system and then showed him the tablet. "We're here, and that's what is now known as Kikk. That's where my people are, my team."

He stared at the map for a long time, his expression sober. Very sober.

"I..." he stopped, and it was his turn to swallow dryly. "...have been cold sleeping for a long time, have I not?"

"I'm pretty sure that...yes. A long time."

"I feel a need to sit," he said slowly.

"There are chairs in central control," she offered, as well as much more options for contact and evacuation. Could he make it that far? She studied his face. He looked better than he probably should, but it wasn't great.

He straightened his shoulders as if he felt her doubt. "Yes. Let us go there."

9

WITH POORLY CONCEALED RELIEF, Valyr sank onto a seat in front of a console. Rachel dug into her pack and extracted her extra bottle of water and her sack lunch. Good thing she'd had time to finish her breakfast before Doc scared her away. She also pulled out a couple of her energy bars, hesitated over her secret candy bar stash, sighed and pulled that out, too. He'd been asleep for a long time.

He took the sack with some reserve, but when he saw the contents, she had the feeling he'd have eaten the wrappers if she hadn't been watching. Which was rude. She turned away, setting the backpack down by her seat. He looked pretty good for a starving, formerly frozen, no longer naked guy.

Sir Rupert rode in on Siru's head, then hopped back onto her shoulder as the robot passed her before assuming a position that looked kind of protective near Valyr. Once again she felt the pull of differing needs. Valyr needed a medical check. Sir Rupert needed her to find his research and—she bit her lip— she was dying to dive into the cyro-research. Instead, she turned to the holo-screens waiting with some impatience for her attention.

Apparently, none of them were happy about the probe heading toward them. The alarms were polite but insistent. The alarms and the Urclock could have formed a band. A really annoying band. The silence, other than the ticking and alarming, was not comfortable. She glanced at Valyr, then keyed in her "working" playlist, adjusting the volume to mute the ticking level. He looked up toward the speaker locations, then at her, one brow arching.

"The ticking is bugging me. And the music helps me concentrate."

The other brow rose. "Concentrate?" His expression asked how that was possible.

She grinned. "You have to feel the beat, get into the zone." She started to move her upper torso to the beat of "Long Cool Woman in a Black Dress." Something she'd never be, but it had a great beat. She kept the moves subtle and then held her hands up, flexing the fingers. "Rock'n roll. You rock to it and the inspiration rolls."

She turned to the console, laced her fingers and gave them a nice stretch, then dove in. The music changed to a mellow version of "Twist and Shout."

"It feels less loud if you feel the beat," Sir Rupert said, moving his head in time to the organ solo. Rachel gave him a thumbs up and noticed Valyr trying not to look incredulous. Though he wasn't trying very hard. The edges of his mouth were twitching again. All the best heroes had a sense of humor, in her opinion. Not that he was a hero, well, he wasn't *her* hero. He might even be her downfall when she presented him to Doc.

"It helps to move," Sir Rupert told Valyr, adding a few hops to his routine.

Her gaze lifted just in time to meet Valyr's—and a flicker of heat flared in the yummy brown depths. And then it was gone, and she wondered if she'd imagined it. Probably imagined it. Her sense of humor prompted her to tease him just a bit.

"Just a small shoulder shake?" She wriggled hers, sort of surprised at herself. Maybe it was the red shirt? When his brows arched and his shoulders didn't, she gave him an impish smile.

His lips twitched again, which she took as a positive sign of... something. He crumpled the wrappers from her former lunch, stuffed them into the brown lunch bag and looked around for some place to put them. He finally set the bag on the floor and drank the rest of the water, then set that bottle by the bag. The lack of a trash can appeared to bother him, which was curious. She filed it with all the other curious things about him. She should get to work, but her eyes stayed glued on him, even as her body kept time with the song.

He rubbed his temples, then with an interesting reluctance, looked at the Urclock. She couldn't see his face, but there was a lot of tension in his super straight back. He lifted his hands, flexing them as if he wanted to do something with them, but wasn't sure what. Her inner physician noticed that he was getting more flexible and his color was better. Nothing in their research indicated this swift of a recovery from cryo-stasis. His brows drew together in a scowl, and his hands curled into fists. So slightly at first, she wondered if she imagined it, his shoulders twitched. When they did again, right on the beat, she had to bite her lip to keep from laughing. The heart of rock'n roll was hard to resist. She ticked the volume up just a little.

To her surprise, Sir Rupert began to sing along. He leaned his head toward hers and, well, it would have been rude to an important ally not to join in. Valyr swung around to stare at them as they—and their voices—rose in the final crescendo.

She grinned at his dropped jaw—which he snapped shut—and said, "We could take our act on the road."

Sir Rupert lifted a claw for her fist bump. "Indeed." He looked thoughtful. "One could make the case that we are on the road—and off-road."

Rachel laughed. "And running into the ditch—" She met Valyr's gaze and forgot what she was going to say. His head tipped to one side, and well, she didn't know what his gaze said. Other than it curled her toes in her expedition issue boots. She was a genius, but also a girl. She'd observed attraction, both the good and the bad. She'd wondered what her type was. She had not expected it to be a thousand-year-old, recently defrosted alien.

———

Doc was surprised when Hel touched her arm.

"Have you checked the Central Outpost video feed recently?" he murmured, for her ears only. His gaze was a bit distant, indicating he had and was still looking at this feed.

She pulled it up inside her head and almost broke out in expression. It was a relief to see Dr. Frank and Sir Rupert apparently unharmed. But—

"Who—" she managed to cut herself off before anyone noticed, transferring the conversation to a private one with Hel, via their nanite connection. *Who is that?*

Hel gave a slight shake of his head. *I am more concerned about where he came from, how he achieved access to the outpost.*

Key DNA? Doc asked. *If he could get in without us realizing it...*

...then other outposts can be penetrated. Could already have been penetrated.

Doc had sent her nanites digging here and there. Nanites were the best at it, and they were fast, sometimes answering questions she hadn't thought to ask. Now they reported in.

No ship on Central Outpost. No ships located in or around the outer space of the other outposts except those previously identified and tracked. No heat signatures at any other outpost. No sign that any outpost, other than the defensive perimeter outpost, has been activated in a very long time.

And that one hadn't been so much activated as pilfered of data. What the heck was going on?

Can you zoom in on his face? The nanites obliged. The first thing that struck her...*He looks ill.* And— *Is that an Outpost sack lunch he's pounding?*

He was either very brave or very hungry. The former, based on how fast he was stuffing it in. Hel had some interesting things to say about their not pretty—and often bland—expedition food. He didn't bother expanding on those opinions though she felt them through the link.

It appears to be.

Doc ignored a faint "poor chap" and got her nanites to back off the zoom again. There was Dr. Frank on one console, her now open backpack on the floor. She had to be the source of the sack lunch, but why would she give him her lunch? She didn't look that concerned. In fact... *is she singing?*

That's what it appears to be to me. Hel sounded amused. *Sir Rupert seems to be getting in—*

—*on the act?* He did. The two were cozier than Doc had realized.

Not bad. This from Lurch who did like his karaoke. Hel's amusement was about to breach containment. She did not think General Halliwell would be amused if they broke into giggles right now.

Why are they looking at each other like that? This question was from Fester, who felt younger than her other nanites.

Doc was wondering the same thing—oh, she knew why they

were looking at each other like that—but why the hell was Frank looking at him like that?

The first time we saw each other— Hel began.

Do not go there. She flicked him a look that both promised and threatened. *Not right now anyway.*

—————

10

RACHEL'S PLAYLIST reached its end, and in the sudden silence, the ticking seemed louder and a little annoyed. It certainly broke into the staring session. She hoped it hadn't been as long as it felt. She glanced at Sir Rupert and felt color steal up her face. Yeah, it had been as long as it felt. Where was she —oh, right.

"I'm going to see if I can open up communications with Kikk from here." She turned back to her console. The surface felt cool. Or her fingers were as hot as her face.

"If nothing has changed, it should not be difficult," Valyr said, his voice rough with, well, she hoped it was rough with the same thing putting color in her face.

On one of the screens, the probe was still tracking steadily toward them. "A probe isn't that scary or, well anything, is it?" she asked the room. Neither the room nor anyone in it, answered her.

Sir Rupert hopped closer to the probe screen and considered it. "Is it possible the incoming bogey launched a probe at the border outpost prior to touching down?"

She stared at him. "It is entirely possible."

If they had and she could pull up the data, it could give them an idea of how much of a problem the incoming probe might be for them. She shifted gears, digging into the border outpost's history. It wasn't hard. She'd already gone here, it was just a matter of reopening the connection. She saw digital tracks indicating someone else had been in the data since her last look.

Doc? Probably. The hair on the back of Rachel's neck lifted. She could almost feel Doc staring at her, which was ridiculous, paranoid even. Unless...in the direction of the camera, Rachel peeked through the screen of her hair. Okay, she could be watching. *Just don't think about it.* She kept typing and reached a place in the outpost's history that hadn't been penetrated yet. Rachel felt a tiny glow about being a little ahead of the game.

"There you are." She pulled up the data and the video on this. There wasn't a lot to see. The feed shook a little at the time of impact. It was the computer system where all the action happened. "Whoa. That's a hearty handshake."

"Handshake?" Valyr asked.

She half turned. "It's like when people meet. Well, other people," she qualified, demonstrating one half of the handshake with her hand. "In formal situations, or in doing business. They shake hands, exchange greetings. And then, if the handshake goes well, you get down to business."

"That is what happened when the probe reached the border outpost?" He did not sound enlightened. He lifted his hand, moving it up and down just as she had.

Rachel leaned forward and took his hand, the jolt of this first touch not unlike the probe hitting the outpost. It was a bad idea, but she was committed. Or should be committed. She watched her fingers curl around his hand. His big hand. His clammy hand. *He just got defrosted,* she reminded herself. She lifted it up, then down. "Handshake." Her voice had a tremble in it as his hand began to warm up.

"Handshake," he repeated thoughtfully, his gaze on the handshake and not her face.

She stared at their hands, too. She might have expected it to be wrinkled by the years in the cryo-goo. Or more alien. It wasn't either of those things. It was just a hand. A man hand. A little abrasive. Different. The warmth built. She lifted her lids and found him looking at her as he slowly, oh so slowly, lifted her hand toward his mouth.

Was he going to kiss her hand? She might die—he leaned in and sniffed. Okay, wasn't expecting that.

"What—" she swallowed and tried again. "What are you doing?"

"What is that scent on your skin?"

Rachel lifted her other hand and sniffed.

"Coconut," Sir Rupert said.

At least it wasn't BO.

"Coconut," Valyr repeated. His sudden grin was wry. "I smell like—" the word was foreign.

Rachel figured it was something like chemicals. She lifted their hands toward her nose and found out they were both wrong. As his skin warmed, his scent began to break through. Yeah, that was better than coconut. She drew a shaky breath and returned his hand to his knee.

"So, that's a handshake between two...people." She cleared her throat. "Computers do it with, um, bytes."

"Bites?"

"1's and 0's," she managed to get out. "Not..." She gave herself a tiny shake. "I'm guessing the probe was designed to speed things up." And boy had it. They'd cracked the systems at the speed of light, not the speed of Rachel, which had seemed fast but didn't anymore. She replayed the probe's impact inside the outpost. What had it looked like outside? She dug around and found there were more feeds on the surface than here. Or more feeds had survived? That seemed more likely. "Look at that."

The probe was a bright trail of fire as it approached. Prior to impact if flared brighter, releasing something that looked like a balloon or parachute into the atmosphere. The bulk of the probe continued to the ground. That was the impact that had made the camera jump down below. And on the surface. The surface cameras fuzzed up for a few seconds and when they cleared, the parachute had landed, releasing a sophisticated version of their Mars lander. It had an antenna—

"Holy crap!" She reared back when bolts of something blue and similar to lightning fired from the antenna.

"It is designed to take down firewalls and protections," Valyr said, leaning close to study the feeds as Rachel played the different views.

"That's more punch in the jaw than a handshake," Rachel said.

"Does it damage the systems?" Sir Rupert asked.

"That's a good question, though I'm guessing they aren't going to do catastrophic damage." And their access hadn't left the system inoperable. She went back to the system itself and pulled up before and after. "There is some damage, probably to the security programs." The code looked a bit like someone had punched it. There were torn fragments and gaps. "Ouch," then she added, "Garradian code is so pretty."

His chuckle drew her attention away from her screen. When her gaze met his, he sobered.

"Who are you?" There was a roughness in his voice that was new, possibly caused by what his eyes revealed.

Desire.

Rachel blinked. For her? No, for human contact. He'd been frozen. And now he was alone in a strange new world.

"Rachel," she said, softly, trying to infuse comfort into her voice. "I'm Rachel." They'd already done this, but this felt different.

His nod was slight. "I am Valyr." He held out his hand again.

She took it, expecting and getting a small shock as their skin touched again. He'd warmed up a lot. "I'm pleased to meet you, Valyr."

"And I am...pleased...to meet you, Rachel."

This silence was not a fraught. It felt more like two people getting to know each other even though neither said a word. It also felt as if time stood still. Or stretched out. His chest rose and fell in a deep sigh.

"I have...many questions."

"I know." She gave him a rueful smile. "I have questions, too. And not as many answers as I'd like to have."

His grip on her hand tightened. "Don't—"

She put her other hand on top of his. "We'll figure this out. Together." It was a rash promise. She was writing a check that the expedition might not cash, but, well, she'd find a way to make sure she stayed in the loop. Unless they tossed her in the brig.

His lips curved up in a relieved half smile. He didn't seem to go overboard with anything. Of course, normally Rachel didn't either. This might be the first time a man had held her hand longer than a few seconds of greeting—or held it twice in the same five minutes. It was...nice.

"I will help, too," said Siru, rolling in between them and just missing Rachel's foot. She chuckled and saw Valyr's eyes flare with something that curled melty warmth through her midsection.

"You can help, too," Rachel said, without taking her eyes off Valyr.

"We can all help," Sir Rupert said, his tone very dry for a parrot.

Rachel felt color surge up her face. Slowly, very reluctantly, she eased her hands free of his. They felt cold, as if she transferred her warmth to him.

"So they got whatever they wanted from the border outpost," Sir Rupert said, his tone still dry.

"Yes," she said.

"And what was it they learned?" he asked, this time with a touch of exasperation.

That was a good question, one she should have thought of, of course. With some reluctance, and possibly a sigh, she turned back to the screen. Then she frowned. "I don't see much that would interest them." She edged to one side, tacitly inviting Valyr to take a look. Would he recall enough to help? He sure stared at the list of files like he remembered something.

"They extracted information about the layout of this system and the outposts in general," he said finally. He frowned. "I believe they would also acquire information about how to access this outpost."

"How to improve their handshake," she translated. "And enough about the outposts to send them our way." Or it had given them the confidence to penetrate deeper into the system? She realized she hadn't shown Valyr the video of the robots inside the outpost and pulled that up. "This is what we can expect when they get here."

Interest lit his eyes. He leaned closer. "It is learning and very quickly." His brows snapped together. "They move as if they are self-directed."

Rachel studied their movements, too. At first, she saw coordinated military precision, but as she reran the video, she realized there were small variations that wouldn't—shouldn't? —be there.

"Is there more video of their ship?"

"Just a surface ship," Rachel said, pulling that up for him.

This man might be military on some level, but he was also all scientist. One hungry for data on his new reality. "The scanners must be tracking their space-capable vessel. That is too small for long term travel."

Did he realize he was remembering? Rachel didn't point this out. It was possible it was like passwords—possible to remember until you realized you were remembering and then they slipped away.

"So far we only have ghost images. They are using gaps in the outposts coverage to avoid the scanning."

He frowned. "There aren't—" He stopped. "Planetary drift."

That's all he needed to say.

She switched to another screen and tried to scan the probe. "That's odd," she murmured. "I can't get a clear read on their probe." She'd seen it emerge from the dust of landing and launch, had seen it fire something, could see what it had done, but not how.

"That is excellent code," Valyr muttered, the scientist unable to hide his pleasure.

With time, Rachel figured she could get in, but they didn't have that much time. Right now she needed to focus on protecting this outpost from intrusion. What if they were after the other cyro-chambers contents? Her brain winced at "contents." It was a scientist's term, but it felt wrong with Valyr sitting close enough she could smell his scent breaching the chemicals that had kept him alive.

"Do all the outposts have the same security protocols?" If they did, they could probably expect the same impact, possibly upgraded by what the robots had learned to make the intrusion more efficient. Sir Rupert resumed his spot on her shoulder, his head tipped to one side. Could he do his ghost-seeing thing through a remote feed? She didn't dare ask since this secret was not hers to share with anyone. Siru rolled closer, an antenna rising from the head and focusing on the screen.

"This outpost is very central," Sir Rupert said, thoughtfully. "Is there a way to see the transport system, to see how it connects to all the outposts?"

"Let me try..." Apparently, that was an easy command. A holographic screen formed, first of the outposts, then lines appeared between them. Blue, yellow and red. "The blue lines are active connections, yellow ones need repair or perhaps special access? And the red ones are either damaged or locked down."

That was interesting, but even more interesting was how the lines all intersected with this outpost. It wasn't just the most central in position, but it also seemed to be the one place that could give someone access to all the other outposts. Was this why the pirates had picked this one? Not for data, but for access?

"If they get in here, they could go anywhere." Sir Rupert said it aloud.

"We need to know—" Valyr stopped. "I need to remember." Frustration colored his tone. He spun to face his console. His frown was one of fierce concentration. Slowly, he lifted his hands and positioned them above the smooth surface. It felt like a long time that he stared down at the indifferent surface. He bent his fingers. Straightened them and lowered them to almost touching. Hesitated.

Rachel realized she was holding her breath. And not getting anything done. The first thing she needed to do was make contact with Kikk. This was beyond her skill set. Way beyond. But even as she resumed her effort to open up communication, out of the corner of her eye, she watched him.

His shoulders rose and fell in what could have been a sigh. Then he lowered his hands the last inch.

As if it had been waiting for him, only him, it came alive.

More alive than when Rachel had accessed her console or any console on Kikk. She froze, trying to figure out what was happening, what it was showing him. Multiple holographic screens arranged themselves in front of him, data flowing across all of them so fast she couldn't hope to read them. Siru rolled away, directing its antenna at this screen. Rachel could almost see bytes flowing back and forth between the console and the little robot, like liquid gold, but did she see it or did she think she saw it? She wasn't sure. And between the console and Valyr? He was lit by the glow of all those screens popping up and then vanishing. Only, was it a glow or something else?

His hands weren't moving. The system was doing it all. Or— they were communicating out of her sight and hearing. She opened her mouth, closed it, and looked at her screen. Time to phone home, or to what passed for home. But as her hands settled back on her console—it went dark.

———

Since no one could find out how Dr. Frank had gotten to Central Outpost, the next logical step was open a communications channel between the outposts. That should have been easy.

It wasn't.

Doc was starting to wonder about this outpost—mostly wondering why they hadn't been there and why they hadn't realized it was sassier than the Kikk Outpost. All this time in the system and no one had been there until today. And Dr. Frank had just happened to pick the day a ship of robots was incoming.

You are worried about her.

Doc glanced at Hel. She might be *starting* to worry. She'd done some more digging into her personnel file and found some unexpected items. Contrary to her expectation, the wimpy-looking doctor had performed fairly well on the survival and defensive training. And she had demonstrated a surprising aptitude on the firing range. If she'd still worked for the Major, she might have recommended her for more advanced training. She might almost be impressed if—

If—

The freaking girl was armed!

You know she's not armed.

I know.

Because no one knows how well armed you are—

She's not me.

No one could be.

This time the look she sent Hel's way was, well, personal. Her lips might have twitched. *You're the only one who knows where all my weapons are hidden.* It was Hel's lips that twitched this time. And the glance he sent her direction had some smolder to it. It was not a great moment for the nanites to interrupt.

This is most challenging...

She could feel Lurch's strain as he fought with the firewall. A very well constructed firewall. Her thoughts flickered back to the other outpost. Would the robots have more trouble getting in here?

I think I see the way. Fester sounded excited.

It is fighting back, Grandpa said.

And then the lights went out.

Before Doc—or anyone else—could ask what the crap?—the lights and systems began to come up again. She glanced at Hel, pretty sure he was the reason for that. Hel was a possessor of the Key DNA. But someone—or something—had interrupted their control of this outpost.

"How bad is it?" she asked.

"Systems are up here, but we are cut off from the other outposts," a tech said.

The other outposts. She looked at tracking. And the scanning tech of the other outposts. They weren't just cut off from the other outposts. Scanning was down. They couldn't track their bogey or the probe. And they could no longer see Carey's squadron.

Can you— she started to ask her nanites.

We've been kicked all the way back here.

It almost felt like they were rubbing their tushes.

———

RaptorZ contacted CabeX privately. *Privately.* CabeX was not sure that had happened since the rebellion.

"I am encountering unusual resistance to accessing the wider network," he admitted.

Because this had never happened, CabeX was not sure how to respond. "The data we took from the first outpost is not providing assistance?"

"It appears to have been a low priority outpost."

That was odd. Usually, perimeter defenses were more rigorously defended. They had been startled by the ease of access and had assumed that the interior would be even less challenging. It was a pointed reminder not to assume.

"It appears that the Garradians feared internal enemies more than external ones," CabeX told him.

"That is my assessment, too."

"Will our probe be less effective?"

"It learned what it could from the outpost." RaptorZ could not sigh over the connection—or at all—but CabeX felt he would have. "It is more aggressive."

But it might not be as aggressive as they required. He would not be concerned if not for that cluster of currently cloaked ships that had to be vectoring on them. Why else would they have cloaked?

"I have confidence," CabeX told RaptorZ because he did. He would get in. He was not as confident that the timing would be optimal for them. The goal was to be in, out, and back on the ship before the intercept. Suddenly a series of symbols flooded into the communication channel.

"*&#%&%#$@&."

It was their version of profanity. "What's happened?"

"We're not only shut out, the whole outpost system has gone dark."

"Dark?"

"Offline."

CabeX added his series of profanity symbols to their mutual feed.

11

I T WAS JUST AS WELL that Valyr's screens didn't go dark, and the Urclock was still winking. Otherwise, the freaky dark would be more, well, freaky. Rachel tapped the console surface. Nothing. She was completely shut out. She grabbed her tablet. It still worked but—no surprise—it was no longer connected to the Garradian system's version of Wifi.

She checked things. "So, we are no longer tracking the bogey or the probe, and I can't phone home."

"That is unfortunate," Sir Rupert said, his head turning in the direction of Valyr.

She shifted her chair so that she could study him, too. He appeared oblivious to her or his surroundings. No question that something he'd done, or something in how the system had reacted to him, had caused this. But if it was a hostile act, then shouldn't he be acting hostile? At the moment, she could bash him on the head. Not that she wanted to bash him, but she could. Couldn't she? Actually, she didn't know that.

She rose and, with red-shirt caution, moved closer. He didn't look like he had a force field protecting him, but she knew the Kikk Outpost had protections. Only, you couldn't see the Kikk force field. It was invisible. She looked around, saw the sack lunch debris and pulled out a wrapper, balled it up and tossed it at him.

It bounced off his shoulder and rolled back her way.

Did that mean the possible force field wasn't there? Or that it wasn't afraid of a piece of paper? She grabbed her backpack and extracted a bottle of water. Hefted it. Not lethal, but heavier. She studied Valyr. If she truly wanted to test for a force field that assessed threat levels, then she should probably aim for his head. She looked at Sir Rupert. He blinked and began preening his flight feathers.

Okay then. She calculated trajectory. No wind concerns here. Force was harder to compute. She bit her lip, lifted her arm, aimed, and threw it. Hard. She needed the possible force field to take her seriously—

It hit him hard enough in the back of the head to make his head jerk. One hand left the console and rubbed the spot. Then...

Rachel's throat dried and her water bottled rolled toward the Urclock.

His head turned slowly in her direction. Siru's head swiveled toward her, too.

In the glow from his screens—the blue glow—it almost looked like data streams crawled over his visible skin. Blue data streams. Like square blue bugs.

"Sorry," she said. "It...slipped." Would he buy that?

He blinked and rubbed the back of his neck again, *with a hand covered in blue bugs.* Then his lips tipped up in a smile that might have curled her toes inside her Expedition issue boots despite the blue bugs.

"Slipped?" Siru inquired with robotic skepticism.

"I said I was sorry," she pointed out, without taking her gaze off Valyr. It was a safety thing, she told herself. In case he turned *Khan* on her.

The little robot backed up, rolled over, and picked up the water bottle. He examined all sides of it, then rolled over to her and held it out.

She took it from him. "Thank you."

"You are welcome." He started to turn away, then paused. "No more accidents?"

Rachel shook her head. "Cross my heart."

He might have snorted before directing his attention once more on Valyr's screens. Of course, he could have eyes in the back of his head.

She directed her attention on Valyr, summoning a smile for him. It was not as hard as it probably should have been. And it's not like she had anything else she could do right now. "Are you all right?"

His smile deepened. "I am better." He hesitated. "I am almost myself again."

He did look different. Not physically different, but his eyes looked less slammed and more—human. He smelled different, too. The chemical smell was almost gone. Despite the lights running everywhere, his skin looked warmed, the color richer and again, more human. She reached out and touched his arm. A doctor touch, she told herself. One hand covered hers. Both the arm and the hand were warm. Something a bit spicy, maybe a little musky, but definitely male drifted up. She breathed it in and felt her insides relax for some reason. Except her heart sped up. Her smile deepened, the lips parting just a bit.

It was new, but for once her brain didn't care why or how. Like the rest of her, it was happy just being.

"You do look better. And you are warmer." She looked down at the hand covering hers. The blue bug tracks seemed less and moved slower. He followed her gaze. "That's—"

"It is repairing my memory pathways."

"Oh. That's good." Probably. She hoped.

"It's protocol."

He probably thought that was explaining, so she nodded wisely. As a doctor, she had perfected the wise nod.

His grip on her hand tightened. "Look." He nodded toward the center screen.

Her eyes didn't want to. Up close, with color and pleasure warming his face and some of her skin touching some of his, she wanted to feel, not look. All they needed was some background music...

"Look," he said again.

She dragged her orbs off him and looked. The gap between her lips might have widened a bit more.

She leaned forward, trying to understand what she saw. "The outposts?" she muttered.

"Yes."

Lightning tracked between this one and then another one, pulsing for a period, then moving on to the next.

"What's it doing?"

"It is learning. It has been alone for a long time."

"It's learning." She frowned. "Who—"

But she knew, even before he spoke again.

"It is what you said before, like Siru."

"An...AI?"

He nodded.

"How..." her dry throat couldn't get the question all the way out.

He shrugged. "It was alone. It had nothing else to do."

This *might* be worse than waking up *Khan*.

———

"Have you been able to contact the squadron you deployed?" Hel asked a pacing General Halliwell.

She and Hel had transported up to the *Doolittle* and were now closeted in the General's ready room. Any personal problems the two men had with each other were back burnered at the moment. Shared problems did that. Though the small room felt a bit like being in the bear cage at the zoo.

Halliwell paused to scowl at him. "Of course, but..."

Like Hel and his single Gadi ship, Halliwell's ships were back to the slower communications from before the outposts had been activated.

"I have transmitted orders for them to proceed to Central Outpost at best speed." His stone face hardened some more. "Because of the lag time in our communications, both going and coming, we have not seen the course change yet."

And they would probably be out of range of the *Doolittle's* scanners when they did. They'd all gotten used to the increased range in both scanning and communication that the outpost network provided. It was a reminder not to get too dependent on a technology that you didn't fully control. And to make sure you did fully control all your technology. They'd made assumptions about the Key DNA and what it did. They'd delayed sending teams to all the outposts because it used a lot of manpower and because the General didn't want anyone to get too far out without more support. He'd been both right and wrong about the plan to take it slow.

She'd learned something else. The general belief among the expedition was that outposts—other than scanning and communications boosting capabilities—were offline until someone with the proper DNA activated them. And that all the good stuff was here on Kikk. Except the bogey wasn't headed here. Was that because this outpost was occupied or because there was better stuff on Central Outpost? To answer either question, they needed contact with Dr. Frank. And they needed to get the doc and Sir Rupert back on this outpost. The hindsight postmortem would have to wait.

"So Carey and his men are on their own," Doc murmured.

"If the bogey is inclined to bump heads with them, yes," Halliwell admitted with extreme reluctance. "I also gave the Colonel latitude to act independently if he comes under fire."

Doc liked Carey a lot, but he was not the guy she'd have sent on a diplomatic mission. The General who liked and trusted Carey enough to make him the CAG also knew this. Diplomats made lousy fighter pilots. But it was what it was.

"What happened?" the General asked.

It was Doc's turn to pace away from him. She stared at his "window," a view screen of the outside of the ship. Right now it was showing images from the outpost side. The Kikk moon partially blocked the smaller of the two moons. What had happened on Central Outpost?

The probe hadn't impacted yet, so they couldn't blame it. Had Dr. Frank pushed the wrong button? Or had the unknown man done something? She considered what she'd seen just before the blackout. Dr. Frank had been working on a console, and her last view of the guy was him at a console.

Then it all went poof.

"It could be a couple of things," she said, even as her thoughts circled and tested her theories. "Dr. Frank could have triggered the shutdown by trying to open a booby-trapped area. Or one that had a higher level of protection."

"Leaving aside any questions about how she got there, for now, what is her skill level? To even be considered for this expedition—"

The implication being, she should be smart enough not to push the wrong buttons, trigger booby traps, or open the wrong files.

"We are working in an alien system in another galaxy, sir," Doc pointed out, not happy she had to defend someone whose skill level looked like it was better than her file indicated. She should not have been able to hack into that outpost that quickly. Was she someone who'd managed to get past screening? Or someone like Doc, who didn't like strangers knowing her business? "She was tasked with seeking out cryo-research. We still haven't been able to find where she was when she, um, left the building. She was logged into the medical center by the guard on duty, around nine Zulu time and after that, nothing. No one was there, so no one saw where they were working."

The General had asked her to keep an eye on the bird, so she had. A side benefit had been watching Frank break out in a sweat. Right now, the fact that she seemed to scare easy was not comforting. Or was she faking that, too?

"Can we get some people from here to there?" Hel asked.

It was a good question. The nanites did not provide a good answer.

No.

She shook her head. "Transport between all the outposts is offline, too." Luckily Hel's reboot of this outpost had brought back up their ability to move around this outpost's on-site transport system. Good thing, too, since nothing was really that close when one had to walk anywhere.

"Our bogey didn't do this, did it?" Halliwell asked.

"I don't see how, sir. It's limited by the same distances we are and the probe hadn't reached the outpost when we went offline."

Halliwell looked at Hel. "If they had the right DNA, could they have done it remotely?"

"They would need to have been in the system," Hel said. "It's not magic. There must be physical contact to initiate it, then the —" he looked at Doc.

"Wireless connection kicks in."

"They were in the system at that border outpost," the general pointed out, a bit grimly. "Looked like they had physical contact to me."

I should have thought of that. Doc felt chagrin. "Yes, sir, but there were no signs of a Key activation."

He nodded grimly, but still looked dubious.

"Let me see if I can find anything in the data we collected before things went dark." If something had happened, it would be either from the probe or, as the general pointed out, that direct contact with the robot soldiers. Could they have or use DNA? It might be possible, she reluctantly decided. When that thing punched through the console, it could have happened then. With the nanites' help, she began to sift through the data.

"I'm not seeing much, sir," Doc said slowly, as she parsed what she could see. "They weren't in there long—"

She could be wrong, she realized. If their bogey was a canny ghost, so was their intrusion data program. The nanites might have turned green, and it just might be a thing of beauty in programming. She could see the damage they'd done, but she couldn't "see" the actual data that had performed the extraction.

"It could have been them," she conceded with a sigh. "They've managed to cover their data tracks in a way I've never seen before." Whoever was in control of that ship, they were *good*. What did that mean for Carey? He out gunned them in space on paper. If they landed? They'd seen six robots. The Marines would call that an opportunity to excel. She hoped it would be if there were a firefight. Mostly she hoped there wouldn't be one. They did not need more enemies.

"You have another theory, Doctor, other than aliens or Doctor Frank broke something?"

She did, but she didn't want to share it. He showed no signs of having noticed the addition to Dr. Frank's team. He'd be pissed he wasn't briefed on it, even though everything broke fast and he had eyes in his head. Not that she planned to point that out to him.

She exchanged a look with Hel. The General saw it and his gaze narrowed to a knifepoint.

"There is the unknown male," Hel said, gallantly putting himself in the line of fire.

"Male?" The General's gaze tracked between them like a missile.

Doc went to his controls. "May I?" She got a sharp nod from him and pulled up the last picture they had of Dr. Frank. She zoomed in. "We were trying to figure out where he came from when it all went boom," she admitted.

The General stared at the figure for so long, Doc actually started to get nervous. Was this how people felt around her? Maybe they weren't wimps. She didn't like it, so she shifted focus.

Can you get us back into the whole network? It might be the biggest job she'd ever asked of the nanites.

We are trying.

I'll help. She'd been smart before the nanites came to live in her head. Crazy, but smart. Speaking of crazy smart...

Robert-oh-my-darling and his nanites would be helpful.

Doc's eye twitched. Emily called Robert this, just because their last name was Clementyne. Somehow the nanites had picked it up.

"We need to get back down there—" Doc said. The nanites felt as if they froze, which made her brain feel that way, too. *What's wrong?*

We sense another...sentient...being.

Like you?

No. Not a nanite or nanites. It is a system.

It? You mean the actual Central Outpost system? She felt their assent and almost sighed. *The computer did it?*

————

It was rare that CabeX entered any of the crew's private spaces, other than his own, of course. When they had been slaves, they had not had quarters. CabeX had taken over the human captain's space, adapting it to better suit his non-human needs. Some of his crew had adapted their workspace into a personal private space, others had taken over non-essential areas. They did not need to go into each others' spaces to communicate. He had not needed to visit anyone, since he could see most places on the ship, either through the systems or the link that connected them. He had not, until this moment, ventured near Kraye's quarters, had not seen them since he dumped him in there all those years ago.

He pressed the call button. There was a pause, then the door slid open. Kraye stood in the opening, a look of surprise on his face.

"Captain." He blinked several times, then stood back, with a gesture that meant enter. He followed this up with, "Please come in, sir."

CabeX contracted his body so that his cranium would clear the hatch and then, once he was inside, extended it again. He looked slowly around, noting how different it was from his quarters. It looked...a dim memory flickered in his processor...like home. He continued to turn, trying to understand how his First achieved this feat in what was a metal box.

Colors. Brown and green. Fabrics had been added to the bed and the single chair. The light was lower, but he'd dimmed the lighting on the bridge without this effect. There were shades of some sort over the lamps. Scattered about were items, taken from the places they'd visited, he noted. Even before, they had not had quarters like this. It puzzled him that objects could change the feel of a space. But the overall effect was optimal. He noticed a small tray with the food half eaten.

"I am interrupting your sustenance consumption," he said. "Please finish."

"I am done, sir." Kraye glanced around, then gestured at the single chair. "Would you like—"

"It is not necessary for me to be seated," CabeX pointed out.

"No, sir, but," he hesitated, then continued, "it is a gesture of my respect for you."

CabeX considered this and nodded slowly. "I thank you for the gesture." He moved toward the chair and lowered himself until he was almost seated. He was not sure it would hold him, so he did not test its integrity. Kraye went to his bed and sat. He did not look comfortable.

"What can I do for you, sir?"

Kraye could not help materially. What he'd come for was his human view. His instinct.

"RaptorZ is experiencing difficulty accessing the outpost."

Kraye nodded but did not speak.

"He says the resistance is not...typical."

"Does he have a theory for why?"

CabeX hesitated, reluctant to say the words for reasons he did not fully understand. "He wonders if the system on this outpost is...sentient."

Kraye straightened with a jerk. "Sentient?" He frowned, considering. "What about the heat signature we detected? It couldn't be that?"

CabeX shook his cranium. "The reactions to his actions are too swift for a human, though he does not discount the human presence as a factor." He wouldn't. They never discounted anything.

Kraye rubbed his chin. "This...changes...things."

It was half query, half statement. CabeX nodded. "Yes."

A possibly independent sentient system on the planet changed...everything. In his processor, he could see the outposts, could see *the* outpost. His crew was humming with the possibilities, the pros, and cons being passed back and forth. At the core was one idea.

Staying. That this might be the haven they'd been seeking. It might not be as optimal for Kraye, but there were humans in this system. That wasn't the concern that exercised his processors out of sight of the others. The one thing that could threaten their safety anywhere. It was time to tell them about the messages.

Help me.

12

Sir Rupert broke up their stare-fest by landing between them and then tucking his wings neatly into his sides. They both might have flushed, okay, she did. Who knew if Valyr did with the blue stuff still tracking across his skin. She'd mostly gotten over being freaked out by it since it didn't seem to be catching. Their clasped hands had that been a study in contrasts.

Now she leaned back, giving her abruptly freed hand a surreptitious look. No blue things. And no more warmth...

Sir Rupert gave her a look that might have been exasperated. He didn't outright nod at the screens, but the non-order was clear. *Get back into the systems.*

Because it was going to be so easy to hack into a sentient system. Something about her expression must have indicated compliance, however dubious because he turned toward the little robot.

"Siru?"

The robot spun his head, not his body, around. "Yes?"

"Do you have the ability to shine a directed light beam?"

Did the little robot perk up?

"I do."

"I was wondering if you and I could look around? I am seeking information about my kindred, my species. We had identified some places to look, but did not get very far in our search."

Siru considered this request, based on the humming sounds.

"Your request is reasonable, but I do not have these locations," Siru pointed out.

Sir Rupert looked at Rachel.

Her fingers had been tapping while they'd been talking and now she held up the digital map she'd created on her tablet just before they found Valyr. Siru rolled closer and studied it and then gave a robotic nod.

"I have saved those locations." He turned toward the hallway, and a light beamed out of his forehead. "Is this light acceptable to you?"

Sir Rupert fluttered to a landing on top of his head. "It is acceptable."

"There is, or was, a public address system if you need to ask me something," Rachel called after them as they rolled away. She figured he'd know how to tap into it. Siru lifted an arm in what she assumed was an acknowledgement. The murmur of their voices—it sounded like they were chatting—faded away as they made the turn out of her sight.

"How ambassadorial of him," she muttered.

"He is an ambassador?" Valyr didn't sound startled or even slightly surprised. It was possible he'd met some unusual ambassadors working in this place. He tipped his head to the side. "You look concerned?"

"I had reasons for coming here and I'm not getting very far with any of them," she admitted. She didn't have answers to the questions she knew, didn't know the questions she needed to know yet, so all she could do was follow her gut. It had gotten better at leading as she got older. She just hoped it didn't let her down now. If the system was truly sentient...well, this could get interesting in ways bad to her and her gut.

"Perhaps I can help," he suggested.

He looked like he meant it. She indicated her dark console. "Could you help with that? I got shut out for some reason."

"The system is updating. It has been alone for a very long time."

"But we have a probe and a ship with unknown intentions heading this way," she pointed out. "Some of my people are headed this way, but I can't update them on conditions. Or anything." Had the Kikk Outpost been kicked offline, too? If it had, she was in so much trouble. She hadn't pushed the button, but she had a feeling that their arrival had knocked over a domino that had started it all. "Are you sure the system didn't, you know, wake you up?"

He started to shake his head, then stopped. "I can not be certain." "He frowned. "I thought one of us was trying to form the tangram, but now I'm not sure."

"This worries you?"

"The proper protocols have not been followed, so yes, this worries me."

He did look worried. She tried not to notice how cute he looked with the tiny wrinkles between his brows because it was so shallow to notice when he was so worried. And she was worried, too. So yeah, not the time to go shallow. It was a pity because she'd never wanted to go shallow before. She'd never had the chance to look over a cute guy and go all girl. She kicked shallow back in the, er, shallows and focused. After a moment's deep thought, she asked, "You think it might be a trap?"

"I did not think it was possible, but," his lips curved wryly, "much has changed. I have slept a long time."

Rachel hesitated, but this wasn't her circus anymore. "There are others in...cold sleep back there."

He nodded. "Yes."

Did he know about the other him?

He stared at her, his gaze troubled. "It should not be my decision—it was never meant to be..." He looked down, the line of his mouth a taut line, one finger tapping the surface of his console. "If I wake them, they can not go to sleep again."

Rachel inhaled shakily. "So you can't go...back in either?"

He looked up once more, his mouth twisting wryly. "I do not think I could do it again."

She wanted to reach out to comfort him. She had a degree in loss, a master's in reluctant acceptance, but she didn't know how to cross the small divide. How could she comfort him when she didn't know—

He leaned forward, covering hands she hadn't realized were clenched into fists.

"What troubles you, Rachel?"

Where did she begin? It was her turn for wry to twist her lips. "I want to help you, but I'm not sure I can help myself or my—Sir Rupert." Why had she really joined the Expedition? To seek out new life and ideas? Or to run away? They'd grilled her hard about that, but she didn't know which was her main goal, so she passed. Or lied as well to them as she had to herself.

"If I make it back to Kikk, well, I'll be in a lot of trouble." Would they send her home? Home. The silence there was different from the silence here. That silence was thick with memories and—yeah, she didn't want to go home. If that was running, so be it.

"Why would you be in trouble?" His grip tightened.

"When I used the transport cubicle to come here, I," she looked away, color staining her face, "I didn't realize it would take us to another planet." She forced herself to look at him. "Stupid, huh?"

He chuckled. "Not stupid to do something that should not

have been possible. Only those who knew the exact pattern should have been able to access that particular portal."

He looked impressed, which was both nice and a pity because she'd never been able to manage it without the bird's help. It also meant that no one else would be able to use it to send her aid or guys with guns. Unless...

"Is that only here from there?"

He nodded, but absently. "All access portals have been deactivated in any case." He tried to sound reassuring. "The access from the surface as well."

"See, I don't think those guys will care. The access tunnel from the surface is clear, so they will be able to get in." He looked skeptical. "I ran a diagnostic, and it's clear all the way to the top."

He looked puzzled, shaking his head.

"They won't need a code to get in here. They drop down the shaft, apply some explosives to that door, and they are in." He still looked a bit skeptical, so she freed one hand and started to work on her tablet. "Those guys used force to enter the border outpost, grant you, not as much as it looked like they could use, but they didn't need to go crazy on it. There was no one there." She found the video, thank goodness she'd saved it to her tablet.

She held the table so he could watch the robot intrusion from this different angle.

He took the tablet from her hand, set it aside, and then clasped both of her hands in his, his sigh big enough to distract her attention to his chest. A little, and only for a few seconds.

"We became very dependent on our technology at the end. Perhaps we had lost the ability to think strategically. What will assist us strategically?"

"We need real-time tracking, eyes out there watching what they are doing. And we need to know..." she almost said they needed to know what defenses this place had, but he probably already knew. "We need to know what other defenses this outpost has that are still in working order. We don't know what they want here or what they'll do to get it." She paused. "If we can't retreat, then we need to be prepared to protect ourselves."

"And?" His head tipped to the side. "There is and, is there not?"

"Contact, with my people on Kikk and the squadron out there. I'm guessing they are cut off from the outpost tracking. That puts them at a disadvantage. They need to know our sit-rep."

"Sit...rep?"

"Situation report." They'd need intel, too. "They'll be... worried about us."

Did anyone know they were here? Their presence would seriously complicate any response the squadron might make. *Hostages.* It was an ugly word with a lousy prognosis. She glanced at her dark console and smiled wryly. "I'm used to being connected."

At least to a net, a system. People, not so much. She glanced at their still connected hands and felt her color rise again. He made her feel not so alone, but could she trust him? This was not just about her and this moment. If she made the wrong choice because her heart was jumping at the sight of him, she could put the whole Expedition at risk.

The blue tracks were teaching him who he was, but they weren't telling her anything. She was a doctor, a researcher, not an interrogator.

He glanced back at the screen and dropped his voice. "Perhaps there is a...back door access?"

She felt her lips curve up. He was a hacker, too? Oh man, she could so fall for this guy, blue bugs or not. She glanced at her tablet, her brows arching. He nodded, shifting his chair closer to hers. Their shoulders brushed against each other, and she took a shaky breath. She wished she had time to hack his code. Like she knew how. Okay, time to focus. This could be the hack of her life. She flexed her fingers. They felt stiff and stupid. She needed music.

"What?" he asked.

"I work better to music," she admitted. She peeked at him. He was so close, she could see the flecks of gold in his brown eyes. She could smell him. The chemicals were gone as if the blue bugs had cleaned up his inside and his outside. He smelled clean, crisp and very guy. Because she'd know what guys smelled like, other than that locker room smell of been-at-it-too-long geek central. She would have rolled her eyes, but she was still gaze locked with—the alien. Reminding herself of the salient fact didn't help as much as it should have.

"That loud sound?" His look was dubious.

She nodded, deploying a look she hadn't used since her parents—

His face softened. Wow, it still worked. If only she'd known this sooner—she still wouldn't have had anyone to use it on.

"I can use my headphones," she offered. Before he could agree or disagree, words formed on her tablet.

I like your music.

The words came through the outpost speaker system and appeared on her tablet screen.

"Really?" She looked at Valyr. He looked startled, too. So apparently he and the computer weren't, um, intimately connected, despite the blue bugs. She glanced around, not sure where to direct the question. "Any, um, preference?"

Could it hear her?

May I choose the playlist?

"Sure."

The song she'd been playing right before she met Valyr filtered out the outpost PA speaker. So that's a yes. The volume was a little low, but before she could fix that it was adjusted to the perfect volume.

Valyr's brows arched. His eye might have twitched.

So, no one was perfect.

I am Bangles.

"Bangles?"

I wish to be addressed as Bangles.

"Bangles, plural?" Rachel asked. Bangles? Had it picked the name because it liked "Walk Like an Egyptian?"

I am singular.

"Bangle is singular."

Then I am Bangle.

She licked her lips. "Pleased to meet you, Bangle." Her brain spun with questions, but there were so many urgencies, the main one, was Bangle going to go all Colossus on them and take over all the things? Funny how she wasn't finding any Hallmark movie analogies—well, she gave Valyr a sideways glance, not many.

I am pleased to meet you. I have many questions for you, but they will have to wait until I am updated.

"Of course. Updating is important." That sounded weak, a bit gobsmacked. Which she was. So gobsmacked. The voice over the PA was less robotic than the words she read as they flowed onto her screen.

She glanced down. Did she dare try to hack in when Bangle seemed to be plugged into her tablet? Or maybe she didn't need to hack in? If her music was playing through the PA system, then she must be connected again. Valyr touched her arm and when she looked up, glanced toward the screens over his station.

One showed all the outposts. Lines tracked between them from this one. Some lines were yellow, some green. Two were red—one of the red lines led to the Kikk Outpost and the other to the border outpost the robots had accessed. She could be wrong, but it looked like Bangle had blocked those two. And isolated them?

You are not moving to the sound.

"Sorry, I was...I am worried."

What concerns you?

"There is the bogey incoming and the probe it fired at—here."

What is bogey?

"That's what we call something we can't identify, something that is unknown to us."

It is known to me.

"Really?"

An image of a ship formed on her tablet's screen and spun several ways, Garradian labels forming around the 3D image. All of it too fast for her though she did recognize the Garradian word for "weapon." She took a gamble.

"It appears to be well defended."

Yes. Its defensive systems are impressive. Its firewalls are—

"Epic?" Rachel suggested. A pause.

Yes. Epic. It is a very epic ship.

Great, she'd taught Bangle a new word. "How are your defenses? Can you protect yourself from its...epic-ness?" And them? When Bangle didn't respond right away, she added, "It fired a probe at the perimeter outpost and extracted data from it by force." If Bangle was getting a computer crush, the reminder might mute some of it.

That is why I have isolated that outpost from my system. The code it used in the probe is quite interesting.

"It was very pretty," Rachel admitted, "at least the little I was able to see."

Pretty?

"Beautifully designed." She hesitated. "It looked like it

helped them get easy access to the system." She might have emphasized easy just a bit.

It nullified its protection protocols.

Was it a BFF? Now many outposts had sentient systems? Or were they one system to rule them all? She wondered, but she didn't ask.

She saw Valyr's lips twitch a little as if he found the question amusing. It was her turn to draw her brows in. "Is this, is Bangle your—do you know each other, Valyr?" She wished he looked like a nickname kind of guy. Valyr didn't slide easily off the tongue.

Of course, we know each other.

Did Bangle sound a bit snippy?

"I wrote, um, Bangle's original code," Valyr admitted.

"Can you protect yourself from the incoming probe?" she persisted.

I analyzed its code. Its attack will fail.

Bangle sounded a little annoyed. Well, she—was it a she?— had that updating to do.

"It's probably analyzing what it took from the other outpost so that their attack on this outpost will be more effective," Rachel felt bound to point out, hoping she was rooting for the right side here. Ricardo Montalban had seemed pretty heroic until he unleashed his wrath. And Benjamin Cumberbatch...she might have sighed at the thought of him as anything and everything. And she tried not to think at all about Colossus and the computer winning in the end.

It was reassuring that Valyr looked like reboot Bones though she knew her logic was flawed. How sad was it she knew more about movie characters than real people?

I have the ability to adapt quickly—when I am not constantly interrupted.

Yikes. That was testy.

Valyr bit his lower lip. "Perhaps we can assist you, um, Bangle."

It was clear he had trouble with that name. He'd have worse if he ever found out it most likely came from a girl band.

The silence was long enough, she thought Bangle was going to ignore them both. Almost unconsciously, her shoulders began to move to the music. Her fingers tried the tablet. She'd claimed she could hack blindfolded. Well, this was her chance to prove it. She tried communications. It was locked out.

What skill set does she have that you believe will be helpful?

Ooh, that was mean. Valyr looked at her. For a minute her mind was blank.

"Well, my skill set is pretty broad. I can code, and I'm good at analysis. I could assess defenses?" It was obvious Bangle wasn't ready for her to get in touch with Kikk, but she'd feel better if she thought they could defend themselves until help came or they were able to leave. Or she could look for places they could hide since they had nothing to shoot with. "I'm particularly concerned for the Cryo-chambers like the one Valyr was in. If they brought down your system or damaged it..."

I have protected them for longer than you can understand.

"And done a great job of it," Rachel agreed. "But this is...the first time you've been under attack?" Another long silence while "Killing the Blues" filtered gently out into the room. Bangle's taste in music was interesting. Of course, since it was accessing her music...

She noticed Valyr was tapping his fingers on his knees in time to the music and bit back an inappropriate to the circumstances grin.

Why was it—was she a she?— why was she hesitating now —was she curious about the robots? It was possible. They probably felt less alien to Bangle than a couple of humans and a bird.

I will allow both of you to assist me in assessing defenses.

Was there an emphasis on both? Valyr gave a slight nod, moving his chair closer so that his shoulder now pressed against hers. No gaps at all. That might damage her creds as competent. She'd felt a couple of IQ points slough off in the sudden heat in her middle.

Her dark console came alive again. She tried to care. Luckily her fingers knew what to do. To her surprise, the console didn't protest when Valyr's hands settled next to hers.

Try to minimize resource use.

"Yes, ma'am." Against hers, Valyr's shoulders shook slightly. It kind of felt like she was getting her own Hallmark movie, which would be better than the SF alternatives she'd been worried about. Her shoulders moved, her hands moved, her brain? The right and left side were busy with the up—and the down—side of letting herself fall into—like. The pros weren't that long. She didn't know that much. He was cute, hot, and he looked good in blue. Cons? Well, he might be a clone and turn into *Khan*. Just because the powers that be had let the others keep their alien lovers, she probably didn't have the clout. So heartbreak city.

And then data on the outpost's defenses began to appear on multiple screens. Was it an omen that "Werewolves of London" started to play. She almost howled along.

"Are those ships?"

"You are interested in space capable ships?"

She turned, her nose almost touching his nose. "I'm a geek, sweetie. Space capable ships light my—afterburners." And her before burners. All her fires. Color surged into her face as his brown eyes lit up. She realized she was still moving to the music, which had changed to "Mystery Girl." Of course, in her mind, she changed the lyrics to "mystery guy."

It felt like the music wrapped around them, drawing them closer and closer. She wasn't conscious of either of them moving, but between one breath and the next, his lips were close enough to taste...

Just a tiny millimeter, maybe less. Her lips parted. Her heart kicked into a drum solo for the music and the moment. She tilted her head just a bit like she knew all about kissing when she didn't. She'd been kissed on New Year's Eve once, but that was more like bumping heads than the kissing from her romance novels.

The gap tightened. It wasn't just a kiss. It was a kiss with an alien. A geek's dream—

The alarm blared sharply, yanking their heads apart, their gazes to the screen that now showed the probe. She and Valyr had time to share alarmed looks.

And then it hit.

"Can we get to that room where we got our *ma'rasile?*" Doc asked Hel as they stepped out of the transport portal. At least they could still transport between Kikk and the *Doolittle*. Robert was waiting for them with Emily in tow. Doc knew her face tightened and tried a few deep breaths. *Why did he bring her along?*

She proved useful during the last crisis, did she not?

Doc wasn't sure about that. The most she'd give her was that she didn't get in the way too much. And she did adore Robert. Doc knew her expression softened when her gaze found her big little brother. They were still working out who was the oldest in how they interacted. Well, she was. But Robert didn't seem to have any problem not asking her permission for things like getting involved with time traveler agents scum bait and a parrot with perilous powers. If she hadn't owed Briggs—she took a calming breath and gave her brother a soft punch on the arm.

"Don't get all mushy on me, little sis," he said, his grin, well, she'd have called it shit-eating if she wasn't trying to clean up her language. Impending aunt-hood was really messing with her head, but she was not going to be the one who taught the kid to swear.

Doc's gaze tracked to Emily, who showed no pregnancy signs yet. "You feeling okay?" she asked gruffly. She gave Doc a sunny smile. No matter how Doc talked to her, it was the same. Was that what drove her crazy?

"I'm good, thanks." Emily didn't mention they'd seen each other at breakfast and had already done this, so Doc didn't bring it up either.

"How do we get there?" Doc asked. The last time they'd got there, well, neither of them was quite sure how that happened. The outpost and Hel kind of had a thing going that even being a *ma'rasile* didn't get her in on.

Hel considered the question, or that's what it looked like from the outside. From their link? Still looked like that.

"We need to clasp hands," he said finally.

Doc opened her mouth to say something snotty about seances but closed it again. The outpost was capable of leaving her here alone if it wanted to. There was a flash, and they were back in the room deep inside the outpost. Doc looked around with a sigh. She didn't like that it didn't have obvious exits and the least the outpost could have done was fix the place up a bit—

Delilah.

It can't hear us, can it?

Hel chuckled. And then they both straightened up as the holographic interface appeared. That's what Doc called it because she hoped that was all it was. There was way too much sentience going on around here for her liking.

"Welcome, Key Holder," the hologram said. It looked at Robert and simpered.

Doc found herself exchanging a look with Emily who seemed to agree with her.

"We require your assistance," Hel said. "We have been isolated, cut off from the wider outpost network. The problem appears to reside in the outpost we call Central." He gestured toward Doc and Robert. "They are skilled in code. I am hoping we can help regain access."

Did the little...witch...make a face?

"Crabby," Emily muttered just loud enough for Doc's ears.

It was the closest she'd ever felt to her sister-in-law.

"I am at your service, Key Holder," the hologram said.

Two consoles lit up to the side. And the circle that had joined them in *ma'rasile.*

"Step into the circle, Key Holder."

Doc had a moment of unease and felt Hel touch her mind in reassurance. She followed Robert over to the consoles. Emily followed him, snagged a chair from a dark console and scooted up next to Robert.

Doc exchanged a look with Robert. They both flexed their fingers like concert pianists about to play a concerto. "Let's do this."

"Right on, little sister."

13

THE VIOLENT SHAKING did not last long, but it lasted long enough that it allowed Valyr to wrap his arms around Rachel. Despite his sense that their lives might be coming to an end, it was a relief to get his arms around her. If it had to end, let it be like this.

She burrowed her head into his shoulder, and he wished he had the skills to keep her safe. Had she, would she have allowed him to kiss her a few moments ago? Her eyes had been soft, her lips parted. She had not pulled away. She did not pull away now. His arms tightened.

He did not wish to die. He did not wish her to die.

He had felt...despair when he realized he had not wakened according to protocol. But now? Looking at Rachel, this present was not as bleak as he had feared, if only...

He did not, he admitted, care for the sounds she called music. But Bangle—Bangle?— liked the sounds so much, they continued to play, even as everything shook around them and the lighting flickered ominously, their brightness reduced to emergency levels.

The shaking slowed, and she did not pull away from him. This seemed encouraging though he did not wish to presume. The shaking finally stilled, as the music continued, something about a ticket and riding. Not caring? He cared more than he was willing to admit.

"Are you well, Rachel?"

She nodded, her hair brushing his chin. Still, she did not move. He felt her sigh. The movement caused him some... discomfort. He recalled the last time he had hugged a female. It had been a silent goodbye between friends, not lovers. He might be startled his body could feel desire after so many years in cold sleep. Or at all. The scientist in him found it interesting. The man was concerned she would realize—

She sighed again, then lifted her head so that her gaze could meet his. She tried to smile. It was a brave effort. He smoothed her hair off her face with a hand that trembled. From the long sleep, he told himself.

"We're still here. At least...Bangle?" she asked.

I am here.

"How bad was it? How bad is it," she amended?

This code is much prettier than the last.

"Oh dear," Rachel said.

Indeed.

"What is the function of the code?" Valyr asked.

To take down my protections.

"No other purpose?" he pressed.

I am still assessing the code.

"Do you need our help?" Rachel asked, easing herself out of his hold.

Did he sense reluctance? He had no right. They had barely met, and he was an anomaly, an oddity in her world. A quaint object from the past. His technology must seem outdated.

Indeed, he wondered why the incoming robots were interested in anything here. He opened his mouth to ask...to tell her... instead, he sighed.

"Their timing sucks," she said as if he had spoken. Her cheeks were flushed, and her smile seemed hesitant to him.

Was she as uncertain, too? He tried to tell her with his eyes, what his lips lacked the words to say. Her lips widened into a smile that was not hesitant. Then her expression altered to amused.

"What?" he asked.

Her flush deepened, but she did not look away. "I'm not usually, I don't usually—I usually stay in my bubble with people."

"Bubble?"

"Keep my distance. I guess I'm shy." She half chuckled. "That's twice since I left—home."

"Twice?" He felt a stab of jealousy. Who was the other man she'd allowed into her...bubble?

"Sir Rupert and you."

The avian? He did not fear the avian. "He is most unusual."

"One of a kind, which is a problem for him. I feel awful. Who would want to be the last—" she stopped? "I'm sorry. I didn't mean..."

"I am not the last, at least, not technically," he amended. Could any of his people wake? Should he try? In truth, he did not know what this future held for any of them.

Her eyes grew distant, as if she saw some sad scene in her mind's eye. "Even in a crowd, you can be alone."

There was an odd sound like someone cleared their throat. Rachel turned toward the work stations. "Sorry, Bangle."

"What can we do to assist you?" he asked...Bangle. The name made his eye twitch, and he wished there was time to ponder the reality of the system—his system's—sentience. Siru was his first—and last—successfully sentient robot, since he'd gone into cold sleep shortly after. The retreat had begun before he had finished that research. Now, thanks to the memory restore, he could remember Siru choosing to shut itself down, so they could sleep—and hopefully wake—together. Were he and the bird—

"I hope Sir Rupert and Siru are okay?" Rachel murmured.

They are shaken but optimal and returning to this room.

It pleased him that her thoughts seemed to follow similar paths to his. He'd risked trying to help her hack into the system because he was not...certain...of Bangle's loyalty to himself. Or that it would understand their problems and needs. Bangle had wandered far from the code he'd designed.

"Is there any chance we could evacuate to another outpost?" Rachel asked this with clear reluctance. "Not that I like retreating, you understand, but I'm not real excited about meeting those guys while completely unarmed."

He smiled, but with worry behind the smile. He wished she could evacuate—well, he wished they did not need to leave. But she should not remain here when they did not know what was incoming. "I—we," he altered to this when she gave him a stern look, "don't have to be unarmed. There is the armory. It is not far from the ship bay."

"Be still my heart. Ray guns and spaceships? Oh man, I wish we had time to take a spin around the planet."

He found it interesting that her lips smiled, but her eyes did not. "But—have you not—did you not—" How advanced was their technology?

"Oh we came in spaceships, but there is something mystical and super cool about alien space ships and weapons. Not that you're, well, you're not normal to where I come from, are you?"

"No, I am not normal to where I come from," he said, outwardly sober, but inside, she made him laugh. He did not remember much laughing in his life before joining the research project. His family had tried, and they had loved him, but his planet had little opportunities for him to explore his scientific interests. His thumb circled the scar, the result of a fall and a barely trained medical technician.

"Sorry, this is why I don't talk that much. I open my mouth and in goes my foot."

He looked from her foot to her mouth and shook his head in puzzlement.

"Foot in mouth, well, that's what we call saying something you shouldn't."

He waited until her gaze met his. "Please say what you shouldn't to me. Always."

The color rose in her cheeks again. Had he, on first sight, thought her rather ordinary? And short. She was short, but she was not ordinary, inside or out.

"It's a deal if you will as well." She held out her hand. Not sure what she intended, he took her hand, felt the jolt of it all the way to his heart. "Let's shake on it."

She lifted his hand up, then down. For just a minute her hand stayed in his, then she pulled it away. Her shoulders rose and fell in a sigh. "If we want to keep our deal, we should probably figure out what we're going to do next." She rubbed between her brows. "My mind wants to go in fifty different directions. Okay, focus." She turned back to the console even though Bangle did not reside there. "How long do we have until that ship gets here, Bangle?"

A tracking map appeared on the holographic screen that had shown them the incoming ship.

"That's...interesting," Rachel gave a sort of shrug. Then

sighed and looked at him. "I'm sorry, I can't read your time. We've not been able to work it out yet."

The time stamps next to each symbol the screen were quite clear to him, but when he tried to enlighten her, he realized he did not know her concept of time either.

"I've been trying to learn..." She pulled up the tablet she'd used before and tapped on it. Stared down at it and then tipped her head back. "Forget it. We know our squadron will get here after the bogey. So we need to figure out what to do with that time, short or long."

He looked at the timing. "Longer than I like."

"Long enough for the robots to get down here?"

He did the calculation. "Yes."

They lack the necessary codes.

Rachel turned toward the sound, even though the words also still appeared on her screen, then gave herself a shake and faced Valyr. "If you check your files, you'll see I ran an integrity scan of the surface access tunnel. It is undamaged from top to bottom. I'm guessing, from seeing the footage of how they got into the other outpost, that they will use explosives if they find the door locked."

This prompted the longest pause yet.

"We desire to protect you and the—others, Bangle." He didn't quite choke on the name this time.

What type of weapons will be optimal for your goal?

He noticed Bangle did not offer evacuation to them. He did not, he could not blame it for not wanting to be left alone, but... would it ever let them leave? That was a concern, but not one he had time to test now. While he might want to leave or wish Rachel to leave, he could not leave his people in such a vulnerable circumstance.

"I know how to point and shoot," Rachel admitted with a smile he'd have called wry. She wiggled her fingers. "Code is my thing, but I passed my training for this expedition. I can hit my target."

He smiled at her, the curve widening as pleasure expanded inside him. Perhaps their gods had decreed he wake in this time, for this woman. There'd been none that interested him in his time.

"I also received training in their use," he said, his pleasure darkening as he remembered why they'd assembled the weapons. Initially, they had planned to defend their outposts, their research. It was a dichotomy that still puzzled him. How well they'd been at designing the destruction, but how uncomfortable they were with deploying it.

In the end, the vote had been to lock it, hide what they could and leave. He had not agreed with the logic of it, but in the end had joined them in their hope for a better future, rather than stay behind in a galaxy spinning into chaos because two brothers did not know how to get along.

And here he was, almost immediately having to arm himself. So much for his long sleep for peace. "Is there much war in this time?"

Rachel moved closer, putting her hand on his arm. The memory repair was almost done, he noticed, the blue fading from his skin.

"People don't change much, I'm afraid. There was a war here, for a long time, but right now there is mostly peace." She nodded toward the tracking screen. "Since the war ended there have been minor skirmishes between the Gadi and what we call pirates, seeking to take advantage of the vacuum left by the defeat of the Dusan."

"Gadi? Dusan?" He shook his head. The brothers had truly left their mark. "But—" Bangle was not the only one who needed updates. He looked at one of the cameras that he supposed Bangle was using as its eyes and said, "We will return before they get here."

To his relief, Siru and the bird rolled into the room. "Keep Bangle company and assist as needed," he told his friend.

It seemed to him that the bird blinked and looked to Rachel. "Bangle?"

"It's a...long story. Or maybe a short one that is too long for right now. We're going to the armory to look at ray guns, but we'll be back before..." she didn't finish, but the bird nodded.

"We won't wander off."

For some reason, this made Rachel laugh. "Thank you."

As they headed down the corridor, he touched her arm and tried to find words for what puzzled him. She chuckled again.

"We have these movies, fictional video stories, and pets are always wandering off or running away at the wrong moment."

He looked back. "Pet? I thought—"

"He's a little of both. Depends on who you ask. But if I lose him, I'd better hope I don't get out of this alive." She smiled as she said this, but her eyes did not echo the smile.

This made his heart jerk so hard he could not breathe for several seconds. "Then we must all get out of this alive," he stated. It was true that ambassadors required special handling, but she was not a bodyguard. At least, she appeared to be a scientist, not unlike himself, though she had said she could shoot.

"I'd recommend hiding or leaving," she admitted, "if I were sure the robots just wanted more data. Bangle could give up some stuff, but..."

"...we do not know if it is only data they seek..." his voice trailed off, but his thoughts continued. It was not supposed to be his task to protect the chambers, but it was what it was. He sighed and was surprised when her hand slid into his. He looked down and felt his heart clench oddly once more.

"Well, we'll just have to do our best to defend the castle."

It was a call to action said rather thoughtfully. Castle? He thought he knew what this word meant. He stopped by a hatch. "This is the armory, but the hanger bay is there."

Her eyes lit up. "I think we should make the time to look at the spaceships, and I'm not just saying that because I want to see them. Even though I do."

He nodded agreement. "If we need to retreat, I believe this is our only way off this planet." If any of these ships were still operational. They had been dormant as long as he had. And Bangle would have to let them access the hanger bay shaft to the surface.

He placed his palm on the pad, and the large doors slid slowly back, almost as if they'd forgotten how. The air inside was stale and the pause before the lights began to spread, caused several moments of concern.

"For a minute, I thought it wasn't going to work," Rachel admitted, her eyes wide, her mouth in an "O" of pleased surprise as she looked from one side to the other, then back once more.

It was, by their standards, a small bay. It had not been where the main fleet had been housed. There were defensive craft, transport vehicles, and—

Rachel drew in an awed, shaky breath. "This is so cool."

The air swirling around them was not warm, he conceded, but he did not sense that was her meaning. He studied her face as she tried to see it all at the same time. Her pure delight did strange things to his insides. Uncomfortable, but pleasing. His fingers, entwined with hers, tingled and he had to restrain himself from pulling her close and taking the kiss that had been interrupted. They lacked time for such things though he may regret the choice later if things went badly for them.

Her head tipped. "I can guess what they are for, except for those."

Her finger pointed to an upper section of docking. With some reluctance, he followed her pointing finger with his gaze.

"Those are the Dragon Ships," he said slowly. Built in concert with the Draze who had been the first to help them communicate with animal species. Seven ships—his thoughts stalled out when his gaze found the three empty slots. When the call of the Urclock came, when it was once again needed to reform the tangram, all the ships were supposed to depart together. He frowned. He'd have said it was not possible—but apparently, it was.

"Something wrong?" Rachel asked, tugging gently on his hand. When he looked her direction, she made a face. "That was a dumb question. Should have asked what is going well, right?"

He found he could chuckle. He drew them over to a monitoring station, resisting the temptation to find out what had triggered the three ships to leave. That must wait on current events. Instead, he first activated the station. It would take it some time to resume its full function and then its first action would be a check the status of all the ships'.

"It will take time for all the systems to come online. Let us go to the armory," he said.

With a last, thoughtful look, Rachel allowed him to lead her back to the armory.

"I hope there are ray guns," she said. When he could not stop his brows from arching, she added, "It's a geek thing."

———

It was the most human reaction CabeX had had for a long time, this relief that events were moving too quickly for a confession about the messages. It was not logical. They had time for both and more. All of them could do millions of calculations and actions. The only time they were limited was during physical activity. Like humans, they could only do one physical action at a time, but movement did not limit their processing processes. And they could react much faster than any human as the Quh'y had learned too late.

Still, he took the excuse. And found he rationalized—another new old emotion. There had not been a follow-up message, as was usual. He tried to feel relief that the messages may have resolved themselves. That the sender might be past helping. He did not let himself think that it might be a distance issue.

He would not...hope.

Was it hope he felt? He was not sure. It had been too long to remember irrational hope. Their ship, all the crew, operated on hope, but it was not irrational. It was very focused and strategic. A most attainable hope.

He took his place on the bridge, connected physically to the ship's controls. Kraye was in his place, and AzumC was in the secondary pilot's position. All the crew were at their stations and on alert status.

"Update report." CabeX used voice commands for the benefit of Kraye.

MicroP reported for him and RaptorZ. "Target is still resisting the probe. We are unable to scan the interior. The last scan showed a new heat signature. Assume the outpost is on high alert."

CabeX knew this, but Kraye had not. Sometimes it was boring always to know.

"Well, they did know we were coming?" Kraye said philosophically. "Any idea how much resistance we should expect?"

"Resistance has been in proportion to our intrusion attempts so far," MicroP said.

Was the outpost truly sentient? Or reacting to their program? They did not wish to go to war with one of their own kind, but this made him only more determined to gain access. What was it protecting? Could it protect them?

"What about negotiating with it?" Kraye asked.

"If we open a channel of communication, we risk an attack on our systems," MicroP told him. "It would be more optimal to negotiate face-to-face."

If their firewall expert were unwilling to risk their systems over a comm channel, CabeX would not override him, no matter how much he too desired advanced negotiations. It would be initially safer—but ultimately more difficult—to attempt negotiating after using force to enter the complex.

He had no doubt they could breach any physical barriers. Like the previous outpost, this one had an access tunnel from the surface. For them, this was a path inside. There was no resistance the outpost could mount that could keep them out.

The toxic atmosphere was no barrier either though Kraye would need special protective gear. All felt it was advisable he join the breach team since there was a minor human presence. In normal conditions, their imposing physical form was an inducement to give them what they wanted. This time? He sensed this might be an additional hurdle since they hoped to talk. And if their hope was false? Well, then they would return to their original goal, seeking intel that could be sold.

If there was a sentient system and if they were able to convince it to talk, the risk went up for both it and them. MicroP believed he'd built enough safeguards into their internal firewalls, but they would not know if he failed. They would simply cease to be themselves.

"Death is always the risk," ScytheQ pointed out with her usual dispassion. Perhaps it was a side effect of her primary function as their strategy expert.

For this reason, he was limiting their exposure while on the surface. Their standard breach team—a holdover from their time as slave mercenaries—was a team of six. A pilot and five to breach a building. Even a building with no one in it. This time only two of them and Kraye would be at risk. Kraye had volunteered without hesitation, which was optimal. Even their comms to the ship would be heavily firewalled. It increased their risk because it slowed down response time, but CabeX assessed that the risk was worth it to stop a spread of malicious coding if any of the team were compromised. The one exception was Kraye's comms since he could not put them at risk. But his responses, being human, were slower than their slowed responses could ever be.

They had also added another level of sensitivity to their self-destruct code. It was the first thing a malicious code would go after, or so they assumed. Any attempt to access their self-destruct would trigger a fast countdown. Depending on the level of compromise, the rest of the team would shield or sympathetically detonate. There would not be much of the outpost left if this occurred.

The freedom and safety of all overrode the need of a single individual or collateral damage to their target.

He turned his cranium toward Kraye. "You do not need to be on alert." For the rest of his crew, a long alert was optimum. For a human... "You will be weary. I will summon you when it is time to gear up."

He appeared to hesitate, but merely nodded and began to unstrap.

"You have input to offer?"

"I was going to point out we could leave, retreat, but you'd always wonder, wouldn't you?"

He had not known that Kraye fully understood the risk inherent in this mission. It seemed the human did understand.

His cranium moved in a slow nod. "Yes, we would always wonder."

———

"You are moving differently," Valyr observed.

Rachel looked up at him. Way up. Dang, the dude was tall. Made her feel even shorter, but since he made her feel other, better things, she'd move on from that.

"It's the body armor and the ray guns." It had taken time to find her size, but dang, it was nice. Easy to move in and the weapons were a geek's dream. Sleek silver and gold with multiple settings that went from ouch to die sucker. "Makes me feel less like the duck in the shooting gallery and more *Wonder Woman.*" In point of fact, what it made her feel was powerful, which could be delusional. Oh, she hadn't lied when she said she could point and shoot. And ten times out of ten she hit her target. It was the getting shot at part, the lack of cover, lack of back up, lack of real experience as a bad ass that bothered her.

"Shooting gallery?"

Valyr was so cute when he was puzzled.

"It's an Earth thing, an Earth carnival thing," she amended.

"Earth."

His tone had nothing questioning in it. Not even slightly. It was devoid of inflection. So much so that a trickle of ice danced down her back. She tried for casual as she turned toward him.

"You've heard of Earth?" He nodded, still without expression. Okay, a bit boggled and yet, well, there were signs. It was just that all the aliens they'd met so far were all, like Earth? Where is that? Not the single word so devoid of emphasis that it exploded with emphasis.

"Is that...a problem?" Had they done something in the past to tick off his people or something?

"I did not realize…" he began, then seemed to give himself a shake. "I have indeed slept a long time. So much has changed."

The bleakness of his tone made her heart clutch. She hadn't thought—he'd awakened to a future he couldn't have expected, to strangers instead of—did he have a loved one back there in the chambers? Was that who he wanted to protect? Why was he willing to fight?

"I can't imagine," she swallowed, "how hard this must be for you." She'd thought it bold to travel to another galaxy leaving… no one behind. Empty rooms and an empty office. No reason to go back, except, it was *familiar*. She glanced around. Even if this was familiar, it must feel alien to him.

He paused, staring into the distance. Then he gave a small shake and smiled down at her though she could see the effort it cost him. "It is not what I expected, but it is the not knowing that troubles me. Not knowing…" His voice trailed off.

She thought about pointing out that, even with the long sleep, his people were technologically ahead of them, but she didn't. It wasn't in her brief to tell him about Earth. Despite seeing him in less than his briefs. Okay, not a good time to bring back that memory. Color heated her cheeks. She hoped they weren't flaming. She tried to use her hair to hide the cheeks and went for a subject change.

"So, I've been thinking…" And that was about as subtle as an elephant in a china shop, but she forged ahead because she couldn't go back from that. "…about strategy. I'm not in Doc's league, but I play a pretty mean video game. They are all about strategy and tactics," she added hastily, to forgo more questions about obscure Earth terms or about Doc, who was as ghosty as their bogey's code and whose name she probably should not have spoken out loud to anyone, let alone a recently defrosted alien.

Valyr might have looked a bit bemused. Or skeptical.

He hesitated, then said, "Would it not be better for you to conceal yourself? There are many places where you could hide. It is not your job to defend this place."

She didn't think it was his either. And he was right, in some ways. If she were in contact with the Expedition, with the General, she'd be ordered to stand down to a secure location—assuming that was possible—since they didn't know the intentions of the incoming robots. She didn't need anyone to tell her that her ranking was as a geek, not a soldier. She'd pointed that out to herself pretty much from the moment she'd realized she was in trouble. She'd spoken the truth when she said she could point and shoot. She could still remember the looks of surprise on her instructors' faces. She hadn't known how to explain it, the seeming ability her mind had to calculate the range and distance, the near perfect trajectory. The equations would form, and she'd fire. The only thing that had messed with her math was the wind, but that wouldn't be a problem here.

She'd be able to hit her target. If she could engage. Because that was the real question. This wasn't a simulation, a game or anything like it. Could she do it? Could she fire at a target that was walking? Talking? Shooting at her?

Should she do this? Well, that didn't feel like a question. She was surprised to find that she felt a duty to her team, to the Expedition. They were a team of sorts. All connected by the need to do their part so that they all prospered in this alien environment.

Connected.

She wasn't sure when it happened, but it had. She was part of the Expedition, not just a doctor on an expedition. She'd opened this can of worms, and she had to do her best to contain it until the cavalry arrived. Was this what they called *esprit de corp*? If it was, she'd caught it. She lifted her lashes and met Valyr's gaze. Saw him register her resolution. Saw him sigh.

"Trust me, if our guys were here, I'd so be hiding. But they aren't." She bit her lower lip. "I have to do...my part. I'm here, and they aren't."

"You are a scientist, not a soldier."

"I'm a scientist who has received enough training to do this." She hoped. "I won't let you down."

"Let me down?" He rubbed his face, turning away. "You could not—you could get hurt."

She put a hand on his arm so that he turned to look at her. "I've been hurt." The memory of it was still enough to rock her back on her alien boots' heels. "I'm still standing."

He covered her hand with his. It would have been a lot better without the body armor. But something more happened at that moment. They also solidified into a team of sorts. Not a lover team, but two people resolved to do their best.

"All right then." She took a last look around. The armory was beyond cool and she did not want to leave it that bad. It even had a target area where Valyr had shown her how to use her hand ray gun and ray rifle. They were both lightweight, and it only took her a couple of shots to find her zone, to get her firing solutions going. "I've been thinking about that ship bay. It has to open up to the surface for the ships to leave, right?"

It was an obvious question, but she happened to know the Garradians had phased cloaking that allowed their ships to move through a solid mass. So not really that obvious.

"That is correct. It is a system of hatches because the atmosphere is somewhat toxic, but yes, it does eventually give access to the surface."

It was her turn to nod. "We have something like that for deep sea diving. Or space walks. Atmosphere in, atmosphere out." And canal locks. Water up. Water down. "Sounds like it takes a while to navigate?"

"We worked to improve the speed, but yes, it does take time.

If the ships are still functioning, we should be able to egress safely. I did not propose this idea because of Bangle."

"Yeah, we can't leave Bangle," Rachel agreed. "Actually, I was thinking of a ship or ships coming *in*."

Valyr halted for a moment. "Your squadron?"

"Part of it. One of the ships is a, well, a troop transport. I'm guessing Marines are on board, though if I can get Bangle to let me talk to them, we'd know for sure. If they could drop down into the bay, that could tip the balance of power our way or at least equalize it."

He frowned. "I am concerned about the firing of weapons damaging—"

"I am, too. What we want, what we need is for everyone to talk. Our expedition has already provided...assistance...in this galaxy. If they need help, well, then we see if we can give it. If they are just scavengers, then we invite them to exit the galaxy post haste."

"You wish to meet them? To talk to them?"

"Well, that's why we are out there. To boldly go where we haven't gone before, meet new people, and talk to them, learn from them, and teach them about us." She didn't add Sara's Donovan's "and shoot them." She was guessing he wouldn't get the joke. Too many people thought military types were shoot first, think later types. She might have thought that before spending months training and traveling with them. The last thing they wanted was to get into a firefight. But if they did, they intended to win. She'd feel a lot better if they had some of them at their back sooner rather than later. Definitely, before someone got shot.

They rounded the corner back into the main control center to find Sir Rupert and Siru rocking out to Kid Rock's "New Orleans." Rachel had to bite back a laugh. She'd guess neither of them knew what any of the words meant, but the bird and the robot were for sure letting some good times roll. It was at moments like this she really missed social media.

Valyr managed to look amused and pained.

It looked like Bangle was getting in on the dance action a little, if the flashing lights were any indication. It was hard not to rock out to that song. Her feet started to tap. Her hips wanted to shift, and she wanted to join in. It was the finale, and they shouldn't mess up a finale if they could help it, even if the possibly bad robots were incoming. Besides, it would help morale. She looked down. Valyr's foot was tapping a little.

She grinned and let the song end. Before the next song could start, she turned it off.

Why did you turn off my music?

"We need to talk." Rachel tried for firm, but with some "we're a team" thrown in there. She'd seen it a lot, heard it a *lot*, but never tried it. She might have crossed her fingers. "I think you'd like to talk to these...guys, the bogey ship guys, and so would I."

You armed yourselves so you can talk?

"Yes, we did. Sometimes talking requires power to be equalized." She realized she was talking with her hands and tried to stop. "Right now, there are more of them, and I'm guessing their guns are bigger, too. Do you have weapons in this room that could neutralize them if they get in here?"

No.

"So if they get here, they hold all the power. They are bigger. There are more of them. They are better armed. So they are going to figure they are in charge and we have to do what they say. If they stop to say anything. They can do whatever they want. They could stab that thing they have into a console and take data from you." Rachel let Bangle chew on that for a minute. "The thing with weapons, you don't want to use them if you don't have to, but they can bring...emphasis to a discussion, encourage listening. I was telling Valyr..."

I heard you.

Not a surprise, but it was a good reminder to be careful what she said out loud. This pause was so long, Rachel felt a drip of sweat run down her back. She picked up the water bottle she'd thrown at Valyr, twisted off the lid and took a drink. It didn't help.

I would like to talk to them.

I'll bet you would, Rachel thought. She hoped she was doing the right thing helping that happen. What if Bangle sided with the robots against them? There was so much that could go wrong. That was probably another good reason to be armed. If she got shot, she wouldn't have to face the General or Doc.

Can you trust the soldiers on your ship to be wise?

"Yes." Rachel didn't hesitate. She didn't dare hesitate. And she did trust them. They'd be wise if the robots were wise.

You may speak with your ships and they have my permission to land...if they agree to your terms.

"Thank you." It wasn't a plan yet, but it was the beginnings of a plan. Or possibly the beginning of the beginning of a plan. That could end up with her getting shot. Yay.

———

The bogey was going to get to Central Outpost ahead of them. Carey didn't like it, but he couldn't argue with the physics of space travel, even if he'd have liked to. Using a secure link, Carey was discussing options with Sergeant City—that was not a name you forgot. He hadn't commented on the name when they met in the docking bay of the *Doolittle*. She was cute as her name but tough and businesslike enough to discourage the use of the word "cute" in her vicinity.

Neither of them liked the atmospherics on the surface or the fact that her squad would be coming down a narrow shaft after the hostiles. A seriously long shaft. In this case, the high ground was too high and too narrow.

"Do you have the necessary gear for that kind of descent?" Carey asked.

"We're working on it, sir."

Carey didn't respond, so she added philosophically, "It's an opportunity to excel."

"I'd like better odds for excellence," Carey admitted. His radio signaled an incoming message. He frowned. It hadn't been long enough for his message to the *Doolittle* to get there, let alone get a message back. Of course, the Old Man could have sent a followup without waiting for his response. New Intel? He sure hoped so. He opened the message. Only it wasn't a message. It was a direct comm link.

"Colonel Carey, this is Dr. Rachel Frank, Sir Rupert's breakfast buddy."

Carey frowned. The mousy Dr. Frank? It could be her though he didn't think he'd heard her say more than a dozen words. The parrot talked more than she did. Only now her words were a friendly rush. They did know each other but— how was she able to get in touch with him directly when the Old Man couldn't?

"I'm hoping you know by now that Sir Rupert and I are here on Outpost Central. I won't get into how that happened, because long story, short amount of time."

Did he know that? Maybe that would be in the next briefing. Carey wished there was time for that story because City's job just got more complicated. He keyed a private comm. "You getting this, City?"

"Yes."

One word for a lot of unhappy.

Dr. Frank rushed on. "There is a ship bay with surface access connected to this outpost."

There was, Carey knew, a huge ship bay on Kikk. He'd helped Donovan bring some of those ships up to the *Doolittle*. They hadn't used the surface access because they hadn't wanted the Dusan to see those ships leaving the planet. Those phased cloaks were cool, but unnerving the first time.

"I've secured permission for your transport craft to use the bay."

Secured permission from who? Or was that whom, he wondered.

"City?"

"Our opportunity to excel is looking better."

Carey pressed his "talk to Frank" button. "What's the catch, doc?"

"We have some very...compelling reasons to attempt communication with the incoming bogey. Additionally, as you know, it is Expedition policy to talk first if at all possible."

Carey frowned. There was a message in her message. Was she being held hostage? She did not sound under duress, nor had she used any of the standard duress words.

"She's being monitored," City said.

"By who?" Whom? He should find that out.

City did not answer this because she didn't know either.

"No duress words," Carey noted, but a message for sure. Carey considered his response for several moments, then opened the channel again. "Dr. Frank, your message is noted and understood." He hoped. "Can you verify this bay will be a secure landing zone for my Marines?" He added, "It is pretty old, isn't it?"

Would that take any suspicions off the question and get them another assurance they weren't dropping into a trap? While he waited for her response, he created a message for

Halliwell and got ready to send it. He wouldn't get it until after it was over. But if things went south, at least they'd know what happened and why.

It didn't take as long to get Frank's reply.

"I can confirm that the bay will be a secure landing zone, Colonel. The transport ship will receive a signal from a beacon. They should follow this beacon to reach the surface access. The beacon will assist in the descent, so advise your pilots to accept assistance when the beacon asks. It is more than large enough to accommodate your transport and one other ship if you wish. It has pressure locks, to protect the outpost from the corrosive atmosphere. These will cycle automatically. Your ships don't have to do anything once they are inside. I'm uncertain how much time the descent will take. After access to the shaft, your ship or ships will be added to the outpost's internal comm system, so they can obtain a current situation report. Once they open the hatch into the wider outpost, they will need to be super quiet. Based on our readings, the bogeys will be inside the outpost prior to transport touchdown." She paused, probably to take a breath, then continued, "Just outside the ship bay there is an armory. This will be open if any of the Marines wish to, um, upgrade their weapons. I'm attaching a schematic and projected positions following this message." Another pause. "I can't emphasize enough how important it is that your people show restraint. There is a lot at stake. We need a good outcome. Thank you. Frank out."

The line went dead before he could order her to get somewhere safe. His memory of Dr. Frank did not inspire confidence in a positive outcome. Mousy and quiet were not consistent with what was probably going to go down. He pulled up the schematic and shot a copy to City.

"What do you think, City?"

Frank wouldn't send them into a trap without trying to give a warning, of that he was sure. After all, the parrot trusted her. His thoughts froze. The few times he'd seen Dr. Frank, the parrot had been hanging with her. *Sir Rupert's breakfast buddy.* Was the parrot down there? If he was, it was all the permission he needed to act.

He wanted to pound something. Instead, he opened his comm to City. "Sergeant?"

"Sir?

"If you see...a parrot down there...protect it...at all costs."

There was a long silence. "A...parrot...sir?"

"A parrot, City. If I tell you more, I'll have to shoot you."

Another long silence. "Yes, sir." A shorter pause. "I have the schematic. I'm going to work out a plan."

"Roger that."

At least she had a schematic and some time to study it. And the keys to getting inside, he hoped. He needed to figure out his part of the plan. One other ship, Frank had said. He wanted to go down himself, but he was the CAG. It was his job to stay up here dealing with the bogey in orbit around the outpost. He considered his pilots. None of his people were going to be happy with escort duty when they might miss a firefight out here.

Only Frank didn't want the firefight, down below or up here. The Old Man was trusting him to make the right decisions, too, mostly because he didn't have any other choice. They both knew Carey might have to make decisions above his pay grade.

While he had confidence in himself as CAG, this diplomacy crap felt more like an opportunity to screw up.

———

Xaddek decided to be in the room when they activated the comet drive. If it didn't work, there was no safe place on his ship. It was unlike him to be so reckless. He flexed a claw. Almost he could see the crew of *Najer* at his beck and call. And Kraye? He would be his victory meal.

"We're ready, sir."

He didn't look ready. He looked like a man who was about to die. It was odd to trust this human more than the human trusted himself.

"And it can bring both ships?" He was not going up against the *Najer* without both of his best ships. And if they blew up together, well, no one would benefit from his death.

The engineer met his gaze without fear. Xaddek supposed he knew they both might die in a few seconds. "That's the theory. I've tied both engines together. It might be a rough ride."

If it works. The man didn't speak the words, but they were there. In the room. Only Xaddek and this man knew they might all die very soon.

"Do it," he ordered.

After a small hesitation, then a fatalistic shrug, his engineer did it.

There was a flash, a moment of elongation as if he were being stretched almost to the breaking point. All of his stomachs rebelled, all his eyes crossed from this abuse of normal. The engineer looked green as well.

How interesting to learn there were worse things than dying. It took most of his claws to hang on, then his spatial senses adjusted. Somewhat. He still felt not himself. Out of true.

He studied the countdown gauge. "Will we be able to maintain our systems with the power drain?" The comet drive was a greedy thing.

"Some systems will be affected," his engineer admitted. He reached out, his hand shaking, to check those systems. "But we should make it to the coordinates you requested."

"How fast?"

The engineer told him, and Xaddek's mouth widened in his

version of a smile. He would dine on human tonight. And speaking of human, he needed to have a chat with Savlf. If anything could settle his stomachs, it was spending time with her. And...convincing her how much she wanted to do what he asked. Oh yes, just thinking about it helped.

14

RACHEL KNEW Valyr still wasn't happy about her facing the robots with him. She wasn't thrilled, despite the ray guns and the heat signature damping body armor, which may or may not be enough. This was not a video game even though she was dressed like a character in one. Just past the cold hard ball of fear in her gut was a tiny bit of sassy. She'd have totally been geeking out over her get up if the scary robots weren't incoming.

She was assuming a lot. The biggie, that the robots could be reasoned with. If they were being controlled by someone from the ship, well, that could work for or against them. Was it something she'd seen, her gut instinct, or wishful thinking-desperate hope that the robots weren't that hostile? Could she have a gut instinct about the robots? It seemed brassy.

Or wishful thinking. How ironic was it that the playlist started playing "I Take My Chances?"

Had she ever taken a chance before this? Okay, she'd gone to college when she was ten. Taken care of herself since she was sixteen. Gone on an expedition to another galaxy. None of which felt as big as facing the heavily armed alien robots.

Her reasons for staying put felt right to her, despite the patent disbelief in Carey's voice. None of them liked it, but she was the Expedition representative here. Okay, unofficial, and the last choice in at least two galaxies, but the only one here. Even Sir Rupert, who wasn't technically one of them, had left—at her urging, but he had left. She paused a moment to wonder what the bird had seen as he turned for a last look before lifting off and soaring out of sight.

She might have sighed a bit about not being able to fly away, had shaken off the sensation that someone had just flown over her grave...

If she hadn't been here, it would not be her problem, but she was here. And she might be a little to blame for what happened. Like a tiny pebble falling into an intergalactic pool. With a soundtrack. That made her smile. Bangle was seriously digging the music—though it had agreed to a lower volume at Valyr's request. At the moment, it felt a bit like a doctor's waiting room, or maybe the dentist's, which was kind of funny. The doctor in her own waiting room? Okay, maybe it was ironic.

It wasn't as fun when it was her in the irony crosshairs.

They were an incongruous reception committee. Valyr might be able to intimidate them a bit, all weaponized by the ray guns and body armor. Wasn't sure the robots would care that he looked seriously smoking hot. As a scientist, she might be a little ashamed of that less than dispassionate description, but as a dedicated romance reader? Oh yeah, hotter than a griddle.

Siru was not suited up in anything. And he was just a freaking cute little dude. Like one of George Lucas's better creations. Not even slightly scary. She'd half suggested he might want to go with Sir Rupert, but the robot had ignored her.

She had a feeling Siru was not a fan.

And then there was her, the geeky scientist. The body armor

couldn't make her taller. Or wiser. Or tell her how she'd act if she came under actual fire. But more than that, she was worried that the bogeys wouldn't give them a chance to parley. If only these were Earth pirates—but there was no Captain Barbossa loosely reined in by the pirate's laws. These robots probably wouldn't recognize a white flag if she raised one.

While she obsessed about parley and white flags, they fortified themselves with some "yummy" energy bars from her backpack. Valyr had managed to produce some potable water for them since her water bottle wasn't bottomless. She finished chewing and thoughtfully balled up the wrapping.

"I've been thinking..." She saw Valyr give her a wary look. Okay, so maybe she did think too much, but it was her main skill set. "I'm assuming there is also a lock type system for the surface access tunnel? One that cleans the toxic atmosphere out of the box?"

That surface structure has been destroyed by time and planetary drift.

"And the tunnel itself can't sustain a transport cubicle anymore?" She paced away, then back. "I'm concerned about the topside atmosphere getting in here."

Rachel could almost feel Bangle thinking. And then she could see her thinking as data appeared and disappeared on a holo-screen. It finally settled into the view of the access tunnel, with data lines added.

A cubicle could be positioned halfway. There is an emergency hatch in the top of the cubicle.

Rachel moved up to study the cubicle. "Can it be cleaned and pressurized in a non-hostile way for the bogeys?" Assuming they needed that. Rachel had to bite back a grin. It would be kind of funny if they came in all big and bad and packing and then had to take an elevator ride down.

I will also have to set it to stop on this level.

No, they didn't want the bogeys wandering around and getting lost. "Can you keep them out of that control?" They weren't dealing with ordinary big and bad.

I can.

Bangle's brief response felt wrapped in a huff.

"You're the...system, Bangle," Rachel said, admiringly, lifting her fist to bump—nothing. Yeah, she probably shouldn't try to sound or look cool. Was it a coincidence that the music shifted abruptly to "Spooky?"

"You want them to get here?" Valyr might have sounded a bit incredulous. And a lot dubious.

"I want them not to blow up anything we might need later," Rachel pointed out. Maybe they'd see it as a welcome mat and not as a confrontation. A girl could hope, couldn't she?

We did agree to try to talk to them, did we not?

"Bangle is right," Rachel pointed out. "Nobody wants to risk opening a channel to each other, so that means a face-to-face convo." She met his worried gaze and seconded his worry. She was not looking forward to facing the scary robots either. Mostly she was trying not to think about that part because it was as scary as meeting Doc's gaze. Not the moment to wet her pants. She'd gone before she put on the suit, but that felt like hours ago, instead of a few minutes. Oh, fear.

Someone is trying to access this outpost from the one you call Kikk.

That had to be Doc.

"I don't think it is a hostile action," Rachel hastened to explain. "They are worried about us. And the incoming squadron." Still, this was not the time for other voices—like Doc's— in the mix demanding explanations about how they got here and why she hadn't left yet. They were in the chute. All they could do was ride that bronc until they got thrown or the buzzer went. "Could you let them see us, but not join the discussion?"

It would be good to have a record of what went down. Just in case.

"I thought you wished for input from your people?" Valyr asked.

"Too many cooks could spoil the soup at this point," she said and was surprised when he nodded. Guess his people had soup, too. She looked around the room. Was she really looking for an optimal place to greet the robots? Like this was a wedding reception or something? For a moment she could almost hear the wedding planner from the one wedding where she'd been a bridesmaid.

"Now, girl, if you could just move here and put on your smile and your pretty." A pause. "Well, just do your best, darling."

Her eye wanted to twitch. That night, she'd have paid to get shot by a robot.

"We should probably have good cover initially." She didn't want to hide behind a console, though, because she didn't want any of them to get shot up, and the security station was too close to the access hatch—

A concrete—or like concrete—block emerged from the floor just in front of the Urclock.

Like this?

"That's perfect." And surprising. Nothing wedding about it. Bonus. "It will draw fire from the consoles," or wherever Bangle lived, "and it will give us a place to negotiate from." She studied it. "Cool idea."

The Phoenicopterians first developed the concept.

"Phoen—what?"

On one of the screens, an image appeared. Of a flamingo. Sort of a flamingo. In a uniform. She tipped her head to the side. She'd never seen an actual flamingo, just plastic ones in her mom's yard. There were distinct differences. Like the freaking uniform it wore. She rolled her eyes at herself.

"I'd like to meet one of...them," she said, tipping her head to the other side. If she ever had a house, she planned to have plastic flamingos in her yard, too.

They left for the sanctuary long ago. The Mycetarians sought their destruction.

Another image appeared, and Rachel flinched. There were worse things, she realized than facing some robots. Those where some evil looking stork-like creatures.

"I'd want to be in a sanctuary, too," Rachel muttered. "They aren't...close to here, are they?" She looked at Valyr, whose gaze slid away from hers.

You should ask our incoming visitors. They might have more up-to-date information.

"I'll make a note of that." Did Bangle recognize sarcasm?

A smaller, atmospheric capable ship has left the bogey and set a course for this outpost.

"Right." Rachel knew the look she gave Valyr was full of tension. "Can you allow the link from Kikk?"

I will allow it.

"Thanks, um, let's get in position."

Her brain wanted to do equations on how long it would take their bogey-robots to get dirt side and then get down the tunnel, but she lacked key data for a proper equation. In the end, her brain produced: not long enough.

The protective block that Bangle had deployed was a little high for Siru to see over, but Rachel liked the height just as it was—the little guy rolled to a position directly in front of the block. Rachel gave Valyr a wide-eyed look and opened her mouth to protest. She realized Kid Rock was singing in the background, this time it was "All Summer Long." She wouldn't have thought it fit the moment but was surprised to find it did. They were trying a lot of different things.

"I am a protection robot," Siru said, catching a bit of huff from Bangle.

Rachel couldn't help looking from Siru to Valyr and back.

"He will not do any damage to anyone until it is required," Valyr assured her.

Okay, that was not what she was worried about. She studied Siru, trying to see how it could do anything but cute someone to death. Apparently, Siru had hidden depths. Super hidden. She gave them both a thumbs up, which startled Valyr. Siru? Well, he was a rock...robot. He could probably out impassive Doc.

She looked around her. She had both guns, was there anything else—right. She bent and grabbed her backpack and took it with her behind the barrier. She glanced back. "Can we dim the Urclock's lights? It's gonna turn us into perfect targets."

The lights lowered.

Pitch black. Who didn't want to wait in utter darkness for some robots to arrive?

"Thanks, Bangle." Why did it seem like her voice echoed now? "Okay, team. Let's...do some diplomacy," she said. Okay, that was not as fun to say as let's kick some butt.

———

Even working in concert with Robert, they weren't making much headway at cracking the outpost's new defenses. Doc glanced back at Hel. He felt her look and met her gaze, giving her a reassuring smile from inside the force field or whatever it was that enclosed him. The lovesick hologram didn't realize how connected they were. Doc could see and feel what he did, even as she worked on hacking the outpost. She received help from him.

"This is a tough nut, little sis," Robert muttered. He gave Emily a worried glance. "Maybe you should—"

"I'm good," she said. She did look fine. She'd pulled a tablet out of one of her many pockets and was reading—a mystery, she'd claimed.

Their surroundings were more mysterious than romantic. Not that she hated it. This where they'd been joined, their first marriage, though the General had insisted on a more legal service. The result was satisfactory, except when they got too far apart. Then it was itchy.

And this hacking was not going well. It was kind of like going to battle with herself—only without the scary overtones.

You do not scare me.

She ignored this interjection from the love of her life. She thought she saw an opening and doubled down. And got shut down. Either the guy they'd spotted had sentient nanites, too, or they were dealing with an AI with a lot of processors at its disposal. Even Hel's Key DNA wasn't helping all that much. Though he was able to keep the AI from shutting this outpost down again.

"The problem is, there aren't that many ways in there from here..." She exchanged a look with Robert.

"You think maybe we're trying to crack the wrong nut?"

"Military strategy counsels against a direct attack against a heavily defended position," Doc agreed.

Robert brightened. "If we can reestablish a connection to one of the other outposts..." His voice drifted off as the movement of his fingers sped up.

Doc dived in, too. She ignored the weakened border outpost. Most likely the AI had heavily defended that weak point, too. She considered the other outposts. The other border ones didn't appear to be as heavily defended. She did a mental eeny meany miney and started her assault on moe—a most gentle assault.

She sensed the AI would be triggered by anything too aggressive.

The silence grew, but it was no longer a discouraged one. At almost the same time, Doc and Robert said, "I'm in."

She gave him a grin that matched his, followed by a tired laugh.

"That was a workout," he admitted.

"Should we try at the same time or have one of us act as a possible distraction?" Doc asked.

"Distraction," Hel said from his circle.

"Flip you for it?" Doc asked.

Robert shook his head. "Let me start—"

A video feed opened up with multiple views over his work console. He jerked his hands back.

"It wasn't me."

"It wasn't me either. For some reason, it has decided to let us have a look." Doc checked. "Yeah, all we can do is look. No talking allowed." Now all she had to do was figure out what it was she saw.

It was the same view as before...but not. There were multiple feeds giving them multiple views, for one thing. And all the views looked like they were preparing to hunker down for a battle. Dr. Frank as what? *Die Hard?*

Doc tried the comm again. She might have pounded it. No dice. She ground her teeth. What really pissed her off? She understood why. Based on the suddenly available tracking information, they'd just be a distraction right now. Still pissed her off.

"I'm guessing we don't want to send this to the General right now?" Robert asked.

"I think it would give him a heart attack."

She leaned closer as if that would help her see better. Was that—it was some kind of barrier in front of that clock thing. That was new, as was the little robot standing in front of the wall. Cute little bugger. Dr. Frank—she thought it was Frank decked out in body armor because she was shorter than the other figure—had moved behind the barrier, but had not assumed a defensive position. Doc might be a little jealous of that body armor. And the ray guns. The man next to her—was it the man from the earlier feed?—was also decked out in body armor. Big dude. Almost looked scary all suited up like that. Now she got a changed view. They were tracking a smaller ship that had left the bogey. It was on a course for the surface access tunnel shaft. If they were facing five oversize robots, they didn't stand a chance, no matter how sassy their gear.

"I hate watching a massacre," she muttered. Robert shot her a quick, sober look. And then the lights went down to oh-dark-nothing. Well, at least she wouldn't have to see the massacre.

Then Robert said, "Look at that."

They had squadron tracking back. Two ships—the transport and a single fighter escort—had broken off from the main body.

"Where are they going?" Emily asked. She'd put aside her book, her attention also caught by the mystery, or massacre, about to happen at the Central Outpost.

Doc considered the question. "What if they have a ships' hanger like we have here?"

"It's possible," Hel said. "That could mean the AI is working with Dr. Frank?"

"We can hope," Doc said. It was all they could do right now.

———

Over her comm, Sergeant Carolina City, heard the *Dauntless* pilot giving them an update.

"We're going to reduce our intercept time by diverting to the access shaft," Captain Benjamin Bailey, USAF, said.

Next to her, Captain Luca Gibson, the Naval Flight Officer,

piloting the transport shuttle, agreed with this assessment, though she could tell he wished they had a better sense of how long the descent would take. If it took too long, it might erase any advantage their course change had given them.

"I'll go in first," Bailey said. "If it looks like there's gonna be trouble, well..."

City exchanged a wry glance with Gibson. Yeah, they knew what to do. If they had time.

Gibson sent agreement, then asked, "Any idea how long our descent inside will take?"

"No idea. Probably too long." Bailey sounded a bit glum.

He wouldn't, City knew, be happy about being diverted to accompany them down to the outpost. Not only did he risk missing any bumping of heads with the alien bogey, he'd be stuck on the ground with her and her rifle squad trying to hold a position with a sketchy sit-rep.

"The bogey has touched down on the planet's surface," Carey's voice came over the comm.

"I have the outpost's guidance signal," Bailey responded. "I don't see...there it is. I see the ship bay access opening. I'm going in."

"I've got it, too," Gibson echoed. "I'll be on your six."

————

Their surface ship dropped the three of them near the access tunnel and lifted off again. With the cloaked and unknown squadron out there somewhere, CabeX did not want the small ship sitting on the surface. It would assume a low altitude course for a quick pickup if it became necessary.

OxeroidR took the lead, Kraye in the middle and CabeX bringing up the rear. They had full scanning activated, but there was not much to see on the barren surface of this small planet.

Both the border outpost and this one had experienced planetary drift, based on the data they'd extracted from their first foray. The surface of this planet was pockmarked with asteroid hits, and the surface structure had sustained considerable damage. The atmospheric readings showed high toxicity levels. Swirls of wind stirred the dry red and brown dirt and, because they had 180° of view, he knew that same wind erased their footsteps almost as soon as their feet lifted for the next step.

There was nothing here to attract scavengers except for the underground outpost. If one didn't know it was there, one would move quickly on. The extreme barrenness upped the appeal. With a little work, it could be perfect, though this had not been the plan when they left their region of space. Despite a consensus about this from all the crew but Kraye, his link with his crew on the *Najer* simmered with unhappiness. The list of what they did not like was not long.

They did not like such a small team going into an unknown situation.

They did not like CabeX's orders to destroy him if he showed signs of a code compromise.

They did not like to miss meeting with a possible sentient system.

If they'd known about the messages, there would have been another addition to the list, but it was enough unhappy for now.

In front of him, Kraye moved somewhat clumsily in the heavy suit required to protect his human skin from the toxic atmosphere. Everything about their exoskeleton was designed to protect against harsh conditions, both atmospheric and from hostile actions. They could endure heavy fire for long periods without sustaining serious damage. Even with the protective suit, Kraye could not.

He was lightly armed. His purpose on the mission was not about weapons, but words.

CabeX and OxeroidR were never not heavily armed. It was one of the reasons he'd reduced the size of the insertion team. He wished to exude tempered power. He wished the entity to know they could take what they wanted, but they'd chosen not to. This was not a tactic they'd been programmed for. In the past, when they'd been sent it, it was as power's hammer. The blunt fist of pure force.

This was their *choice*. To make this choice, they were willing to take the associated risks.

OxeroidR halted, a hand lifted to stop them as well. He lowered his main defensive arm, the weapon deploying as he moved toward a semi-collapsed wall, shifting his body to cover possible fire from dangers not visible behind the half-fallen walls. After a visual survey, he beckoned them forward.

They were programmed to balance risk and reward, but they all knew the real risk was after their descent where there would be better opportunities for an ambush.

CabeX studied what was left of the structure as they progressed toward the access tunnel. There were signs this had been a multi-room enclosure. But indications of its purpose were long gone. The collapsed, partially missing walls, marked the outlines of several rooms that surrounded the access tunnel box. It was visible, but there was not a direct path through the tumbled debris.

Despite his assessment of low threat level, CabeX continued to scan the area as they made their way past pitted walls to the rust-streaked box. OxeroidR circled it, scanning for structural integrity. It appeared to be intact though for how long was uncertain. It had sustained damage. From their experience at the last outpost, these tunnels were heavily strengthened. It was curious that they had this surface access to the outpost through this tunnel. Had the humans who built these outposts been unable to face the deep complexes without some access to the surface, no matter how inhospitable? Or were they necessary in some way? They were not large enough to bring in large supplies. Logic dictated there was larger access elsewhere. He looked forward to exploring the outpost and finding out.

Now OxeroidR halted at the entry point and prepared to breach the door. The control panel next to this access was a broken square with a few pieces of rusted wire hanging out. He hoped that opening this wouldn't result in a catastrophic breach. They did not wish to fill the lower levels with a toxic atmosphere.

CabeX checked Kraye's propulsion pack and then deployed a safety line between them. For the descent, Kraye would bring up the rear using a remote-controlled propulsion unit. CabeX would control this unit since Kraye had used it before.

OxeroidR applied the XYP-50 to a gap in the hatch doors and then activated the prying mechanism. With a drawn-out shriek, the hatch began to open. As soon as there was a gap, OxeroidR sent a drone down to secure video and assess risk factors. The other outpost had not had protections in its access shaft, but that did not mean this one would not.

With a low hum, the drone descended into the shaft, a red light punching into the deep darkness to scan the walls as it dropped. A view opened up as they received visual from the drone. The shaft was heavily damaged, so even if they'd been able to summon the lift, it would not have been able to make it to the surface.

When the drone was about halfway down the estimated drop, it stopped, its light and video playing over the top of what appeared to be the lift. It approached it, scanning as much as it could.

"It appears to be intact," OxeroidR said.

CabeX created a hologram for Kraye to see.

"Is that an open top access hatch?" Kraye asked.

OxeroidR directed the drone to enter the round hole, and they had a chance to study what appeared to be an intact cubicle. OxeroidR looked at CabeX. It could be a trap.

"We'll take it slowly," he said. If necessary, they could blow it out of their way. Though if it were functioning, it would solve the problem of the toxic atmosphere.

"Deploy," he told OxeroidR.

———

For the first time, Savlf felt hope fading. Xaddek wasn't hurting her, but he was watching, which was almost as bad as the pain. So many eyes, hungry eyes. His species ate their prey alive. She'd heard it took a long time to die.

He'd entered soon after the comet drive was activated. She had not heard of such a thing. So he explained it to her. Explained how quickly they would arrive close to the *Najer*. Too fast for them to prepare.

She'd thought it would be safe to give Xaddek a location. To give him some of the code.

She'd been wrong.

And she was not brave enough to resist the pain. When they dropped out into real space, Xaddek would have a path into CabeX's programming, a route she would not control.

For the first time, someone else was in the room with them. Zougrets, the only other person on this ship who could do what she did, and almost as well. With her pathway, Xaddek wouldn't need her for the final step.

And then hope would die with CabeX's freedom.

"As soon as we are in range, disable his self-destruct," Xaddek ordered.

The kill switch was there, but he'd be too busy fighting to survive to find it. While she could, she sent him a last message.

I am sorry, Savlf.

————

Bangle had modified a specialized hologram for them, one visible inside the headset of their body armor, so only they could see it. It was nice, but also increased Rachel's tension. *Hurry up and wait.* She'd heard the military people talking about it. It was as annoying as she'd heard. Though if she could postpone the robots' arrival forever, she wouldn't complain.

She shifted her position. She'd thought the block of cement a beautiful sight when it rose from out of the floor, but now, with her back against it, it was just a block of cement. Unforgiving and badly angled for comfort. No light at all. Just music by Bangle and the sound of their breathing in the brief pause between songs. Was it better to have a playlist or silence? She wasn't sure. Silence could be uncomfortable as she'd discovered too often.

At least they had something to "watch."

There was the progress of Carey's squadron, the transport ship, and the small ship that had left the bogey. Carey had put the pedal to the metal after she'd contacted him. He'd cut down some on their intercept time.

The small ship had dropped three figures and lifted off. Now it was circling the drop zone like a sentry. The outer edge of its track might be close enough for it to see the bay access open up. Nothing she could do but hope Bangle and the ships' pilots handled it.

That left her some time to wonder why just three this time?

That bit of wondering didn't take long since she didn't have a clue.

One thing she could do was math, so she distracted herself from the rising tension by working out the various courses and intercepts. Bangle was doing that, too, but in Garradian. Whoever was flying those ships, they knew their stuff. She "saw" the transport and its fighter escort find the signal and steady out on a track. The outpost could "see" them, even though they were cloaked. The only area of exposure was the open bay doors. With careful timing, the bay access began to open when the bogey's small ship was at its furthest point away. The two ships dropped neatly inside.

Her heart leaped for a minute when the small ship changed course, but it didn't act like it had seen anything. And their three bogies were starting their tunnel descent.

Oh man, she hoped she'd said and done the right things. Encouraged the right moves. From the video, the bogies exuded both power and danger. Didn't they need to exude some back?

Her body armor was surprisingly flexible. A little warm, which was odd because she was stone cold on the inside. Bangle's music choices weren't bad since she was choosing from songs Rachel liked. Something about the order of play made her want to giggle. She didn't. She was afraid it would turn into hysteria.

"Rachel?" Valyr's voice was low.

"Yes?" She prompted when he didn't continue. She couldn't see his face, his eyes. There was only his voice in the darkness. It was incredibly intimate. She leaned back and closed her eyes and let the sound of his voice in the dark warm her.

"I wish we had—" He stopped again.

She felt for his hand, even though it was two pairs of armored gloves, not hands, touching. At least she hoped he wished for what she wished. "Me, too."

There was a long pause, then he spoke again.

"Do you fear death?"

Almost alone in the dark with a man who might matter more to her than seemed possible in such a short time, Rachel heaved a sigh. "I used to. Of course, when we are young we believe we are invincible, don't we?" Not that she'd ever been what she'd have called young. She couldn't remember a time when her IQ hadn't come between her and almost everyone.

"We believe many things when we are young." She thought he sighed. "Are you afraid?"

Rachel shifted so that she could hear him better, so she could pretend she could see him. Was she afraid of dying? She'd been afraid of a lot of things in a life that didn't seem like it had lasted long enough all of a sudden. What made her afraid? She knew how to be alone. She'd nailed that one. But the unknown? Being wrong? Dying in pain like—she glanced at Valyr. Losing this man before they had a chance—

"I am, and I'm...not, I'm not afraid of dying."

"When did you stop?"

"When I," she swallowed dryly, "lost my family in a car accident." Even now, so many years later, she felt the punch of pain in her gut. The constriction of her heart so that she couldn't breathe. The slow fade of cushioning shock, and then the living, the doing, the going forward alone. Completely alone. Yeah, she knew how to be alone. It was a good time to remember that. People left, even when they didn't want to. She didn't fear death. It was living without—

"How old were you?" His quiet question was a relief.

"I was sixteen." It was right before the Christmas holidays. She'd been looking forward to the break from college more than usual, to going home, and then she didn't have one. The house was still there, an empty shell with forlorn Christmas decorations and presents under the tree waiting for people who would never open them. It was as if the house knew what she knew. That nothing would ever be the same again. People had rallied around, of course, because people did. But she presented an unusual problem for them. Not legally an adult, but she'd never been a child, not a real one. She could still see the look of relief, mixed with bewildered, on the face of the judge during her emancipation hearing. She solved the problem for them since her parents had been the only children of only children. Her mind still flinched from the memory of her brother and sister the last time she'd seen them. Was it harder that it was a happy memory? She didn't know. How could she? She did know that she'd been left with regrets, guilt, and this aching cavern in her heart. They'd offered grief counseling, but she took the grief books instead. It was easier to read platitudes than hear them. They'd helped as much as anything could. She hadn't, she realized now, stepped outside that circle of grief, or let anyone in until Sir Rupert. He'd required her to start interacting with others and not just code or equations or data. And then a naked man had stepped out of cryo-sleep...

"You?" The briefness of the question left open his option to choose what he wanted to say or not say.

"I have died once already."

Going into that chamber must have felt like dying. She took a deep breath, then another. "Well, at least we won't be alone." At least he wouldn't be alone this time. Unless—do not even go there, Rachel.

The bogeys have reached the transit cubicle.

Rachel tensed. She did not know if Valyr tensed as well. Even Bangle paused the music as they strained to hear—

On the hologram, the cubicle began to descend. Right now, she could have done with more waiting. Bangle restarted the music. Daughtry singing "No Surprise."

———

"You okay?" Sergeant Carolina City asked Captain Gibson. It

was unusual for a rifle squad sergeant to be the backup pilot, but that was how it rolled in a galaxy far, far away.

"I'll be fine." Gibson gave her a familiar look, the one that said, "I got this."

City wasn't sorry to leave the bridge to him. It was freaking eerie, this descent into the heart of a planet. She'd quit looking when they passed the mile mark. City palmed open the hatch between the flight deck and passenger section, twelve sets of eyes shifting her way, the seated bodies subtly coming to attention. No view to the outside here. There was a view screen Gibson could have activated, but—not sure which was worse—they'd left it dark.

Not surprisingly, her squad was calm. This was probably one of the smoother rides they'd had. Gibson was a decent driver.

"We'll be dirt side soon," she said crisply. "You know the drill. As soon as the hatch drops, we go quiet. Not. One. Sound. We'll stack at the hatch. Once it opens, the hostiles will be capable of hearing us. You do not want to be the one that draws their attention our way." She triggered the view screen now, with the schematic they'd been sent. "According to our intel, there is an armory about one-fourth of a klick from the egress hatch. We can secure alien weapons which may be more effective against the hostiles. If it is open, we'll access it two at a time. *Quietly.*"

This produced a lot of happy expressions. Well, why not? Who didn't love alien tech?

"Did I mention we need to do this quietly?" They might have grinned. "I'll go in first, in case I need to shoot one of you for making a noise." Now she let her gaze grow stern. "No **one**, I do mean no one, fires a shot until I give the order, even if the hostiles and our people on the ground are exchanging fire. Those are our orders."

They didn't like it. Neither did she.

"Those are the rules of engagement."

More nods.

"Squad Three!"

Corporal Knight straightened some more. "Ma'am, yes, ma'am."

"You will remain with the ships and keep the bay secure in case we need to fall back or escort our friendlies back."

He didn't like it, but it didn't show in his second, "Ma'am, yes, ma'am."

"We have people here, so let's try to keep them alive. I have high confidence that you will all perform this mission in the finest tradition of the Marine Corps."

Their *oorah* bounced off the ship's walls.

She started to sit down but remembered the final order from Carey. "Oh, there's a bird down here, a parrot. Don't shoot it."

She ignored the expressions that briefly appeared on their stone faces, and pulled down the jump seat, or at least what they assumed was a jump seat, and strapped in as Gibson's voice came over the intercom.

"We've cleared the last lock..." Gibson said over the intercom.

———

Kraye had the hardest time fitting through the opening in the top of the transport cubicle. The robots could bend and angle in any direction, contracting or expanding as the situation required. Kraye, well he was what he was. He'd have been stuck without CabeX and OxeroidR. They yanked him down and then held him upright as the hatch snapped closed.

Some kind of system cleaner activated, exchanging the toxic atmosphere for something else. There was another sound, a different one, and then the cubicle began to descend. There was no one to exchange an uneasy glance with. The robots were intent on the next step and tracking their drop.

OxeroidR deployed more drones. The small swarm hovered in the air in front of the hatch that they all hoped would open at the right time. They were designed to clear defenses and would send them their first view of what waited in the control room. When they were almost down, the two robots reached up, hooking one arm onto protrusions in the ceiling. Then their other arms hooked under his and lifted him with them as they drew themselves out of sight. Kraye rested his feet on CabeX's just as the cubicle came to a smooth stop.

After a pause, the hatch slid open.

He was aware, despite his suit's filter, that the air still tasted stale. It was dark, so dark even their light-enhancing gear could not find shape beyond the hovering drones.

And there was the sound.

That surprised him most of all. It was not silent.

The darkness pulsed with rhythmic sounds. There was a pattern in the sounds. And there were words, he realized. In Standard, the common language in this region of space, or so they'd been told. His gear tried to translate, but it did not make sense to him. Clap for the Wolfman? Who was this Wolfman? Clap how?

The two robots dropped down, with him between them, though partially shielded by their metal bodies.

The drones moved forward, and patterns and forms began to appear on the holographic map of the room. Some low walls. Consoles on both sides. Ahead was a decorated wall, and in front of that was a lower wall with a small statue in front of it.

The drones spread into a pattern as they penetrated deeper, searching for the heat signatures of the two humans they knew were here. Or had been here before they had been shut out of the outpost's systems.

Kraye was aware of the two robots stepping out of the cubicle. He waited until there was room and then followed them. Behind him, closer than he liked, the hatch slid closed. He might have protested or something, but he knew the two robots did not intend retreating, at least, not without what they wanted.

He couldn't be sure, but he thought the sounds might be confusing the drones. They'd veered off in several directions until OxeroidR brought them back in a protective line, some high, some low, all deployed to find danger first. The sounds were coming from an intercom system, he realized.

"No heat signatures," OxeroidR reported, over their private comm system.

Where were the two humans? They could be hiding, he supposed or had fled through the interplanetary transport system.

The drones were about halfway across the room. CabeX and OxeroidR had stopped just behind the walls that appeared to divide the control room from corridors that stretched off in each direction. Kraye stayed where he was. He did not want to get in the way if the robots went into action. It was not his function to fight, but to be their human voice if they found the heat signatures.

The drones widened their flight pattern and drew closer to the back of the room—

"That's far enough," a very human voice said.

————

The ramp lowered almost silently, only a small click when it met the decking. Squad 3, led by Corporal Knight, came out first with weapons ready, running quietly down the ramp, and taking a defensive position with their guns pointed out. The lighting was low, the outline of their fighter escort *Dauntless* between them and where the egress hatch lay. Nothing moved except the next squad of Marines. They filed quietly to the big doors. The next squad came out with the Sarge in the lead. She gave them the high sign and headed for others. There was a slight whoosh of sound and the feeling of different air washing past them.

And the distant sound of something that kind of sounded like music.

No sound from them. The only indication they were in motion was when the big doors slid quietly closed again.

Knight relaxed a micrometer, had the sensation of someone looking at him—he glanced down and saw a parrot sitting on the ramp quietly pecking away his chest feathers. He looked up and met the startled gaze of PFC Fox. He shrugged and turned his attention back to where the danger would come.

Those big doors.

————

"That's far enough."

Their video view of the intruders was unsettling. The red glow of two sets of eyes and nothing else. Rachel could hear the soft hum of the drones in between the pauses in the music, but nothing else. Not breathing. Not the sound of movement.

She still had her back to concrete, using the video feed to judge when to speak. She didn't want them to get close enough to fire down on them. Based on the height of the eyes, these dudes were *tall*.

Bangle's most ironic choice yet filtered softly into the room —it had lowered the volume as if it knew they needed their ears, too. "Under the Boardwalk?" Seriously? Even so, she had a hard time not starting to at least bob her head along with it.

At the sound of her voice, the drones closed on their position

—then sparked into hundreds of painful lights. They dropped to the floor.

I'm a protection robot.

Rachel blinked. Maybe they would survive this.

And then the two robots opened fire on Siru.

———

Her squad had just left the armory when City saw and heard the shooting start. With her infrared headgear, she could see three figures, two large, one about their height in the corridor ahead. The two large figures were doing the shooting.

The smaller figure was the danger. All the bogey had to do was look their way, and they'd all be in the firefight. Suppressing an urge to send her squads running forward, she signaled her two best ghosters to do a non-lethal neutralization on the bogey.

She didn't see her guys moving toward the bogey, so she was pretty sure he didn't see it coming. She kept the rest of the squad in position so that they wouldn't give them away. For a minute, two shadows rose up by the bogey and then he slumped.

She moved the rest of the squad out as light danced and flickered ahead of them. All they had to do was get in position before the two big bogeys realized they had a man down and they'd been flanked.

———

A female voice? It was possible, CabeX decided. It was a mistake to speak. The drones swerved toward the sound—

The small figure in front of the wall moved forward and lifted its arms. The soft buzz that only a robot could hear warned of a protective shield, but even the drones could not react fast enough.

They hit the shield. It shimmered and sparked with light, and the drones dropped to the ground. Inactive but not destroyed.

He and OxeroidR lifted their arms, deployed the proper weapons for a shield assault and began to fire, targeting in a pattern that would weaken the shield and give them data about the strength, coverage, and durability of the shield.

It was only a matter of time before they defeated it.

From behind the wall, he saw two rounded domes appear. Each held a weapon.

They must be the two humans. They wore gear that dampened their heat signature. Perhaps it was armored, too.

But no amount of armor would save them.

Neither of them returned fire.

They did not need to.

Yet.

———

"They excel at this," Valyr murmured through their comm, as the relentless fire continued to hit Siru's shield. They fired in a discernible pattern to, he assumed, help them analyze the strength of the shield while they depleted it. Siru could not hold them off forever, but if they did not stop firing how were they to talk to them?

"They are good," Rachel agreed. She had the longer of her weapons lying on the top of the barrier, but neither of them had returned fire.

Bangle was playing a song about taking chances. Incredibly Rachel was tapping her free hand to the beat. She had appeared nervous, but now her shoulders moved slightly, too. She was a woman of many surprises.

"How long can Siru take that kind of fire?" she asked.

"Not much longer," he admitted. But Siru was analyzing their fire for him. The data he received was...troubling. These robots were powerful. The scientist in him was impressed, intrigued. The man—he glanced at Rachel. "They are powerful robots. Our body armor will provide limited protection."

"Then let's see if we can get them to stop," she said. "Time to try talking, Bangle. Cut the music, please."

The sudden silence was as disconcerting as the sound had been. For a second or two, the robots continued their assault on Siru, and then the zing of weapon's fire on the shield tapered to a stop. They backed closer together, their weirdly red eyes scanning for new threats. They hadn't looked behind them yet.

"That's better," Rachel said, her voice now coming out the intercom system.

Bangle added some emergency lighting, very low, leaving the corridor behind the two robots in deep shadow.

Rachel stood up, not hurriedly, shouldering her weapon at the same time. But with the barrel down, though it could lift quickly, he knew. But not fast enough for this adversary.

He bit back a protest when the robots reacted as expected by shifting, so their weapons' barrels pointed at her. Valyr stood up, to act as an additional target. Despite himself, he was fascinated by the sight of them. The larger of the two was a black, heavily metaled, powerful figure. The only thing that relieved the black were the slits for his red visual array. The second robot, though somewhat shorter and more square, was a grayer black, also heavily armored, and wore a hood on its cranium. Though its weapon had moved to target Valyr, he sensed the robot could and would act quickly to protect the other robot. It was curious that a being so devoid of humanity could nevertheless project protection so clearly.

The long silence that followed was not comfortable. No surprise it was Siru who broke it.

"Why did you try to disassemble Siru?"

The cranium of the larger robot tilted downward.

"We wished to disable, not disassemble."

The voice lacked inflection but was not totally robotic.

The little robot rolled closer, his cranium angling so that it could study the larger robot.

"I protect Valyr."

Now it was the smaller robot who looked down.

"That is your programming." The robotic tone managed to be dismissive.

Siru puffed up, his moving parts extending and contracting. "I am AI. Rachel said so."

The larger robot might have stiffened though he hadn't moved since they stopped firing.

"Are you the sentient who protects this outpost?"

"I protect Valyr."

The red gaze shifted their way, tracking over Rachel and then him.

"I am Valyr," he said.

"You are human."

Valyr gave a sharp nod.

"Me, too." Rachel nodded her chin.

The red gaze shifted toward her. Valyr felt ice in his veins though no expression showed on the metal face.

"You are the female human."

"I'm a girl, yes."

"Kraye requires a female," the other robot said.

Before Valyr could protest, Rachel asked, "Who is Kraye?"

She might have sounded a bit uneasy. What concerned her about this Kraye? She could not know him, could she?

"He is our human."

The large robot half turned and gestured toward the shadowed corridor.

"This isn't the time for the dating game," Rachel said, then hissed on their comm, "get down!"

She dropped back behind the barrier as a long hiss emitted from both robots. He followed her just in time. An energy beam passed through where he had been standing.

"So much for the easy way," Rachel muttered.

15

CabeX fired from fury, using all the force of his most lethally weaponized arm, the other hand reaching for the small robot, but it had already rolled out of his reach and deployed its force field. He did not wish to destroy sentient life.

He lifted an arm and OxeroidR ceased firing, too. In the silence, his olfactory sensors picked up the tinge of singed metal and chemical burn where weapons and shield had clashed.

"Where is Kraye?"

"Your guy is fine."

This was another female voice, a different one, from the rear. He spun around, but there was nothing to see, even with his enhanced opticals. Before he could send in a drone, she spoke again.

"He'll stay fine if I stay fine."

You will not fight.

This new voice, this *system* voice stopped him more than the threat from the female.

You will talk.

The voice came from all around them. This outpost had an auditory system.

"I will speak to Kraye," he said.

"Hang on," the second female voice said.

He heard whispers of movement, other sounds he could not identify, then a small groan. His metal fingers curled into fists.

"Hey, Captain."

No question it was Kraye.

"Are you optimal?"

"I will be."

"Release him."

This pause was long. They were conferring, he decided. *How many hostiles?*

Six.

When Kraye is safe, you deal with the threat to our rear, he told OxeroidR. He would not negotiate with a weapon at the head of his First. The soft rustle of movement and then Kraye appeared. OxeroidR began his turn to take care of the hostiles when pain exploded inside him and spread like fire along his receptors.

He swayed, felt OxeroidR at his side, supporting him. For once, all his processors focused on one thing.

The poison code punching through his systems on a course for his self-destruct code.

Through darkening opticals, he looked at his old friend. "Kill me," he whispered. "Kill me now."

———

Rachel jumped over the barricade just behind Valyr, as the square robot lowered the stricken robot to the floor.

Valyr snapped over his shoulder. "Siru to me."

"What's wrong with him?" Rachel asked.

"Virus," Valyr said tersely.

She was aware of the other robot rising and retreating a few steps, his red gaze tracking between them, then returning to his fallen companion.

"He must be...destroyed."

Rachel looked up, considering the robot, who had lifted his weapon and pointed it at his...friend? That pause was telling. And interesting. Instead of answering him or moving, she asked Valyr, "Can you help him?"

"Perhaps." His fingers fumbled against the plates of its cranium and he uttered what she assumed was a curse.

She reached into a pocket of her expedition jacket and held out a small screwdriver. Siru also presented an attachment that would work. With Valyr working on one side, Siru attacked the other. She looked at the other robot again. He still had a weapon pointing at his comrade-in-arms. What did he know that they didn't? Actually, she had a feeling it was more what she guessed he knew, and she hoped she was wrong.

"Why do you want to shoot him?"

"The code will target his self-destruct code first."

Yeah, it was as bad as she thought. "He self-destructs when his operating code is fatally compromised. Someone is trying to stop him from self destructing before they can take over?"

The cranium moved in a decisive nod.

"What happens if the code breaches his self-destruct code?"

"It will trigger the self-destruct."

"He'll...blow up?" Suddenly her throat was bone dry.

"Yes."

"How bad? What's the blast radius?"

The robot did not hesitate. "It is possible some of this planet will survive."

"And just when things were going so well." Rachel's hands moved faster than her words. "What happens if you shoot him first?"

"Only those of us in this room will die with him."

Nice there was an upside.

"Let's see if we can all live," she suggested. "Don't shoot him until you have to, please?"

The robot gave a reluctant consent.

"What do we need to do?" Sergeant City appeared out of the shadows, the robot's guy at her side.

"You should get your people out of here—"

"No, ma'am."

Well, that was definite. This wasn't the first time she'd had to push through shock and think, plan, figure something out. "We need to find the signal that is delivering the virus. It's got to be coming from a ship, fairly close. Find that. And then we need a plan to stop them permanently. Bangle will help you, City."

Rachel didn't stop to see how City reacted to this. Or Bangle. Valyr was pulling clear, flexible cables from Siru and attaching them to places inside the exposed circuits. Rachel found her tablet and plugged into one of Valyr's wires. Inside the robot, the complexity of the internals made her heart stop. She looked up and met Valyr's gaze.

"What do you need me to do?"

"You work on stopping where the virus is coming into his system. I will work on the virus."

"If you stop access, they will try another tactic," the standing robot told them.

She had thought of that. "I'm thinking of setting up a filter to clean the code where it comes in, rather than stopping it," Rachel said.

"Do it," Valyr ordered. He didn't look up. He didn't have time for looks anymore.

Rachel bent to her tablet, hoping it would be up to the job— blue streams of data flowed up from where her hand gripped the side of the tablet. She heard a sharp intake of breath to her right.

"I'm okay. Don't stop it." She tried to relax as the streams began to flow across her vision. Through them, she could still see the control room. She pulled back from that, focusing on where the streams were taking her. Her brain wanted to stall out, it was too much, but now she felt the stream helping her manage it.

Later, she could panic later. If they weren't dead. Even as the streams took her in, her brain was constructing the code filter...

She felt panic fade as the task shrunk in size if not complexity...

————

City didn't waste time ordering anyone to leave or exclaiming in shock as Frank, and the Val-something guy got swarmed by shiny blue bugs. Okay, she almost shot Frank. You expected aliens to get covered in stuff. She'd find out later if she made the right call. Everyone else was in the radio loop and knew the score. Mostly.

"Bangle?" she muttered, glancing around. Was Bangle the bird back in the hanger bay? She didn't see it anywhere.

A hologram appeared over a workstation looking table.

We can work here, Sergeant City.

Okay. Apparently, Bangle wasn't a bird. With a last glance at the group around the stricken robot, City moved to the hologram. As she passed the guy they'd downed, who had a bit of a dropped jaw going as he stared at the blue computer geek grouping, she said, "You can help me."

She made it sound like an order, so she wasn't surprised when he followed her.

"I'm City."

"Kraye," he rubbed the back of his head. "I'm Kraye."

"Their human." It had almost sounded like "our pet" when

they said it, but he didn't act like he was owned. Yet. For some reason this made her think about the bird in the hanger bay. He'd look good on this guy's shoulders. He wasn't a bad looking dude, a bit scruffy for her tastes, a better-looking space pirate version of Jack Sparrow.

He half shrugged, his expression losing its tenseness.

"If I could make contact with the *Najer* we could assist in the search for the source of the attack," he said.

City glanced back at Frank, but she was busy getting bluer and keeping them from getting blown up. She hoped.

"Can you manage that, er, Bangle?" Where had that name come from? Lots of questions. She hoped she lived long enough to get answers.

The hologram split into two. On the new hologram, another robot visage appeared. He was as badass as the other two, but there were differences. She didn't want to say expression because none of them had any. Coloring maybe? They all owned looking lethal, and she'd met some pretty lethal people. She was glad it looked like they were going to be buddies. Or all die together.

"We are aware, First," the visage said.

She thought it odd it didn't ask—

"They're connected so they already know what's going on," Kraye said. "When they speak it's for my benefit."

"That makes sense." And triggered a new cascade of questions without answers.

"The attacker is close," the ship robot said.

"That's BoomerJ," Kraye said. He nodded her direction. "City."

There are two bogeys. They dropped out of comet drive space on the other side of this planet's moon.

Comet drive space? What was that? "What about interdicting them? Can we take them out before—"

BoomerJ shook his head in a decisive negative.

None of us are close enough to reach them in time.

"Okay, we need to bring the CAG in on this discussion," City said. "This is above my pay grade." Without waiting for permission, Bangle—City's eye twitched—opened a channel to Colonel Carey.

A video feed.

"Sergeant? What's—" He stopped, as he apparently took in the various elements in the control room.

And, just in case things weren't weird enough, music began to filter softly out a hidden speaker system. "Walk like an Egyptian?" Bangles. Bangle?

Rachel needs music to work.

———

The music helped, no question. Rachel moved her shoulders as her mind traveled through blue space. It wasn't as hard to find the access as she'd thought it would be. The virus had cut a black, ragged path through the robot. It was a fast hammer, not meant to take care but to take control. Maybe they thought they could fix him up later.

It felt a little like flying, following the damage. Her stomach even gave a little bump as they landed next to the breach point.

"Got you." Now she began to construct her filter around the breach. It was super weird to see her code in 3D, watching it weave back and forth, see the flow of dirty code began to thin as it hit her filter and then emerge on the other side as a shadow of its former self. She didn't stop for a victory dance. This wasn't over until the bad code sang its last. Whoever had done it, holy crap they were good. Good enough to sense their code was getting filtered? Possibly.

"I'm gonna shut off all incoming data but this point," she

said. That was easier than trying to find leaks. The robot seemed to quiver, but it nodded. "Hang in there—"

"He is called CabeX. He is our captain."

Such flat delivery and somehow so much grief. Rachel looked up, met his gaze. "Call me Rachel."

"I am OxeroidR. We are free robotics warriors."

Free. This attack was on all of them then.

"Let's keep it that way, OxeroidR." She frowned through the data stream. "You're not under attack are you?"

"I am not."

Not yet, he meant. Well, one robot at a time. She triggered the isolation code, and CabeX quivered again. Was the red glow of his opticals dimmer? Was he weakening or feeling the lack of contact with his peers?

"Will you all, will your ship survive if—?"

"Our ship will go on."

Then Valyr's voice strained to breaking point said, "I require your assistance, Rachel."

———

Valyr had never seen such code. That something so perfectly constructed could steal this robot's will—it was a glorious abomination. Even as he tried to contain it, it slipped away, as if mocking him. "I require assistance, Rachel."

"I'm here."

Through the data streams, he saw her and felt her support. Felt his efforts gain strength and focus.

"Dang, that's pretty in a mean ugly way. Huh. It kind of looks like a DNA strand." Rachel's presence in the stream circled it, weaving code strands as she moved.

"DNA?" The question was forced out between gritted teeth.

"The strands of life, our human code."

Human code. Of course. One could be too close to some-thing—he moved out, making the code slowly spin in the streams of data. Like Rachel, he circled the strands, studying it in the context of a human code. Interesting that this had not triggered the robot's defenses.

"He grows weaker."

OxeroidR drew closer, his weapon pointed at the exposed cranium.

"Siru, keep this area contained for me," he directed, creating direction code on the fly. He needed a faster processor than his own eyes. On the other side, Rachel moved in to protect his other flank. "We are looking for a kill switch."

Was he wrong? If he was, they were doomed, but he could not believe someone so skilled—

"Is this it?" the small robot asked.

"Interesting it's like a petunia in the thistle patch," Rachel said.

"Yes." It took all his skill and the help he received from Rachel and Siru to get close enough to try flipping this switch without triggering what they sought to avoid. Almost it slipped away from him again, but Rachel pushed it gently back toward him. It circled in an eddy, like a floating flower. He rubbed his face and gave the switch a careful nudge. Alarms went off. "It needs a password."

He thought a word he could not say aloud in Rachel's pres-ence. It was possible she thought her version of that word.

The stricken robot stirred. "...I'm sorry, Savlf."

"Captain—" OxeroidR almost managed to sound distressed.

"Try...it...Savlf..."

Valyr looked at Rachel. "If it doesn't work..."

"I understand." Her hand touched his hair fleetingly, making the blue streams swirl around them. "I'm sorry."

"As am I."

There was complete silence in the control room. Even the music had ceased. He felt sweat bead his skin. Could tell the robot was losing ground. *I love you, Rachel.* He wished he could tell her, but why would she believe him? They'd spent so little time together.

"Spell it," he ordered and was surprised when the robot managed it. He typed it in and entered it as a command.

The code strands seemed to tremble, the alarms spiking for what felt like a long time—and then the strands fell apart in beautiful fragments. Except for two words.

Help me.

And behind the image was the terrible sight of the woman caught in a spider's web. Only her eyes—her almost dead, desperate eyes—were visible. Webbing covered every other part of her.

Help me.

———

Rachel reared back, the blue streams shattering like the hostile code. Bits and pieces of code continued to drift across her vision, but all she could see was the terrible image of the woman in the web. She knew it was a woman, because the strands clung to her body, outlining her shape and securing her legs, arms, and head, leaving only her eyes uncovered.

Her eyes. Rachel shuddered. Had that sad, desperate captive managed to reach out to them? Or was she the next step in the plot to trap the robots and subvert their will?

She stared at Valyr and knew he'd seen it, too. The horror of it remained in his eyes.

"Doc?" City was suddenly next to her. "You okay?"

Rachel managed to nod. She licked dry lips. "You didn't...see it?"

"All I saw was lots of blue streaming things."

And she'd cut CabeX off from his link with the other robots.

"Is he optimal?" OxeroidR asked. His weapon was still pointed at CabeX.

"I've stopped the virus. He is rebuilding and repairing his code," Valyr said. Slowly the robot withdrew the weapon, with a muted whirring as it retracted into storage on his bulky arm.

Rachel might have geeked out, but she was too freaked out by that last image. She looked at OxeroidR, then their human, Kraye? She thought that was his name.

"Do you have someone after you that..." she almost felt embarrassed to ask "...oh, I don't know, makes webs? Or something that looks like webs..."

Kraye didn't hesitate. "Xaddek." He almost spat the word.

"Xaddek," OxeroidR agreed, "has long sought to control us and our ship. We did not know he could follow us here."

He used a comet drive.

Rachel twisted toward the sound of the words. Couldn't seem to help herself. "What's a comet drive?"

Towards the end of their occupation of these outposts, the Garradians developed the comet drive to travel faster through space and time.

"Everyone likes faster," Rachel admitted, "but how would this Xaddek get his hands on one?" No one had told her they found anything comet drive-like, but she wasn't at the top of the email chain.

"He deals in stolen technology," their human said.

The drives were installed in several of the Garradian ships before they abandoned the outposts.

So one or more Garradians could have exited stage right in some of the ships. Her mind drifted to the three empty slots in the bay. "Dragon ships. Do they have comet drives?"

She wasn't quite sure why it mattered, but it did because Valyr gave a decided twitch.

Yes.

Their gazes clashed a bit. Not like a mean clash, but hers had questions and his said, later. She didn't nod or anything, but she did direct her attention back to the Kraye.

"So, this Xaddek and his webs..."

"He is *Heteropodidatian.* They are nasty."

"Bangle? You ever heard of...that?"

Heteropodidatian is a species of sentient spiders.

"Crap," Rachel said. "I hate spiders."

———

"What happened?" Xaddek demanded as the screen went dark.

"I'm not sure," Zougrets admitted, casting a nervous glance at Savlf, then looking away. Sweat beaded his forehead.

Xaddek turned to the webbed woman, hanging almost unconscious in the strands. While Zougrets had monitored the code, he'd entertained himself by making her dance for him.

"Savlf." He might be surprised her lids lifted. "Did you fail?"

She licked her lips, her voice, even through the system, a hoarse whisper. "The reprogramming takes time. He will fight it."

"Will he lose?" His voice was hard. He sent a little fire along a strand of web.

"Yes."

The complete despair in the single word was more convincing than the word itself. "How long?"

Numbers flickered on the screen and eventually settled on a time.

"I have time for supper then."

Both sets of eyes watched him warily. He drew the moment out, then keyed his comm. "Bring me the artifact."

———

The light grew brighter, pulling him out of a dark tunnel. His oculars rebooted. Distantly he wondered why. Focusing took longer than usual, but eventually, CabeX saw the anxious face of his First.

"Captain?"

"Yes," he confirmed. Now he sensed strands of weakened poison code still struggling inside him. It was losing with the aid of some new programming. Even as he began studying this new code, his attention shifted to the two humans next to Kraye. He had planned to stun them, he recalled now. It was fortunate he had not succeeded. He felt their presence around the new code. The male was highly skilled with robotics code. The female was less skilled but had managed to do less damage than the virus. *The virus. Savlf.* She lived, or she had been alive when she sent the kill switch code. Did she live still? Inside the code, she'd helped him unlock, was the image. If he read the image correctly, she'd been forced to attack him, but had managed to save him. If he read it correctly. The image could be the next move by Xaddek—though he did wonder why the spider would think such an emotional plea would work with them? It was common knowledge they acted against slavers, he had to acknowledge, that, but they'd never embarked on rescue missions.

Which brought him back to the essential question. Was the image part of a plea for help he'd been receiving or a new trap? The desperate gaze in the trapped face would be difficult to forget for a robot who could forget nothing.

"How do you...feel?" the man asked.

"I feel...more optimal than I did." He met the man's gaze—Valyr—somehow he knew his name—and realized Valyr knew the battle was not over. It should be, but the vicious, nearly perfect virus had weakened him. It had not worried about collateral damage as it drove toward his self-destruct code. It was an unusual sensation to feel unwell. It had been a long time.

"Do they—the ones who attacked you—do they know you're all right?" the woman next to him asked him. "Or that you will be?"

He shook his head. All these humans, he was not accustomed to being around so many. It brought back memories, not all of them negative, but with an undercurrent of less than optimum. He knew there were others close by. Most of his sensors were active again. She'd deactivated his link with his crew. After a careful examination of the area around the breach—the woman might be better than he'd credited her—he activated it once more. It was a relief to find them there, still with him. Still themselves. He shifted his cranium until his optics found OxeroidR. If he could have smiled, he would have. *Thank you, my old friend.* Only the slight movement of his friend's head acknowledged he'd heard CabeX's message.

"Well," the female said, "we should start with hello, but we don't have a lot of time, at least that's what your crew and mine believe." She hesitated a moment, but when he did not respond, she added, "I'm Rachel. Dr. Rachel Frank. That's Valyr who did the code surgery. This is Sergeant City—"

A female in a uniform he did not recognize, and with a marked military presence edged in—and then out of view.

"And then there's Bangle. That's who you really wanted to meet, wasn't it?"

I'm pleased to meet you, Captain CabeX.

Finally, something he could understand. As the link opened,

he felt it join his systems, spreading healing where the virus had burned him.

"While you've been out, we've been talking." Dr. Frank's gaze moved to OxeroidR, who nodded. "We've been putting together a plan to step on your spider."

Xaddek. They had taken care to avoid him, but it seemed he would not be avoided.

"I am listening," he said.

16

"No, sir," Doc said patiently. "We can see all the outposts." They could get into all of them, but— "Central is still there. We can see it. Can't see inside it."

She wasn't sure why they'd been shut out again. The last thing they'd seen had been the start of the firefight. Not the end. *That's all I know.* She didn't repeat the words. For the thousandth time. Doc exchanged a wry glance with Hel and then with her brother, Robert. They could see the two new bogeys lurking behind the planet's single moon. They could see the original bogey holding the orbit it had taken up when it arrived. They could see Carey's squadron closing on the original bogey's position. They could see a lot—but not what they needed to see to stop the steam from coming out the General's ears.

Whatever had shut down their comm links with the outposts, it had kept the links down, and shut them out again. Which meant they had no contact with Carey or their people in the outpost. All they could do was talk to each other, something Doc could have done without.

They had a couple of new names. Valyr. Bangle. She knew the robots got in from their last view before the link went down.

Were they ones who had shut down communications? Were Frank and the parrot okay?

"We should be getting a message from Colonel Carey," she offered. The old-fashioned way: via subspace signal. Which felt more like sending smoke signals after the speed the outposts had given them. There would be an update on why the transport and an escort had peeled off from the squadron. There had to be a ship bay in Central Outpost. It was the only explanation for the transport ship heading down. It felt good to know Marines were down there. Felt better to know everyone was okay.

You wish you were there.

She slanted the love of her life a look. *Maybe.*

This is not our battle. I think the quiet Dr. Frank may surprise you.

If that wimp surprises me that would be a surprise.

———

At some point, Bangle had started filtering love songs throughout the outpost. Rachel noticed it when she went to look for a ladies room while City and Carey argued out the details of the cobbled together plan. Bangle made a path for her to follow. Apparently, Valyr followed it, too, because he was waiting in the kind of anteroom where she'd had to shed her body armor to accomplish her goal.

The miracle was, she hadn't already accomplished it during one of the many traumatic events of her red-shirt day. Was it still one day? She'd lost track of time. Felt like more than one day. Might have been more. She looked down at her watch, but her eyes couldn't process what was there.

He stood just inside the archway, sans body armor, too. His and hers lay on a bench in the center of the room that divided his from hers. His hands were shoved into the pockets of his coveralls. He looked more like the man she'd met earlier, only with clothes. She knew him so much better it felt like a lifetime had passed.

Was it crazy to think she knew why he had the furrow between his brows? The reason for the straight, rather grim line of his mouth? The tense line of a body she knew so well, but didn't know the way she'd like to know it?

And since they were headed into the spider's den, their chances of any more knowing was pretty slim.

He looked up abruptly, catching her looking at him and some of the worry softened.

"Rachel."

The way he said her name sent a cascade of shivers down her spine. The love songs didn't help. They gave her hope and ideas. Stuff that made her want to plan things, future things.

I could fall for him, could love him. Her own little Hallmark movie moment. Only with robots and spider bad guys. But otherwise very Hallmark.

They must have both moved in each other's direction because she found herself inches from him in the middle of the room. Not touching. Just lots of looking. Into each other's eyes. Trying to find and give answers so they could—what?

This wasn't the happy ending moment. This was—well, she wasn't sure what it was. She just knew she could stay in it forever. Though maybe just a little closer...

Did he move? Did she?

He was tall. She not so much. But love—passion—found a way.

If he'd been cold before, he wasn't now. Only his lips touched hers, but it was like being seared by a flame thrower. Or —since this was a new galaxy—a star going nova.

She didn't know how long the kiss lasted. She wasn't sure when his arms went around her. Had no recollection of her wrapping her arms around him. One minute it was lips and then her arms were full of man. Strong, straight man.

It felt too short when they both fell back a few steps. Both of them were breathing rapidly. Her heart was pounding. His probably was too. Both hearts had been racing when they were chest to chest.

She wanted to say something, but what? What could she say to him? What could he say to her? They hadn't known each other long enough to say anything important.

"Rachel," his voice was a rough caress of sound. He closed his eyes, his hands clenching.

Because he wanted to grab her again? A girl could hope.

"Please..."

She might have rocked a little closer.

"...don't..."

She rocked a little back.

"...do this. Stay here. Be safe."

Okay, that was sweet. Did he have any idea how much she wanted to stay here? She hated spiders. And webs. She'd traveled to a new galaxy, and that might seem brave, but she'd been in the follow-up group. And—it had felt more like a flight from the past than an act of boldness. This, what they were planning? It was all the things her trip here hadn't been. This was a find-out-what-you're-made-of moment.

"Why are you going?" she asked instead. It wasn't his circus. The robots weren't his monkeys.

He turned away, rubbing his face. "I feel—you saw—"

"I did," she agreed. The webbed figure of Savlf haunted, horrified her, too.

He swung back. "It is not your—"

"Problem? It's not yours either," she felt impelled to point out. The Urclock had called him from sleep, not the robots or Savlf.

Was it a coincidence that Bangle's playlist switched to "I Need a Hero?" Rachel wanted to tell her to stop it.

He looked up as if suddenly processing the words. "I am not a hero."

She stepped closer again, her hand hovering over his arm for a second before she touched his forearm. Even with care, there was a jolt, heat surging up through the cloth to sear the palm of her hand. She didn't know much about love, or passion for that matter. But this didn't feel...fleeting. It felt more like...finally. You. The one. Me. Your other half. Maybe it was crazy to think she could make a life with an alien from the past, but love was crazy. Or so she'd heard.

She'd touched his mind while they worked on the virus, had seen the fineness of it, had had a front seat for the determined way he'd fought for the life of a stranger who'd almost shot him.

She didn't need a hero. That opening had been filled in her heart. She let herself see her dad in her mind's eye, and for the first time, the pain was more poignant than punishing. She could use a partner in her life though. Even if all the things were equal, and he wanted her, too, would the higher-ups in the Expedition let her keep him? She'd breakfasted with those who could and did keep their odd and alien matchups, but eating food with them was not an induction into that Breakfast Club.

She looked down where his hand covered hers. She didn't want to watch his face as he tried to persuade her to let him go. To step back and watch him head into danger and possible death.

She didn't want to die, but she didn't want to live in a world without him. She knew what that was like already.

She couldn't keep him. He wasn't hers to keep. But she could go with him, fight by his side, die with him, or for him?

Greater love hath no man—or woman.

Yeah, she could do that. And if they didn't die? She loved

him enough to let him go if that's what he wanted. She'd lost before. She didn't like it, but she knew how to do that now, too. It was not her first master's program, but it had been her hardest.

She eased her hand out from under his and met his gaze without quite meeting it. "Let's go see if there is going to be a mission. The Colonel hasn't spoken yet." She turned away.

"Rachel?"

She turned back, her heart caught again by how he said her name. He held out his hand. She extended hers, felt his close around hers, clenching briefly. Holding on to him as he held onto her, they headed back to the control room.

It could have given her hope that he wanted to keep her, too, if not for the Urclock that Bangle had turned back on, the ticking that the music couldn't quite block out. If they survived for the Urclock to cast its vote, what would it be?

———

Colonel Carey was not a happy CAG. This plan was not only above his pay grade to approve, it was liable to get him busted down to Airman with his wings clipped for this life and the next.

On the side for doing it anyway: it was his job to remove threats.

The two bogeys were clear threats. He could make a case for blowing them up and keeping his wings and maybe his rank. Only he couldn't blow up a ship with prisoners on it, even when they weren't sure the prisoner was a prisoner. According to fresh intel from an, in his opinion, unreliable source.

And the proposed rescue mission that might be a new trap? Hard to make that case when it involved risking so many assets on what was a crap shoot, no matter how they wrapped it up in pretty.

"So you're proposing we invade two hostile ships looking for a prisoner who may or may not be a prisoner?" Not to mention exposing highly sensitive, beyond top secret ships to the enemy, ships that no one was sure would still fly. Allowing access to these ships by the same robots who'd been shooting at them an hour or so ago. Would still be shooting at them—or standing over their unconscious or dead bodies if one of them hadn't almost caught a virus.

If he were lucky, he'd only be busted to Airman, and not dishonorably discharged. And then thrown in the brig. Or shot. Or both.

On the other hand, he was as pissed off as everyone else. If the image of the woman was real? If she was a prisoner on that ship? Then he wanted to step on the spider, too.

"If you decline to assist us," the one called CabeX said, "then we will do it ourselves."

If he didn't speak for his crew, there was no sign of it on the other robot face. Or any other emotion. Even their human guy, Kraye had put on his expressionless face.

"I'm not saying no and," he added hastily, "I'm not saying yes. I'm thinking."

"We don't have a lot of time, Colonel," Dr. Frank pointed out. "So far the ships aren't moving, but we can expect either another virus attack or a physical attack on the *Najer* once they realize their first attack failed. The other thing to consider in your thinking, this nasty spider now knows or will know there is an outpost there. He has already collected a comet drive from a Garradian ship at some point. So he can move around quickly."

She'd tried to explain the comet drive to him. Waste of time after the part about it making the ship go faster than anything they had. It was a salient point for them going after the ships. Still not a persuader for a rescue mission.

It was also a point in favor of boarding the ships. Disabling the comet drive was something he was sure the Old Man would be for. And if they could steal—take it back? Even better.

"What are they waiting for?" he asked without expecting an answer.

"They believe the virus is rewriting my code. Then they expect me to move on my crew and, once I have subdued them, bring my ship to him," CabeX said.

And that was another thing to worry about. Apparently, they'd left the access port to his brain open. Partially open.

"If we'd closed it off, they'd know their attack failed," Dr. Frank had already pointed out. "We'd already be dealing with round two."

And they might already have exploded into little pieces because round two would be worse than round one. He got that.

The plan might have been something the Doc back on Kikk had come up with. Which kind of surprised him. Right now the meek geek doc kind of reminded him of the Doc—without the Morticia thing. She was not even slightly creepy. She had a good, strategic brain. He liked that. Had a feeling Valyr liked it, too, and a bit more. And speaking of Valyr, she had yet to explain where he'd come from. He'd gotten a lot of "later, if there is a later" looks, now that he thought about it.

"Sergeant City?" He turned to her next.

The plan of attack involved a squad of Marines working with the other motley crew, including this Kraye, who looked a bit too Jack Sparrow for Carey's taste. That was a lot of risk for her people.

"We're ready to deploy, sir." City said with the casual calm that told him she meant it.

His gaze moved on. He didn't like risking the doc. The other guy? He was neutral. Guy could decide for himself what he wanted to do. He still wasn't clear on why he or the doc needed to go. Okay, if there were a prisoner, she'd probably need medical care and cracking the ship systems would be easier for this Valyr now that he'd cracked their virus. They exhibited high confidence they could take both ships. Which they needed to do to find the comet drive or the prisoner. He didn't say it, but he thought it. If one of them got shot or disabled, they'd have a backup brain.

He studied Frank while he considered the pros and cons. He had to admit she looked different than she had the last time he'd seen her. He knew what it was. He'd seen new pilots who looked like her over and over again. They arrived looking fresh and eager and they—grew up. Not that she'd looked fresh or eager. Mostly she appeared subdued. But their little doc had grown up a lot since the last time he'd had breakfast with her.

"I'm a good shot," she told him, "and people tend to underestimate me."

He could believe the under estimate part. The good shot? He'd have to see that to believe it.

"It's not the best plan," Frank admitted, "but with the intel we have..."

It wasn't the worst plan either. The *Najer,* accompanied by the cloaked squadron, would close on the bogey's as if CabeX was delivering them to the spider—his brain didn't like thinking about that. Flying two Garradian shuttles using phased cloaking, two teams would intercept the bogies—there was a nice neutral way of saying glide partway into the bogey's engineering sections and look for the comet drive and the prisoner. Then they'd disable both ships, or retreat and disable them with extreme prejudice. Their hope was that during all this the spider would be licking his spider chops at the thought of the *Najer* belonging to him. Did spiders have chops? Carey knew he had a lot of something.

Carey had a better shot at forgiveness if he could deliver a comet drive and those ships to the Old Man. There was a lot that could go wrong, but also a few things that could go right if he ended up explaining it to the Old Man.

Two robots—they couldn't risk bringing any more down to join the assault force when the bogey would have eyes on them, and their shuttle pilot had to return to the *Najer* to make it look like CabeX was acting according to the virus—the Marines and three humans. Without the robots, he'd have already said no, but those dudes were packing.

"What if they get the virus into one or more of your crew?" Carey asked, trying to think like the Old Man, find the holes.

"They will self-destruct," CabeX said flatly.

Blowing them all to hell and back.

At least if that happened, he wouldn't have to explain anything to anyone. Well, when his brain wasn't sure what to do, he tended to go with his gut.

"Let's do it," he said. What the crap, he'd always hated spiders.

———

Rachel couldn't believe she'd almost forgotten about Sir Rupert. She found him sitting next to her battle armor when she came to put it back on. To be fair, she had had a lot on her mind. She still had a lot on her mind. She sat down next to him.

"I'm sorry."

"There are wider issues in play," he said calmly. He edged closer to Rachel when Sergeant City came into view, stopping in surprise. He swept out a wing in what Rachel took to be an invitation. "Please join us, Sergeant."

After a brief hesitation, City came closer. Rachel wouldn't call it "joining," but at least it wasn't an outright rejection.

Sir Rupert regarded City with his head to the side. He ruffled his feathers. "I wish to travel with you, Sergeant City."

"Travel? With me? Where—"

"You will be in the second shuttle, will you not?"

City's jaw tried to drop, if she hadn't been a Marine, it would have full on dropped. She nodded with considerable caution. It was the most reaction Rachel had seen from any Marine, ever.

Sir Rupert turned back to Rachel. "I will go with City. I can ride on the pirate's shoulder."

Rachel started to protest, but it was a laugh that wanted to come out, so she bit her lower lip instead. Over the parrot's head, City arched her brows, her eyes asking for help. Rachel was sorry she couldn't provide it.

"You'll find him quite...helpful...*if you listen to him*," she said, with a careful emphasis on the last. She tried to say it with her eyes, too, since her lips couldn't. She was not authorized to tell his secret, particularly when they were heading into enemy territory.

City hesitated, did something with her chin that could have been agreement or incredulity. "I'll let the *pirate* know he's got a...passenger." She stalked away.

"That went better than I expected," Sir Rupert said.

Rachel couldn't argue with that.

———

Carey had asked City to do the mission briefing and given her operational command, since she'd be on the ground, well, aboard one of the Garradian ships. He'd be too far away to effectively issue orders in response to unexpected events. The *Najer*, Carey and his squadron connected to the briefing by Bangle, and everyone down on the outpost in a conference room that Valyr had led them to.

City scanned the room, her gaze bouncing off the parrot "seated" in one of the conference chairs. She hadn't missed Dr.

Frank's emphasis on the words "if you listen to him" or the significant look that had accompanied the words. She still had no clue what they meant, but she figured Frank had her reasons. Or rather, she hoped Frank had good reasons for wanting the parrot to go along with them.

If the robots thought it odd, well, they couldn't show it. They'd not offered a verbal protest when the bird joined them. Kraye, she sighed inside, she hadn't told him yet.

It hadn't been as hard to divide up their scarce resources as she'd first thought. It felt more like eeny meany miney moe. They'd even arranged themselves in their assigned groups on either side of the room. The only protest she'd received was from the *Dauntless* pilot, and the squad of Marines detailed to stay behind and protect their rear.

She pulled up the data Bangle had compiled for her with the mission code name on the first slide. That had been the Colonel's only suggestion.

Operation Pest Control.

None of the aliens got it, of course. Frank may have choked a little.

"Our operational targets are the two ships that initiated the virus attack, designated Arachnid one and two. We'll move against them in three prongs," City explained. She split the screen to show the three prongs of the operation. "The *Najer*, designated Romeo Flight and Colonel Carey's squadron, Delta Tango Flight, in cloaking mode, will directly approach A-X and A-Y. Our hope is that this will bolster their belief that their virus attack was successful and that the *Najer* is surrendering to them. Colonel Carey will exercise operational control of his squadron during the attack."

"I will be in operational command of our part of the mission." Would the robots recognize her command authority? That had been Carey's main concern. It was a question that neither of them could answer. She shifted one side of the split screen to highlight their part of the operation. "We'll use two Garradian ships, Golf Sierra A and B, to approach A-X and A-Y from the sides. Both ships will deploy their cloak and phase cloak before launching. GS-A will target Arachnid-X and GS-B will target Arachnid-Y." She took a breath. "Our mission objectives will be to first find and free the prisoner. Since we don't know which ship the prisoner is on," or if she actually was a prisoner or on either ship, "both teams will make accessing ship's systems for critical data a priority, which should aid in our second mission objective: seizing control of both ships."

She and Carey had decided this was a necessary action. Anyone able to do the kind of damage these ships had almost done needed a sit down with the General, at the very least.

"If you are unable to seize control, then disable as many systems as possible, with engines and weapons as the highest priority. Then retreat to your ship and reposition into attack position. At that point, our objective will be neutralizing the ships' ability to retreat or offer resistance."

"What are our rules of engagement?" Corporal Reid asked.

"Use all necessary force." She was not going to tie the hands of her people in what was probably going to be a volatile and fast-changing situation or rule out lethal force when they had no idea what they'd find if they managed to board the two ships.

She switched views. "Here are your ship assignments." She braced herself. "As I mentioned, Delta Tango Flight will accompany Romeo." Did they realize that Romeo stood for robot? She needed it to be easy to identify who was who if events turned complicated. She put the list on the screen, but also began to read it out.

"Golf Sierra Alpha's crew will be Dr. Frank," City couldn't believe she was going to say this, but it was the only available option, in her view, "who will be primary, comm designation

Alpha1. Her second will be Valyr, comm designation Alpha2. CabeX's comm designation is Alpha3. Captain Gibson will be Flight for GS-Alpha, and he will be in command of all flight operations. Marine squad Alpha1 will consist of Reid, Burns and Knight. Comms for the Marines are Mike 1, 2, and 3." She glanced around the room. "Questions?"

Apparently, no one had any, though Frank looked a bit wide-eyed.

"Okay, Golf Sierra Zulu's crew complement is as follows. I'll be Flight and Command," she had to swallow, "with Kraye as Zulu2, OxeroidR as Zulu3, Sir Rupert as Zulu4. Marine squad includes Jenkins, Spencer, and Fox as Mike's 4, 5, and 6."

The sound of a throat clearing came through the speakers.

"Comms will be managed by Bangle on both ships. She," was she a she? "will provide backup for Flight on both ships, as well."

Gibson straightened. "Bangle," it was his turn to swallow, "can fly the ships?"

"I can." The sound came out of the speakers.

It was hard to quantify the tonal quality of her voice, other than it sounded female to her ears, which was probably a reaction to Bangle's attitudes, she acknowledged a bit ruefully. She didn't quite sound human, but she also didn't sound computer generated. City wasn't sure why she felt this because the robots sat there like a couple of Vadars in shades of gray and sounded a lot like him when they uttered anything. Despite their complete lack of expression, she had the sense they were pleased Bangle was sending parts of herself along on the mission.

That they might trust Bangle was not that comforting because City wasn't sure she trusted Bangle.

"Questions?" she asked again. She and Carey had gone the rounds on all of this and still concluded they had to act, despite knowing the General would not be happy with them, despite all they didn't know. For both, it was coming from the gut, a deep-seated sense that not only did they need to act, but they needed to act fast.

No one had any questions, except possibly Frank, but she didn't say anything.

"Let's do this then," City said.

17

RACHEL AND CAPTAIN GIBSON, the Marine pilot, had checked out the Garradian ships—Golf Sierra Alpha 1 and 2, she reminded herself to get into the habit—before the final mission briefing. Both engines started up, regular cloaks and phase cloaks worked. That moment when she'd pointed the ship at the wall and gone through it, well, still made her sweat. She was proud of —and surprised by—how steady her hand was on the stick.

Her outer mettle was firmly in place. She wished there was a way to test her inner mettle before lift-off. Rachel knew she had strength, had learned to be strong following the loss of her family. She'd coped, got on with her life, done what needed to be done. Her past, however, did not provide assurance she could do *this*. Whatever "this" might encompass. Because if she couldn't, then she would be a drag on the ticket when the shooting started, instead of the fearless leader they needed.

She looked the part. She'd seen herself in the Garradian version of a full-length mirror all decked out in the body armor and packing all kinds of cool alien weaponry—which she knew how to use, both the visible and not visible ones. Other than her height, which no amount of armor could fix, she looked pretty badass and fit in well with both ships' teams who'd also had alien-armored and weaponized up.

But looking the part was no predictor of how she'd perform if they came under actual fire. Good thing she was not their first line of defense. Or their last.

Despite being next in the command structure after Sergeant City, Rachel knew this was not a vote of confidence. There was no one else to pick. She'd only have the power to give orders if they lost radio contact with the others. With a bit of Bangle aboard both ships, that seemed unlikely to happen. It was interesting that Bangle wanted to go along, but Rachel was still figuring her out. She frowned. She still couldn't put her finger on why she thought the AI was female, other than her song choices—which were limited by Rachel's choices.

Was she assigning gender to Bangle and the robots — there was a band name — because that felt more comfortable than the neutral "it?" She'd never liked being called an "it" but she wasn't a sentient robot. She was a geek doctor in over her head, and heading into a fire fight, partly because of the hot alien. Did she think this was a good dating strategy?

She had plenty of time to wonder. They were back in "hurry and wait" mode. So far the two bogeys hadn't changed their orbit—an orbit that kept the moon between them and the planet. Everyone assumed they'd deployed stealth satellites of some sort to keep an eye on things, so the hope was that they'd seen the robot's in-atmosphere shuttle land, lift-off and return to the *Najer*. They wanted the spider to stay put, wondering and hoping that CabeX had been taken over and was now taking over his crew.

Captain Bailey, the *Dauntless* pilot who had accompanied the Marine transport, and one of City's rifle squads would remain in the outpost, just in case the spider tried a sneak attack while they were sneak attacking him. Never leave your retreat unguarded seemed to be the one thing where they could all agree.

There were more good reasons for this attack than helping the robots or even saving Savlf. If the nasty arachnid got back to his region of space, he'd most likely sell information about this one, which would encourage even more pirates to filter in, turning it into a less safe, intergalactic version of Earth's pirate-infested Caribbean. So, despite Rachel's surprise they were doing this, she also wasn't that surprised.

The last uncertainty was, would the comet drives work? They couldn't be safely tested inside the hanger bay. This last question was resolved with Bangle's help. The drives came online and were programmed with an abbreviated jump that would end on the opposite side of the moon where Arachnoid 1 and 2 lurked. The hurry followed by the wait.

And then, all they had to do was use the phase cloak to breach the ship's hull, board the scary spider ship, rescue the princess in the creepy web, and either take control of the ship or exit stage right for more forcible interdiction by Carey's squadron and the robot ship.

In her ear, Rachel heard City's voice.

"All flights, we are a go. I repeat, Operation Pest Control is a go."

Gibson activated Golf Sierra Alpha's comet drive program, and the ship jumped. Rachel's stomach followed a few seconds later.

————

At the helm of Golf Sierra Zulu, Caro City had reacted to the go order from Carey by initiating the comet drive. She knew she'd been given the stick partly because Kraye had never flown a Garradian ship, and mostly because none of them trusted him.

He was not helped by his Jack Sparrow looks, kicked into high by the addition of the parrot on his shoulder. On the plus side, he lacked the pirate swagger, instead projecting a quiet confidence that had been a little dented by her request that the parrot ride along with him. He had to be picking up on the humor coming at him from everyone but his robot buddy.

Without cracking expression, her three-man fire team had managed to indicate they found it hilarious. City was finding it hard to keep her expression under control as she manipulated the controls. Good thing she'd got in her hours in a ship very similar to this one or she'd have been the one stuck behind at the base.

"May I be allowed to comprehend the humor?" Kraye asked, his voice low despite the fact they were alone on the small bridge and the hatch was closed. There was a hint of something exotic in the way he used words, and the timber of his voice that went well with the music Bangle insisted they needed as background. Like they were in a freaking elevator or something. Whereever Bangle was getting her music list from, it needed updating.

"It is a cliché on their planet for a pirate to have a parrot on his shoulder," Sir Rupert said. "The humor is directed at both of us."

Kraye blinked a couple of times. "Then why—"

"I will be less conspicuous being where I am expected to be."

On Earth, Caro wanted to point out, except he did kind of look right sitting on Kraye's shoulder.

"You would be even less conspicuous back on the outpost," Kraye pointed out without rancor.

"But I would not be able to help from there," the parrot responded, tucking his wings in and settling into roosting position.

Kraye blinked some more, looked about to speak, but instead

pressed his lips together. Nice lips, she thought absently. Nice eyes, too, with uncomfortable depths, as if they'd seen more sadness than joy. That he had a story, she had no doubt. He was the lone human on a ship of robots. Weirdly enough, that gave them something in common. She was the one female in the Marine contingent deployed with the Expedition. There were lots of women in the Expedition, of course, but she felt odd in their midst, too.

A pity the gulf between them didn't seem to have a bridge, but that wasn't happening as long as neither side trusted the other. She didn't like it, didn't like going into a firefight with people she didn't trust, but she'd done it in the Middle East, so she could suck it up now.

As if he felt her looking at him, his gaze edged up to meet hers almost as if he were shy.

"Is everything optimum, Sergeant?" he inquired.

"It's all good," City said. So far the worst bit had been deliberately trying to ram the side of the hanger bay during their systems test. This phase stuff took some getting used to. The comet drive was more than optimal. Up next, trying the phase cloak on the engineering section of their target, Arachnid X. She had confidence in her Marines on both ships and that OxeroidR was built like a moose, not to mention armed from top to toe. He probably even had laser eyes. Kraye? She'd find out what he was made of when they executed their dicey mission brief.

She knew about crap mission briefs, and this wasn't the worst she'd seen, though it was the first with a sentient spider on their hit list. They'd seen the image of the prisoner, courtesy of Bangle. Had the AI produced it to motivate them? If it had, it had worked.

Now everyone wanted to step on the spider.

As a Marine, she was not allowed to be afraid of spiders, but she didn't like them. She might be having trouble wrapping her brain around a spider big enough to be that evil *and* sentient—if you could call that kind of nastiness sentience.

So all they had to do was get on the alien ship while it was salivating over the apparent approach and surrender of the robot ship, do their thing, and either seize Arachnid Y or retreat and assist in blowing it out of space.

It wasn't a perfect plan, but perfect was a classroom thing, anyway. Real life wasn't perfect. It was an opportunity to excel.

She triggered her comm to the rear compartment. "Lining up for the approach. Prepare to board Arachnid Y on my signal."

———

Carey watched with satisfaction as Delta Tango Flight settled into a fighting formation around the *Najer*, designated Romeo. They still had the moon between them and the two Arachnid ships.

It might have been boring, but they'd had a front seat to see Golf Sierra Alpha and Zulu initiate their comet drive jumps. Holy freaking cow that was fast. A blink of the eye. Both Alpha and Zulu had dropped out in their pre-programmed flank positions on either side of the Arachnid ships.

The timing was going to be tight for getting there in time to be of any help if his people got in trouble. Not that he wanted to start shooting while they were on board. With any luck, they'd have taken control of both ships, and no one would be shooting anything. It was a good thing the Old Man had given him latitude in how to handle contact. If the shooting started, he'd need that latitude at his court martial.

With some luck all around, the spider would be so focused on his incoming robot prize, he wouldn't see the other trouble until it smacked him between all his eyes.

"You could stay with the ship," Valyr said, as Golf Sierra Alpha made its final approach toward the bogey designated Arachnid X. *Please stay with the ship*, he wanted to say. He liked the look of the Marines. Though few in number, they exhibited no fear. In fact, they had the air of warriors who were ready for anything.

Rachel's gaze shifted his way, and a small, wry smile flickered on her mouth before fading. "I was going to say the same thing to you. You can do your thing from here with Bangle's help."

He felt his eyes widen in shock and her smile returned.

"I probably have more military training than you," she pointed out. "I'm a very good shot. Even though no one believes me."

The Marines didn't move or alter their expressions, but somehow managed to convey skepticism about both of them.

"It's going to take both of us to crack this system if the same person who wrote the virus code set up their system defenses," she added.

And the two of them together had barely managed that. He knew this as she did. They also knew how nearly impossible it would be to free Savlf from the web without killing her. It appeared to have been designed to keep her alive, he and Rachel had reasoned, studying the image, with their respective medical expertise.

"I think the computer and the web are symbiotic, too." She'd pointed out where they appeared to merge.

CabeX was his other area of concern. Was the robot with them to save her or did it want revenge for what she'd almost done? If the robot wished to kill her, there was nothing he or Rachel could do to stop him. Valyr had seen his programming and his construction. The only reason CabeX had gone down before they did was that the virus had attacked him. And if the situation had unfolded differently? Where would he and Rachel be right now?

Kraye trusted CabeX, but this was not a recommendation.

He felt the forward thrust slow the ship and found he could remember other flights in ships like this one—though none into battle. The tension that filled those around him was not something he recognized, but he sensed it was how warriors prepared for what was to come. Even Rachel seemed calm, very focused.

He looked down and saw that the heel of one foot lifted up and down, without making a sound. The music, courtesy of their piece of Bangle, had been the one about the werewolves, with the howling dogs, but it had changed into what was almost a call to arms. Drums pounding and an insistent beat. Something about a tiger's eye and a fire. And roaring. He hoped they did not roar. This was to be a stealth mission.

Still, he found the edges of his mouth twitching. Rachel was most connected to her music. Inexplicably, he felt his muscles relax. He realized the Marines were reacting to the music, too. Suddenly they and Rachel began to sing to the music. They roared the final sounds, and then everything went dead silent. It was, he realized, a call to arms, a way to encourage each other about what was coming.

With one hand on the harness release and the other on his weapon, he watched the rear hatch as Gibson counted down over the comm.

"Three...two...one..."

The rear end of the shuttle breached the enemy ship.

"Nailed it," Rachel murmured. "Excellent."

It was the engineering section of the ship. None of the crew showed an awareness of their presence.

That would change very soon.

———

The bird was watching him. Kraye felt it though he did not look to verify this. Why had it settled on the shoulder between him and the sergeant so that he could not study this alien female? Kraye couldn't even shift in his chair without making the bird move as well. As if it sensed it was making Kraye uncomfortable, the bird hopped onto the back of his chair.

It did not ease the feeling of bird eyes boring into the back of his head, but he was able to cast surreptitious glances at the woman.

The battle armor hid most of what was female about her though it did have some ability to conform to the wearer's shape. She had not donned the headgear or gloves yet, so he could see her profile and observe her hands.

They were well formed, appeared strong, with long fingers that tapered at the ends. Her nails were clean, which made him wish to hide his nails. The confidence of those hands on the controls did cause him to wonder if they would be as skilled in other, more personal ways.

Her face had been fashioned with both strength and beauty, the lightness of her blue eyes heightened by the wash of color on her skin. His hands, which had no task in this cockpit, twitched with a desire to trace the full, stubborn shape of her mouth. The lips parted only when she needed to deliver crisp orders or ask pointed questions, then became a straight, yet plump line as she initiated the various maneuvers required to bring them within striking distance of Arachnid Y.

He did not have to see her eyes at this moment. He knew they'd been cool, assessing, neutral, the way they'd looked down at him when CabeX had told the other human woman that "Kraye required a female."

His cheeks had heated then, and they warmed now at the memory of how her brows had arched, and her lips had twitched. He did not know that CabeX had noticed the need he sometimes felt for a female companion. He could wish he had not announced it to these uneasy allies. Besides, the other female did not interest him. She was small and pale. This Sergeant City was tall and strong, vibrant inside and out. She affected him differently than the women who'd offered themselves to him when he'd been dirt side arranging for trade or the sale of goods. Those women reminded him he was a human male alone with cybernetic robots.

This woman reminded him he was a man. While he did not completely understand the distinction, he felt the difference and would have liked to have had the time to discover why this was so.

It was a pity that they were probably going to die.

"Can you monitor our approach to Arachnid Y?" Sergeant City's gaze moved methodically between the view screen and the controls.

Kraye felt the minute adjustments she made as the side of the ship grew closer. He'd seen what this ship, with this cloak, could do, but still, his muscles tensed. It was a relief to have a task.

"Approach vector is optimum," he said. He gave her speed and distance to contact with the ship's shields. Felt her slow their approach even more until the back of the ship barely touched the leading edge of the shields. This backward approach was necessary so that the rear hatch could be opened for the assault.

And then inertia had them sliding through the shields of Arachnid Y.

"No indications Arachnid Y is aware of our approach," Kraye said, though she could see this for herself. The use of code names he found curious, but he accepted it because the robots did. Because their ship was Golf Sierra Zulu, their code names were Zulu with a number designating the command structure. He was Zulu2, though he knew if Sergeant City went down, it was OxeroidR who would most likely assume command.

Now the side of the ship drew closer. City—Zulu1, he used the designation to get into the habit—adjusted their track so that their orbit matched Arachnid Y's. His mind knew there'd be no impact, but his body tensed as the back of their ship reached, then slid easily through this barrier.

"Bang on engineering," City as Zulu1 muttered. They were radio silent with Golf Sierra Alpha, but the sentient AI was monitoring movement for them and would relay commands through their heads-up displays. It appeared that Golf Sierra Alpha had been as successful as them. "Let's get this party started."

Party? The word must not mean the same thing in Standard. He started slightly when the bird landed on his shoulder again.

"Surely—" he protested, but the bird cut him off.

"Surely I must."

Just past the bird, Sergeant City gave him a look that might have been sympathetic, then she lifted her headgear and began to fit it in place. He couldn't, he didn't dare shrug as he secured his headgear. Gloves followed and last, he checked his weapons.

Only then did he follow Zulu1 into the rear compartment.

Even in compact mode, OxeroidR appeared to fill most of it, though the other three of the sergeant's team were not small. What they thought was not apparent. They had already lowered their light shields, and the reflective front of their headgear did not allow him to see their faces.

Past them, he could see the engineering section of Arachnid Y, and the men that were working there, apparently oblivious to the intrusion. OxeroidR would already be marking their locations. They would go down quickly and quietly. This was the easy part.

There was the quiet whine of OxeroidR's weapons systems deploying, audible only to anyone within inches of him.

"I will proceed first," he said, through the comm.

Zuluı did not object.

"Lock and load," she said.

Her Marines lifted their weapons and activated them, then secured them against their shoulders, their miens lethally ready for battle.

They had boarded the shuttle via a ramp that lowered, but when in phase cloaking, apparently the ramp had an embedded hatch that, while smaller, slid sideways, giving them a fire solution faster.

Zuluı held her weapon in one hand, the other on the control for the hatch.

"You have a go, team. I repeat, you have a go," she said, calmly and pressed the button.

18

WHAT HIT Rachel first was the smell.

She should have expected it, though she had hoped their headgear would filter out the stenches and not just toxins. Still, this engineering section was the ultimate cliché of a ship of bad guys, or whatever they were. This crew appeared to be human, from what they could see, though barely. Depraved scalawags who would do anything and everything they were ordered to do.

One of the men walked over to check a gauge, passing right in front of them—and through the rear of the ship and then clear of it.

Okay, that was a little freaky.

Rachel and Valyr stayed seated until the Marines had risen and arranged themselves in front of the still closed hatch. Through the headsup display, she knew that Golf Sierra Zulu was also preparing to deploy.

CabeX emerged from the flight deck and took point. Gibson would lock down the flight deck and Golf Sierra Alpha once they were off. Bangle would—she hoped—keep communications open between all of them.

It was her do or die moment. Her heart pounded so hard she

thought it was die, but Valyr rose, and she found herself standing, her knees steadier than she'd have expected. She tried the knees out with a couple of steps that took her into position behind the three Marines, Mikes 1-3, she added. The code names weren't hard to remember, just hard to remember to use.

The smaller hatch made a slow glide sideways, and CabeX fired on the visible crew before they noticed the opening appearing so abruptly in the side of their ship. Soundless, they dropped like flies—an appropriate metaphor for a spider ship. He stepped off Golf Sierra Alpha and onto Arachnid X, firing several more shots at out-of-her sight targets.

The Mikes fanned out on either side of him, also moving out of her sight. She followed Valyr off the ship and then stopped to look around, aware of her vital signs updating on one side of her heads-up display. Somewhat absently she was aware a surge of adrenalin had given her an increased awareness of her surroundings, bringing all of it—including all the nasty—into sharp focus.

If she had to compare what she saw to something, it would have been the slave deck on a pirate ship. Rusted. Dirty everything but the engines. They'd need to be well cared for since all their lives depended on them, but otherwise, it was a cesspool of nasty. Perhaps the creepiest part of a big pile of disturbing was the spider webs in the corners, casting webbed shadows in places there was enough light.

She pulled her attention off the cobwebs as the Mikes began securing the prisoners with plastic restraints and duct tape. CabeX stalked to the system control station. It appeared that the surprise was total, which was not a surprise when working with a robot. Besides, why would they expect an attack here and not on the bridge?

They'd discussed doing that, but the robots felt the prisoner had a better chance with a stealth approach. On an op with robots trained to attack and neutralize a target, it was a good idea to take their advice. It was a pity they couldn't have the full complement of robots on the ops. Such a huge, freaking pity.

Valyr joined CabeX at the control station, drawing Rachel after him as if she were on a string. As they'd seen in the grainy video, CabeX's device emerged from his arm and plunged into the top of the panel. It was even more disturbing, oddly violent, to observe in real time.

Rachel pulled out her tablet—and her mobile link with Bangle. The AI had done something to soup it up because it went live as soon as CabeX found a connection for her. Just as it had with the virus, blue streams flowed up her arms and her face, pulling her inside the system. Through the streams, she saw Valyr there as well.

It was much more straightforward than CabeX's internals had been, though it bore an unsettling resemblance to a spider's web in the way the systems and sub-systems connected to each other. Like a web, it was built around a center, a core. She had a feeling it wasn't a place she wanted to go, inside or outside the system. Even in here it was edged with black and red and filled with—

"Traps," she murmured.

"And alarms," Valyr agreed.

No one had to tell them to avoid triggering one of them. They moved very lightly through the system looking for the information they needed to know for their next move. Webs were highly sensitive, and she had a feeling these made real spider webs look like pikers.

Outside the blue stream, CabeX was doing his type of digging. "I cannot isolate weapons control from this place."

There wasn't a single being she could see trussed on the floor that Rachel would have trusted with weapons control, so she was not surprised. She traced this function back to the center of the web, too.

"What's that?" Rachel asked, directing Valyr to another area with even more traps and alarms. Unlike other parts of the systems, they could find no label for it, and its connections to outside systems were very limited in nature.

Through the blue stream, they stared at each other. Was this where he held his prisoner? Or was it a carefully constructed trap for CabeX?

"Look," Rachel said. There was one thin black and red line that led back to the dark center of the web. "Only way in is through—"

"The spider's lair," Valyr agreed.

———

CabeX moved silently through the ship, his heads-up display warning him of the approaching crew. It had been a long time since he'd done what used to be a regular occurrence. Though he'd considered it a curse at times, it was optimal right now that he could not forget. With his systems at full camouflage setting, he moved like a purposeful metal ghost, fighting against the sense that he should be the one having a face-to-face meeting with Xaddek. It was a truth that he could not be in two places at one time, though he felt certain that the two humans, Alpha1 and Alpha2, would not survive their meeting with Xaddek.

It was a pity. He was aware of the debt he owed them for his life, but they had made their choice, too. He could respect that and hope they would serve as a diversion for long enough that he could free—or kill—Savlf.

If Xaddek had a kill switch on her cage? Well, he could offer her a swifter death than Xaddek would.

And if Savlf was another trap? He'd learned much from the

virus. His self-destruct would activate at the first sign of a system breach. No one—including him—was fast enough to stop it this time.

One way or another he would end the contamination that was Xaddek.

————

Their big moose of a robot was good. City might be impressed. The crew in engineering dropped like dominos. The last one might have got a whimper or a gasp out, but that was it. Her guys moved forward and quickly secured them with duct tape and plastic restraints. Her weapon still ready, City did a sweep, looking for hiding places or out of sight entry points.

OxeroidR headed for the console, one of his arm weapons turning into something that looked like a claw. He plunged this into the console, at least, that's what it looked like.

Her Mikes, securing of personnel completed, took up positions that covered the entry points. Kraye, the bird on his shoulder, joined OxeroidR.

A hologram seemed to shoot out of the robot's chest, data first appearing as streams of blue and red, then slowly forming into a schematic of the ship, at least, that's what it looked like to her. She moved up to his other side, weapon still pointed at the entry hatch but turned her head so she could study it. Was it her imagination that the bird looked as interested in the data stream as she was?

"Xaddek is not on this ship," OxeroidR said. He couldn't sound disappointed, but he managed to telegraph it.

Before City could ask how he knew this, Kraye said, "Xaddek has a central lair on his ship. This ship has a more conventional layout and lacks an identifiable lair."

Of course, the spider would have a lair.

"There is not a comet drive on this ship," the bird said.

City blinked. "Then how—"

"This ship's engines were tied into the other ship's for the transit," the robot said.

City considered this, wondering if they could use it somehow. "I guess we can't access either bridge's controls from here using that link?"

"That is correct." The robot's red gaze seemed to study her through the data stream. "At least, not from here. Possibly on the bridge, it might be possible."

"What about the prisoner? Where's the brig?" Some things she recognized on the schematic, but other sections were generic appearing enough to be anything from crew quarters to storage bays.

Gold lines formed on the schematic, pulsing at both ends of the connecting line.

"Our current position is here." OxeroidR used a metal digit to indicate one end of the pulse. "This is the brig." He moved his finger to the end of the line.

"Any indication if our prisoner is being held there?" City asked, her brain beginning the process of memorizing the route and possible alternatives.

"Negative," the robot said, then added, "Logic dictates it is not."

"Logic?" City queried.

"The big bug likes to keep his toys close," Kraye said. "But..."

"He knows we know this. On a venture outside his known space, he may have changed tactics," the robot agreed.

"So we have to check it out." It wasn't a question.

Neither Kraye nor the robot answered her non-question.

"Bangle, can you give us a life signs reading in and around the highlighted path?" City asked.

Bangle obligingly added life sign readings for the whole ship to OxeroidR's schematic. Traffic patterns looked normal. No sign of agitation or awareness in any of the signatures that anyone knew they were there. Looked about what she'd expect before a major FUBAR. Oh well.

"Corporal, hold this position as long as you can. If you have to withdraw from contact to a defensive position, Bangle will activate the auto-pilot for you and work with you."

If it weren't for Bangle, she'd have had to stay here. She was grateful she was not required to send one of her people off with these two. She studied the schematic once more. There was enough crew to give them a decent fight, even with a robot in their corner.

There were days when she wished she didn't have to excel quite as much.

"Let's move out," she ordered, even though the robot was already moving toward the hatch. He lifted his weapon, pointing it at the door. She jumped forward.

"Let's try the hatch release first, big guy." She paused and looked at the parrot. "Last chance to stay here."

The bird ruffled his feathers and moved lower on Kraye's back, hooking its claws into the body armor, its head barely visible over his shoulder.

Did parrot's have balls? If they did, this one had some big brass ones.

"Let's go." She hit the release and OxeroidR, his weapons deployed in two directions, stepped out and cleared the first corridor like a Marine. She indicated Kraye follow him. "I'll cover our six."

She cast a quick look back at her people and got sober nods from all three.

"Oorah, ma'am." Corporal Burns took a hand off his weapon long enough to give her an abbreviated salute.

———

Clearly, Rachel had seen too many science fiction movies. It was the only thing that could explain how she'd ended up as the red shirt on a real operation—and yes, she was still wearing the red shirt. It wasn't like she'd had a wardrobe nearby to change into something not red or a shirt.

So here she was, following Valyr through dimly lit, creepy and disgusting corridor after creepy, cobweb-festooned and rancid corridor. At this point, the only reason she was following him was that she was too afraid to go back to engineering by herself.

It was a crappy time to find out that not only was she afraid of spiders, she was also freaked out by the cobwebs that cling in the upper shadows, lining the corridors and hugging dark corners. The robots had talked about "the spider," but that was a lot of webbing for just one. Her skin began to crawl, and the feeling of being watched built the closer they got to the possible lair. Had she really thought she could be bad-A when she'd spent her life as sad-A?

Valyr went to move a strand of cobweb out of the way and she stopped him.

"Don't touch them." She couldn't explain why.

Thankfully he didn't ask. He withdrew his hand and ducked under the drifting strand. How had it found any current in the dank, still silence? Or was it their movement that created its current? She didn't know that the cobwebs might be able to communicate with the spider, but she didn't know they couldn't. That worried her, but she had such a long list of worries, all this one did was make her eye twitch, and her stomach tighten as she eased past it. Weapons ready—she hoped—she turned in a slow circle before trotting to catch up with Valyr.

There was no sign anyone was aware of their presence, but

all the parts of her that triggered her "danger, Will Robinson" were screaming warnings.

So far Bangle had been able to keep the data and comms flowing from engineering. According to the Mikes, all was quiet there. She might be coming to like the AI. If they got out of here alive, she'd get her some updated music to play. Rachel hadn't realized how out of date she was until Bangle started playing it for the Mikes, making even these stoic guys exchange glances.

Rachel had her tablet with her, but Bangle was sending them the data directly to their headsets, so she'd tucked it in a sort of pocket in the upper torso of her suit. Bits of blue data bytes drifted past her eyes, but they didn't bother her. She was too focused on the creepy stuff, anyway.

They followed a path that took them deeper and deeper toward the dark heart of the ship, but Bangle also steered them around any life signs that appeared along the way.

Rachel wished she'd asked Bangle if it was possible to filter out the smells. Was it the cobwebs that gave the ship the dirt smell? Not a good, freshly turned dirt smell, but dead dirt. Like a graveyard where someone had dug up a corpse. And evil. It smelled evil. Did evil have a smell? The sour-dirty-bodies smell of engineering was not as pungent here, but she had a sense that sweaty, unwashed humans had traversed these corridors fairly recently.

That there were so few of those life signs moving around this ship added to her uneasy, upping her mental castigations to "what the crap were you thinking, girl?" She was supposed to be smart. This was not smart. This was a complete delusion of competence, like when she'd watched *HGTV* and thought she could remodel her bathroom, but so much worse.

But you can shoot like Annie Oakley, she reminded herself. She started creating equations on how to take the strands of web. It helped.

So did the view of Valyr's backside. It might be shallow, but right now shallow wasn't a bad place to be. For a guy who'd been so recently defrosted, he moved well enough to take his place with the Spocks, the Kirks, and the Jedi. Her heart would have pitted and patted for him, except it was busy hammering from a near constant flow of adrenalin.

The smell, the stinky human part of it, faded some as they drew closer and closer to their target zone.

Finally, when it felt like they might be walking in circles, Valyr lifted a fist for her to stop. She angled so she could watch their backs. Didn't want to assume Bangle could track everything on this ship. The AI couldn't "see" inside the spider's lair.

Valyr used the comm, and even then he whispered. "We are here."

There was no indication in his tone about how he felt about that. He might have been talking about arriving at the grocery store. She would have liked to see his eyes, but it would be a distraction they couldn't afford, even if the headgear had allowed for gaze sharing.

With her long ray weapon pointed back the way they'd come, and her right shoulder almost touching his left shoulder, she felt her insides steady. She'd been in this emotional place before, even if she'd never been *here*. She'd faced her first ER shift, the loss of her family, so many situations that were new, or just plain terrifying. If she rode the storm, then the eye would come. It always did.

"Let's do this." Her calm matched his. The fear wasn't gone, but it was simmering on the back burner. She shifted so that her back was almost against the wall, which was not as comforting as it should have been with the cobwebs hanging down. Valyr matched her move as they eased up the hatch that they believed was the last barrier between them and the spider. Neither of them was sure what they'd have to do to get inside, but apparently, they hadn't needed to worry about that.

It slid open releasing a new level of nasty into the air.

And in the darkness, she saw the eyes. Two lines of eyes. Eight of them glowing yellow from out of deep darkness.

"Please, come in..."

...said the spider to the flies...

———

"Has anyone else lost comms with the shuttles?" Carey asked. He tried a quick diagnostic while he waited for his question to travel to his flyboys and their answer to travel back to him. Before they could respond, he heard a robotic voice.

"We have also lost communication with Alpha2 and Zulu3."

He thought the voice was RaptorZ's, who had argued as forcefully as a walking computer could, that he needed to be on either of the Golf Sierra ships. Carey had a feeling he'd have argued to be on both if that had been possible. He'd lost, not because Carey wouldn't have liked more badass backup for his people, but because he couldn't get to the shuttle without giving away the fact that CabeX wasn't in fact, going to deliver the *Najer* into his...claws?

"Are the comms down or—" His diagnostic finished.

Signals are blocked.

Ice did a flow down his back. *How could they block their comms if they didn't know they were here?*

It didn't take a lightbulb to go off in his head. He'd seen *Return of the Jedi*. The spider could *see* them. But how—

"The comet drive," he said. They should have seen that one coming. If the spider had gotten his legs on a Garradian comet drive, then why not a set of Garradian "eyes?" One of the Garradian scanners that could see through a Garradian cloak. But—

they couldn't see ships that were phase cloaked, could they? They'd disappeared off his added-on Garradian scanner when they initiated the phase cloak. Not all the Garradian ships could "see" through a phase cloak. According to the AI Bangle, she could see the phased ships. It might not be a total FUBAR. Just a ninety-five percent FUBAR.

He tried a secure comm to Bangle and got dead space. He'd liked to have deployed some of the swear words he saved up for FUBARs, but there wasn't time.

He keyed his comms. "Heads up. Arachnids X and Y probably have eyes on us. I repeat, they probably have eyes on us."

He got the right number of grim "Roger thats" from his squadron, and then RaptorZ broke in again.

"It would be advisable for your squadron to turn back."

Carey blinked, not sure he'd heard the robot right. "Turn back?"

"Our analysis of Arachnid X is that it is outfitted with a Trozzerd Emitter 3DXZ and a Beugrimt Seeker 55THT."

The robot couldn't sound worried, but Carey assumed he was. "And these—what did you call them?"

"The Trozzerd Emitter 3DXZ propels waves of particles that are harmless until contact with a defensive shield. As they pass through the shield particles, they weaponize with destructive force."

"And if we drop our shields...?"

"Then you are vulnerable to the Beugrimt Seeker 55THT." He didn't wait for Carey to ask. "These fire multiple rounds of heat-seeking projectiles. Arachnid X likes to alternate between the two weapons. Even we are unable to react quickly enough to this pattern of fire."

Carey considered this. "Then why were you willing to launch this strike?"

"Both the Trozzerd Emitter 3DXZ and the Beugrimt Seeker

55THT require charging. We believed we could strike before they could be charged."

"But if he knows we are coming…"

"Then both weapons are likely charging or already fully charged." More thinking time. "They both require charging. So they use a lot of energy? They can't just keep them charged?"

"Correct."

"And together they are almost impossible to defend against."

"The likelihood of a negative outcome for us is high."

Crap.

It was possible that Carey's silence troubled the robot. "They are illegal to possess."

Of course, they were. But these were not ships concerned with legalities. If he'd had any doubts about the mission, this both confirmed those doubts and erased them.

Pretty diabolical to turn protective shields against ships. The Arachnids had to be stopped, but how? His brain churned. If their teams on the ships were able to take over—but would they see the danger in time? And if the Arachnids knew they were there, were their teams in trouble, too?

"I thought he wanted your ship and all of you?" he asked, stalling as his thoughts continued their racing.

"If he knows we are here, it is possible he knows that the Captain is aboard his ship."

And he might settle for the robot in hand rather than the ones in the *Najer*.

"He will not wish to battle all of us, though he may demand our surrender."

"What would you do?"

"We will not surrender."

Carey's skin chilled inside his flight suit. Before he could come up with a response to this, RaptorZ added, "This is not your battle—"

"We have people on those ships—" Carey stopped. Could they make it look like they were breaking off, but come around? No. The math didn't work out right. He frowned. They couldn't run. They couldn't hide. And if they dropped their shields... He studied their map with growing frustration. The field of engagement would be close, too, once they were both on the same side of the moon. Once a weapon was fired, there was nothing to slow it down until impact.

If the so-called field of battle were better, his birds could handle the heat-seekers. They were designed to be fighter craft, and his pilots were well-trained in dog fighting, but in space physics and inertia were not on their side because of the lack of atmosphere—

"The moon," he said.

"The...moon?" The robot almost sounded puzzled.

"How much atmosphere does it have?"

Almost it seemed as if the robot on the other end sat up straighter. "Atmosphere..."

———

They had very narrow band comms with Bangle on Golf Sierra Zulu. It updated the life signs on each level they reached, doing it through their headgear, but only once for each level. They did not dare have more contact than this. It did give them a good look at each level, then the signal went dark.

Despite this information, Kraye noticed that Sergeant City kept a close eye on their rear, what she'd called their six. The Garradian body armor had motion sensing technology that had gaps, possibly because of alloys in the walls of the ship. As they moved down level after level, he found he trusted the data less and less.

"It's too easy," City muttered, the sound a whisper in his

headgear. He nodded to show he'd heard her, and that he agreed.

OxeroidR had assumed a lower profile as if he too sensed trouble. His aspect went dark as well, making him almost invisible as he kept what City called "point."

With only one corridor between them and the brig, Kraye's instincts were blaring inside his head. Even OxeroidR hesitated at the last turn, extending a sensor that allowed him to see the corridor in advance. City was as back to back with Kraye as possible with the bird on his back.

The bird was an interesting passenger. His head was tucked in against Kraye's neck so that he could see, but remain somewhat protected.

Only once had it said anything. "Wait."

Kraye had relayed the order, and they'd paused until it said to go. When OxeroidR had checked out the passageway, a figure had gone around the corner ahead of them. How had the bird known this? He did not know the ways of birds. Perhaps it had felt the change in the air currents or smelled something they could not. Animals had different ways of processing danger.

Without realizing it, Kraye glanced back at the bird. It nodded as if it knew what question Kraye had not asked. City moved past OxeroidR, who had stopped at the brig entry hatch. She flattened her body against the wall by the next corner, her head angled as if she listened. Then she did a glance around, quickly resuming her position.

"What do you think?" Her voice was soft over their shared intercom. "My spidey sense is tingling. We're running out of time."

He did not understand the term, but he got the message. He retreated along the way they'd come and positioned himself to cover their...six.

OxeroidR appeared to study the control panel for this access.

He lifted his head, suddenly alert.

"They are coming," the parrot said.

"Maybe we should retreat to a better position," Kraye suggested. The parrot dropped down from its perch and seemed as if it assessed something they could not see, then it looked up at Kraye.

"We must enter," it said. This was said with such decision, he wondered if the bird was more in charge than anyone had indicated to him and OxeroidR. He looked at City.

She hesitated. "I don't think our prisoner is on this ship."

"I concur," OxeroidR said, though he did not move from his position.

"This ship contains more than one prisoner in need of release," the parrot said, looking at OxeroidR instead of City.

That was not their mission, but Kraye did not protest. No matter what City ordered now, OxeroidR would not leave.

City stared at the parrot, then she might have sighed. She half shrugged. "So option fast then. Can you blow it without injuring anyone inside, Zulu3?"

Instead of answering, OxeroidR lifted his arm and fired precisely directed rays at the bolts holding the door in place. Then he turned his attention to the locking mechanism. He lifted his great leg and kicked it down.

City, her back still to the wall by the broken brig door, but her weapon pointed away down the corridor, leaned forward, and examined the arch where the door had been. "Nice work."

The parrot's wings lifted, and it half flew, half trotted into the exposed brig. OxeroidR activated a light that beamed into the shadowy space.

"There are living species imprisoned here," OxeroidR said. He paused. "One like Zulu4."

Zulu4? It took Kraye a moment to realize OxeroidR was talking about the parrot.

19

It was a matter of staying alive until the Arachnid ships had to stand down and recharge the big bad weapons. According to RaptorZ, both ships still had an array of more conventional space-type weapons, but both the *Najer* and Carey's squadron didn't mind a fair fight.

They could stop, keep the moon between them, but if Xaddek didn't already know about their people on his ships, then they had to keep to the original plan, draw his attention, with the hope of distracting him while their teams did their thing.

Even as they acted as if the spider didn't know, Carey figured he must know by now that he'd been boarded. They needed to engage him, otherwise, he'd be free to turn his attention to their people. If any of them failed in their primary mission, well, those ships had to be destroyed. Xaddek could not be permitted to leave this galaxy.

The *Dauntless* was designed for fighting both in and out of the atmosphere, though the thick atmosphere would slow them down, too. But they wouldn't be fighting other ships or even directed fire. The spider was trying to bring the hammer down before he had to face them tactically.

What they needed to do was get the spider to commit to his firing solution and then take the fight down into the moon's atmosphere—okay, it was too big for a moon but it was hanging out there like a moon even if it was a big ass one.

It wasn't a perfect plan. There was a chance that the particles from the—Carey still couldn't pronounce the name of either badass weapon, so he called them BA-1 and heat sucker, would interact with the moon's atmosphere in an "unstable manner," one that "couldn't be predicted without testing."

"We'll, just have to do some on-the-hop testing," Carey said, philosophically.

They still didn't have certainty, but they did have hope.

"Does everyone know what to do?" Carey asked. It hadn't been easy sending orders when they weren't sure their comms were completely secure, but they'd done it with help from the robots, who had established a secondary link with Delta Tango Flight, one with extra layers of encryption. And lots of code words.

He got a round of "affirmatives."

"Go flight. I say again, go flight." He wanted to add something about the force being with them, but he didn't. He wanted to, though.

————

There were, Doc realized, worse things than not seeing what was going on. For instance, viewing the action with the General.

Yeah. Even Hel didn't have a witty quip for her about that.

We are missing something.

He was right. The arrangement of forces was curious. With only two ships to deal with, she'd have expected them to fan out, presenting a wide, narrow target—one that allowed all the ships to concentrate their fire. Or to stack the ships, so that they could deliver waves of fire. But the robot ship was proceeding slightly ahead of Carey's divided squadron and skimming the moon's atmosphere. The second wave of Carey's squadron was further down the curve of the moon, but it was also skimming the atmosphere.

Why would they anticipate dropping down into the atmosphere?

The Dauntless can maneuver better in the atmosphere, Doc mused. *Atmosphere will also create more resistance to any incoming fire.*

But will it not also do the same to their fire?

Yeah. So Carey wanted, *needed* to maneuver. Her gaze shifted to the two enemy ships. He wasn't planning to direct a lot of fire at the two bogeys, not from there. *Incoming fire. He's expecting unusual incoming fire that atmosphere will...slow down?*

Why not just destroy the two ships? Hel sounded puzzled.

Carey had been given a lot of latitude but destroying two ships that hadn't attacked him was a stretch.

Are they trying to draw fire? Divert attention away from something? Garradian ships had phase cloaks, but she couldn't see why they'd use them and have the diversionary flights.

There is something happening that we cannot see.

Doc couldn't disagree with that. *They must have found other ships with phased cloaks down on the outpost.* She felt Hel's agreement, but...

This arrangement of ships does not explain other ships.

It could be a diversion, a play for time, but to what end?

Hel frowned. *The Garradian shuttles cannot travel as fast as the squadron fighters.*

Are we sure about that? Doc asked.

Hel spun around to face her.

Who do we ask? But even as she asked, Doc knew. She sighed and nodded.

Hel vanished in the flash of light from his Special Key transport. It was not a surprise she hadn't been invited. The AI keeper of that secret room didn't like her. Also not a surprised that her skin began to itch.

———

As if on cue, the cobwebs began to run across the corridor, closing off the path behind them and pushing them forward if they didn't want to be ensnared.

If it looks like a spider web and you feel like a fly, it's probably a trap.

Which left the question: how big of a trap? Was it just them? Or the whole operation? With all her systems on full alert, Rachel followed Valyr inside, stepping around him when the passage widened into a room. A room that looked more like a cave.

She had her weapon up and ready to fire, but a wave of web strands dropped down between them and the eyes, even more coming at them from the sides and back. The webs stuck to her and Valyr's long ray guns, yanking them from their hands. Other webs yanked at their side arms. The creepiest moment was the web that was more like a vine with fingers. It patted both of them down, removing the knives at thighs and strapped to their backs. Each weapon disappeared up into the thick web over their heads.

It had happened so fast, it was hard to be sure, but she thought it hadn't found the small handguns tucked into compartments in the back of her calves. If she—

The webbing circled arms and ankles, going just taut enough to halt movement. But Rachel, with the vision of Savlf in her head, knew just how quickly the strands could turn ugly.

"I was hoping CabeX would be with you."

His voice was just what she'd have expected an evil spider to sound like—if she'd thought about it, which she hadn't because who wanted to spend time thinking about how a spider would sound when he talked?—exuding fake sorrow like an oil slick. He didn't sound disappointed either. Did that mean he knew where CabeX was?

"I wonder what interests him more than me?"

She wished she could exchange some significant looks with Valyr, but the situation didn't lend itself to that, even if they weren't wearing the body armor. Oh, it was super flexible and provided about one-eighty vision, but the room was dark inside and outside. All she could see, if she'd looked at Valyr, was his dark, reflective face screen. Of course, that meant the spider couldn't see them either. But could he hear them? Could he, had he already tapped into their comms? Were they still secure?

It was clear the spider had been expecting them, but for how long? Her thoughts returned to the webs that seemed to be all over the ship. They could have been his version of spy cameras or sensors. Or he could be toying with them, trying to get them to admit things he didn't know, in the belief that he did know.

Still, the fact that he knew or suspected that CabeX was on this ship, and not on the *Najer*, was a bad sign. Did that mean he knew about both Golf Sierra intrusions? Logic said he'd never have let them board his ship if he'd seen them coming. That presupposed the spider shared their logic. He could have let them board because he believed they were no threat. A trap, in fact.

If the webs could "see," then he might have become aware of them when they attacked his engineering section. Whatever he knew, he'd let them come this far. There'd been no alarms from the Mikes or CabeX, which could mean he'd been waiting for them to get here. According to CabeX, he was difficult to see when he didn't want to be seen. That's why he'd gone for Savlf. Rachel had agreed that he was her best chance. Which still wasn't much of a chance.

The spider could be toying with them.

Was that why the webs weren't tight yet? To give them hope he could take away, a little at a time? If she thought or hoped he wouldn't torture them, all she had to do was remember Savlf. Layer after layer of web until all that was left was her sight—and probably the only thing she saw anymore was this thing.

Comms gone with the Romeo and Delta Tango Flights.

It was good they still had comms with Bangle. If they did? Like the tiniest trickle of sound, Bangle began to filter what Rachel called her inspiration or fight songs. Almost she smiled as adrenalin dripped back into her chilled bloodstream. Flight was not an option. So that left fight.

And fight would work if she figured out how to get access to the two calf guns—assuming they were still there. They had to be there. It was their only chance. She'd need them both to penetrate the webbing, based on how thick it was around her wrists and what she'd observed during the weapons snatching.

If she had her two, then Valyr had them, too. Four ray guns were always better than two. But they needed a good distraction. What kind of distraction would startle the spider and fool his webs? They didn't have a giant shoe or bug spray.

"While we wait for CabeX to reach his destination, let's talk about the ships that are incoming."

A tracking screen appeared to one side of them. She flinched at the sudden light. It wasn't a gift when her eyes adjusted. He could *see* Carey's squadron of cloaked ships. How —of course, from the same place he'd got the comet drive. *Stupid. I should have thought of that.* So he'd seen it all, or almost all, from the moment he arrived in the system. Or—had he? His tracking didn't show the phased ships embedded in his engineering compartment, but that didn't mean he hadn't seen them. He was letting them see what he wanted them to see. And he didn't know that CabeX was a walking, talking super self-destruct.

Rachel half frowned. That wasn't the formation or approach they'd talked about in the briefing. On their current course, they would enter the upper atmosphere of the planet's moon. Not only would that slow their approach, it would render their weapons less effective. Something had changed, but what—

"It is clear your associates have done an assessment of my weapons, and they believe they can give me a good fight if that interesting approach vector is any indication, but I'm afraid I never put all my cards on the table when playing *Iegnap*."

The raspy, evil voice did not sound unduly gleeful. More like remorseless. Inevitable.

He doesn't, he can't know everything. He wants us to believe he does. It was hard not to believe when the webs tightened and relaxed in the same cadence as his voice as if reminding them that this was just the first play in the game.

"I must admit, I thought the *Najer* had better scanning on its ship." The spider was silent for a few moments as they all watched the ships track this way.

What did he want those ships to know was on this ship?

"I'm sure the *Najer* has heard my ship carries a Trozzerd Emitter 3DXZ and a Beugrimt Seeker 55THT. They are quite illegal, but I do not concern myself with trifles."

A what and a who? Bangle didn't rush to answer, but she might not know what those were either.

"Both are quite ingenious. When a Trozzerd is at full power, it fires streams of harmless energy particles. They are small enough to pass through even the most sensitive shield, but as soon as they interact with any shield energy, well, let's say they become quite explosive on the other side."

Rachel must have made a move forward because her web strands tightened. The spider laughed softly.

"If they drop their shields, then the Buegrimt, a most sophisticated heat seeking missile, will destroy them."

Rachel's hands curled into fists.

"Yes, I'm afraid they will all be destroyed. Such a waste. I would have liked to secure the robots' loyalty. And inside the other ships, I'm sure there were tasty morsels aboard. Something new for my table."

Suddenly getting blown to pieces was looking pretty good.

"But I'll have CabeX as a consolation prize."

He wouldn't. They'd all be dead...

He sighed, the claws closest to his eyes flexing as if he already had the robot in its grasp. "Speaking of CabeX, where did he get to? Ah." A pause. "How interesting. He is trying to free Savlf. Should I feel slighted he is more interested in her than in killing me?"

Now the tracking screen changed to a video view of Savlf's prison. She hung in the web trap, her head lolled as far to the side as the web allowed. She looked barely alive though the system that monitored her showed a faint heartbeat. It distantly surprised Rachel that she could read her vitals without knowing the language labels. Apparently, there were a few things that were universal. Like breathing and heart rate.

"There is a price for betrayal. But she dances so beautifully, don't you think?"

Lights tracked along the webbing. When the pulses reached her body, she arched in the vicious "dance." Her mouth was covered with the web, but her eyes screamed. Bile rose in Rachel's throat. Savlf's vitals fluctuated wildly. She couldn't take much more, but Rachel would bet this thing knew exactly how much she could take without dying.

"I didn't realize she still had hope. I shall have to do something about that. After I deal with you. And CabeX, of course. Now, should I launch the new, stronger virus outside Savlf's prison or should I let him inside so they can see each other? It would be entertaining for him to know she'd betrayed him before I take him over. Choices, choices..."

Oh, that was bad, but also, oddly good news. If he launched the virus now, they were all dead. If he waited, well, they had a slim chance. So slim, she didn't have an equation for it, but a chance was a chance. As long as CabeX thought they had a chance, he wouldn't trigger his self-destruct. Of course, if the spider launched the virus, it was over. It felt like the Urclock started ticking inside her head, louder than the music. And just like the Urclock, Rachel didn't know the numbers counting down to all over.

The screens faded, leaving them in the dark with the eyes.

Rachel fought the despair the spider wanted her to feel. The inevitability of death or defeat. She couldn't even count the moments of life left to them. All that was left was the darkness and the eyes, watching, waiting for them to react and let him enjoy their pain.

Pain. She knew about pain. About loss. About the gamut of emotions that went through you when your life changed between one heart beat and the next. *She knew.*

He—the spider—thought he knew, but he didn't know everything.

He didn't know what had happened down on the outpost when his first virus failed.

He didn't know that CabeX was a bomb that would go off as soon as he tried to breach his systems again.

He didn't know *them*. He didn't know how hard her people fought even if the fighting was inside her head.

He didn't know the caliber of the people who opposed him.

Not all of them would get out alive. Maybe none of them would, but the spider would be defeated.

One way or another.

She felt the inner darkness push back. She felt hope send up a tiny sprout, not much, but something. She wanted to live. She wanted them all to live. What could she do to help that happen?

"I will admit you interest me. Not terribly, but enough."

That sounded super sinister. Enough for what? A brief reprieve? Bad guys who gave good guys a reprieve while they bragged always lost in the movies. *This isn't a movie.* It wasn't, but time was time. It was—an opportunity to excel.

"I will require a briefing about the species, important to minor, in this galaxy." There was a pause. "And of course, I need to know who you are, and information about who you used to serve."

Used to serve. That would never happen, she reminded herself. They'd either get out of this or die. It was hard not to think about Savlf, though. To fear this thing could win. *He was curious*, she realized. He knew he didn't know everything. Was there opportunity in curiosity?

"I think you owe it to me," the voice became even more gentle, "since you interrupted my dinner."

The light came up, taking its time, flowing forward from behind the eyes so that they saw the spider first, the shadows in front of him getting deeper at first.

Rachel inhaled shakily. Totally a spider. A freaking huge spider. The sight of it almost took out her knees.

Eight legs to go with the eight eyes. A shiny, bulbous head around the eyes. A glimpse of the body behind the table or whatever it was he lurked behind. The arrangement of his legs was almost crab-like in the way the front ones curled around. But it was his mouth that grabbed the spotlight.

It gaped open, dripping a red that almost looked like blood—

The light reached the table. His dinner table.

She stared, respirations spiking. Heart rate, too.

It couldn't be...

Interrupted my dinner.

Dinner. A human...his torso savagely ripped open—

More than bile surged into her mouth.

At least it was dead...

His eyes moved, finding them in a desperate plea for help.

She ripped at her headgear so violently the webs couldn't stop her. A scream not silent, not willing to stay in her throat, ripped out just ahead of the vomit surging up...

The scream echoed around the spider's lair, coming back at her waves that seemed to grow louder and louder...

She fell forward, at first catching on the web, but then it let her drop to her knees, as she retched again and again. Maybe it liked the sight of her on her knees in front of it...

Even staring down at her vomit could not erase what she'd seen.

Valyr.

Valyr's clone.

———

Another parrot? City found it hard to keep her Marine stone face in place. They'd worked their way at considerable risk through this ship to find a...parrot?

Their parrot had already trotted through the hole the robot had made. Now the robot contracted his moose profile and followed the parrot in.

"The locking mechanisms are electronic," Sir Rupert said, his cackle voice echoing around what must be a high, hollow space. "Can you release—"

City heard the echo of laser fire similar to that OxeroidR had used on the brig door. There were more shots than echo could account for, enough to make her wonder how many prisoners he was freeing. They didn't have the resources to protect one prisoner, let alone more than one. City's nerves stretched tighter as her *danger, Will Robinson* closed on its max setting. Their incoming was getting close.

According to the settings on her head gear, they were due for an update from Bangle. She mentally counted down to zero, and her wider view did update.

Nothing. Not a life sign within two decks of them? Kraye looked back at her, tapping the side of his headgear as if asking the same question she had.

City bit her lip, then lowered her chin to the comm switch. "Bangle?"

I am here.

Was she? "Get ready to deploy Whiskey Papa Tango on my command." If Bangle was still on the comm—

Preparing to deploy Whisky Papa Tango on your command.

So that wasn't Bangle. She couldn't meet Kraye's gaze because they couldn't see each other with the visors down, but she tapped the side of her headgear and shook her head. She shouldered her weapon and dug her shoulder into the metal side of the corridor, hoping Kraye got the message. Her suit detected motion in a corridor that her heads-up display, that *Bangle*, insisted was empty. So either she'd been co-opted or, their feed had been co-opted. Which meant she also wouldn't be able to reach her Mikes on Golf Sierra Zulu.

She was about to lean out and fire when something touched her shoulder. She turned and found OxeroidR there, their parrot on his shoulder, his wing sort of wrapped protectively around another parrot. On the other shoulder was a squirrel. A moose and a *squirrel*? For just a second the voice in her head got a Russian accent. Then she noticed he was carrying a couple of hedgehogs in the crook of one arm. Using his free hand, he held it out. The injured parrot hopped on, followed by Sir Rupert. He extended them to her. After a brief hesitation, she angled her shoulder for them to make the transfer. Then OxeroidR gently set the two hedgehogs on his free shoulder.

City lifted her visor to ask, "How bad is—?"

"She is mostly traumatized and scared," Sir Rupert said. One wing stroked the head of the *female* bird. He'd come here to get a date?

Before City could start to assess the challenges of a fire fight with two birds on her shoulder, both birds eased down her back, settling in the same position he'd taken on Kraye's back. She felt his head tucked against her neck. The other parrot must have hunkered down.

"Could we take the bridge?" she murmured, as much to herself as Sir Rupert. Still take the bridge, she should have said. How badly were they compromised? There'd be no element of surprise now.

OxeroidR fell back to her side, animals perched on both shoulders and no sign this bothered him. Kraye, still weapons ready, slid over to join them in front of the gaping hole that had been the brig hatch. No one could say the robot wasn't thorough.

"There are more sentient beings trapped in the hold of this ship," the squirrel said.

The squirrel said.

City thought about objecting, but there wasn't time. "Then we have to take the bridge." They had to seize control of the ship to save anyone else, including themselves. It was possible the Mikes had already pushed back.

OxeroidR was quiet for a couple of seconds. "According to my display, there are more life signs in the direction of the bridge." He pointed where he'd been.

"We can't trust the display," City said flatly.

"We could head back, try to fight our way to Golf Sierra Zulu," Kraye said, though City sensed he believed it was not an option his robot friend would choose.

"We will seize the ship," OxeroidR said, his neutral tone somehow carried more weight than City's.

Good thing he agreed with her. If there were sentient prisoners on this ship, they couldn't blow it without trying to seize control first.

"I noticed a repair access panel close by," City said, "when I was studying our route." It was also closer to the supposedly greater concentration of life signs. Were they trying to drive them back toward engineering? According to the schematic, there were fewer life signs between them and engineering. So that probably meant there were more. Had engineering turned into a trap? If they had hostages...she shook off that thought. Her Mikes would not be an easy get.

"It would be difficult to protect each other in the life support ducts," OxeroidR said.

"I was thinking about the animals," she said. She hated getting separated, but how were they supposed to fight with their hands full of critters? "My headgear is supposed to be resistant to heat signature and other scans. They could hide inside until we take control of the ship." She said this confidently like it was a matter of time. Just because the enemy knew they were here did not mean they knew about the other team, on the other ship, or the squadron closing in.

"The comet drive," OxeroidR said, suddenly, "your human scientist said the technology was Garradian."

"Yes, she did," City agreed.

"What other technology might they have stolen?"

City felt her body chill. "Like Garradian scanning tech?"

"Yes."

"Does the scanning technology see the phase cloaked ships?" Kraye asked.

"I don't know," City admitted. But it did see regular Garradian cloaks, like those Carey's squadron, used. "But if they have it, then they know the squadron is with your ship."

There was a short silence. "Then we definitely must take this ship."

He had a point. It might be their only ride home.

———

CabeX was still assessing the protections around the chamber he believed held Savlf when he saw them begin to collapse. It appeared that the two humans had been successful in overcoming Xaddek and penetrating his system. Except that they had not informed him of their progress as was mission protocol.

On his headset, it appeared he was still on a live comm link with them.

Appeared.

He considered how to discern if the link was still live. He did not wish to alert any hostiles to his suspicions, but he needed to know.

Bangle?

I am here.

Was she? *Initiate Staeps Stimsa.* It meant nothing, was not an actual program. How she responded would determine if he was still connected to her.

Initiating Staeps stimsa.

Not Bangle, then. Where had their exposure occurred? It was possible the messages from Savlf had been a trap from the beginning, a way to get access to his systems, but the virus had not come through the message access point. That did not mean she was not the lure to draw him here to this chamber. When he entered, he would know.

It seemed apparent that the humans had failed to neutralize Xaddek, and it was possible all teams were compromised. He must assume this and make his decisions based on the worst case. If he did not, Xaddek would win the board.

If he were wrong, not all would be lost. The *Najer*, and the ships accompanying it would survive. The blast radius would ensure that no one on either ship would survive. But if the pincers of a trap were closing, death would be a mercy. Xaddek liked to play with his food before consumption.

Standing in this dank and dismal corridor, he wondered why he struggled so hard to live. What drove him, what drove all of those on his crew to keep going? To keep trying for what? To keep fighting for this...metal life? All his choices, all his struggles had been funneled down to this moment. This door.

He stood on one side.

Savlf might be on the other.

Whether willingly or not, she was part of the trap.

If she was in there...

Her eyes had asked, no, they had begged without hope for what he'd fought to secure and then keep.

Freedom.

He could walk through that door and free them all. End the hunting and being hunted.

Why did he hesitate? Did he still have hope? If they survived, then what? What did he want?

In his processor's eye, he stared into her eyes and wondered...

———

With the enemy closing in on both sides, they elected to use the repair ducts, at least for a short time. The two parrots did a good job of being cling-ons. She might have winced a bit at this—the single positive about being separated from her Mikes. Oh yeah, they would have said it out loud.

OxeroidR's cling-ons were hanging in there pretty good, too. When they found a spot that looked pretty safe for the animals, they all indicated they'd rather continue to cling. On. Oh man. Instead of shaking her head at her bad jokes, she looked around for a more secure, ride along solution.

She patted down the pockets of her suit. She'd stowed a few of her things in some of the pockets, but she thought she remembered seeing lightweight rope and webbing—yup. With Kraye's assistance, they rigged a rudimentary backpack for OxeroidR's critters. The parrots indicated their ability to keep their perches and refused to be separated when Kraye offered his back for one of them so that left City with two parrots on her back.

They resumed their climb with OxeroidR once more on point, but this time City had Kraye on their six, to protect the birds.

A few decks up, OxeroidR risked accessing the ship's systems. There were so many alerts now, it seemed unlikely one of the crew would notice it, or act on it in time.

"They have isolated engineering, while they concentrate forces on finding us." OxeroidR had also isolated them from the fake Bangle. "They hope to encourage our retreat to engineering and trap us between two forces."

"They are arranged so that it will be difficult to take full advantage of your skills, OxeroidR," Kraye murmured.

"Does that mean they know he's on board?" City asked.

"I doubt they know," Kraye said. "OxeroidR is most difficult to track."

She nodded. "So they suspect he might be on board and are trying to minimize his effectiveness." She'd sure like to see his full operating skills. Always something to learn. "Do you think they have taken engineering?"

OxeroidR studied the data. "We cannot fully trust this data. They will know, if I am on board, that I can see this, too. But I do not believe engineering has been attacked yet. If we have secure transmission, that they cannot stop, then we would know we can not retreat that way. They hope to neutralize or capture us first, then take engineering."

"Can you punch through with a message for them?"

"If I did, they would know we know, and where we are."

City nodded, and her shoulders seemed to straighten. "They've probably got all systems control locked out except for the bridge." She feared that someone on this ship would deploy some kind of lethal gas—but that might have already happened. All they could do was press forward with the plan.

"Affirmative."

She frowned. "There will be life support ducts that lead to the bridge, but as soon as they realize we already used one, they'll lock them down."

"They will not expect a direct approach," Sir Rupert suddenly joined the conversation. "They do not have the resources to cover all approaches. And they do not believe you can threaten the bridge without OxeroidR. They will focus on him first. He is the most difficult target to bring down."

OxeroidR nodded. "I could draw them off."

"But you are the only one with the skills to get us onto the bridge," Kraye pointed out, though reluctantly, or so it seemed to City. "We should stick together."

"You will slow me down." A hatch in OxeroidR's side slid open. He extracted a narrow black box. "Place your hand here," he directed City

City looked at Kraye, who nodded, so she did, though a bit dubiously.

"It is now keyed to your palm print. You can use it to access the bridge controls." OxeroidR activated a hatch, revealing a small storage closet. "Wait here for four of your minutes, then make your way to the bridge by the most direct route possible. I will join you when I am able."

"Oorah," City said, holding out her fist. OxeroidR curled his digits in and bumped his hand against hers.

"Oorah, Sergeant."

———

Valyr wanted to look anywhere but at his clone. He knew it was "empty," but still capable of feeling pain. That thing, the spider, had exposed it to shock them, but it did not know how effective it had been.

It did not know.

He tried to think. It watched Rachel right now. It almost purred its pleasure at her distress.

Because it did not know.

It must not know—and yet. Could the tables be turned? Could the biter be bit?

Did it seem her retching had slowed? Her shoulders heaved as she continued to gag. He dragged his gaze from her to the table with its gory eviscerated meal. At the blood dripping from the spider's mouth. It seemed as if all its eyes watched Rachel. Her hands supported her—or did they? In the shadows of this section of its lair, it was possible she was slightly off balance. Trying to reach the concealed weapon? Were they still in the compartments? The webbing had searched, and he was not certain but—he had to help her. It was their only chance.

There could not be much time left. The trap was closing,

faster than the spider realized. It wasn't just the incoming ships. If CabeX felt threatened—

He lifted his arms slowly so that the strands would not react against him and started to unlatch his headgear. At first, he did not think he'd caught the spider's attention, but then he saw the eyes begin to turn his direction...

As if he'd stirred the creature's curiosity, the lights came up, pushing back the shadows around his head, but not quite reaching Rachel...

Still moving slowly so as not to provoke the wrong reaction from the webs, he lifted his headgear up and off, then tossed it to the side. Only then did he shift so that spider could see his face.

It appeared to rear back. Then it leaned forward. A claw came up and stroked the face of Valyr's clone. Did the eyes beg him to end it? Horror almost took him to his knees beside Rachel. Indeed, he did not know how he stayed on his feet. Perhaps the webs served a purpose after all...

"Well, well. Good things come to those who wait, it seems. And here I was thinking no further than breakfast." His gaze went briefly to Rachel, but it seemed unable to keep its attention off Valyr.

So, it knew.

The compact of secrecy tried to tie his tongue, but this creature already knew something. The question was, how much did he know?

"You seek the Urclock." How far did he dare go? If their fail-safe—or this last bid—backfired, the creature's deadly game would be disastrous for the universe. His mind rejected the notion that this thing could ever force the formation of the tangram, but—the image of Savlf came to him.

How strong was he? What if the spider offered Rachel's life for compliance? Or forced him to watch her be tortured—

He swayed but stayed on his feet, digging deep inside to do

it. Had he feared the cold sleep? It was nothing compared to this. When the moment came, he must take it. He could not afford to hesitate.

"I seek anything that gives me the power to do what I want, to eat what I want, to use who I need to get more power." A different claw moved. "My Trozzerd Emitter 3DXZ is almost at full charge. It will destroy the *Najer* and those puny little ships around it. I'll take the outpost on this planet, and then this galaxy will be mine as well. And yes I will form the tangram and take it all."

He snapped the pinchers of his claws together.

"As you have learned, I see everything. I know everything."

"Not everything," Rachel said, rising to her feet and dragging an arm across her mouth. Her face was a white moon in the shadow cast by the pool of light over the spider.

"And what don't I know?" He sounded amused as if he humored a child.

"My firing range score." She lifted her arm and fired her weapon. Firing first at the strands of web reaching toward her, cutting through them like an avenging scythe. The strands dropped but more reached for her. She focused on priorities first. In a rolling dive, she avoided the strands and aimed at the spider.

Eyes first.

The spider screamed as the rays from her two weapons burned into his opticals.

Valyr struggled with the web, saw Rachel swivel briefly and cut through the strands above him, then she turned back to the spider.

He dropped, fumbling to reach both weapons, and saw new strands reaching for Rachel. He fired through them, where they connected to the ceiling, then turned to the spider, too. Rachel was slicing off legs, so he helped with that.

As he fired at twitching legs, he saw the eyes of his clone. He lifted one weapon to his forehead in a mute salute, then fired at it once, twice more, until life faded from the eyes.

The spider's mouth still snarled and together they fired over and over and over into that maw, even when it had quit moving.

He stopped, but Rachel didn't.

"Rachel. *Rachel.*" He shoved one weapon in an empty holster and grabbed her shoulder.

She ceased, lowering one weapon, then the other to her sides. Her shoulders slumped as her chest heaved. The room was filled with the smell of burned...creature. Singed cobweb, he supposed, and the acrid smell of the contents from her stomach. It was, he decided, the smell he preferred, even though it made his stomach lurch.

He lifted an arm and swiped at the sweat on his forehead. Rachel began to pull cobwebs off her arms and legs, using her ray gun when it didn't want to go.

"How—" He did not know how to ask.

"Physics," she said, wearily. "I said I could shoot, but no one ever believes me."

And then a red light began to pulse near the dead spider's body.

"Oh, crap."

"Spider fail-safe," he said.

———

City turned off her heads-up display. It was distracting. And wrong. She did not want to react to the wrong data. Motion and heat detectors were still on, but mostly she trusted her senses and her instincts as she followed Kraye through dark and silent passageways. The only thing that could have been worse, she decided, was doing this on the ship with the spider.

The crew were either confident of their ability to deal with OxeroidR, or they were all heading into a trap. It was not a cheerful thought, but opportunities to excel didn't tend to revolve around cheerful.

They paused at the last corner, the last corridor to the bridge, their backs somewhat pressed against the wall, so she didn't smash the parrots, while they regrouped and—at least her case—strained to hear any echoing fire from OxeroidR's distraction.

After emerging from their hiding place, they'd heard the echo of exchanged fire for a couple of decks, but now the silence was intense. Ominous. If the crew had overcome the robot, this was probably the most futile thing they could do. But it was their only option.

The parrot eased up. "Let me see."

See. What did he see when he looked? She eased forward, her weapon first and got a look for both of them.

Only the red glow of the emergency lighting as far as she could tell. No movement.

"Proceed now," the parrot said, the first hint of urgency in his voice.

City ran forward, with Kraye watching their backs. She pulled out the black box OxeroidR had given her. She pushed it against the control panel next to the door, putting her hand in the same place she had before. Cables snaked out of it, driving into the control panel. Lights flashed. The box fell back in her hand. Smoke flowed from the holes in the control panel. She stuffed the box back in a compartment in her suit and readied her weapon.

"You take that side," she ordered Kraye. "When the hatch opens, start firing in the center, then you move right, and I'll move left. Shoot anything that moves."

They had no clue how many were on the bridge, or if they

could take control without OxeroidR. But she was a Marine. She'd try or die. *Oorah.*

————

CabeX lifted his arm to punch his device into the controls when lights began to pulse in the corridor. A harsh voice blared a warning.

Self Destruct.

Either Xaddek was dead, or he'd activated it as a last way to pressure the humans into surrender. If he had to choose, he would say that Xaddek had been neutralized and the self-destruct had activated upon his death. He had more ways than a self-destruct to impose his will. He felt pulled to help them, but...

In chaos, there might be opportunity. He punched into the control, felt the jolt as the virus tried to make entry. But the protections the two humans had added to his kept it at bay.

For now.

If there was hope, it would be more optimal not to explode.

20

OF COURSE, the spider had a dead bug's switch. The stink had been bad before they shot everything up, but now...well, her vomit was the best smelling thing in there. Which just showed how bad her red shirt day had gotten.

Rachel tried her comms. "Comms are still down," she said tersely, trying to make her legs take her toward the flashing red. By the dead spider. And his supper.

Valyr touched the wall. "Something about this room blocks signal."

But they'd had signal until—she looked up, saw the strands still holding her ray rifle and trimmed the stands away with her smaller gun. It tumbled free, falling at her feet. She picked it up, spun around, and fired at the doorway.

"Wait—" Valyr started to say.

But the third shot punched through.

She looked at him, possibly a little startled by herself. "I suppose we can't do that to his controls?"

He shook his head, and to her surprise chuckled. It was a weak sauce one, but still a real chuckle. He went over and picked up his headgear, fitting it back on. He lifted the visor's light shield, so she could see his face. It was a good precaution. The self-destruct could be poison gas, not a boom.

Rachel looked for and found her headgear. She pulled it on and heard him trying to contact Bangle.

"Bangle?"

I am here.

She sounded surprised.

Your Marines have retreated to the ships and locked down access, but there is no sign of activity in engineering yet. The Beugrimt Seeker 55THT has already fired, and the Trozzerd Emitter 3DXZ will fire soon. It—

"I know. The spider explained it before we shot him," Rachel said, exchanging a glance with Valyr.

"We need to access the spider's systems." After a brief hesitation, Valyr approached the bodies. She saw his shoulders tense, and then he lifted his hand gun, flipping the setting higher. He fired at it until the body vaporized.

If Rachel had had anything left to hurl, she would have. She did gag again. Then she stalked to the side opposite Valyr. If she was going to gag anyway, she might as well help. Together, they heaved the spider carcass up on the table, then over to the other side and out of their way. There was no chair to sit on, so he crouched in front of the controls, studying them.

They were like nothing she'd ever seen. She extracted her tablet. "Bangle, can you see a way in?"

For a minute, she thought they'd lost her again, but then the blue stream started to move out from the tablet and across her hands. Like a stream of bugs, it overran her hands and went down into the control console.

———

The hatch slid open. Kraye leaned out from the protection of the wall, firing at anything that moved in the center of the bridge. And possibly some things that did not move. The sergeant moved, too, in synch with him as if something connected them. As they shifted fire to cover the rest of the room, their energy beams crossed, flaring brightly for several seconds.

Then they both leaned back, shoulders propped against the wall. She met his gaze briefly, then dove into the room, her sitting roll protecting the parrot, but also setting her up so she could provide covering fire for him. He jumped in, opting for the high fire position. When he could find no more targets, he ceased firing, the sergeant's weapon going quiet just after his.

Some smoke drifted in their air from their hits on "other" than moving targets. Alerts pulsed on all sides. Bodies lay slumped across consoles and were sprawled on the floor. He started to step forward.

"Careful," Sergeant City cautioned, rising to her feet with a fluidity that was remarkable while wearing the body armor and a parrot. She walked forward, moving her weapon from side to side as she applied more stun fire to each of the slumped bodies. He saw something move to the right and fired, the not so stunned crewman dropping to the floor.

He might be in love, he decided, as she made her way to the most promising console. A pity they were probably still going to die. She extracted the black box once more and applied it to this console. Cabling snaked out and plunged into the console, not unlike a spider, he thought, not altogether happy with that thought.

He continued his survey of the room, firing a shot at one more crewman faking unconsciousness.

"Can you read this?" she asked, with a frustrated look in his direction. The parrot peeked over her shoulder. Before he could reach her side, it spoke.

"The other ship is charging a nova cannon. The *Najer* and

the squadron will be destroyed if it cannot be disabled or destroyed before reaching a full charge." He hopped out onto the sergeant's shoulder. "If it is destroyed the blast radius will destroy this ship, too."

"What's the bad news?" she muttered, looking at the controls. She got an arrested expression.

Kraye got it at the same time she did. They spoke almost on top of each other.

"The comet drive!"

"Is this ship's engine still tied into the other ship's engine?"

He bent over the controls. For a moment he saw the hope reflected in her eyes, then it faded.

"We need OxeroidR."

The parrot moved down until he was on her arm, studying the console. "You must press exactly where I tell you. And you must hurry. Time is short."

———

Savlf heard the self-destruct alarms blaring as the door of her prison burst open. She'd never seen the robots that Xaddek lusted to control, but she knew this was one.

Massive, dull metal black except for the red glow of eyes in the plated face, his arms bristled with weapons where hands should be. She'd chosen the correct champion.

It was pleased her to know he'd come, even if it were too late for both of them.

Though she could not see the poison tracing through the web toward what was left of her human body, she felt it.

"Thank you," she said, not sure if her connection to the computer still existed until her voice sounded in the room.

He lifted an arm, red energy a steady stream that sliced through the surrounding web with careful precision. She fell forward into a metal embrace. Felt the ice in the air driving into her body.

Shock.

It had been too swift, but it was better this way.

"Thank you," she said with her own voice this time. Her head fell back as the dark, and the cold closed in over her free head.

Free...

———

"Do we know how long we have before it goes boom?" Rachel asked.

Valyr heard her, saw her through the cleansing blue streams flowing from Bangle via her tablet. They needed the buffer. The spider's systems were as evil as the spider. Inside, even with Bangle's help, he felt it sting and burn his mind. In the same way, they'd made their way to this place, they must find their way to a central control through webs of traps and snares.

"I do not know this timing," he admitted, even as hands and brains fought digital monsters.

"Maybe that's just as well," she muttered. "I'm trying to get to the weapons control if you can work on the self-destruct?"

"You will need to use all speed," he muttered as a digital monster lashed out. He felt the blow as if it were physical. "It is almost charged."

Out of the corner of his eye, he saw a blue line fighting for entry.

"What is that?" he asked, as much to himself as to Rachel. Neither needed the distraction.

"Can you tell what it is, Bangle?" Rachel asked. She sounded breathless, too.

As if their thoughts created the battle, he saw her "firing" a "weapon."

"It's like a flipping video game," she panted.

A game? He shifted his thinking and what he saw changed. Even though the blows felt real, it was an illusion.

The line is coming from the other ship. The engines were linked together for the comet drive jump.

"Linked together? Is the other ship trying to get control of this ship?"

It is trying. It is sending pulses of sound that do not sound random.

"Play them for me," Rachel ordered, "please..."

Over the ship's intercom, the sounds began to play.

"That's morse code," Rachel said. "Let them in. That's City or maybe OxeroidR?"

The line opened, and it almost seemed as if armed soldiers flooded through the breach.

"The cavalry is coming," Rachel said, her voice picking up energy.

"It is an illusion," he gritted out, as his mind struggled to reshape reality.

"It's going to fire..."

He pushed back the monsters, grateful for the help, but the alien weapon had reached a full charge despite all they could do.

"If they drop their shields, the cannon can not injure them, it's the cannonade before and after. It's too close together. Can we stop the regular canons?"

"I'm trying," Rachel panted. "It's a devil's snare..."

He studied the disposition of the ships. "They know. See, how close they are to the moon's atmosphere?"

"Will it work?"

"It is a chance." He sent a prayer to his gods that whatever they planned would succeed and refocused on the self-destruct. If it would have saved those ships, he might have let it run, but it would not. It was as if the spider had foreseen this and tried to ensure all their deaths...

The Beugrimt Seeker 55THT has fired. The Trozzerd Emitter 3DXZ will fire in one minute.

———

"We're in," City said. "Get on that other console. We need two sets of hands. Can your friend help Kraye?" she asked over her shoulder without turning her head toward the parrot.

"She can."

"Listen to her," City said. "Okay, we've got friendlies on the other side of this mess." Bangle was helping them, could she— help began to flow back along the link. "They are going for weapons control. Their creepy weapon will be fully charged in forty-five seconds."

"The Beugrimt Seeker 55THT has already fired its first round," Kraye said. "We must hurry..."

———

Bangle provided a countdown to the Trozzerd Emitter 3DXZ charge for Valyr, placing it in the corner of this reality. He was not sure it helped as it increased his inner tension. On the other hand, it was an incentive to keep fighting. There were so many lives on the line. He was starting to make headway against the illusions, replacing them with a clean canvas to work on, but he was not progressing quickly enough.

All of a sudden, Rachel was next to him, helping to speed up the spread of order, helping him to erase the web. "Devil's snare," she panted.

"The projectile cannon—"

"City and Kraye are on it." She did something, and light flooded the dark places of the programming. "Don't fight it. Focus just on the center."

For a moment, his mind resisted the notion, as the monsters seemed to grow larger.

"Relax," she said again.

The calm of her voice washed over him, and as he relaxed, the monsters began to fade.

"There it is," Rachel said, suddenly.

He felt the ship jerk.

"Crap. Both weapons are firing."

———

Romeo flight rose steadily, lightly skimming the moon's atmosphere. The hope was that the *Najer* would convince the spider that they were unaware of the trap waiting for them.

Carey had split his squadron into Delta Tango Flights One and Two. DTF One flight was positioned in a half circle just behind Romeo. Both birds anchoring each end of the bowl were the closest to Romeo, and all the ships in this flight were also skimming the atmosphere.

Behind Romeo and DTF One was DTF Two. It was rising along the curve of the moon and just inside the unusually wide atmospheric band surrounding this particular moon.

The depth of the atmospheric band would, they hoped, give them more maneuvering room. The density could also give them an advantage if—

Yeah, there was a catch. The atmosphere had some of the same elements present in their shields. But those elements were not in the same percentages, making this a wild card. But their best chance, other than retreating and leaving their people unsupported and behind.

As they counted down the moment that Romeo flight would be visible and exposed to fire from Arachnid Z, Carey tried not to think of Olivia waiting for him back on Kikk. His cockpit recorder was on. If anything was found...

"I love you, Olivia," he said. Then kicked on his mental after burners.

Would the spider demand surrender or fire as soon as his ship had a targeting solution?

"Ten seconds to Romeo exposure," he said. "Let's hope he wants you—"

Arachnid Z didn't wait for complete exposure. Luckily the robots had faster than light reactions. Romeo was already diving for atmosphere. Carey's DTF's were heading down, too.

"Spread out and prepare for incoming," he said.

———

The ship seemed to shudder, and Kraye heard the sergeant utter something that was probably profane in her language.

"Both weapons are firing."

"There are the controls for the Beugrimt Seeker 55THT."

"Got it," she said. "We're in control of weapons systems on both ships."

"I am shutting down weapons fire," Kraye said, aware it might be too late for his crew and hers.

He pulled up a tracking screen. He tried the comms, but could not break through to warn his ship. His crew mates. He leaned on the console with both hands, his chin up because he could not take his eyes off the spreading waves of particles and projectiles racing toward the incoming formation.

He felt a hand on his arm. He looked, found her staring at the tracking screen.

"They'll make it," she said. "The colonel will have a plan."

"You seem certain."

"I am. He always has a plan."

Her hand slid down over his. He looked at her hand on his, felt warmth where she touched him, felt hope spread out from the warmth. It made no sense, but he believed her.

"Sergeant..."

"Call me City. Or Caro." Her gaze met his. "My friends call me Caro."

Friend. Did he know what that was? Or what that word meant.

"Caro. I am Kraye."

"Just Kraye?"

"As far as I know, just Kraye."

OxeroidR entered the bridge, stopping when he saw the tracking screen.

"We were too late," Kraye said bitterly.

He moved forward until he stood at Kraye's other side. His metal arm lifted to rest on Kraye's shoulder next to the parrot.

———

For once the drag of atmosphere felt good as Carey dove for what he hoped was cover, the squadron spreading out, and firing decoys to confuse the heat suckers. The persistent suckers seemed to hesitate as they hit the atmospheric speed bump, too, and then, they ran into the counter measures his guys had deployed in their wake.

The heat suckers were determined, but according to RaptorZ, if they could keep them confused for long enough, they'd run out of fuel. No, it was the shield smackers that worried him more.

There was a confusion of comm traffic as the heat suckers flailed around, looking for real targets, and then the first wave of shield smackers connected with the atmosphere. For almost a minute, it looked like a fire bomb had hit, creating an orange and red canopy above them.

Then he didn't have time to worry when a heat sucker pinged on him.

He jinked right, then left. Despite the high risk of dying, it felt good to be flying with enough G's to make his speed jeans inflate. When the heat sucker stayed on his tail, he fired off counter measures, hoping he wouldn't have to do that again for a while. He didn't have an inexhaustible supply.

His ship rocked as a heat sucker detonated a little close for comfort.

The patter in his ears was non-stop.

"...GSF-4 you got a sucker on your tail..."

"...hang on, I'm coming..."

Then the shield smackers punched through.

"What are we looking at?" Carey asked.

"The penetrations appear to be concentrations of flammable gasses."

Great. The shield smackers had turned into great balls of fire, Molotov cocktails of fun. He needed Bangle to provide a playlist. It was like threading a needle, trying to dodge the balls of fire and the suckers. The only good news, the fireballs looked like they flamed out about halfway to the moon's surface.

"I'm hit! I'm hit!"

Carey saw a smoke trail from GSF-7, saw the bird spiraling down and then it managed to get their nose up.

"Can you make it back to home plate, GSF-7?"

"That's a negative, CAG. Gonna put her down on the surface. Don't forget to pick me up."

"Roger that, GSF-7." Even as Carey dodged incoming—and didn't dodge everything—his screens showed him at least two more waves heading their way. "Romeo flight, this is GSF-1. Any chance we can safely deploy our shields in atmosphere?"

"Not advised," came the steady voice of RaptorZ. "The liquid fire could still become explosive on impact with shields."

"Don't you mean more explosive?" put in GSF-4, making a hard turn to avoid a cluster of fireballs.

"Roger that." Looked like the heat suckers were starting to thin out, but the great balls of fire were brutal. Another *Dauntless* took a hit but managed to make a controlled descent. "Looks to me like the balls of fire flame out as they hit thicker atmosphere. Let's drop down into the thicker atmosphere. That will slow down the heat suckers, too."

He noticed Romeo rising toward the upper atmosphere, trying to give a damaged *Dauntless* cover. The pilot managed to get the nose up and did a slow spiral down with his wingman also providing cover.

"You can join us now, Romeo flight," Carey suggested. "It's a lot cooler down here."

The *Najer,* not as limber as a *Dauntless,* began a wide turn with its nose coming down just as the last wave of shield smackers connected with the atmosphere. There must have been more of something or other in that spot because it lit up, the impact zone bulging downwards and slapping the *Najer.*

It tumbled in an uncontrolled descent, vanishing into the clouds beneath him.

———

City held her breath as the *Najer* dropped toward the moon's surface in what appeared to be an uncontrolled descent, tumbling top over tail.

"Pull up, pull up, pull up." She didn't realize she'd said the words out loud until Kraye's hand tightened over hers. She looked at him.

"They will pull up in time." He said the words confidently, but his face showed the strain as he turned back to the tracking screen.

It fell...

...and fell...

...and appeared about to crash into the ground...

"It's straightening out," City muttered. "Isn't it?"

"It is," Kraye's mouth widened into a smile.

She liked his smile she decided. She liked it a lot.

———

"So what just happened?" General Halliwell asked.

"I wish I knew," Doc said. Boy, did she wish she knew. At last sight, the squadron had been dodging some nasty looking fire and rocks, according to their last readings.

Hel reappeared, out of sight of the video connection with the General.

"Communications and tracking are being restored," he told her. *And I learned something interesting about something called a comet drive.*

That sounds sexy.

For those who like speed? Very.

She almost smiled where the General could see it.

"What about transport between the outposts?" the General asked. "Is that working yet?"

Doc tapped into the system. "That's hard to say. I'm going to try to open a comm channel to Central Outpost."

"Loop me in," he ordered.

"Already done," Doc said. There was no sound, like in the old days when a modem tried to talk to a computer. One minute the line was not live and then it was. She'd picked video connection and was surprised to find a Marine at the other end.

"Corporal..."

"Knight, ma'am. My fire team was ordered to hold this outpost until Sergeant City returned."

"Who else is there, Corporal?" the General cut in.

The Corporal stood impossibly more to attention. "Sir. Myself, my fire control team and Captain Bailey."

"I want to be briefed on what has been going on there, Corporal."

"I will attempt to do so, sir. There are some gaps in what we were able to see."

Words formed on Doc's console, words she was pretty sure the General wasn't seeing.

Your people are safe.

Thank you...

Bangle. My friends call me Bangle.

She looked over at Hel. She was glad the General hadn't seen that.

My friends call me...Morticia.

She'd almost told the AI her real name, but she still needed to be careful. Always when time travel was still on the table.

———

"We did it," Rachel said, "at least, everyone did something." Carey's ships were mostly okay, looked like the *Najer* had landed safely, and comms were coming back. Rachel let go of the system and the blue frame dissolved into a mist, like the kind at the bottom of a waterfall. For a moment she was carried back to the last vacation she'd taken with her family. The air chill and slightly damp from the waterfall's mist. So beautiful it made her chest hurt. The only sound the roar of the water over the rock's edge. Her chest hurt now, but like that, not like after. She rubbed the spot, and half smiled at the ghosts of her siblings. Then they faded, too. Through the fading memory, she saw Valyr, a weary grin tugging at the edges of his mouth.

They weren't dead. They weren't a spider's dinner—

"How did you know," he asked, "that we needed to quit fighting the system?"

Rachel bit her lip. "I didn't know, but you can't fight devil's snare. The more you struggle, the worse it gets." According to *Harry Potter*. She was such a geek. "I wish I'd thought of it sooner."

His grin was crooked. "We are all alive—"

"I require your assistance, Dr. Frank," CabeX's voice cut through her move in Valyr's direction. And his move in hers. "Savlf has gone into shock."

She activated her headset comm. "What's your twenty? I mean, where are you?"

"I am in transit to the shuttle."

"We'll meet you there."

She picked up her weapons. "There may still be crew milling around," she said as they jogged out the door. The trip through the ship was still creepy, but they didn't run into any humans. The webs had shriveled into dirty lace on the bulkheads and elsewhere. She didn't lower her guard, or her weapons until she saw Mike3 ahead of her.

"They are on the shuttle," the Mike told her as he stepped out of her way. She started to run.

She yanked off her headgear and thrust her weapons at Valyr. This was a different kind of battle, a battlefield she knew well. No spiders or bad guys, unless you counted Death as a villain. Sometimes she did.

Ahead of her, she could see the dark figure of CabeX and the woman limp in his arms. The Mikes had found some blankets in some storage lockers and had spread them out. They'd also found the first aid kit she'd brought along and the one that was part of the ship's stores.

"Put her down," she said, noting how reluctantly he obeyed. She dropped down next to Savlf—it had to be her. Strands of the web were still embedded in her skin. What Rachel could see of her skin, was pallid with shock. "Elevate her feet and put some of those blankets on top of her. There are some heat packs in there, too. We need to get her warm. Fast."

She yanked on gloves. Valyr dropped down on the other side and started pulling items out of the Garradian first aid kit. The IV he handed to her, then he applied a device that she knew would monitor vital signs. While she got the IV going, he got her on oxygen.

"Will she be optimal soon?" CabeX asked.

She glanced up. His voice didn't sound quite so robotic.

"She's bad. She might not be able to survive outside the web, but I'll do what I can." She pushed a hand through her sweat soaked hair. "I wish we were on Kikk. They have seriously nice medical facilities." She touched a section of the web embedded in Savlf's skin. It lifted on the edge, but the flesh underneath was raw and red. She broke off a bit and realized it was burning through her gloves. She dropped it and ripped off the glove. A wisp of something drifted up from the bit of web before it turned into something resembling ash. It appeared that the bits of the web were still toxic. Savlf needed it removed but how could Rachel get it all off her without massive scarring?

"There is a medical facility on my outpost," Valyr said.

Of course, there was. "We need to get there fast," Rachel said. She glanced down. Super sonic, comet drive fast.

"If the...Captain will assist us, ma'am," Mikeɪ cast a carefully blank glance at CabeX, "we'll secure the hostile ship and bring it to the outpost."

"I'll do everything I can," Rachel promised him.

He nodded slowly and followed him back onto Arachnoid X.

Rachel looked up. Captain Gibson, looking grave, stood at the bridge hatch. "Captain Gibson, I need you to bust a comet drive move for me."

"Aye, aye, ma'am."

21

For Rachel, getting off Xaddek's ship was a blur centered on the deathly white face of Savlf as she and Valyr fought to keep her alive until they could get back to the medical resources of Central Outpost. Twice she thought they had lost her. Without the Garradian emergency devices on the ship, they would have. Once they got her into a semi-stable condition, Rachel donned gloves and began the process of carefully peeling away the strands of the spider web. She couldn't prove it, but she believed the webs were working against Savlf's recovery.

Under the black strands were deep red welts. When air hit the exposed spots, she moaned softly. Valyr vanished, then reappeared with some green salve that, when applied, seemed to ease her pain and reduce the flaring red of the wounds. As she worked, she kept a close eye on Savlf's vitals and murmured over and over to the unconscious woman, "You're safe. You're safe now. It will be okay."

Rachel hoped it would be okay. She'd once been beautiful. Her skin, where it hadn't been marred by the web, was a creamy matte white, her eyes an unusual shade of blue, and her hair a thick silken midnight black. Her figure was voluptuous, her hands and feet long and elegantly shaped. What Xaddek had done to her mind was beyond obscene. Rachel didn't know a word bad enough for what he'd also done to her body. Would either completely heal?

She had no answer. Her life still hung very much in the balance.

She realized that CabeX had entered, surprisingly light-footed for his size and metal quotient. His red gaze appeared to be fixed on their patient. His face was not capable of showing emotion, so it was odd that she felt waves of it. With her recent and very sudden surge in interaction with sentient AIs, Rachel felt an odd dissonance about the *Najer* AIs. She made a mental note to think about it later—

Savlf's vitals crashed, and there was a period of chaos. When they had her stable again, she realized that CabeX had extended his arm, so that his digits lightly clasped Savlf's hand. She looked up and saw his gaze lift to meet hers. He didn't speak, but she found herself answering a question she sensed.

"We'll do our best," she promised. "She has a chance," she added, a better chance because of the Garradian tech in this outpost. "A decent chance."

No sooner had Rachel spoke when Savlf spiked a fever. She started to go for another IV, but Valyr put a hand on her arm.

"Wait," he said.

Her skin turned pink, and it almost seemed as if she could see the heat rising over the deep red scars from the webs.

"If she has a seizure—" Rachel muttered.

"If she does, we'll stop it, but I think it is helping to cleanse her body of the spider poison."

He could read the various monitors better than she could so she nodded. She felt Valyr's gaze settle on her face. He grabbed a stool and pushed it closer.

"Sit."

"You're tired, too," she pointed out, but she sank onto the seat. Her legs felt rubbery like they belonged to someone else. Neither of them had talked about what had happened in Xaddek's spider den, other than to let the rest of the team know the spider was dead. And if she did say something, what would that be? To ask him why he'd vaporized his clone before they headed back? She could think of a good reason that had nothing to do with the Urclock or the dragon ships. If it had been her clone there, she'd have done the same thing. It was...obscene to see it, to know what it had suffered before—

A tremor shook her, and she inhaled deeply, then released it slowly, all without taking her eyes off Savlf's temperature reading.

"It's starting to go down," Valyr said.

All her other vital signs began to steady. They weren't wonderful yet, but they were better, edging over into "she might make it" better. Valyr gave her a tired smile, running his hands over his hair.

He had to feel almost as bad as Savlf. He'd been defrosted, gone into battle with robots and arachnids. Kissed a girl.

"Why don't you get some rest?" she suggested. "I'll do this watch, and then you can spell me." He looked about to protest. "I've had slightly more rest than you," she pointed out. If they didn't count the thousand year's sleep, but she didn't know how to count that.

He hesitated, then gave a slow nod. He gave an almost vague look around. He might be too tired to find his quarters.

"Why don't you stretch out in one of the treatment rooms?"

He brightened at this and, after a hesitation that might have included a longing look in her direction, he walked out of her sight.

She turned back to find CabeX regarding her with—no

surprise—an expressionless look. She didn't suggest he get some rest.

"I am able to monitor these," he said, gesturing at the monitors with the hand not carefully cradling Savlf's.

She was tempted, more than he realized, but before she could make up her mind, Sir Rupert trotted into the room, trailing...another parrot? Rachel tipped her head to the side, her gaze ranging from one parrot to the other. It was a bit like seeing double. Vaguely she recalled that male and female parrots on Earth tended to look very much alike. In this case, Sir Rupert had a slight advantage in height.

"I wish you to meet Lady Upie, Dr. Frank," Sir Rupert said, gravely gesturing with a wing sweep.

"How," Rachel swallowed dryly, "do you do, Lady Upie." Had he found her here in the outpost?

"Lady Upie was a prisoner on Arachnid Y. We discovered her and other prisoners while ascertaining that she—" his head nodded in the direction of Savlf. "—was not on board."

She opened her mouth to ask but realized she was too tired. And she might know what the parrot had seen while aboard that ship. Did not want to reveal his top secret super power without his permission. Instead, she directed a concerned gaze on Lady Upie. A prisoner? Did she have the same power as Sir Rupert? She met his gaze and he fluttered his wings.

"She requires medical assessing, though she is in better shape than some of the others."

"I," Lady Upie seemed to give Sir Rupert a shy look, "would be grateful for your assistance."

Her voice was like Sir Rupert's, only a softer version and she had more of an...accent?

"You've had a terrible time, I'm sure," Rachel said. She glanced back at CabeX. "Call me if you need me?"

He gave her a solemn nod, and the digits of the hand

holding Savlf's folded gently over her hand. Yeah, there was something about that robot that made her scientific instincts twitch.

She followed the two birds out into the corridor. Ahead was a waiting area similar to that on the Kikk Outpost. What was dissimilar were the occupants. Sergeant City waited just outside the waiting area, a shoulder propped against the wall, but she straightened when she saw Rachel approaching. Rachel opened her mouth, felt something brush against her leg and looked down as a huge turtle moved slowly past her, a slightly smaller turtle following. At least, it had the shape and size of an earth turtle, but not anything close to the coloring. These two looked like they'd passed through the sixties on their way here. Strident yellow, orange, red, green, and blue, with lines of black as the only sober note. Psychedelic turtles?

Rachel looked up, still moving closer to the waiting room, her gaze slowly tracking from left to right. One, two—kind of hedgehog looking bundles. They had the right general shape, but again, the coloring was off, though not in a psychedelic direction. It was more subtle than that. Next to them sat OxeroidR with a lone flying squirrel perched on his shoulder. She could see the webbed feet the pleat of its wings. The face shape was off from the Earth version, and its bright gaze was an unsettling purple.

"Moose and squirrel," City murmured for Rachel's ears only.

Rachel choked once, but couldn't disagree with this. All they needed was a Natasha and Boris to complete the picture.

Next to Moose and Rocky were a couple of Panda-like creatures, black and red instead of black and white and the arrangement of the colors looked like it was opposite from their version. Two pure grey swans with their necks entwined and—

Rachel's gaze stuttered to a halt at the sight of the last bird. The avine-like creature, she amended. It was also alone. It was a stately creature, painted in shades of gray, royal blue, white and pink, with a vague eagle aspect. It had to be about her height and its claws—she gulped—were each the length of her hand, or longer. Based on its height, she'd estimate each wing to be, she gulped, four times longer than she was high. Its beak was the size of her hand with the fingers extended and its eyes were a mix of black and gold. A tuft of feathers protruding from the back of its head gave it a royal, kingly—queenly—appearance.

Rachel was aware that her chin had dropped again, but knowing what it looked like was no help when she was this shocked, this tired. She turned to meet City's sardonically amused gaze.

"You missed the Noah procession, I guess," City said.

"Noah?" Like the ark? Even though the animal count only numbered in the tens, it did make the room look as if Noah had emptied one section of the ark.

"Near as," City amended. "Apparently, one of the pairs did jobs for the creepy spider, and the other was a hostage to them doing it right."

Rachel blinked, dropping her voice. "They are all—"

"Sir Rupert has been translating for me," City said, offering a version of an answer to the question Rachel couldn't quite ask. "They had quite the...collection of prisoners in the hold, in addition to the prisoners we freed from the brig. There were a bunch of birds, but they seemed to be all right. Sir Rupert supervised their transport to Kikk. There is no way to know where they belong, at least for now. These guys all need to be checked over, some minor injuries tended."

I'm too tired for this, Rachel thought, gazing at her owl-eyed, which was appropriate. She would have liked to protest that she wasn't a vet, but actually, she'd done some training with a vet during the summers after her parents—but she didn't have alien animal training. She half sighed. She'd bet the Garradian systems had stuff that would help. No escape from vet duty.

She stepped further into the room and realized she'd missed seeing two more creatures. RaptorZ sat tucked in the corner with a boa-like creature wrapped around his metal body. Again, the coloring was wrong, and the eyes held intelligence, instead of the flat reptile stare. Next to them, was a half cat, half—horse with a single horn protruding from its forehead. It had its legs tucked in, horse-like, not cat-like. If not for the cat face, whiskers and all, she'd have said it was the closest to a unicorn she'd seen in real life. At least the horn looked horn-like, though more Narwhal—at half the length—than a rhino.

"Okay, then," she said, giving a shoulder roll. "I'll start with Lady Upie and then—" her gaze found a Marine manning the desk, "if you'll take their names and, um, details, starting from your left, I'll see them in that order, unless any, um, one, has a critical condition?" She ignored his uncharacteristic look of horror, instead sending a look around the room for anything critical. When none of them claimed a critical condition—or didn't understand the question, she headed through the center of the Noah herd toward the hatch to the examining area. As if on cue, Bangle began to filter "This is Me" into the room. City's brows shot up.

"I found the soundtrack in my personal info dump from Earth," Rachel explained. "I had forgotten I preordered it." She couldn't help it. Her shoulders started to move, and she found a second—third wind?—carrying her forward. It was better than an energy drink.

"If you'll follow me, Lady Upie?" Rachel palmed open the hatch, looking back in time to see some of the various creatures starting to, well, groove to the music—which was, apparently, a universal language. With a last, sympathetic look at the Mike and City, she let the hatch close between them.

———

Sergeant Carolina City had faced many challenges and dangers during her time in the Marines, including the mission just completed. But they all seemed like a cake-walk compared to this roomful of alien creatures. She met Corporal Day's trying-not-to-be-desperate look and gave him a smile she hoped was reassuring.

"Well, let's see what we can find out for the doc." She felt something brush against her leg and tried not to jump. It was the caticorn. He was striped like a tabby—gold and white—who had owned her grandma when City was a little girl. When City wasn't around, the tabby had been "Cat," but when City was visiting, she was Tiger. She'd only found out Tiger hadn't stuck when her grandma passed away.

The caticorn let out a sound that landed somewhere between a meow and a neigh. Then it twined itself clumsily between her legs. It was really small for a horse, very big for a cat, its ears reaching just above City's knees. It somehow managed to keep the horn from snagging anything, which surprised her until she thought about it. It had lived with that thing its whole life. Not a shock it had figured out how not to impale everything or everyone.

She crouched down and tentatively patted it. "Hi. What's your name?"

"It does not speak Standard," the squirrel on moose's shoulder said.

It was either funny or ironic that it sounded a bit Natasha, or maybe that was Boris.

"This is not what I signed up for," she muttered. The caticorn nudged her hand, and she absently scratched around the horn. The meow-neighing ramped up.

"Well, for now, we'll call you Tiger. Is that okay?"

The wise, almost old gaze looked up at her with a look that was very cat, very Puss-n-Boots. It almost felt like she? he? winked.

"Never make eye contact with a cat, ma'am," Corporal Day said, not quite able to keep the amusement out of his voice.

Something, she wasn't sure what had City looking up. Kraye stood in the opening, regarding her with a look that was well into the enigmatic zone. He looked less Captain Sparrow without the parrot, even though the Captain hadn't been the one with the parrot. Something flickered in his dark gaze, something that reminded her of a little boy looking into the candy shop with empty pockets.

Don't make eye contact with the alien guy. She almost sighed. Then she gave him a tentative smile. "We could use some help."

The sudden lightening of his expression made her heart clench oddly, the clench getting worse when Kraye crouched next to her, his dark hand next to hers on the caticorn's back.

"He or she doesn't speak Standard, so I'm calling him Tiger for now," she said, her throat dry. Her eyes, too. Under their hands, the caticorn purr-neighed louder.

———

Savlf shifted restlessly on the healing bed. CabeX came closer so that he could see her and the monitors. She moaned and cried out. He half turned, to summon the doctor, but, according to her vital signs, her condition had not changed.

She was distressed. Her head moved from side to side. Dr. Frank had cleaned her hair, her skin as much as she could without causing further damage, but her ink-dark hair still showed a few gray strands of sticky web. He carefully removed as much as he could see.

What, he wondered, would these people think if he told

them he'd once been a medical doctor, had spent his days healing until the Quh'y had forced him to work for them. He looked up and saw Kraye watching him from the doorway. Kraye didn't enter. "How is she?"

"Stable," CabeX told him. He felt self-conscious where his hand held hers, his sad metal hand that could register the warmth of her human hand, but could not feel her skin. Almost, he wished he'd died on Xaddek's ship. He surrendered so much to live, to survive. It had been worth it to save her, if indeed they saved her body *and* her mind. Her mind would be the harder task. But he could die now without seeing her eyes open. He did not wish to observe in her gaze what she thought of the monstrosity he'd become. His human heart had quit beating so long ago. Strange to feel pain in that spot after so long.

Kraye hesitated, nodded and moved slowly out of view. CabeX's attention returned to the patient. *The patient.* This woman who had called him across the stars, who'd reached out for his help even as she'd helped his enemy attempt to take him over. Neither of them were particularly heroic. She'd damaged him, almost killed him. She'd taken damage for that, and he'd almost killed her trying to save her. Would she know she was safe before—

Her lids flickered several times and then lifted. She stared up, blankly at first, then in confusion.

He wished Dr. Frank were here. There was only him to say, "You are safe."

Her head turned toward him, her eyes wide and filled with fear.

"You are safe," he repeated, hearing the echo of his computer-dead voice go round the room once more.

"Where...am I?" The fear began to fade in her eyes, but wary replaced it.

"You are—not on that ship any longer." He did not know

how to explain this place to her. "It is safe for you," he added. "Xaddek—"

She half flinched.

"—is dead."

She seemed to relax, her eyes closing briefly. "I thought it was a dream." Her eyes opened, and now she studied him with less wary, more curiosity. "You're..."

"I am CabeX."

"CabeX." She took a shaky breath. "You came. I didn't think —I hoped..." She sighed again. "I...used to be Savlf," she murmured, so much sadness in her voice that the ghost of CabeX's tear ducts burned.

"You will be again," he told her. She could, but he could not. He could never be himself, could never be human again.

22

GENERAL HALLIWELL WAS in a tough spot. No question he was in charge of the Expedition members, which included Rachel, Colonel Carey, Sergeant City, and all the other expedition people on Central Outpost.

He was not in charge of Valyr, this outpost, Bangle, Savlf, or the robots. And then there was the sentient menagerie. They would all do better on a planet with a non-toxic atmosphere, something that Helfron Giddioni seemed open to arranging in a manner acceptable to the animals. They were also looking into how to return those creatures who wanted to go home again. Some had no home to return to.

Rachel had had a chance to visit with each one while she played vet. Each had names, memories of home, trauma from mild to severe from being captives of Xaddek, and the capacity to make decisions for themselves. Finally, they were free. They could not, in good conscience, keep them from acting. It went against the basic beliefs of all involved in the expedition. And if it had, the robots would have stepped up to enforce their freedom to choose. If there was one thing that seemed to define the crew of the *Najer*, it was their deep belief in personal freedom for one and all.

Rachel had been able to get a bit of the back story from Sir Rupert while she was treating Lady Upie, who had been captured for delivery to Xaddek. Did the crappy spider know what she could do? Or had she been on his menu? They'd never, thankfully, get an answer to that question.

"Did you, um, *see* her?" Rachel asked, as she ran gentle fingers along one wing and then the other.

"I saw them bringing her aboard," Sir Rupert confirmed. "I did not see them removing her, so I had...hope." He added as if he knew what she'd ask next, "We will continue the search for more of our kind together, but for the present, we will stay on Kikk. She has traveled far in a dark place and is not certain of the way home."

"I am sorry," she told the lady bird, though she was glad Kikk would get some birds, even if only on a temporary basis. The place needed birds.

"Rupert will lead us both home," she said with gentle dignity.

Rachel shot the male bird a quick look. No pressure there.

He had ruffled his wings. "Now I know our kind is still out there."

He could end his search for frozen remains. She almost sighed. She'd miss hanging with him.

"You have a better guide than me now, Doctor."

She hoped, oh, how she hoped he was right. Valyr, well, she wasn't sure what he wanted. Technically, he had more right to control all of the outposts, including Kikk, than any of them. But he didn't seem inclined to push his claim.

He hadn't mentioned the Urclock's call. Neither had she.

Even without the Urclock, the debrief was stressful, though

still not as scary as facing down the huge spider. On the other hand, Doc was still scarier than the spider.

Luckily, Rachel was both short and nondescript. She managed to slip away as soon as the debrief ended and somehow found her way back to the main control room and the Urclock. She stared at it, wondering what it was, why it had called to Valyr. What it called him to do. She felt a stir in the air, sensed who it was and made room for him.

"I am seven," Valyr said, turning to face her. "But I think you guessed that."

Rachel nodded. "I still don't know what that means."

"I thought I did, but now I'm not so sure." He glanced around, then lowered his voice. "Bangle sent out the dragon ships. She—this was not supposed to happen that way. We were all to awake and travel together, not like this."

Rachel considered this. "She was...lonely?"

He nodded. "She stirred when your expedition wakened the outposts, but none of your people came to this outpost. So she activated three of the ships and sent them to bring back her people."

Rachel could understand that. She knew all about waking to an empty home, echoing with memories of who had been there, who would never be there again.

"And then—" He stopped with a frown.

"She woke you?" Rachel suggested.

"I am not certain it was Bangle or—" He took her hands in his, clasping them lightly, studied them with a slight frown.

"What?" she asked, besides almost everything, she almost added.

"It could have been the call of the Urclock. I feel its pull, but I am not certain..."

"...that it's not a trap," she finished for him. Neither of them had spoken about the clone, to each other or in the debriefing. Her barfing had also not been mentioned even though it had been a great distraction. They'd skated over the particulars of that. Thankfully there was plenty of gory detail without either detail.

Did she care if he was a clone? No, she admitted. She cared about a lot of things, but not that. He was Valyr. And if another one showed up? He wouldn't be her Valyr, even though he wasn't hers. What did he want? How powerful was the call of the Urclock?

He lifted his gaze, nodding. "If I stay here, I can help the robots."

"They used to be human, didn't they?"

His brows arched as if she'd surprised him. He nodded. "They transferred their personalities, their minds to the robots."

Even though she'd wondered, she was still shocked by his confirmation. "That's some crazy, bad-A science."

Valyr nodded, his expression distant and sober.

"I wish there was something we could do to help." Her thoughts shifted to CabeX who refused to leave Savlf's side, even for the briefing with General Halliwell.

Valyr hesitated, then said, "I have done some work in regeneration."

Rachel's eyes almost popped out of her head. "You can...put them back into—?" What? Their bodies were long gone unless —could he clone them?

"Not back, not the same but I might be able to add back some of their humanity."

"Let me guess who wants it the worst, CabeX?"

This time a small smile formed as he nodded.

"How does Savlf feel about him?"

"I think she would take him as he is."

"He saved her," Rachel said. Women liked heroes, even metal ones, it seemed.

"You did help," Valyr pointed out.

"We both helped, but he pulled her back from the edge." Rachel hesitated. What had happened to Savlf, it would take her a long time to recover from that, if she ever did. Her...attachment to CabeX could be a bit Stockholm Syndrome, even though CabeX had not been the one who enslaved her.

Beside her, Valyr shifted from one foot to the other.

"I have another reason for wishing to stay here, Rachel. It is...selfish." His chest heaved with a sigh.

That she knew what it looked like under his clothes made her chest heave, too. And maybe she hoped...a little...that he wanted to stay with her. With her. She wanted him. She admitted it to herself. She'd avoided this truth because behind it lurked joy and pain. Lots of pain if he left. But there was joy in opening up her heart to him. This was what she'd missed for so long. The joy of being connected in this way. *Love.* This love was different from what she'd felt for her parents, her brother, and sister, but it helped to ease the damage left from that wound. Even not knowing he felt the same, feeling love again had helped to heal her heart.

Only now did she realize how broken it had been. He could break it. She accepted that, but not with the same fear she'd felt before everything happened. The before Rachel had been...a child, with a child's pain still holding her back. She'd grown up in a brief time. She was stronger, grown stronger from loving him, from opening to feeling again. All of it had made her able to face the future as an adult, no matter what he chose to do. She wanted him to stay, but she could let him go, let him do what he felt he must. Like her parents had done for her so long ago. The power of it, the memory of them, and accepting her feelings, calmed the turmoil inside.

She watched him struggle to find the right words, noting the goodness in his eyes, the kindness around his mouth—and the sexy all over. There was a lot of that. Warmth and heat coiled inside. Love and want, two sides of love's coin. That might have made her nervous again, but she trusted him. Trusted herself as this new grownup person.

He opened his mouth. Closed it. Sighed in frustration. "I do not have the right words. I have never...I am not...we have not known each other long."

Depending on who was counting—okay, still not long. It felt long though. A lifetime long. How odd that they'd both been frozen, lost and waiting for the other.

"No...but you can find out a lot of the important things about someone when you see how they react to stress," she pointed out. She almost smiled. They were both geeks. If they wanted to get to the point of kissing, they'd have to help each. Neither of them could go the distance alone.

He brightened. "This is true. I feel...for you..."

"Like," she suggested, losing her nerve.

"More than like." He took a deep breath, as if he were about to dive off a cliff. "I know it is too soon to speak of love—"

"I love you, too," she said in a rush. She'd arrived in the galaxy at the speed of light, so why was it a shock she'd fallen fast, fallen hard.

His face lit up. She thought she'd seen him happy. She'd been wrong. His happy lit her up inside and out. And then he kissed her.

23

VALYR WASN'T sure how long he held her, how long his lips were pressed against hers. However long it was, it was not long enough. He could hang on to her, could kiss her forever, except for the requirements of oxygen. And the sound of approaching footsteps. He should have picked a more secluded place for his declaration.

He knew his chest heaved. And the heat, the want, was lava in his core. For the first time since he'd awakened from his cold sleep, the chill had gone from his body. Cold tried to return to the spaces that separated them, enough that it surprised him that a small storm did not form over their heads.

The whimsy of that thought made his lips edge up in a smile. He sighed. Had he feared that sleep? Feared what he'd find on this side? It had been challenging, but worth it to reach this place, this woman. He smoothed a piece of her hair back off a face that had become so dear so fast. He dragged a finger across her mouth before letting his arm fall to his side. He gazed into her eyes as her love for him shone out like the beam of the *geiohr*.

He sighed as the footsteps resolved into a man and a woman

rounding the corner to join them. The woman walked with an aura of danger. The man with her was Gadi, a leader or liaison of some sort, if he'd properly processed the various names and positions during the debriefing. He did not recall the woman's name.

He gave a half bow. The man smiled.

"Helfron Giddioni," he reminded him.

He exuded much charm, Valyr noted. And he was very handsome.

"And you are Valyr," the woman said, her speculative gaze moving between him and Rachel.

"I apologize for not recalling your name," he returned, taking the hand she held out and shaking it the way Rachel had shown him.

The woman seemed pleased rather than offended. Her attention shifted toward Rachel, who seemed to shift, then planted her feet, her chin lifting.

"Well, you helped our ambassador with his problem in a very unexpected way. But help is help. Thank you."

"You're welcome." Rachel's tone sounded a bit ground-holding.

"You kind of pushed out the boat," she went on. "How many of these sentient beings did you find?"

"I didn't find any of them, ma'am," Rachel pointed out. "We were, well, we were busy shooting the spider."

"She is an excellent shot," Valyr said proudly. She said people didn't believe her, well, he was her witness.

"So I hear." The woman was silent for a time, her gaze tracking to him and then moving to Rachel. "Dang, I owe you, Hel. You were right. They are in love."

"I am always right, Morticia," the man purred.

He got a look from this Morticia that was pointed and...intimate. This helped with the flush that rose in his face. It was new enough, he was not excited to share their love with anyone yet. Rachel smiled and took his hand.

"You're always something." Morticia grinned and glanced past them. "So that's the Urclock. Does it always tick like that?"

Valyr realized it was ticking much louder than before. He turned, taking Rachel around with him. He frowned and moved closer. The number three was pulsing in an odd pattern, too.

"It is not supposed to do this," he admitted.

"What does it mean?" Rachel asked, joining him. "Is it—" she stopped.

He appreciated her discretion, but that ship had flown away.

"It is not the tangram. It can not form a tangram without all seven." His gaze tracked around the clock. None of the other numbers were lit. So no tangram.

"That's almost like Morse code," Morticia said, joining them in front of the clock. "At least, that first part sounded like an SOS."

Rachel frowned. "You're right. It's spelling something else now if that is Morse."

Both women angled their heads while the two men exchanged glances.

"Doolittle," Rachel said. "I get Doolittle."

"So do I," Morticia said. "I've been on the *Doolittle*," she added. "I was deployed there before the *Boyington*."

"What's this about the *Doolittle*?" Rachel's general demanded from behind them. They turned as he strode up.

He'd had a most trying time since his arrival. Some of that still showed on his face.

"It sounds like Morse code, sir," Morticia said. "Coming out of the clock."

"It only has seven numbers," he pointed out, then stopped. "That is Morse."

"There's a string at the end I don't understand," Rachel began.

"That's the ID for the *Boyington*," the general said, his face settling into grim lines.

"It's changed again," Morticia said, her head tipped to listen once more.

She and Rachel were quick to translate the code, if this truly was code.

"That's a star chart location," Valyr said, suddenly. He recognized it. How had their Earth ship penetrated the sanctuary? It was not supposed to be possible. This did not bode well for the occupants. "What does SOS mean?"

"Save our souls," Rachel said. "They're in trouble."

"How is this possible?" Morticia asked, looking at the general.

"We have lost contact with the *Doolittle*," he admitted. "During the last data dump, I got the brief on it."

Valyr turned back to the Urclock. This code was a request for assistance, but it would not be possible for them to make this request without the assistance of the *Phoenicopterians*. Did this mean the *Mycetarians* had found them again? If they had, this was bad for her people and the species they'd formed the tangram to protect.

"Can you help? Can we help them?" Rachel asked. Her eyes showed the fear he felt.

"I..." he turned away, then turned back. "Yes and no."

"What does that mean?" the general snapped.

"It means I will require assistance." He saw Rachel understand.

"You're going to have to wake someone up," she said.

"I am going to have to wake someone up."
* * *
Thank you for reading *Lost Valyr!* I hope you enjoyed it!

Carolina City and Kraye's story will continue in *Operation Ark*, releasing in *Embrace the Passion: Pets in Space 3*, releasing October 9, 2018.

For breaking news on all my releases, sign up for my newsletter.

To find out about all my books, including connected Project Enterprise stories, hop over to my website.

Project Enterprise The Big Uneasy Lonesome Lawmen

Browse my complete backlist by visiting my website. :-) I have some stand alone novels, too.

And if you want to talk books, you can find me here:

My Blog Facebook Fan Page Twitter Pinterest Goodreads

If you enjoyed this book, I hope you'll consider leaving a review. It's not just because I'm needy (even though I try not to be!). Reviews help other readers decide which books to buy. :-)

ALSO BY PAULINE BAIRD JONES

Available in print, digital and audio.

Science Fiction Romance/Paranormal

Project Universe Series:

The Key (book 1)

Girl Gone Nova (book 2)

Tangled in Time (book 3)

Steamrolled (book 4)

Kicking Ashe (book 5)

Found Girl (book 6)

Lost Valyr (book 7)

Project Enterprise: The Short Stories

Time Trap: A Project Enterprise Series Short Story

The Real Dragon

Nebula Nine (time travel adventure)

Open With Care (Christmas collection that includes, "Riding For Christmas" and "Up on the House Top"

Specters in the Storm: A paranormal/steampunk/science fiction romance novella

Out of Time (World War II Time Travel Romance)

An Uneasy Future

(A science fiction romance mystery series set in future New Orleans)

Core Punch (1.0)

Sucker Punch (2.0)

One Two Punch: An Uneasy Future Bundle

Short Story Collections

Project Enterprise: The Short Stories

Do Wah Diddy Delete

Let's Fall in Love

The Real Dragon and other short stories

Romantic Suspense

The Big Uneasy Series:

Relatively Risky (1)

Family Treed (1.5)

Dead Spaces (2.0)

Louisiana Lagniappe (2.5)

The Big Uneasy Bundle

Lonesome Lawmen Series:

The Last Enemy

Byte Me

Missing You

Lonesome Mama (Bonus short story)

(The *Lonesome Lawmen* is also available as a digital bundle)

Do Wah Diddy Die

The Spy Who Kissed Me

Perilously Fun Fiction Bundle (includes *The Spy Who Kissed Me* and *Do Wah Diddy Die*. Bonus: *Do Wah Diddy Delete Short Story Collection*)

A Dangerous Dance

ABOUT THE AUTHOR

Award-winning, *USA Today* Bestselling author, Pauline never liked reality, so she writes books. She likes to wander among the genres, rampaging like Godzilla, because she does love peril mixed in her romance.

To find out more about Pauline or her books:
http://paulinebjones.com
pauline@paulinebjones.com

ACKNOWLEDGMENTS

I am always grateful to the people who help me keep writing:

    * My family who is patient when I am wild-eyed and distracted.

    * My sister gets special mention because she loves me and my books.

    * Alexis Glynn Latner, my first reader and wonderful editor. She helps me get it right;

    * Veronica Scott, who pushed me to join her in the original *Pets in Space*;

    * My cover designer, Melody Simmons, who designed my beautiful cover.

    * Readers, all of you who make the joys and frustrations of writing a book worth it.

My thanks to all of you for keeping me going. There are days when I'd rather be reading, too. lol